Printed by Createspace KDP, An Amazon.com Company
Published by Farquhar Publishing
Copyright © 2021 Loulou Farquhar. All rights reserved, including
the right to reproduce, distribute, or transmit in any form, or by any
means. For information regarding subsidiary rights, please contact the
Publisher.

Website: farquharpublishing.com
Email: linton@farquharpublishing.com
ISBN 978-0-9935525-7-1

I0549068

This book deals with suicide. While the author has taken great lengths to
ensure the subject matter is dealt with in a compassionate and respectful
manner, it may be troubling for some readers. Discretion is advised. If you
need help please go to https://www.opencounseling.com/suicide-hotlines to
find your local support.

Although this book is in no way affiliated with or endorsed by Twitter,
my thanks go to the Twitter team, and all its fabulous users for being the
inspiration for this book.

TABLE OF CONTENTS

TWITTER ME PINK

PROLOGUE

A lone figure sat motionless on a bale of hay, staring down at the *Browning* handgun sitting on their lap. Anger and sadness coursed through their veins, as freezing hands caressed gunmetal. An index finger gently squeezed the trigger. It seemed a fitting day for it. Dark demonic clouds slunk across a daytime sky, though you'd never have known it wasn't night. Lightning cracked and echoed throughout the empty surrounding fields. Ice-cold rain hammered down relentlessly.

Dark thoughts rained constantly through the mind, making it impossible to think rationally. It had been a long three weeks and so much had happened. He'd been up and down the full scale of emotions, and it had been multidimensional, and exhausting. Nothing had seemed to bring the slightest shred of comfort. A dull aching pain lurked at the back of his head. This particular gun had been used many times before, but never on a human. Held in the hand it felt like it *needed* to hunt something. Murderous thoughts strangled the brain which controlled the index finger which squeezed so dangerously. It was right that it should be today. It was loaded, and had been carefully cleaned and checked. Gentle hands raised the gun.

Yes, now... his mind said, firmly.

The howling wind screamed, *DO IT!... DO IT!...*

***

1

I was being held down whilst a bright light shone through my eyelids. Someone was speaking a language I didn't understand. My mouth was roughly opened, and something was forced inside. I struggled futilely, my screams stifled by the tube inching down my throat.

Even though I couldn't understand the words, I recognised the atmosphere, which hung heavy with amplified sounds. Alien beings shouted incomprehensibly all around me, and I began to gag. Heavy duty tape was placed over my mouth, stopping the vomit from exiting. My frantic, blinded eyes pleaded with them, as elongated fingers pinched my nose together, cutting off my only air supply. I attempted to resist, feebly, even as the life began to slip from me.

***

My eyelids slowly flickered open. My vision was blurred; I was finding it hard to focus. My chest rapidly rose up and down. I tried to scream, but my throat was too painful and my mouth seemed extremely dry. Opening and closing my eyelids a few times helped me to partly regain my vision.

I realised I was staring at an old yellowing ceiling. Fear still had its grip on me, as I hauled myself up into a sitting position. My eyes scanned the room.

I'm in hospital, a hospital ward...

My eyes settled on the figure asleep in the chair next to my bed. It seemed to be a wild unkempt creature. It had very dark, frizzed hair, battered into all directions, and creases covered its beautiful Don Lorenzo Suit.

My eyes widened. *Nora? But it can't be...*

A dream, apparently I was in a dream, and this was what he would look like if he never made the effort. This was the Jekell's Hyde side of Nora, wild and uncaring. Stubble lightly frosted his skin. I decided it must be a clone. This version even slept in a chair! It started to move, and say my name;

"Lauren!"

They have replicated his voice well...

He leaned closer to the bed. "Lauren?"

"Yes?" I croaked thickly, through the pain in my throat from the alien experiments.

The clone of Nora stood. "Are you alright?"

I nodded my head slowly. He drew his hand back, slapped me sharply on the cheek, and then followed that up quickly with a tight hug.

"Don't 'choo ever do that to Nora again. You're not supposed to leave Nora alone in this mad, cruel, world." He pulled away from me, his Cuban accent unusually calm, quiet and clear.

It had not been a dream. It was real. The coin I'd flipped had landed on HEADS - Run away forever. Only something had intervened...

SURPRISE, SURPRISE!

Nora looked hurt, tired and worried, all in one expression.

"You cannot just run away," Nora placed his hand on my heart. "You think it's easy to be Cuban, Gay, *and* Black?"

His gayness far outshone his skin tone, which I just took for granted and was never an issue for me. This however, was not the case for Nora's father, Hector Noel Sanchez. He was a stallion of a man, and fiercely proud of his Afro Caribbean heritage. The fact that his only son was probably gayer than a Christmas tree brought big shame to all the family. Hector was exceptionally proud that he had made his own money and was among some of the wealthiest men in the world. Black and Cuban, he was not prepared for his son to compromise any of it. He often said to Nora "We have to fight even harder, from all sides. I would never tolerate anything different."

I had only met his father on one occasion, and very briefly. He seemed to me to be all at once; huge, sexy and terrifying. Nora hardly ever spoke of his parents, and kept no photos of them on display in the house.

Nora took my hand. "Our lives are for living, for taking our pain, and using it as a tool to help us build a happy, honest life.

Like any tool, pain must be used wisely and correctly, or it will only become a burden. Of course this doesn't apply to me *not* telling my parents I am gay. I'm having too much fun with them trying to make me straight, and I'm no fool when it comes to their money."

This was the wise, all-knowing Nora. A side he rarely showed. A chink in his glamour armour!

I squeezed his hand and managed a weak, embarrassed smile. "I've never seen you like this." I croaked painfully.

"That," he dramatically waved his free hand. "is because I have not had to sit, waiting to see if my best friend in the world will live or die." He lowered his head and spoke into his lap. "Pills, Lauren. Pills..." He raised his head up to face me. "They pumped your stomach."

Now I understood the pain and discomfort I was feeling as I remembered. I felt ashamed. I couldn't even kill myself properly.

"Fight, Lauren! You must, *siempre,* always fight.

"I don't have it in me, Nora."

He squeezed my hand "Oh yes you do. You decide what you have. You chose to give up, because it's easier. I understand. But choose the fight, because this is freedom."

It sounded like something Nick would have said. My eyes filled with tears.

"*Cariño*... you have been given a second chance. Now you can fight. Nora will help you." He smiled, and his kindly brown eyes soothed me. He sat back in his chair, and I managed to slowly pull myself upright.

A noticeably pretty nurse came in, and seeing me awake, came over to the bed.

"Ah, Miss Bowman. You are awake."

I reached over and poured myself some water.

"How are you feeling?" she chirped.

Dead inside, but alive it would seem... , I thought, as I gulped the water down.

A mumbled "Alright" was all I could muster.

She nodded, primly. "Doctor will be round soon," she informed me in a clipped tone, and walked away.

"How long have I been here, Nora? When did you get here?" I began to ask more but he held up his hand to stop me, crossed his legs, and leant back.

"Nora will tell you everything, *todo*." He paused, and drew a deep breath. "So, your Aunt Patty found you. She'd fallen asleep downstairs. The poor woman, she is *loco*. She blames herself."

I bit my lip. *Poor, poor Aunt Patty...* A thing like this could unbalance her delicate world for years. I'd been selfish, and I'd committed a selfish act. Back then, in that moment, I had only been able to think of the pain within me, but now, faced with the consequences, shame again engulfed me. Nora's hand stroked mine.

"Lauren. It's not your fault, grief can cause wars. So when you get here in the hospital, she calls your parents. They call Jonathan and he calls me. We all came up here together in your Father's car and arrived early this morning. Your parents are staying at your Aunt's, and your brother is trying to get a car to rent. We both got a hotel."

Oh, great! The whole family's here. Pile it on...

"Anything else?" I enquired, stupidly thinking that maybe, somehow, Nick knew and had called.

Nora looked round furtively from side to side. "Well," His

eyebrow arched. "There was one more thing."

For one, tiny moment, I thought I was right, and managed a smile.

"It's about your brother."

My smile evaporated.

"For the past three weeks he's been living in your flat, *si?*"

"Oh, okay. Yes?"

"Well... Oh, *chica*, this is hard! Nora doesn't like to be a tell-all." He hesitated, fidgeting.

"For God's sake Nora, how bad can it be?"

"It's *Innis*. Innis has moved in with him." He gasped suitably, and sat back, satisfied.

Oh, shit. That *bad...*

"Shit! Oh, fucking shit!" I said aloud in disbelief.

Nora just nodded slowly.

Scottish Innis was my brother's best friend. Originally from *Thurso*, a small town with historic importance, in the highest of highlands, his thick intangible accent mystified most people who attempted to listen to it.

Innis and my brother had met ten years previously, when they both happened to be bungee jumping in Norway. They shared magic mushrooms, in order to heighten the experience, and became firm friends.

Innis, like my brother, was a huge Brain. He was a chief petty officer in the merchant navy. Here was a man so brilliant that he had to be contained in a submarine, working under the sea. He could have worked his way up the ranks easily, but was happy instead to remain where he was.

Innis and my brother had always been human drug-consuming machines, and when the two of them got together, they broached subjects and situations that mere mortals would fear to tread anywhere near. This debauchery could go on for days, as they pumped anything they could get their hands on into themselves, through every possible orifice. Their alien brain's intellect never seemed to diminish throughout these self-inflicted, ritual onslaughts.

I only needed to have a cigarette, and I'd forget my own phone number.

Innis' ruddy cheeks were a result of the clean Scottish air, and gave no hint of his decadent lifestyle. Slightly thinning strawberry blonde hair fell in front of twinkling mischievous grey eyes, and his smile was set in a permanent grin.

"*Nae* time to brood," Innis would say.

Sporting perhaps some of the biggest ears in Scotland, he would tell people "*Ach*, that's the reason the Navy took me on; I can *hear* enemy radar." Every action he made was big, bold and decisive. When he walked, he marched, and when he was speaking he virtually barked at you.

During his spare time he made robots – advanced ones that spoke and did certain tasks. His house, (that Nora and I had visited only once,) was filled with them.

Nora found Innis very disconcerting to be with, just as Innis felt awkward around Nora. He *tried* to feel comfortable, but you could see it took an intense effort.

For the sake of my brother, Nora didn't harass Innis, as he would have harassed others. I think that deep down, Nora was a little scared of Innis, and granted him a rare respite from his gayness. We had always had great nights out together, and Innis was extremely generous. He had a heart of gold, and I was very fond of him.

However, there was one thing I hated about him, a straight male compulsion which Jonathan was also afflicted with – to leave in his wake a chaotic mess and an unkempt house, permanently in disarray. Initially I'd been rendered incredulous upon seeing his house and the results of his bad habits. I'd assumed that being in the Navy would have made him tidy and orderly, but when Innis was aboard land, an animalistic highland gene kicked in, and he just about seemed to manage to be able to use a bath and toilet.

The thought that he and my brother had been living in my flat for nearly three weeks filled me with a cold terror, and gave me a prickly sweat on the back of my neck.

I stared at Nora, who was brushing his trousers down with his hands, trying to remove the untidiness of himself.

"Oh, Nora, I know how much you hate hospitals."

Nora had once told me that when he was young, about fourteen years old, his parents were travelling abroad as they often were, and his *Grand-papi* had been taken very ill. Nora had insisted on going with him in the ambulance, and had then spent two lonely days and nights at the hospital in Cuba, keeping vigil while his *Grand-papi* had the audacity to die five times.

Nora would collapse, crying, each time someone came to tell him he had passed away, and then laugh and clap upon being told he was in fact alive again. By the fourth time Nora thought it all nothing but an exquisitely cruel joke. On the fifth time a comfortable madness had unfortunately settled, and when told that his *Grand-Papi* was once again dead, but had in fact *not* been successfully resuscitated this time, Nora began to laugh hysterically, and jumped up, shouting- "Thank God! - Finally, the son of a bitch is dead. *Con Dios*!" Cue more dancing and laughing.

When his parents finally arrived, Nora's father, Hector, upon hearing how his son had reacted, had struck him viciously across the face. Whereupon Nora had said to his father "If I had known the old bastard was going to take so long, I would have stayed at home, wanking." For which he was bashed again, even harder.

Nora told me that later he had repeatedly ejaculated all over the seats of his father's Mercedes. And that included wiping it all round the steering wheel.

Nora looked up from the creases in his trousers. "Being in hospital is like having a dog constantly pissing in front of you – Disgusting, darlink."

We both looked over to the entrance of the ward as raised voices drew our attention. A male voice came from what looked like the Doctor. The pretty nurse who we had seen earlier was by his side holding a bunch of folders. As he moved round the ward she would hand him the corresponding folder. I counted round, quickly. I knew I was the last in line, and I was not relishing this encounter. Nora and I both watched him as he slowly navigated the ward, and finally reached me. The nurse handed him my folder and he opened it, revealing nothing on his face. A face that had years of wear and tear etched into it, no doubt from the stress of having to give constant bad news to people. His grey-steel hair was short and thick, and a matching moustache sat on top of a decently stiff upper lip. At about six foot five, he struck an impressive figure, and being a doctor obviously suited him.

He looked from his notes, to me, then to Nora, and back to me. "So, Miss Bowman, how are you feeling?"

"Well, my throat and stomach are pretty sore, but apart from that, I'm fine." I didn't mention that my heart was broken, and my soul shredded.

'Well there's bound to be a bit of soreness after a stomach pump."

More shame shifted through my body.

"An appointment has been made for you to see our resident psychiatrist. It is entirely up to you whether you keep it."

His tone suggested that he thought I should. I couldn't be bothered to tell him that I would never go to one of *them*.

"Now, normally you would have been prescribed some sort of medication, but in your condition, this will not be possible." He looked me straight in the eye.

"Okay, Doctor."

His lips pouted slightly. "Mm. Now what *does* concern me greatly, is how underweight you are. It is very unhealthy. When you come back for your next appointment, I will expect to see great improvement in this area."

I just nodded, though I had no idea why I would want another appointment.

The doctor turned his attention to Nora. "Are you her friend?"

"Si, *Señor.*"

"Please could you try to make sure that Miss Bowman's diet is as healthy as possible? Lots of vegetables, fruit and potatoes, yes?"

"Of course, *Señor,*" Nora answered, doing his best to show his concern.

The doctor handed the folder back to the nurse.

"So, Miss Bowman, I will see you tomorrow, before you are discharged. You can make an appointment at the reception on your way out."

Again I just nodded vaguely, I didn't really know what he was talking about.

His expression and voice took on a very serious air. "You are extremely lucky that your babies were unhurt. Maybe that's a

11

part of the reason you are in here. Again, this is why I strongly advise you see the psychiatrist, and put some weight on."

I just carried on nodding glibly at him, before one solitary word came screaming back at me.

BABIES. He said Babies...

ALL CHANGE

I cocked my head crazily, and stared at Nora. He looked frozen in time.

Babies, plural. Not one, that means two, or more!...

My eyelids stretched open and I felt my eyes bulge out, before Nora and I reacted at the same split second. He leapt from the chair and let forth a high pitched scream, while I shouted; "DOCTOR!"

All the women on the ward looked over towards us. Nora was fanning himself and hopping from foot to foot, chanting -

"Puta Madre! Puta Madre!"

The exiting doctor and nurse turned on their heels and re-entered the ward. His stride brought them quickly back to me.

"Miss Bowman, what on earth is going on? There *are* other women on this ward."

"Doctor, I'm sorry, but I, er, I..."

"Yes, yes? - And Sir, please, will you sit down?" he asked Nora.

Nora did as he was told, with his hand clamped over his own mouth.

I took a deep breath. "Sorry, Doctor. Did you say 'babies'?"

His lips pouted again as he sucked on that imaginary dummy. "Yes. Am I to take it that this is the first time you are hearing this?"

"Two, are there two babies?"

I will assume that is a yes. Yes, you are seven weeks pregnant, Miss Bowman. With twins."

I heard a small cry escape from behind Nora's clamped hand.

"Twins? Two? Inside me? Two?" I directed my questions to no one in particular. "Two?... Two?..."

"Yes, Miss Bowman." His thick grey eyebrows rose. "Twins. Not octuplets, septuplets, sextuplets, quintuplets, quadruplets, or triplets, but twins, meaning *two* babies."

I was in too much shock to react to his supercilious pomposity. I simply held up two fingers to Nora, whose hand was still firmly in place on his mouth, as if he had just been told that he was carrying the babies himself.

"But, but, I haven't got any idea how this has happened!" I aimed my protest at the Doctor.

He took my folder, read from it, and then looked at me. "Well, at Forty-three years of age I would have thought there was no need to explain."

I frowned "I understand the concept of the birds and the bees, but I have a coil, an IUD fitted."

"Then you received some very determined swimmers. We have of course removed the coil."

Nora finally removed his hand "Her boyfriend is like a Greek god. Twenty-three years old." He sighed, beside himself thinking of the image of Nick.

Oh Nick. Beautiful, stunning, father-to-be Nick...

"And yes, plenty of sex would also contribute towards the unusual failure of your contraceptive device." The Doctor's moustache hovered as he allowed himself a momentary smile in his otherwise un-humorous profession.

I narrowed my eyes at Nora, who raised an eyebrow in his, 'Really darlink, do I care?' kind of way. He began to pat his hair, moulding it carefully into shape. The normal Nora was coming back.

"So Miss Bowman, now you understand my concern about your health. If you intend to keep these babies you must take care of yourself."

I could only blink incredulously.

"So, I must continue my rounds. I am outrageously behind. Please think about everything I've said, and I'll see you tomorrow."

He turned and strode off. As soon as he'd gone, Nora pounced onto the bed and placed a hand on my stomach. He looked me straight in the eye.

"*Bambinos*, Lauren. *Bambinos. Doble! Gemelos! Es muy especial.*" His voice sounded soft and soothing and my eyes filled with tears. He hugged me and allowed me to weep.

"What's wrong? - Hey, Nora." The sound of Jonathan's voice stopped me from crying immediately.

"It's just an emotional moment for me, knowing your sister is alive," Nora answered as he released me from his protective hug.

I managed a weak smile."Hi, little bro."

Nora sat back down to let Jonathan see me.

"Fucking hell, Sis." My brother bear-hugged me.

15

I could see Nora, as he mimed locking his lips, and throwing an imaginary key away. I relaxed a little. I didn't want anyone knowing my news just yet. My mind went back to when my brother had just turned up at my flat and told me I was in love, and I'd asked how he could tell. "Because you're *glowing*," had been his reply. *Glowing*, the word everybody uses when, guess what? Yes, when you're pregnant. Must be the number one word everybody uses to describe mothers-to-be.

Jonathan released his grip. "Fuck me, you gave us all a fright. It's none of my business why you did it, but please don't fucking do it again."

All the time his big wide smile brought sunshine to an acrid atmosphere. He laid across the bed, resorting to child-like behaviour in the uncomfortable situation.

"So, Jonathan darlink. You got a car?" Nora asked, before returning to his self-preening.

"Yep, it's a beauty. *Mercedes*."

Nora nodded approvingly.

"So, Mum and Dad are having an awful time at Aunties. I fucking love it, its pure comedy gold. Shit! I do love Aunt Patty."

I managed another weak smile, and I knew I would always feel a little guilty for what I had done to her.

"So, how's it going at the flat?" I asked, daring to go there, even as wild thoughts raced through my mind. Not only would I have killed myself, I would have taken two other lives with me. Even though I had never wanted children.

What a mess...

My brother's voice came back into focus. "So, I hope that's okay?"

"Sorry, I wasn't listening. Hope what's okay?"

"About Innis staying." He raised his eyebrows and fished a packet of cigarettes out of his pocket.

Before I could answer, the pretty nurse from earlier came swiftly over to the bed.

"Sir, if you wouldn't mind not sitting on the bed?"

My brother stopped swinging his legs, and surveyed her very petite figure and pure white-blonde hair, that sat neatly in a bun under her nurse's hat. Big baby blue's matched her starched nurse's outfit and completed her sexiness.

My brother gave her his best big sloppy, *help me*, boyish smile. "How could I not comply, when someone so pretty is asking?" He got up, smartly.

She blushed, and fussed about straightening up my covers, even though they didn't need it. My brother also had an ability to charm, and his subtle American accent only accentuated it. He took a cigarette out of the packet and she looked at him in a reprimanding manner.

"Oh, I'm not going to smoke it in here, Nurse." He leant forward and read her tag. "D. Urmsham. So what's the D stand for?"

She blushed again. "Daisy," she replied, in a small buttery voice meant only for him.

He has her...

"D-a-i-s-y," Jonathan repeated, slowly. He momentarily transfixed her.

"Well yes... So, please - no sitting on the bed. And you'll both have to leave soon, visiting hours are almost over," she said, sounding official.

"I'm her brother, Jonathan," he announced, and stepped

forward, giving her a kiss on the cheek, before turning to me. "Going outside for a smoke." He placed the cigarette in his mouth, film star-ish, and nonchalantly walked off. Nurse Daisy Urmsham followed.

Nora had been merely sitting and observing quietly.

"Thank you for not saying anything. Please, Nora, I don't want anyone, and I mean *anyone* knowing about this."

"I say *Nada*, nothing. My lips are sealed, unlike yours, darlink." He laughed, naughtily. It was the first thing to make me smile.

"Oh Nora! Never leave my life."

I caught him off guard, and his mouth opened slightly, underneath glistening eyes. He stood and came over to me.

"Cariño," He kissed my forehead gently. "We will fight. Get your strength."

Jonathan returned, looking very pleased at himself "So, I got nursie's phone number, and we're going out tonight."

"Of course," Nora said. "We really must be going now."

"Yep, it's all good, I even got a date." His clear blue eyes twinkled.

"It's a hospital, Jonathan, not a dating agency." I said, with a fringe of humour on my voice.

My brother leant in to kiss me goodbye. "Shit, who said it isn't, big sis?"

I watched them leave, all the time wishing they wouldn't. I knew my own premonitions would invade my brain, and indeed they did.

***

18

Nick was shouting at me for not telling him about our babies. My mother was administering her judgement.

"How can you, at *your* age? Don't be absurd, darling."

David was there, pointing and laughing at me, while Angela constantly screamed in the background. Sergeant Cole sat behind a long high bench, wearing a judge's grey wig on his head. He looked stern and unforgiving. He smacked down the gavel he held in his hand, and his deep booming voice began to chant; "JUDGEMENT DAY!"

Jenny Setterton, my arch nemesis, was typing, taking down all my confessions. A bright light shone down above her head. The Doctor was here again, except the Doctor was Nick.

"So, have you managed to kill the twins?" he asked me, with a twinkle in his eye.

***

I woke up sharply, sweating and hyper-ventilating. The ward was in darkness, save for a faint light coming from the nurse's desk. I was pleased I hadn't cried out during *that* horrific nightmare.

Really, I should have known I was pregnant…

During the early weeks, I hadn't once questioned where my normally regular-as-clockwork period was, as apparently I didn't care about such trivia. My condition also explained my recent behaviour. My hormones had been rampaging through my body.

Now in some way at least Nick was here with me. The babies had survived so far with their fight for life, and I decided then and there that life is what I would give them. Nora was right - **Fight**.

I knew now what I had to do.

FAMILIAR VISITATION

After breakfast the following day, I fell into the dark milk of sleep again. My mother's voice came to me in another nightmare.

"Lauren! Lauren!" My arm was being shaken, and as I fluttered my eyelids open, there in full technicolour was my mother.

Shit, it isn't a nightmare...

"Well thank goodness!" she said as she let go of me and kissed me dutifully on the cheek. "Really, darling. Was all this necessary?" She said it as if I had changed the room round.

As always, she was dressed immaculately. That day she was sporting a turquoise blue two piece suit with black lace trim, complete with matching hat and a handbag, which she opened, removing a handkerchief and placing it on the chair before sitting down. My father played with his hat, nervously turning the brim of it in his hands. He moved forward and kissed me on the forehead, just as Nora had done the day before.

"Hello darling. We've all been very worried about you," he said quietly as he stood next to my seated mother.

"Sorry." was all I could muster.

"Yes, as well you might be, young lady," my mother interjected, the pitch of her voice rising an octave higher.

I always felt incredulous that my mother was forever telling me to grow up, whilst she talked to me as if to a child.

"Your father hates hospitals." she announced.

Surprise filled my father's face, and we both knew she meant herself.

She sniffed the air, and crinkled her nose as if there was no doubt that the place would infect her. "Everybody knows you get ill when you come to hospital."

"I think it's the other way round, Mother," I challenged her feebly. She gave me one of her looks, and I retreated.

"Anyway we are not here to discuss these things. Already we have spent two unwholesome nights with *your* Aunt," she complained, making it sound as if this Aunt only belonged to me. "Well, we will be leaving right after this visit. The car is packed and your father and I will not stay there a moment longer. Enough of this *silliness*, Lauren. Put this boy behind you, and maybe please try to grow up."

In my mental dictionary, under the word, **Suicide,** was the definition; *Silliness*. I opened my mouth to protest, but knowing it would be futile, I simply nodded.

"Of course we would more than welcome you to come and stay with us over the next few days, but I have told the neighbours you have been to a health farm."

That made me smile, as the last thing I looked like was a glowing picture of health.

"I would not advise you to stay with your Aunt, as I fear she is quite mad." She closed her eyes, shook her head and sniffed in a ladylike manner.

I loved my parents, but hell would have to freeze over before I lived with them at this particular moment in my life. I wondered what had happened at Aunt Patty's.

"I cannot even begin to describe it. Lionel, please? I will let your father explain."

Again, my father looked surprised. Caught off guard, he coughed to clear his throat. "Mm, well, mmm, well..."

"Oh, do come along, Lionel!"

My father's neck turned pink behind his tightly done up shirt collar.

"Well dear, which incident would you like me to...?"

My mother interjected. "For god's sake, Lionel! That foul deed, this morning?"

My mind boggled.

"Mm. Yes, dear. Of course, well, mm, your mother and I came down to breakfast,"

"- and we all sat down," my Mother interrupted professionally, as she took over the story she had asked my father to recant.

"All of us squashed unhealthily around that Bohemian table," she recalled, as her nostrils flared distastefully. "being served slices of cardboard. I ask you darling, vegan bacon? Apparently it's made from some kind of bean bacon!" She scoffed at the thought of it. "Bean bacon. Whatever next? Poodles made of cheese?"

I tried desperately not to crack a smile.

"Giving a grown man that... Well it is simply not good enough."

"It really is alright, dear." My father cut in with concern in his voice. He was trying to placate my mother. It didn't work.

"It really is *not* alright. Well, if that wasn't bad enough, then well…" She paused.

My father took her hand. The suspense was getting to me.

"Mother!"

"Well, we all had cups for the tea, your Aunt Patty had a small clear glass, and she... she simply drank the contents in one go." A small cry escaped her. "Well, darling. I just assumed it was apple juice, and when I enquired if maybe your father, and I could have some, oh dear. Well, she just came out with it. She said - 'What? You would like some of my urine?'"

My mother sat back, and removed another handkerchief from her bag. A smile teased at my father's lips.

"My own sister. Every day for years," she spoke into the hanky. "Mad, I tell you. It's sent her mad. The very thought that your father and I would want to drink her urine. Absolutely disgusting."

As she placed the hanky over her mouth again, I, like my father, was trying to suppress my laughter. I was imagining my Aunt jumping up onto the table, knickerless. Her wild hair flailed as she squatted over a shot glass and urinated into it. The mental picture warmed me, and brought some humour back into my life. Jonathan was right. God bless Aunt Patty. I exhibited the appropriate look of alarm for my mother.

"Yes. She tried to defend this lunacy; she said it was good for you. Your Grandmother once told me a story, that when your aunt Patty was very little, she was in a pushchair, outside a shop, when," She faltered as she looked round the room, and lowered her voice. "A stray dog lifted its leg, and urinated on, well…"

She let it hang in the air. I tried to make a face that showed I understood, but that a dog pissing on a buggy was beyond my comprehension.

She waved her hanky, "Oh, darling. Please. Well, some of the urine went on dear Patty, and clearly made her one of the mental people."

Don't smile, don't smile... was all I could think.

"So you see, darling. We cannot stay there. I already caught her the night before trying to re-align your father's... what was it, dear?"

"Chakras, dear."

"Yes that's it. With crystals. I don't even know what *Shakr-arse* are, but the word sounds very Arabic to me." She rose, lifted the handkerchief off the chair and threw it into the bin by the side of the bed.

"I will not be a party to a satanic ritual, urine drinking, and Shakr-arse."

Neither my father or myself bothered to correct her.

"It's simply not very Christian, or even very British."

I had never seen my mother go to church, but again it simply wasn't worth the debate. She squeezed me very gently as she gave me her farewell air kisses.

"Please try to look a bit more human, darling. It is a terrible reflection on me and your father "

I nodded. My father hugged me, whispered that they loved me, and then I was alone again.

I turned my thoughts to being as positive as possible. The nurse came over and told me they would be keeping me in for one more day, and that the Doctor would see me before I left. She looked very happy, which helped me to keep my positivity.

Nora and Jonathan came to visit me that evening. Both remarked that my mood had lifted. Jonathan only stayed ten minutes because he was meeting Nurse Urmsham. That gave me and Nora time to talk properly.

"Nora, I'm going to Devon to see Nick."

Nora was back to his usual immaculate self. He was wearing a *Wong Foo* red snakeskin shirt and trousers. A *Louis Vuitton* emerald green bag hung from his shoulder. A matching jacket held a pale pink silk hanky in its top pocket. There wasn't a hair out of place. His face was smooth and scented. He clapped his hands together gleefully.

"You going to tell him about the *bambinos*?"

"No, Nora. I want Nick to come back to me because he wants to. *Needs to*. Not because he has to. That wouldn't be real love, Nora, just empty commitment. Nick has at least shown me that it must be real or not at all."

I could tell that Nora thought I was wrong.

"And then he says No, *entonces*?" He held his palms up.

"Not sure yet, I'll have to see when that happens. One step at a time, Nora. That's all I can manage."

"*Poco a poco*. I understand. When do you leave?"

"The nurse said tomorrow morning. They want me to stay one more night."

"Okay, darlink. Me and Jonathan will come and pick you up." His hands held my face and he kissed me on the mouth.

"Nora's going now. She's gonna cruise Norwich." He let out his familiar cry - "*Aaiieee!*" and was gone.

***

My sleep was less fitful, and my mind focused on Nick. I dreamt we were at the big oak tree where we had gone for our enchanted picnic, except this time we were a family and even more laughter and love filled the air. Happiness flowed between us.

***

When I awoke, fresh hope surrounded me and fuelled my every movement. I wanted to leave. I texted my brother to tell him I was being discharged at ten a.m. and he was waiting faithfully with Nora as I passed through the reception.

The doctor I'd been seeing passed by, spotted me and stopped.

"Ah, Miss Bowman. I've made an additional appointment for your ten week check up. As you've explained you do not live here, so the appointment will be at your local hospital. You will receive something through the post to that effect. Your appointment with the psychiatrist is here at the hospital, and you know my views on that. The check up is to determine the babies are healthy. You still need at least four weeks rest."

I kept nodding until he strode off. I looked over at my brother who luckily for me, hadn't been paying the slightest bit of attention. I collected up all the paperwork and we left.

Jonathan told us what an awesome night he'd had, and that he'd definitely be travelling up to see Nurse Daisy Urmsham again. In the car on the way home Nora tried to convince me he should take care of me at his house. He kindly reminded me I had no responsibilities to attend to. I turned down the help, not knowing what was about to happen...

HOME NOT SO SWEET HOME

Life crept back into me during that car journey home. Jonathan told us how much fun nurses are. Daisy had definitely made an impression on him. Nora said he was disgusted at the lack of bum-fun in his own life lately, and insisted he'd be rectifying that as soon as he got back to London. His phone constantly made a trilling sound. Nora tittered, or made sad faces depending on the notifications.

"So I suppose you want your bedroom back then, big sis?" Jonathan cut in.

"Oh, I hadn't even thought about that. Oh shit! Of course, you've got Innis living there now."

"Well, I could crash in the living room and I'm sure Innis could get a hotel for a few days. Especially under the circumstances."

"Does he know what happened?"

"Fuck, yes. I kinda freaked out when I got the call from the folks. He was there."

He got out his cigarettes again, lighting one skilfully whilst he drove. Nora wasn't able to drive, and always said life was hard enough without that nightmare.

Faintly, in the background I heard Frankie Bubbles singing *Desire* on the radio. In the back seat, Nora turned and looked at me. I took his hand and squeezed it to signify that I was alright.

"It's number four now," Nora whispered.

"I'm pleased," I whispered back, and I was. Maybe by now, Nick had told his family he had written the lyrics. Everyone would be very proud of him, even if they *had* been written for a slut.

For the rest of the journey I re-told the story of the pee drinking, in-between Nora's phone incessantly going off. Jonathan laughed so hard he swerved the car a couple of times, and Nora screeched hysterically.

"Priceless. Fucking priceless," Jonathan concluded, and chuckled as he tried to light another cigarette.

"Once, I had a boyfriend who liked to be pissed on. Nora thought - Okay, why not? But when you sit having breakfast together the next morning, normally its *muy romantico,* no? Well, for me that spell was broken when I remembered that only a couple of hours before; I was pissing on his cock."

All of us tittered at the thought of it.

"Well it's gotta be better than the other one," Jonathan called back.

"What's that?" I asked, and quickly wished I hadn't.

Nora looked stunned. "*Que pasa?* You don't know?" He wrinkled his nose, and his mouth set into a straight line. Perfect eyebrows frowned together.

"The dirty log ride!" Jonathan shouted. Nora giggled. Still, I was not getting it.

"Sucking the arse turtle!" Nora suggested as he joined in. "*Aaiiee*! Yes."

"Chomping on the chocolate snake!"

Nora screeched and came back. "Bum takeaway."

The penny finally dropped, and I held my hands up. "Okay, okay, I get it. That's enough."

Nora giggled. "The brown eyed butt sucker!" He just couldn't help himself.

Jonathan roared with laughter.

"Enough, both of you!" I shouted, loud enough to be heard.

"Sis, we're only *pissing* about. Don't go all prim."

Nora laughed at my brother's terrible pun.

"It's rare, but on certain subjects, yes I am prim and this is definitely one of them."

"So you won't be -"

"Jonathan!" I shouted.

"Alright, enough. I promise," he relented, and began fumbling for his cigarettes.

I sat back and noticed Nora still had a silly grin on his face. "I was thinking of starting a band, maybe. Called *Captain Fudge and the Packers.*"

I couldn't help but crack my serious face, and we all roared with laughter. Nora looked at his phone for the hundredth time.

"Okay, I admit I'm curious, what's going on, why all the messages?"

Nora preened his hair, and exuded an air of pomposity, "Well it's *Twitter*. I'm Big, baby. Everyone loves Nora. They're all asking advice on fashion, Love and commitment."

The idea of Nora advising anyone on the latter topic made me smile.

"I'm *'Nora's Pearls'*. I shoot my pearls of wisdom over everyone." He splayed his arms open above his head theatrically, while his phone kept bleeping.

"Well, please can you silence your pearls for now? We're nearly there. It's the only place I can call home, and I'd appreciate it as tranquil as possible."

"Of course, darlink. *No pasa nada.*" He switched his phone to vibrate.

"Innis will give us a nice warm welcome," Jonathan chirped.

Please don't let it be as bad as I fear...

I clutched my heart, and tried to have hope. Nothing, absolutely nothing would have prepared me for what I was about to discover. *Nada.*

***

As we pulled into my street, the air in the car was dense with tobacco smoke. Every time I had pressed the button to bring the window down, Jonathan, who had full control in the front, would close it. From inside this Gypsy fortune-teller's crystal ball, the smog made me aware of the new lives inside me. I supposed that the smoky atmosphere was not good for them. I felt sure my attention would be drawn to these spoilers many times over the next few months, although it still didn't seem real to me. I took a moment to steel myself before I got out of the car. Jonathan got out vigorously and bounded up the steps with ease. He opened my apartment door just as Nora and I got to the top of the stairs and recoiled back, as one. The smell violated our senses. Both of us entered the flat like two old ladies about to go on a rollercoaster for the very first time. We clutched each other's arms with terror. My first step into the hall actually made my eyes water. Nora sobbed like a child, and put his free hand over his mouth. Jonathan led the way and walked into the lounge, nonchalantly.

I imagined that this is what it would have been like when they'd opened a tomb in ancient Egypt for the first time. A rancid belch of old stale air hung heavy and encompassed everything. A giant pile of revoltingly dirty clothes sat on the floor at the far end of the hallway, very close to the bathroom door.

Plastic bottles neatly lined the skirting board on the other side of the hall, and ended with what looked like my best glass measuring jug. Both of us crept towards the front room, trepidation in every step. As we entered, my mouth opened involuntarily as I tried to take in the pantomime before me.

There wasn't one inch of space left on the sides, floor, table or furniture. Condensed un-breathable air hung even denser than in the hall. Nora performed little coughs behind his hand as I took the minimum of tiny breaths so as not to pollute myself. I found it hard to tear my gaze from the construction which sat centre stage on my table, and rose at least two feet high. The only materials used seemed to be sanitary towels, tampons and thick silver duck tape, which held it all together.

Something struck Nora's leg, and caused him to scream involuntarily. We looked down and saw a small robot, holding a tray with cigarettes on it.

"*Ach*, don't mind him. That's Ronnie."

Innis' unmistakeable Scottish voice cut through the mist, as he stepped out of it and hugged me tightly. He followed that up with some hard manly slaps on the back.

"So, you're better then?" he shouted at me, and returned to give me some more crushing hugs. Within my eyesight I could see more than forty overflowing ashtrays, countless plates with unknown contents on them and many pizza boxes, some with slices still inside. White fluffy bacteria seemed to be crawling over some of them.

Ennis finally released me. He spun around, shook Nora by the hand and gave him a sharp slap on his shoulder. "Awright?" he asked, acting as politely as he knew how to.

Nora nodded. "*Hola* Innis."

I could tell Nora was as least as appalled as me at what he was seeing. My eyes settled on the sculpture again.

"*Ach*, what you see here, is a crude replica construction of NASA's six four eighty global weather station." His red apple cheeks rose proudly above a winning smile. A much taller robot strode past, accidentally hitting a chair on its way. Its little electronic voice sounded like it was saying "*Whisky and Coke.*"

Innis bent down and turned him round,

"And this is Russell."

Jonathan stepped expertly through all the clothes and different items that were strewn about. He was holding a bottle of bourbon in one hand, and two clinking glasses in the other. Two lit cigarettes were clenched between his teeth. Innis took one cigarette and both the glasses.

"Thought we'd all have a drink?" Jonathan said.

"Not for me," I snapped, angrily.

"Or me," piped Nora.

Nora and I had our own reasons for not accepting. I imagined Nora's to be hygiene.

"Oh, not even a little?" my brother hung his bottom lip out.

"No, honestly." I shook my head vehemently.

Innis began pouring one for each of them. "I would offer youse a tea or coffee, but I don't think there's a clean cup."

The room must have contained at least twenty-five cups, nearly all of which I didn't recognise.

"Yep I know it seems like there are a lot." Jonathan coughed as he spoke." We went out and bought some more. Fucking shit loads in there." He flicked his heavy blonde fringe towards the kitchen.

Nora and I shuffled forward as one. It was as if we'd stepped into one of those TV programmes where people are clearly mentally ill and doing all kinds of bizarre and unsavoury things. In the kitchen mugs were stacked all over the floor, but a small path led to the kitchen sink. Nearly four weeks of washing up was piled high, precariously balancing on itself. A large fly landing on them would have caused it all to fall. A layer of cigarette ash dusted everything and the hob rings swam with rancid fat one inch thick.

Nora took out his mobile, gently. He took a photo and began typing rapidly.

"Are you seriously tweeting this?"

"Of course, darlink. This is too good not to. Hashtag *#SquatScum #CouncilSlag*."

"Nora, please. This is *my* home that I pay for. You can be such a snob sometimes."

He stuck his nose in the air, as if to prove my point.

I looked down and jumped as Russell the robot walked between my legs, announcing "Whisky and Coke."

Astonishment coursed through me. *How could humans live like this?...*

I peered at my brother, admonishingly.

"Deep in the jungles of Thailand, there is a place called the Golden Triangle. It's filled with Opium dens, with stick thin people in them. They lay in their own shit and puke, with cockroaches everywhere, and even *that* looks," I opened my arms to illustrate my point. "...more sanitary than this!"

My brother pulled his *'I can't help it'* face.

"I *dinnae* think they dens have robots in them!" Innis shouted through the haze.

I wanted to use the bathroom, but I was scared witless.

"I'm going to the toilet, there had better be nothing there." I glared at the pair.

Innis and my brother giggled like school girls. I tightened my grip once again on Nora's arm.

"Please, darlink. Don't make me come with you."

"If you love me you'll do it."

"Puta Madre! Si, si, vale, vale."

We attempted to navigate our way back through the living room and inched forward into the hall as we passed the stench soaked pile of clothes. My hand lingered on the bathroom door handle. A small cry escaped from Nora. Pushing down I opened the door just as Nora began to cross himself, mumbling,

"Santa Maria."

An unexpected welcome awaited us. The air seemed aesthetically pleasurable. Nora and I exchanged glances of renewed ease. Right in front of us was the toilet, which at least looked clean and sanitary. We released our grip on each other slightly. I had thought that would have been the most offensive article. Unfortunately it was evidently there deliberately to lull us into a false sense of security. We rounded the corner to where the bath and basin were. Between them sat a mysterious object with flashing fairy lights all over it, two tea light candles, and some other artefacts I couldn't quite make out. As I took a step toward it, Nora pulled me back.

"*Por favor*, I don't want to know."

I let go of Nora's hand and took another step, looking down at this new installation .Between the candles sat some M&M sweets, one of each colour. Two pound coins and half a block of blue cheese seemed to serve some integral purpose. The pretty fairy lights blinked on and off.

"What the..." I began, and trailed off as I gazed at this occultism. It began to reveal itself to me.

"No, it can't be."

I turned to Nora, who had his hands clamped together in front of him.

"I think it's… a giant shit," I finally managed to say, as I returned my attention back to it, and squinted through the lights.

Nora squealed. "No way, *es imposible!*"

I stood back. "It is definitely a shit. I've never seen anything like it. Why here? Why not two steps further, where the toilet is?"

"'Cos there's no way that is fitting in the toilet," Nora tittered, getting his mobile out again.

#BigShit #CacaGrande

A splashing noise came from the bath. We screamed and

ran from the room, slamming the door behind us. Out of the corner of my eye I saw something move on the hall floor. We looked at the pile of clothes and saw definite activity.

I screamed, then Nora screamed, and his soprano cry shook the whole building. We bolted back into the front room.

"Rats. Fucking rats in my flat!" I shouted at the pair of them.

Innis and my brother looked surprised.

"Rats? They're not rats, they're Lobsters," Jonathan said.

Now it was my turn to look surprised.

"What, in my hallway?"

"What? I have no fucking idea what you're talking about, Sis. Why would there be Lobsters in the hallway?"

"Look this is getting us *naewhere*." Innis spoke, and Nora's attention was distracted by something behind us.

"And is that a giant shit in my bathroom?" I asked.

Another scream from Nora delayed the answer. I turned to see the clothes pile from the hallway walking towards us. I joined Nora, screaming, and both of us belted them out. The thing stopped moving.

'SHUT UP!" my brother bellowed, and we did.

"For shit's sake." My brother walked towards the clothes heap.

"This is *Irene*. Didn't you see her in the hall?"

I was wild eyed. The twilight zone had arrived at my home.

"We met her on one of our nights out. She normally lives on the street. We thought it would be charitable to give her somewhere to crash."

He beamed as if he had saved an entire race. There was no response from Irene. I could make out a small, well worn face, nestled inside at least seven layers of hooded items. The outermost was a purple knitted hoodie with fur trim. From deep within, Irene grunted. Pallid red, ultra-dry hair stuck out randomly from the hoods. Evidently, stale urine combined with cigarette smoke was the perfume of choice for Irene. She got up and shuffled towards the kitchen, farting twice along the way. I gave my brother one of the foulest looks I could.

One of our nights out... I shivered at the sound of those words coming from Jonathan. Once, he and Innis had been missing for nine days. I had been worried sick. They were eventually found in *Johannesburg*, South Africa. Neither of them knew how they had got there or even why they'd wanted to go.

That adventure had earned Innis a tattoo that said;

I Love Cocks

on his forearm. He'd gone mental about it at the time. "*Ach*, a submarine full of men, an' me with this."

He went to another tattooist and had them add a backwards C adjoining underneath the existing one, cleverly changing it to;

I Love **S**ocks.

My brother had said that that was just as gay, he who'd also acquired an inking; A thickly set Gypsy man's face was tattooed on his left buttock.

At the time, I went so apeshit about it that they hadn't gone A.W.O.L. since. Their minds glistened like diamonds, circuit boards in pure symmetry with each other and protected by walls of kryptonite against the permanent onslaught of human stupidity.

Irene trawled through the floor of crap and back out towards the comfort of the hallway.

"What the hell is going on?" I demanded, in full anger mode.

37

"*Ach*. Sorry hen, but she's kin. Well she's a *weegie* anyhew, and she reminds me of me Ma."

The goodness in his heart showed through his words. I felt myself soften slightly.

"Okay, Innis. But I'm finding all this a little hard to take in. I'd sit down, but I'm not sure where the furniture is, under everything."

One chair had apparently become the place where all the pants came to die.

"Oh yes, and is there a giant shit on my floor in the bathroom?"

Both men smiled broadly.

"*Ach*. Ay, It is. A real beauty. *Nae* one knows who did it," Innis said, sounding ridiculously proud.

"We preserved it by spraying hairspray on it," Jonathan said, joining in.

Nora let out a small disgusted squeal. I pulled my head back and gagged slightly. The latter information disturbed me even more than the original revelation. The thought that Irene the tramp could have done it only befouled the deed even more.

"So that's there in the bathroom, and there's a hobo living in my hall?"

"Technically it's my hall, as I'm paying to live here."

My eyes became slits as I walked towards my brother. "Are you fucking joking? And where are these Lobsters?" I suddenly remembered about them, and thought of Nick. That day at Warbling cottage, when he'd caught me sunbathing naked.

My temper simmered fiercely.

"Oh, there in the bath." My brother replied, and his nonchalant attitude made my rage bubble over. I turned to him and prodded my finger sharply into his ribs. Innis was turning Russell around again, where he'd become entrenched in a bundle of pizza boxes.

"Whiskey and coke."

"This is not how I imagined my homecoming to be when I said you could live here, little brother," I shouted, poking him sharply again. "I thought you'd exist as a normal human being. Not perform a vivisection on my flat. You're wallowing in foulness. It's one big septic tank, full of excrement. Frankly I'm shocked that even that homeless woman would want to stay here.

"She *doesnae* like to use the lavvy." Innis cut in.

Jonathan jumped to her defence. "Actually Irene's rather tidy. She takes a pee in the jug then saves it in plastic bottles. After a while she takes them all and throws them on the soil somewhere."

I remembered the glass jug in the hall. I didn't want to ask what she did with the other stuff. My face started to feel hot. Nora had stopped moving, clearly fearing contamination from everything around him.

The smaller robot with the cigarettes bumped into my leg. I screamed at my brother.

"You've fucking gone too far! I mean it. Fucking sort it out." I started to cry.

He came over and put his arms around me.

"Shush, shush. Sis, I'm sorry. Okay, maybe it is a little out of control."

Innis had already begun to tidy up. Jonathan looked at me, flushed.

"We were gonna get a couple of cleaners in. I didn't think you'd see it like this, but well, circumstances change."

His face wanted me to forgive him. His boyish freckles danced across his skin.

It was hard for me to stay angry at him.

"I know very good cleaners. *Buena. Muy buena.* Nora will sort for you, darlink."

"Cool. Thanks, Nora. Appreciate that. I'll sort out all the payment," Jonathan gushed.

I suddenly felt exhausted. I looked at Nora.

"So if you don't mind, is that offer still open?"

Smiling and nodding, Nora clapped his hands.

"Jonathan, can you give us a lift please to Nora's? I'll be staying there a while."

***

Twenty-five cigarettes later we pulled up outside Nora's house. As soon as we got out, Jonathan pulled away, as he shouted out the window: "And thanks for sorting out the cleaners Nora. Make sure they're good looking."

Nora's smile was like a Cheshire cats'.

"Oh, I will, darlink."

We walked up the outside steps. He put the key in the door, and opened it to reveal the smell of clean salubrious air.

"So who are these cleaners?" I asked.

"You will see. *Aaiiee!* So naughty."

We stepped through into his beautiful existence.

GETTING BETTER ALL THE TIME

Nora was right, this was what I needed...

I was stretched out in a huge tear shaped marble bath, which
was set to a gentle bubble. I had chosen the Hibiscus oil from
the array provided. Under the black onyx shelf that they sat on,
was a gold card that informed me which oil did what. It said
that Hibiscus was good for relaxing. The gold taps had golden
cherubs for handles that you pushed back to pump out boiling
hot water. A radio played classical music by the side of the main
control panel. Normally that wasn't my thing, but that day it
seemed appropriate to the surroundings and my mood.

There were leather cushions embedded into the bath so
you could lay at most angles and be comfortable. For the first
time since I came out of hospital, my mind and body relaxed
completely.

One of the first things I did once I'd settled in at Nora's was to phone my Aunt Patty. She'd been very upset. The laying on of hot stones, two coffee colonic irrigations and endless chanting, had not helped her despair. All I could tell her was how sorry I felt. I told her that my mind had been decayed then, and that now I wished it had never happened.

She had sobbed, churlishly, as she apologised for not coming to the hospital, and told me she suspected it would upset her bowel movements for weeks. We ended the call by sending our love to each other.

I called my parents briefly and let them know where I was. Nora let me choose my own room, and I opted for the one with a four poster bed and large windows that let in lots of light. Birds and butterflies adorned the walls, and everything was in pale summery colours. It was also one of the least furnished of all the bedrooms; after all, I worried about my clumsiness constantly.

Nora let me have time to myself. I fell asleep still dressed, and when I awoke the room was dark.

I opened my overnight bag, removed what little clothes I'd grabbed, and decided to take a bath. Once submerged, I pushed one of the Cherubs gently with my foot and released more hot water. I allowed my hands to roam over my stomach, which seemed perfectly flat and normal.

You would never know there were two babies inside...

As my mind pondered that paradox, I stayed calm in the tranquil atmosphere. Ironically, I had protected myself from this my whole ovulating life. If anything I'd always been overly cautious when it came to birth control. David had been right that day in *Frannie's* cafe when he'd said I didn't want children. Now I was incubating two of them. The thought of childbirth terrified me, let alone the concept of being a mother.

Maybe a single mother? Oh, Nick. What are you doing? Can you feel something is wrong?...

42

I allowed a couple of tears to splash over my cheek, before I wiped the rest away. My heart still felt hollow, as reflected in my appearance when I looked in the mirror.

I was so shocked by my own face, I vowed to take more care of myself.

Nora announced his presence, came in, and sat on the edge of the bath. His perfectly manicured hand dangled into the water and gently swished it round.

"How are you, darlink? Hungry?"

"I'm fine, why? Are you going to cook?"

Nora looked at me, sharply. "Are you *Loco?* Me cook? *Por favor.*" He tittered to himself.

"I'm not really hungry. I'm still so tired. After this, I think I'll just go back to bed."

"Okay, darlink. But you must eat, for you and the *bambinos.*"

"I will. Sleep now. Eat tomorrow. Promise."

"*Vale, cariño.*" He removed his hand from the bath, leant forward and kissed my forehead. "Nora's going to take very good care of you." Somewhere downstairs his phone started bleeping, and he left hurriedly to check it.

True to my word, I slept heavily after my bath, without dreams or interruptions. It was a desperately needed deep sleep.

***

A light knocking on the door stirred me. I poked my head out of the covers and opened my eyes. Bits of sleep clotted my vision.

"Nora, you don't have to knock. Just come in."

I rubbed my eyes to clear my sight. I heard the door open, and then a strange voice.

"Good morning, madam. If you're ready, I have some breakfast for you."

It wasn't Nora's voice. I sat bolt upright and I saw it was a beautiful man.

"I am Apollo," he said, and nodded with firmness and self-possession.

"Greek god of music, poetry, art, medicine, sunlight and knowledge. I'm here to take care of you."

This god was dressed in character, in the classic short white toga, clasped together at the shoulder with a laurel leaf. A thin gold cord ran round his waist and tied in a bow. Dark hair curled around the edges of his face framing strong features. He was a commanding figure. This was no boy. I managed a whispered "hello," as he placed the tray on the bed, then he opened the curtains.

Nora came in and sat next to the tray, which was laden with fruit and a variety of teas. He looked sensational. He wore a buttercream silk shirt, a *Don Lorenzo*, with a slightly high collar, which extenuated his neck. Pearl cufflinks glittered. He crossed his legs, and adjusted his pale salmon trousers. The movement made them look alive. They were made from the most delicate fur. I knew they would probably be *Gaultier*. He always managed to choose the colour of clothes that complemented his perfect skin tone.

He helped himself to a coffee "I see you've met Apollo." He glanced at him as if he were his next human meal.

"Yes," I answered, and smiled.

Apollo stood at the end of the bed, "Will that be all?"

Nora put the coffee down. "Could you please go down to the kitchen and bring the strawberries up. I've forgotten them."

Apollo nodded and hurried off to do his master's bidding.

'So this is your way of looking after me," I said, helping myself to a slice of apple.

"Of course. What, you think I'm going to do it? No way. Not when I can pay for it. He is going to live here and help with things around the house. I got him from an agency called *Maid in Heaven*."

He passed me his mobile and asked me to take a photo of him as he lounged next to the strawberries. I took two pictures, then handed back the phone.

"*Gracias,* darlink. Hashtag *#stylishbreakfast.*"

I sighed, resigned already. I knew this tweeting wasn't going to stop. In fact, I had a feeling that *Nora's Pearls* were going to grow.

He took a sip of his coffee, just as Apollo came back into the room and handed Nora a large bowl.

"Your strawberries, Sir."

"Apollo, please open the top window."

As Apollo did that, Nora took a strawberry and rolled it around his mouth, sucking it as he viewed the Greek god intensely .

"After all, Lauren. I'm your friend and you need this."

I knew he was talking about himself, but I appreciated the gesture nevertheless. I nibbled at the fruit.

45

"So when you say *you're* paying, you mean your parents?"

"Of course I do, darlink. I'm costing them a fortune."

"Will there be anything else, sir?"

"No. *Gracias*."

Apollo left the room.

"*Aaiiee*, so naughty, but so necessary." He smiled with pure wickedness.

"You really are incorrigible, Nora."

What's the point of having rich parents if you can't squander their money? As their only son, I feel duty bound."

"You really do put your father through it."

"I *am* wicked to Hector, but he must pay for not allowing me to be myself. For his money that always comes with conditions, and for my mother who is being weak and letting him do all this."

"I don't mean to point out the obvious, but you aren't standing so tall yourself when it comes to egging your father on."

"Darlink! I am not the accountable one." He waved his hand through the air.

"I must admit, I can't imagine you being poor."

He gasped. "I should strike you for even saying that word to me. Then I would just be an irritating black hispanic fag. Instead of an infinitely interesting and culturally rich queen."

He sipped his coffee, his little pinky finger sticking up in the air. I knew that deep down he wouldn't have cared about the money if his father would only accept him, for just being himself. Why is it that some of us always seek such approval from our fathers? Some people crave acceptance, and need that kind of love that only a father can provide. While for other people, it's the mother's love they miss. It's a bit like; Are you a cat or dog person?

For me, it was my mother I wanted to please, and Nora needed his father to connect. We were clawing our way through life, hoping the next claw would be the last claw, to final acceptance.

I poured some tea, instead of going for my traditional mandatory coffee. I wondered again if I should cut down on caffeine.

Fucking hell, and so it begins. I am now in that club. The parents club. One of them. A Maureen Little...

I thanked God I wasn't going to work.

I was already thinking about them. It was only bound to get worse, and in my case, doubly worse.

Fingers clicked in my face. "Hola, hola! You are *vamos*."

"Sorry, I... Never mind. Well honestly, at this moment in time, I'm pleased that you have money," I sipped my tea. I didn't want to already become someone that never shuts up about their kids.

"Very good. You change the subject. You think about the *muchachos*?"

"Yes."

"Tell me, please. I'm so excited." He popped another strawberry in his mouth.

"I took a fair amount of drugs, Nora. I feel guilty about that, not to mention all those sleeping pills as well. I'm nearly forty-four, and I'm a walking disaster who can't even keep a goldfish safe."

"You are in fact a beautiful human who will be a fantastic

mum. Don't worry, they are already strong. You cannot feel guilty over what you did not know, and the most important thing is that you have me."

He soothed some of my fears, and I started to enjoy my breakfast a bit more.

"It's normal that you think these things," Nora said, wisely.

"I must try hard to act more mature."

"You know, change can be good, but don't ever lose your inner child. It's very important. But you already know that."

We both sat there for a few moments, just eating and being. I was enjoying the beauty and freshness of my surroundings, although I still had many questions.

"...And you know what I'm like about pain, and what do you think it will do to my body? Two giant melons travelling down a tube the width of a pea?"

He choked. "Sounds disgusting. I don't think your tube will be that size afterwards." He laughed gaily at my prospective misfortune.

I continued to eat. The selection was fantastic, and I ate more than I'd done in weeks.

Nora gave me Apollo's mobile number. "Just call when you want him. No need to talk. He will... just come. Oh yes. He *is* going to come. *Aaiiee*!"

"I will need to go back to my flat to get more clothes soon, but not if it's in the same state as it was."

"*No problemo*. The cleaners go tomorrow. We can get a taxi, and go and see how they doing."

"Thanks, Nora. You are on it."

"*Si si*. I'm *on* it," he mumbled slyly. There was a strange tone in his voice, but I couldn't place it's meaning. "Okay, darlink. I will leave you now. I have just remembered I have something that needs cleaning."

He left me with the tray, and I didn't see him until the next day. I called Apollo a couple of times. The first time he was an hour late. His hair and laurel leaves were all over the place. He was breathless and red-cheeked. So, it seemed Nora had enjoyed his second meal of the day. The next time I called for him, Apollo looked even worse. He virtually threw the dinner at me, and I didn't see him again until the next day.

At nine a.m. the next morning I didn't even get blessed with an appearance from Apollo, but merely a simple knock on the door. On the other side I found a tray with my breakfast on, while in the distance I could hear small cries of pleasure.

While I ate and bathed, I thought about when I should go to Devon. My heart said '*Go, now...*' but my head spoke more rationally. I needed to get some strength back, and in three weeks I had that appointment at the hospital.

Could I wait three weeks? Or should I go and come back quickly? I could miss it altogether. It is almost my birthday as well, and what a present. Yes please; Twins, for my forty-fourth birthday. A big fat belly, and a twat to match...

Just as I was going to go and find Nora, he came to me, beaming and immaculate.

"So, can we get a taxi now?"

"Well, that's perfect timing. That thing you needed cleaning must have been very dirty."

"It was filthy, darlink."

We both giggled, and instantly I was in as good a mood as Nora. Once we were in the taxi we chatted quietly.

"So when are you going to Devon?" Nora asked.

"I'm not sure what to do yet."

"You have that check up, and the psychologist appointment," he dropped casually.

"How did you know about that?"

"Nora sees everything. And?..."

"For one, I don't need a psychologist. I can heal myself. I've done it before, and two, it's miles away at the hospital in Norwich."

He took a small silver round case from his bag, opened it and checked in the mirror that he was still perfect.

"You do what you like," he said, running his finger along his left eyebrow.

"Don't worry. Soon we are visiting *su casa*. Then we can have some fun." He snapped the case shut.

"I know you're up to something, Nora," I warned him, but I was enjoying the mystery as it made a good distraction.

***

We pulled up outside my flat. I hadn't phoned to warn them. I had the spare key and didn't feel it was necessary. After I'd pressed the doorbell three times, I produced my key, and stared abstractly down the street. That was when I saw the small pink car, with the words *Maid In Heaven* written down the side.

'Nora. You didn't," was all I managed to say as I flung the door open. We gasped, and lurched back.

There stood my brother. He was wearing a full horse's bridle. The bit was in his mouth, and reins hung down each side of his body. To complete the look, a little saddle was strapped to his back, and he had a brown patch painted over one eye. He held a carrot in one hand, and was otherwise, totally naked.

He spat the bit out "For fuck's sake! I'm well busy, and Innis is too scared shitless to move a muscle."

"For god's sake, Jonathan. My neighbours will have a fit."

Nora held his hand on his chest, his mouth slightly open. "So you are a little pony?" Nora giggled.

"What? I'm a fucking horse, if you don't mind."

"Can we please go in?" I asked, whilst frantically trying not to look at my brother's tackle.

He turned round and walked up the hall. The little saddle squeaked as he went. Nora made little horse neighs, and I did the *clippity-clop* sound.

"Funny," Jonathan called back.

"I'll need to use the little girl's room in a minute." I shouted after him.

Once in the bathroom, I noticed that Irene was no longer there, and yes, as a result it did smell better. I could hear a *Hoover* and went towards the sound. My lounge was a hive of activity. Before me were three *Angels*, all busily cleaning with their heavenly bottom cheeks boldly on show. All three men wore pure white leather chaps and a small set of white feathered wings. Their upper torsos were painted gold, as were their genitalia, for none of them wore underpants. One of the men was bending over, vigorously polishing the table, and from behind him I could hear weird noises. Upon investigating I found it was Innis. He was sat on a chair by the window, his feet off the floor, and a laptop open right in front of his face.

"Innis!" I shouted over all the racket.

He slowly lowered the laptop. He had the look of a man about to be anally gang-raped by a flock of angels. He was in full fear-mode, trying desperately not to look at the full sets of shiny gold bollocks that swung before him.

I turned to dish out some admonishment to Nora, but he'd gone to see the angel in the kitchen. Personally, I thought my flat had never looked so clean. I didn't really care how many free range cocks there were flying about.

"I'm *sweatin'* it here, mon." Innis rasped in his thick Scottish accent.

"Innis, I think you can put your feet on the floor."

" I *dinnae* want tae be asked to lift ma feet."

One of the angels passed by with the vacuum cleaner, stopped and cleaned carefully round the traumatised Innis.

"That's the third time that *laddie's* done that." His neck and whole face was bright purple, and he was sweating profusely. Sure, Nora had been so cruel, but I was finding it hard to suppress my smile.

My brother came back in, by now dressed normally, but still with the patch on his eye. Nurse Daisy Urmsham was with him, wearing her uniform.

"So, this nurse does not ride bareback. *Aaiiee!*" Nora laughed at his own joke, walked over to them and air-kissed Daisy on the cheek,

"Darlink, call me Nora."

"I suppose all this is your doing?" my brother asked, pointing to the angels.

Nora simply raised an eyebrow and took another photo, saying; "Hashtag *#maids #GoldenBalls*"

"Hello," I greeted Daisy. I hoped she wouldn't mention anything about me.

"Hello," she answered simply, in her fairy voice.

Jonathan sat down, slapped his lap and indicated that Daisy should sit on it. Like an obedient little bird, she fluttered down without protest. At the most she probably weighed forty-five kilos. I betted to myself that she could eat and eat. For some reason girls that petite normally can. When they say; "I really don't know where it all goes,"

I had always thought; *Well, they can probably shit their own body weight. Just because of the smallness of their frame, that has nothing to do with the size of their number two's. I eat like a horse and poo like a rabbit. There's tiny women all round the world creating giant mountains in their own bathrooms...*

"Hello, *hola?*" Nora was saying.

"Oh, sorry. I wasn't listening."

Nora tutted. "The cleaners have finished. Are you satisfied?"

"Yes, very." I beamed at the three waiting angels, and their gold penises shone back at me. As they bent down to get their stuff, we all heard a groan from behind the laptop.

"Fer fuck's sake, mon."

Nora insisted he escort the maids out, while I collected a bunch of my clothes from the bedroom. I could hear Innis' raised voice and my brother laughing. Poor Innis.

So, evidently my brother was seeing Miss Urmsham already. He must have gone to pick her up from Norwich. By the time I re-entered the lounge, Jonathan was in the kitchen and Nora was in an armchair, examining his nails. Innis had moved to the sofa next to him, laptop still stuck to his lap and his skin a deep shade of red. Daisy was still sat in the same chair.

"I'm making a drink. Do you want one, sis?" my brother chirped.

"Er, Nora? You having one?"

"No, darlink. *Estoy bien.*"

53

"No thanks, then. We'll go, and let you get on with your stuff."

"Jonathan, darlink? Can you call us a taxi?"

Minutes later a taxi was bibbing it's horn. We said our goodbyes and my brother saw us out.

I asked Nora to go ahead, and get in the cab while I had a word with Jonathan.

"When are you taking Daisy back to Norwich? "

"Tomorrow, why?"

"Oh. Can I come with you?"

My counselling appointment at the hospital was the next day. I'd been thinking of it a lot. Was it fate? Was I meant to go? I would never, ever normally go and see a shrink.

"The hospital made me an appointment, to talk to someone. About... Well, you know."

For a minute he didn't know, and then realisation hit.

"What time is it? I'll come and pick you up."

We made the arrangements. In the taxi, I managed to tell Nora I would be out most of the next day, in-between the constant beeping of notifications from Twitter, and laughter from Nora. I knew it would start to wear thin with me very soon. He roared and slapped his hand on the seat.

"Okay, so what is it with these pearls of yours? For instance, what was so funny just then?"

"*Aaiiee!* I just told my fans what happened in the flat, so funny."

I crinkled my forehead. "Oh, really. Who are these fans? And I hope you don't give out any personal information."

"Darlink, of course not, my fans, well there are virtually four hundred and twenty-five thousand of them, waiting for my pearls of wisdom, and my pink news." Nora pouted and smoothed his hair down.

I had clearly offended him, although I was staggered at the huge number of people that followed him. He placed my hand on his leg,

"I'm sorry. I'm sure all your pearls are fantastic. Shoot me one now." I smiled, and his leg released its tension.

"Okay, darlink. *Por ejemplo*, I tweet; Don't go cruising in Victoria Park, London, at night." He let it drop, without explaining.

"Okay, you've got me, very clever ploy. Is it really dangerous?" I asked, now genuinely interested.

"No, not at all, but the lighting is that terrible fluorescent kind that makes the people look like ghosts, or very sickly. So it's not a good place for being sexy."

"Okay. I see, not what I was afraid of, but yes that sure is informational."

"Yes, stuff like that. What restaurant not to eat at, homophobic food, what colours not to mix..."

I couldn't help but laugh. "Homophobic food? My mind is boggling."

"Plum tomatoes are one of the worst, but everybody knows that." He waved his hand dismissively through the air.

We pulled up outside the house.

"Don't worry about tomorrow. I will be busy."

As soon as we got back he did indeed get busy. I heard the muffled sounds of ecstatic shouting again, and there was no maid service for me. I spent most of the evening contemplating my appointment.

GOOD COUNSELLING

I was beginning to wonder why I was here. I'd only been waiting fifteen minutes, but time seemed to be suspended whilst I waited for my counselling session, in some kind of holding pen. I was surrounded by an entourage of continually performing patients, that included the classic, (and everyone's favourite,) the *Wanker*. This one happened to be an old man in a wheelchair. His carer tried to get him to stop shouting, but it literally fell on deaf ears.

Then there was a woman in her mid-thirties, who was apparently made of the colour grey. Her clothes, hair and skin tone were all the greyest of greys. She rocked gently back and forth.

She needs to see a funeral director, not a councillor...

The was a girl in her early twenties who I thought wore her madness well, until after about five minutes she began to ask me, in particular, some aggressive questions.

"Why don't you just fuck off?"

My initial reaction was to shrug, not sure myself. She did actually have a point.

After she'd asked me five or six times, however, I wished *she* would fuck off. The room we were in had allegedly been designed for us fragile, volatile, people, clinging to the thread between madness and sanity. If you were feeling depressed when you came into this room, then you sure would want death to come and take you after five minutes in here. In fact you'd will it, beg for it even. At least hell would be more colourful than this. Who had deemed the colour scheme to be all these shades? There were shit-brown chairs and puce-green walls, the shade of snot from a very sick baby.

I stared at the old posters. Nearly every one of them had a photo of a person looking distressed, and another person trying to cheer them up with either a hot beverage, or a caring hand. They began to depress me, so I looked at the name on the psychiatrist's door.

Dr Smith. MD, Ph.D, Psy.D.

I imagined a very sedentary, middle-aged, slightly sweaty and extremely balding man.

The *'Fuck off'* girl began to encourage me again, and this time I decided to take her advice. I arose from my chair that seemed to be made of nails at the exact same moment that the doctor's door opened. A quite attractive, tanned man in his early thirties was seeing an elderly woman out. He smiled but his face still showed genuine concern.

"Thank you, doctor."

"You're welcome, Mrs Plate." His voice sounded exotic and intriguing.

Mrs Plate scuttled off.

"Miss Bowman, please."

"Here!" I shouted, putting my hand up as if he was taking the school register. He gestured to me to come into his lair, and without the slightest hesitation I complied.

58

The room was just as I had imagined it, unlike the man who was seated in front of me. Hippy beads adorned his dark skin. Thick, almost dreadlocked hair cavorted round his head. He glanced at the notes on his computer screen.

"You don't look very much like a doctor," I said, doing my usual nervous thing of filling in the slightest silence. He turned his attention fully towards me, and for some unknown reason I shuddered.

"Is that a good or a bad thing?" he asked, and his smile entranced me.

"I - I don't know. It depends on what you're going to do to me."

"What do you think I am going to do to you?"

"Aha! So you must be *Doctor Smith*. I've seen how you people operate on the telly, answering questions with questions," I told him, sounding triumphant.

"Is that what I'm doing?" He toyed with me in his strange accent.

I chose not to reply.

"I am *Doctor Hyam Baber*. I'm a fully qualified psychiatrist. I've been working here once a week for two months now, and I've got another four more to go. "

He was perfectly demure and relaxed as he continued to study me, and I didn't feel uncomfortable.

"Am I supposed to say something now? I've never done this before."

"It is up to you, Miss Bowman," he replied, the colourful pattern on his shirt full of life.

"Well I didn't think you looked like a Smith. Do you mind me asking where that name comes from?"

"But of course not, I am an Israeli," he answered. His mannerisms were so tranquillising.

"Are you one of the people that wear those little hats?"

My question made him smile broadly. "I see your knowledge of Hebrew culture is cutting edge."

Normally I would have felt embarrassed at my total lack of wisdom. Instead I began to chuckle, and he joined in with me.

"Well, I have to say I am pleasantly surprised. I had an idea in my head, and I was determined not to comply. I really don't know why I'm here."

"Well for one thing, it's free, and perhaps you had a need to be here, anyway."

His relaxed and easy manner made me feel like he was already a good friend. All my preconceptions and defences were gone, having evaporated away, and I had no idea what I was going to do now.

"Well. I think you must have seen my notes and you know why the hospital made this appointment."

"Yes, I've seen them, however you can use this one hour for whatever you want. It is up to you. Maybe you don't even want to use words?" He leant back, hands in his lap.

"My story is quite simple. I fell in Love."

"I often find, Miss Bowman, that Love is never simple."

"Please, call me Lauren."

He tilted his head slightly to indicate that he would.

So I told him about Nick and David, from how I had met Nick, right up to the present time - pregnant, with Nick's twins. The whole time I was talking he didn't once fidget or look uninterested. An aura of sympathetic understanding radiated from him.

"So there you are, all in quick time. So the diagnosis is dial M for madness, I suppose?" I concluded, trying to use humour to cover my nervousness.

Hyam leant forward and pulled me into his positive force field.

"Lauren. It sounds to me as if you have been through a lot." He paused to give me a reassuring smile. I noticed his eyes were dark green, similar to Sergeant Cole's. I wondered how *he* was, and if he was still with Jenny. It was the first time I'd thought about either of them in a while.

"I could tell you my overall impressions from everything you have just told me," he offered.

"Yes. I would like that," I said, and I meant it.

"Everything you relayed to me was said as if you were saying it all about someone else. You seemed very casual and matter-of-fact."

"Well..." I stammered, not knowing how to react. "How does it matter how I say it? Surely it's the words that are important"

"Yes. The words are important, *and* so is your manner of speaking them. You casually tell me that in the past you have lost a child, and you are now pregnant, and that you tried to take your own life. As if we were neighbours hanging out the washing, and you were telling me over the fence."

I was taken slightly aback. This wasn't turning out to be as easy as I'd thought.

"I don't see it like that. I am telling you factually. I have dealt with these things, and I'm simply relaying the information to you."

"I believe you feel like you have dealt with things, in the most appropriate way you could."

61

"Which was...? Well, you're the Doctor," I concluded, with a hint of bitterness.

"Lauren. I am here to try to help you. It's possible for you to resolve and change some negative life patterns. I am not here to judge you." His kind words swam within the texture of his accent, and soothed my defensive nature.

"Please, Hyam. I would like to know what you think."

"I have no doubt that you are in Love with Nick. Opening your heart and letting Love in has obviously been difficult and traumatising. Nick has clearly opened a lot of old wounds, especially as he is David's son."

He stopped talking and let his evaluation hang in the air. I thought about what he'd said, and without realising, tears filled my eyes.

"It *is* hard and painful. I did let my feelings in, and it ended up even worse than before. I expect you think I'm wicked for what I have done." Tears rained from my cheeks.

"I stress again, I am only here to help, not judge. You have suppressed so many emotions. Love can also be glorious, joyous and enriching."

"I haven't suppressed any emotions. I honestly have dealt with them," I argued as I wiped away those pesky tears. He handed me a box of tissues.

Shit, I bet he gets through a lot of these...

"I think you are being brutally honest with yourself. Your protective reaction is a coldness, a hardness. You are repressing your rage. There is actually a right time for anger. I am not advocating violence, but venting at the right moment in the right way can help you to release negative emotions. You've taken your pain and internalized it. Maybe your coldness has made your defences stronger but it can also be most detrimental and self-destructive. However, back then, you were a teenager, you were young and vulnerable, and you were dealing with adult

62

complexities, which even adults have trouble mastering. You did what you felt was best at that time."

Wow... His words were blowing my mind. I was trying to keep up.

"Okay, so if that is the case, what can I do about it now?"

"I don't have the answer to that question."

"But you seem to have all the answers, so why won't you tell me?" I could hear myself starting to sound angry and desperate.

"You must face yourself, Lauren."

"Am I sick? I feel normal, well maybe not normal exactly, but maybe you can define that for me." I was becoming confused. "I did deal with it, I told you." I repeated parrot fashion what I knew.

"I feel you may have what I would call *Arrested Development*. It's a natural side effect of trauma at an early age. You are an intelligent woman and well travelled, and yet it sounds like you have lived your life as if you were a nineteen year old. It's no coincidence that that's the age you were when you and David finally split up. You are letting the past control your present. You have the power in your life. You are not driven by external forces, out of your control. In fact you happily relinquished control over and over again," He paused, and I could only sit and stare at this Jewish Guru. "That's possibly why you reverted back to your oldest self-harming habits; not eating or caring about yourself. This is what led you to try to end your own life. You clung to the old emotions that were so familiar to you and deemed yourself unworthy of happiness and love, but you *are* clearly deserving, Lauren. Allow yourself some Love." His face shone with honesty and grace.

I cried hard. Very hard. I tried to take it all in, but his words rang true, and I instinctively trusted him.

"Protecting yourself by denying yourself Love and trust is ultimately negative, and spiritually harmful."

I sniffed and sobbed. "If, if that is the case, then how do I change?" I asked, and blew into a tissue.

"How would you want to make that change? I am merely suggesting some self-reflection, during which you address some of the issues that arise within yourself. Allow some Love in your life."

"I do Love Nora. He's my best friend." I protested, as I tried to justify myself and show that I was capable of love.

"You seem to have no friends apart from Nora, who is a gay man. No women or female friends. Do you feel that it is quite lonely and perhaps it's unhealthy for you and stops you from building relationships?"

"I've never really thought of it in that way, but I get hurt the least, the less people I have in my life, which I suppose is my self-protection."

His concerned look took on a smile, as I received my first lesson in self-enlightenment.

"There is a lot to think about. Your words have made some sense," I said, and I definitely felt better, somewhat calmer. I'd been given something special from this man, and I knew better than to discard it.

"I'm so sorry, Lauren, but our time is up."

An edge of panic started to rise up in me. *How will I cope without Hyam's wise wisdom?...*

"Now? But it went so fast. I need more. How will I do this? What if I forget what you've told me?"

"You won't forget. The main theme will stay with you. You have all the control." He sounded so convinced.

"Yes, I do. That was exactly what you were talking about. I was trying to hand it over to you again."

He beamed, and I knew I was on the second step to enlightenment.

He stood, and so did I. However, I really felt like I didn't want to leave his aura.

"I don't know about other psychiatrists, but I think you've chosen the perfect profession."

He blushed.

"It's silly, but I'm finding it hard to say goodbye," I said quietly.

"*Toda*. That's 'thank you' in Hebrew."

I lingered at the door, and as we shook hands, a thought came to me.

"Do you see patients privately? Can I pay?"

I never thought I would be asking that question in a million years, but I'd never felt anyone's help could be so valuable. I wanted to cherish and nurture it. I was prepared to drive to Norwich, shit, even Outer Mongolia if I had to.

He is a gift, Lauren, sent to you in your time of need...

He looked pleased.

"I do. You can. It would be an honour to be your psychiatrist."

"I bet you say that to all your patients."

My god, Lauren. You're flirting with him...

He walked over to the desk. Sauntered perhaps, but even that would be the wrong word. Moved by the breath of god?

Shit, Lauren Bowman. What is happening to you?...

I felt humbled, a feeling that I had only felt since I'd met

Nick. As he walked over I noticed he was wearing open-toed sandals and light blue baggy genie's trousers.

"Here is my number. The sessions will still be in this location, but I hope it was me that helped and not the room."

I laughed like a girl as I took his card.

"Definitely not the room."

"Call me when you're ready."

"*Toda,*" I said. I beamed, now that I thought myself fluent in Hebrew, and left.

I sat in the local park, waiting for my brother to call me. He was still with Daisy. I was going to ask him to bring me up to Norwich again, and while here I would go and see my Aunt Patty, and try to rectify some of the damage I had done. I felt different. I couldn't pinpoint it exactly but as I sat there, I allowed myself to examine my life, crying for the baby I had lost all those years ago, and for the new lives I now held responsibility for. My bitterness was dissipating. I began to release my ice-queen grip on myself. I felt certain these changes were going to be permanent.

TURNING THE CORNER

Over the next three weeks I saw Dr Hyam Beber twice a week. My brother continued to see Nurse Daisy, and both of us were getting completely different fixes. His was physical, mine was spiritual. I had no idea why Hyams' words had such a profound effect on me, but I'd begun to examine myself, in a critical and unbiased way for the first time ever.

I had decided to wait a while until I went to see Nick. I was regaining my strength and returning to being a human. I wanted to address the issue of babies. Hyam was shocked that my only concern was the pain of birth, my body changing, and becoming one of *them*; The Parents Pool. We had been talking about that in our last session. I intended to wait for my ten week check up before going to Devon. I didn't tell Hyam that. I wanted to wait and see what happened. It was enough just trying to digest all this information about myself.

Back in London, I could not shut up about Hyam. I went on and on, driving Nora mad. "Seriously, Nora this guy needs to be Prime minister."

Nora was not impressed.

"My parents made me go to a psychologist. He told me to stop being Gay. *Coño.*"

I agreed that was some shit advice, and assured him that Hyam would never say that. He eventually snapped and forbade me to talk about him.

My brother did the same. By the end of the first journey back home, he told me: "That's fucking it now. Enough about your guru Jew."

My aunt Patty had already had a session with the good Doctor, after I'd telephoned her to explain that I would visit her the following week, and told her why I was going to Norwich. Every week I would visit her house after my hour's consultation, and our coven of two witches would vigorously and enthusiastically talk about Hyam Beber. It helped to heal the wound between us, and was a small but important connection I would always have pooh-poohed before. Until Nick had come into my life, *Spirituality* had been just a swear word to be mocked and sneered at. Now I opened my mind and soul and allowed a small shred of Hippy-ness to enter me.

When Nora got agitated, I even said to him;

"You need to be *Hyamized*," and then I tittered at my own piquant wit.

He screamed at me, told me he was going to puke, and warned me I would have to leave his house if I mentioned anything more to do with him. My clumsiness had even abated, as I tried to be more aware of myself. I still managed to break two priceless vases, but Nora didn't care. The previous maid had gone and that week's replacement from Maid in Heaven was *Bacchus* - god of wine, madness and theatre, as he informed us, salaciously. He was Russian, very brisk, and turned out to be the biggest queen of them all. He devoted nearly all his time to Nora, just as his predecessor had done. My favourite maid was the following one who worked during my third week of recovery; *Eros* A.K.A. *Cupid* - the god of sexual desire and attraction. The agency had definitely picked the perfect god for us that time. He was the only one who could resist Nora's advances. He genuinely seemed to take his job seriously, and often tried to help me. His cooking was excellent, and we got on very well. Nora got a little jealous, but secretly enjoyed the chase. Eros told me his real name was *Danny*, and that he lived not far away with three other gay male friends. His chiselled elfin features were very striking. He told me his mother was Swedish, which answered some questions. He spoke fluent Swedish, and I enjoyed listening to him speaking it.

68

I tried to convince Nora that he should keep Eros on as long as we needed him. I reminded him that Eros had been hired to take care of me, not for Nora's bum fun.

My brother told me at the end of the second week's therapy that Innis had gone back to sea in the giant metal penis. Jonathan thought that the cleaning angels had probably scarred him permanently, and that maybe Nora had gone too far. Still, we both belly-laughed when he told me Innis had said that polishing would never be the same again for him. I imagined Innis constantly showering, sobbing and scrubbing himself with a pumice stone to get clean.

Jonathan said that Nurse Daisy had got a hold on him. He told me he had never met anyone like her. She lived in the nurse's home and he was thinking of renting a place near the hospital. He could easily afford it. I said that if he felt that strongly, he should.

By the third week of therapy, all I wanted was to see Nick. I wasn't brooding; I just had a simple need. I had told Eros/Danny nearly everything, except that I was pregnant.

"That sounds so romantic. You should write a book about it. When are you going to see this Nick guy?" he asked as he folded the towels. We were engrossed in talking. My tests were due the next day, and then three days later, Jonathan was taking me up to Devon so I could see Nick. Nora had reacted as if he was mortally wounded, and told me he didn't like not being involved in this particular Love plot, but I reminded him that he was the only one who I trusted to know about the babies, and that even in London he stood out like a sore thumb, let alone in rural Devon. I'd told him that Jonathan was the best choice. Nora had relented, but he'd insisted I needed to be in disguise, and told me he would at least help with that.

"I'm going in three days, so over the weekend I'll pick my undercover outfit."

Danny sighed, and held one of the towels to his chest. At five foot five inches, he did not cut an imposing figure, but his manner, and prettiness made up for it. His hair was blonde like mine, but almost white. He looked truly angelic. He had a fake tan, and told me that if he didn't add some colour he would have looked like a puddle of sperm.

"Do you really think you have to go in disguise? Is it really that bad?" Danny asked. He came over and sat on the bed.

"Yes, it is. If anyone there recognises me, it's game over. Then Nick will find out quickly. I need to see what's going on. Three weeks is a long time and anything could have happened."

"Yes, that's true, but won't he recognise your brother?"

"Yes, but no one else would." I explained as I ate an amazing lunch that Danny had prepared. Apparently, all the maids had been told by Nora that I'd had a nervous breakdown. I didn't want the world to know what I'd done, and Danny agreed. He had asked me what caused my breakdown, and I said it had been brought on by everything that had been happening. He too had looked up his 'The One,' on Facebook, and had been shocked to see his ex was married to a woman, and had a child with her. Discovering this information had given him nightmares for weeks.

Nora was out, and I was reading in my room one day when Danny came in. He let me chat for a while about my Miracle Guru, and seemed to like it, but I was still aware that he was being paid a very good salary.

"I will be gone next week, but honestly I'll be dying to know what happens. Can we keep in touch? Is that too rude?" he asked.

His soft, delicate and well looked after hands touched mine.

"I would like that, and yes, I'll let you know, unless it's not good news. Oh, I'm not sure what's going to happen, but please let's stay in touch." I dropped my knife. The thought of going to Devon was putting me on edge.

"Sorry, Lauren. I didn't mean to upset you."

70

"Then don't, bitch!"

We both jumped at the sound of Nora's voice.

He stood in the doorway looking viper-ish. His slitted eyes were transfixed upon Eros, who jumped as if he had just been stung.

Nora sauntered into the room and bent down to kiss me on the forehead.

"I don't pay you to upset my friend, and I definitely don't pay you for sitting on the bed."

Without saying a word, Eros quickly and quietly left the room.

"Darlink, I wish you wouldn't cavort with the staff."

I laughed, and began to take the piss. "Cavort with the staff? What, pillow fights and tickling?" I teased, still laughing. "Piss off Nora. For one, you definitely don't pay him, and secondly, put that gay jealous pride away. For you it's just a ball slapping competition."

He smirked and removed his golfing gloves, which he often wore even though he had never played the game in his life. Once my father had come round and seen Nora dressed from head to foot in golfing attire, including the hat. My father asked,

"What hole do you play off from?"

Nora seemed both amused by the question and taken slightly aback.

"Lionel, darlink. You *are* full of surprises. I play with whatever hole you like."

Luckily my father hadn't understood, and left me having to explain the rules of golf to Nora, who found it eternally amusing.

Nora became benign as his smirk turned into a smile.

"Well in one way, darlink, I am paying for it. *Bastardo!*" He ran his index finger along his eyebrow and sighed with the boredom of being alive. "Still," he said, clapping his hands. "*Mañana* you have your hospital appointment. We can ask to see what sex they are."

"I don't want to know, Nora. I only want to know that they're healthy. I don't care what sex they are."

"Oooh!" Nora pouted, but carried on smiling, just happy to be a part of it all.

"I have been out buying wigs and make up for your transformation," he said slyly.

"We can't make it too hard or I won't be able to make myself up." I finished my lunch and placed the plate on the floor.

"This is why you need me with you. Nora just blends into the background."

"Blend. Sure, yes, *blend* is the word. A black guy dressed like a peacock, who's gayer than *The Wizard of Oz*, in a tiny village in Devon. They call you *The Chameleon*. Blend? Haha!" Laughter leaped from me, and eventually Nora joined in.

"Anyway, I will call you every day, Lauren." He reached for his mobile, called Eros and asked him to come upstairs.

Danny knocked gently on the door.

"*Si? Entrar!*" Nora called out.

Danny's face peeped in and his hair seemed to radiate light.

"Can you take these plates, and bring us up some *Lapsang Souchong* tea?"

Eros did as his master bade him, and flashed me a very quick glance as he skipped out. Nora and I chatted idly about the next day. By the time Eros came back with the tea, he was humming a tune in an effort to lighten the atmosphere. It was a very familiar tune. One I hadn't heard for three weeks. *Desire.*

He chatted while he poured.

"Oh, I just love that song, Desire. Its number two in the charts now. *'Valentines spin in my brain',*" he sang.

Nora's body became erect. I knew he was going to say something. "Yes, me too."

I smiled warmly. "Good, it deserves to do well."

Immediately after he'd left the room Nora asked if I was alright.

"As Hyam would say, it's better to have and embrace, rather than hide and ignore. I can't ignore the fact that the song was written for me, and yes, it does make me feel a little sad still, and I can't hide my feelings about it, but also now I'm thinking; Shit, that was written for me. What a beautiful gesture that was."

Nora looked as if someone had just opened their bowels in front of him.

"*Puta madre*, Lauren. He isn't Jesus. You're on this fucking hippy cloud, sprinkling your little fortune cookies of shit."

I hit him on the arm, and he screamed melodramatically.

"So I hope you'll both be very happy on your own little Fantasy Island. *Aaiiee!*"

We both giggled like young girls.

The rest of the day we relaxed. The only other event was my mother calling to inform me that my father and his best friend, *Rupert Douglas Mountshaft*, or *Duggie*, as he was known by only the closest of friends, had been accepted into the *Lawns Golf Club*. To my mother, that was life changing news. She would be in her natural surroundings at the golf club, rubbing shoulders with local gentry such as *Admiral Pickering* and his wife, *Maud*, who owned *Pickering's Pies*.

The boss of the local pub, *The Cock and Pea*, was a member, not to mention the spectacular *Lady Crumb*, head of the Girl Guide association, who one year had been featured in *Fox and Hound* magazine, with her amazing sponge cakes and exotic pickles.

I let her talk for a good hour, name-dropping names of people that I'd never heard of, but I was pleased for her that she had achieved this coup. The last thing she informed me of was that Jonathan had a girlfriend. This as yet unidentified woman had apparently answered the phone at my flat. Of course my mother had sent my father round to see what this jezebel was doing with her baby boy. Luckily, my mother found out that her name was Daisy, which is one of my mother's *good girl* names. If she'd have been a Rachel, a *bad girl* name, she'd have had to go. My mother kept a list of bad names, and not only for women. A *Dave* would never have even made it past her front door. Also Daisy was a nurse, which my mother considered to be one of the oldest and noblest professions throughout history. Unlike prostitution, which would be akin to, say, teaching dance, or so my mother thought.

She had already called Jonathan and arranged to have tea on Sunday. He and Daisy were going to my parent's house. I could imagine my brother swearing and cursing, but he knew it was ultimately just easier to do her bidding.

I told her virtually nothing except that I was still at Nora's, which of course she already knew. I would never tell her about the counselling. Especially about Hyam. Just the word *Israeli* would make her assume I was being hypnotised and groomed into becoming a terrorist.

The next morning I was ready by ten-thirty. Danny served me breakfast, and I was aware that I probably seemed unusually quiet. He didn't question me, and answered me softly when I asked what Nora was doing.

"He's getting ready." Wrinkles flawed his normally perfect skin and let me know he was concerned.

As I sat on the bed thinking about upcoming events, Nora burst through the bedroom door. He was dressed in a dark purple crushed velvet suit. A big hat was trimmed with dark pink feather trim, as was the jacket. His gold-toed shoes sparkled, and a gold topped cane was a perfect accompaniment for that perfect seventies pimp look.

He leant back, one hand on his hip and the other on the cane.

He's got the wrong event...

"Nora, we're going to a hospital so I can have all manner of cold objects inserted into me. Not so you can drive me to the nearest Street corner."

"But this is one of my *Vivianne Westwoods*," He stepped forward. "And I know exactly where we are going. Darlink, I am adding a dash of colour to their otherwise drab environment."

I sighed. To argue with him would have been absolutely futile.

"*Como esta?* You are worried?" He asked as he sat next to me.

"Not exactly worried, but well, in a week I'll be forty-four. It's natural to be concerned." I gave him a reassuring smile. "But I'm happy you are coming with me, even if you do look like *Ali G*."

Nora preened himself and looked happy to be of service in my time of need.

We caught a taxi, and once again hospitals were in my life. This month's major feature; *Hospital - The Movie*. This time however it wasn't Hyam I was waiting to see, and the noise and smells seemed to attack me and alert my attention to the clinical-ness of it all. Nora strolled with his cane as if he was meandering through Kew Gardens. He'd actually been right. He was indeed a well needed giant splash of colour in that depressing environment.

The next few hours were only the beginning of what I was to expect in the next few months. I was stabbed by long painful needles. I was expected to produce cups and cups of piss, grunting and groaning as I squeezed every last drop from my tired bladder. I had freezing cold hard metal objects put up my vagina. We walked to the ultrasound waiting room, just as giant globules of lubricant slid out of my pussy from the last set of tests.

"Why do they have to put so much in?" I complained to Nora. "I mean it's not like they're going to insert their whole arm." At least I was making him giggle.

We arrived at the latest holding pen. About fifteen pregnant women gaped at us, incredulously. I sighed, anticipating a long wait ahead. The mandatory chairs felt as if they were made of pine cones. Nora sat down, legs extended, and both hands clasped on top of his cane. He smiled and nodded at the bemused women. One of his specialties was making other people think he was a *someone*. An actor, an eccentric millionaire or perhaps the son of a celebrity.

I felt sulky that I had to wait, and slumped down hard on the chair. A hugely loud and long moose call yodelled forth unexpectedly from my vagina. All that lubricant had created and trapped air bubbles, which produced a legendary fanny-fart that volleyed round the room. Nora gasped. I pulled my head back and my eyes bulged. I was scared stiff of moving in case any more air escaped. All fifteen ladies and girls' intense attention settled on me like a blanket of astonishment. Even in the privacy of my own bedroom, I'd always dreaded the wet, air-propelled pussy queef.

The chair was *so* uncomfortable. Just as everyone had settled back down, I moved slightly and coughed involuntarily. Again, there was a rasping sound like a carthorse's sneeze. I sat in a puddle of wet shame for the next forty minutes enduring the looks of contempt.

Finally, my turn came. Nora led the way. A short well-rounded nurse, advanced in years, told me to get up on the bed. She applied more dollops of lubrication onto her hands. *Oh shit, not more?...*

"Pull your top up, please." she asked, very matter-of-factly.

Thankfully, she smeared the lube on my stomach and placed a small scanning device onto it.

Nora and I looked at the pixels on the screen, and the nurse pointed at the two little shapes in my tummy. I could quite clearly make out their tiny bodies.

"There are the heartbeats," The nurse said, and Nora screamed.

"Everything looks good. The twins are the same size."

Nora squealed again.

"Are you the father, sir?" The nurse was genuinely asking him.

Up until that moment I'd been in a kind of state of shock. The scan made it all so very, very real.

Those tiny little hearts beating...

I didn't know if I could talk without crying.

Oh, Nick. I wish you were here to experience this...

Eventually laughter took a hold of me as I wondered how anyone could mistake Nora for the father of my children. Only with a turkey baster, at fifty paces and blindfolded, would that ever happen.

"*Aaiiee! Madame, tu eres Loco!*" Nora screeched, joining in.

We knew the nurse was pissed off at us by then, but neither of us could deny it was funny. In fact we took the joke with us, through the rest of the time at the hospital, and all the way home. Our faces ached with amusement, and by the time Eros opened the front door it was obvious we were both in very good spirits. My fears had been half quashed. I had to wait seven days for the test results, but at least I'd be in Devon and that would take my mind off of them. The scan had changed something in my mind, now I'd seen the twins inside me. I wanted to call Hyam and tell him, but I knew that would seem a bit needy.

I'll tell him next time...

I was trying to be more mature, and I knew I was responsible for the consequences of my own actions.

I'll need these newly acquired skills to cope with being a mother. A Mother...

The title did not seem to suit me in that role.

I will think of one that's more apt. One thing I'm sure of is that it should not become my only title. I won't put my life away in a little box, and devote everything to motherhood, whilst I wait for the little body snatchers to grow up and leave home. My dreams are after all, still only dreams…

Even at nearly forty-four, there was still a lot I wanted to do with my life.

The biggest changes will be dependent on what Nick wants to do. When I know that, then I can think more about the future. The hardest thing would be not to tell him about the pregnancy. If he doesn't want me back, it would be easy for me to use the babies against him, in my moment of weakness, but I need him to come back for me of his own accord, without knowing he's a father...

The potential for damage was great, and all this thinking was tiring me out, especially in the hot Juniper oil bath. It had been a long day. I pressed the gold cherub tap and steam roared upwards joining the cloud that hung in the air. The Turkish steam bath atmosphere soothed me. I opened my vagina and allowed the hot water to flow up inside me, cleaning out my very sticky love tunnel of lube. The sensation made me moan gently as my sexuality raised its lovely lonely head.

Hi, remember me? The thing that makes you feel sensational? I need attention too...

My hand lingered on my long forgotten clitoris, but some part of me resisted.

Come on, give in, treat yourself...

My pussy filled with pumping blood in anticipation of the onslaught of a good overdue meat-pounding masturbation. My fingers slipped inside.

I imagined that Nick was standing at the side of the bath. He was dripping wet, and a white sheet wrapped round him and clung to his body. His hand was under the sheet playing with his cock.

My fingers went into overdrive at the thought of that. I began to manically wank, hoping an orgasm would come before cramp did.

Orgasm thankfully took first place. I thrashed around in the water bellowing like a constipated bear.

"Fuck yes!" I shouted out gleefully, pleased all my effort had not been for nothing. On the contrary, my hormones were racing, and I felt *sooo* good.

Danny came running into the bathroom.

"Oh my god, are you alright? I heard shouting."

I was more than alright actually.

I grinned. "Yes, I'm fine, Danny."

That night I slept deeper than I had in a long time. That bloody bear wasn't constipated any more.

***

The next day was Danny's day off, and *The House of Nora* was left to fend for itself.

Nora thought it was the perfect day to get me in disguise. I sat on the beautiful fourteenth century stool, in front of an equally stunning vanity table and looked at myself in its mirrors. It was covered in mother of pearl with ivory legs, hand-carved mahogany flowers, and fans adorned it. Nora informed me it was from the Spanish Revolution, and that this piece had been specially commissioned for Princess Isabella.

"It's priceless." He waved his hand, nonchalantly.

"Maybe because you see it every day in your bedroom, you take its beauty for granted." I proposed.

"Ha! Of course I do, darlink. Look around. You see a palace. I see a toilet." He pulled an unhappy face.

"Fuck off, Nora!" I said, and smiled.

He laughed casually as he began to get out all the stuff he had bought for my trip to Devon. He was in *Queen Heaven*. He'd bought bags and bags of stuff.

Dressed in a *Sherman Hill* dark blue tracksuit, he'd lifted his hair slightly, and dared to let his afro relax naturally. He hummed happily and I was relaxed. He covered the mirrors and told me it would be more fun that way.

As he whipped the covers off for the first time, I released a small involuntary cry. I was wearing a bright red wig, and tons of makeup.

"Shit, Nora. I'm trying to blend. I look like fucking *Cher*. I'm not entering stars in their eyes."

He pulled a face as he went to re-cover the mirrors.

"No. I think its best I see," I protested. He pouted at me, but left them off.

He took some of the makeup off, and put a blonde wig on me.

"Yes, and I don't get it. I am a blonde anyway," I said, and he giggled at my unintentional joke.

"So why should I bother to tell you, Blondie?" Nora replied, nudging me. "Well, okay, it's because you have a fringe, and this wig doesn't."

"Oh right, so what you're saying is that no one will recognise me without my fringe? Yep, that's brilliant Nora. If the whole village is stultifyingly stupid, it's in the bag. Not a soul will see through your master disguise."

He poked out his tongue, hit me on the head with the back of the hairbrush, and started tutting.

The next wig was black, and I hated it. We eventually settled on a shoulder length mousy-brown one, with a fringe. I wore fake glasses with a black frame, a knee length green skirt, and a white shirt with a dark green jacket. It was nothing like how I would ever normally dress. *Blend...*

I kissed him on the cheek. "Yes, this is the one. Oh, thank you, Nora."

He beamed beatifically. "So, honey, you go and get ready and rested. I am going out cruising, and I won't be back until tomorrow. Eros will be here if you need anything."

That was the last time I saw him until the next Monday morning just as my brother was picking me up. I was in my outfit, ready. He staggered past us on the stairs, clearly still totally shit-faced, and hugged me tightly.

"*Buena suerte. Besos, besos.* You better call Nora. Oh, remember your name is Janet!" he shouted, before turning and going into the house.

I got into the car, and embarked on a journey that would change my life. Finally, I was going to Devon to find Nick. This time I was Janet, but I wanted to be Lucy.

DEVON REVISITED

My brother had bought Daisy Urmsham with him, and as he explained:

"I'm not fucking staying for days in *Buckwheat Nowhere* with nothing to do."

Daisy giggled. In fact, she seemed to giggle at everything he said. I was pleased I had the protection of the back seat. My brother hadn't liked the idea of going to Devon to find Nick one bit. He was only coming with me because he was concerned, and thought it could be bad for me, although he finally conceded that it was good to close this chapter of my life. I hadn't explained the purpose of the journey was for me to try to get back with Nick.

"I've no fucking idea why you're dressed like that." he shouted back, one hand loosely on the Mercedes' steering wheel.

"I don't want people to recognise me, and my name is supposed to be *Janet*," I explained.

Daisy turned and fixed her puppy dog look on me. She was grinning inanely, which made me feel unnerved.

"Isn't this nice?" She said, still giving me her *Children of the Corn* stare. "Isn't this nice, Janet?"

Was this chick for real? " Y-e-s," I assured her, with a slowly growing smirk.

She turned back round, unperturbed.

"This is going to be *soooo* much fun!" she shouted, placing her hand on my brother's leg.

"Sure is," he replied, and those two words set her off giggling for the next two miles.

As the beautiful countryside began to rear up around us, so did my nerves inside. All the counselling sessions in the world couldn't soothe them. I tried not to doubt the decisions I'd made. I still felt excitement at the thought of seeing Nick, but trepidation at the possibility of seeing anyone else. My disguise was good, but I felt sure Nick would instantly know who I was.

I haven't even asked my brother where we're staying. Oh crap, I hope he booked somewhere...

I interrupted their idle chatter. "Where are we staying, Jonathan?"

He turned down the music playing on the radio. "You're gonna love this, its above a pub called *The Thirsty Nun*." He laughed, she laughed. I did not.

So maybe I should have checked. What was I thinking? *Elderton* - population; ten gossiping women, twenty fisherman, and a cow called *Wally*. Nightlife: Two pubs. Hardly a metropolis, and not the best Bed and Breakfasts in the world. At least we weren't staying in *The Dry Thrush*. Out of the two I supposed I would rather be in *The Thirsty Nun*.

I began to recognise the landscape, and shortly afterwards we pulled into the familiar surroundings of the village. My heart was beating so loudly I felt certain it could be heard by anyone nearby. I told my brother that the pub was on the corner as you came into the square. Nurse Daisy Urmsham said how pretty it all was, and how happy I must be to be back. I was beginning to view her as something like a young enthusiastic Red Setter; eager to please, but stupid enough to eat their own poop.

My brother parked, and got two enormous suitcases out of the trunk. They looked as if they could easily hold enough stuff for a two month stay.

"Bloody hell! We're only going to be here a few days," I complained, even though the truth of it was that I had no idea how long it was going to take.

"Well, you see ah got my other two bitches in these," Jonathan explained, putting on an American homey's accent.

That set Daisy off tittering again.

I was too weary to discuss post-modern feminism. We all went into the pub, which had the lounge round the side, where I remembered they had played darts that disastrous night back then. Tonight was very quiet. There were two old men from the fisherman's posse, and that was it. A huge tree of a man was serving behind the bar. The night I was here before, there was a peroxide blonde woman whose name I couldn't remember.

"Yes. Hello. I booked two rooms for one week in the name of Bowman," my brother said.

I faked a hacking cough. I was incredulous that he had used our real surname, after I'd gone to all this effort.

"One of them Yankees, are you?" the barman asked, his booming voice matched only by his appearance.

Jonathan tilted his head at this giant tree of a man.

"Yes, sir. You sure got that right, sir," and saluted him smartly.

He could really put a convincing American accent on. I suppressed a smile, and of course Daisy giggled.

The man's huge cheeks lifted his big mouth up into a smile. His hands were like shovels.

I bet his cock is the size of a hazelnut...

"I'm John. People round here call me *Little John*!" He roared with laughter. "Cos I'm so big!"

I didn't know if he felt like he had to explain that because he thought we were American, or because our little group seemed to be as stupid as mud. He had a deep voice and a strong Devonshire accent, and his laughter made my hairs stand on end. As if to confirm his size, I took a small step back. I forgot my case was there, and tumbled backwards, landing with a hard bang right on my arse. I let out a wounded scream. Little John took two giant steps and lifted me up as if I was a tissue.

"Oh! Careful there, miss. Don't fall over yourself." He placed me back onto my feet. The pain in my coccyx was excruciating, but I gritted my teeth and smiled through it.

Little John went back round the bar. "Let me get you all a complimentary drink, and then I'll get the keys. Can't have you going back to America without plenty of Devon hospitality inside you!" He sprayed us with booming laughter.

My brother and Daisy had a whiskey. I asked for a lemonade, even though I wanted a whiskey for the pain and nerves.

"What's with all this no fucking drinking?" My observant brother asked.

"I'm on a de-tox," I lied. *A nine bloody month de-tox. Shit, this is going to be hard...* "Okay, if it will keep you happy, I'll have a white wine spritzer." I am only human after all, and my bum was killing me.

When we'd finished our drinks, Little John got the keys, and directed us to our rooms. He pointed up a tiny rickety staircase, which clearly would never have taken someone of his build. The only man I had ever seen before who was that big was Shannon's Father, *Flynn*. The memory made me feel sad. I hadn't talked to my longest friend for more than two years.

What would she say about what I'd done? Our lives are so different now...

Shannon had gone on to great things, becoming one of the best vets any animal lover could hope for. She worked in England and in Ireland, where she had met her husband, Paddy. I had met up with them, and found I liked him a lot. He was also a vet with his own practice in Southern Ireland.

Shannon had told me: "We fell in Love when we were operating on a dying dog." I guess it was one of those moments that you had to be there to appreciate it.

She was so successful that she had been picked to go on a regular TV programme called *Vets To The Rescue*, by then in its third year. I had seen her on it a few times. Now both of us were caught up in the tangle of life, with time running as fast as ever.

When I get home I will call her...

Our rooms, if you could call them that, were right next to each other. You couldn't even have swung a cat in mine. My head almost touched the wooden ceiling, there was a tiny single bed and the whole floor was on a slant. An ancient wooden wardrobe dominated the room, next to a small hand basin that was *so* small I didn't think even one hand could fit in it. I opened the wardrobe, half expecting to see *Narnia* at the back of it, and hung up my only other outfit, which was almost identical to the one I was wearing. I sat on the bed hoping I would make contact with Nick as quickly as possible. My feet were killing me. Why I'd let Nora talk me into wearing heels, I didn't know. I began to think that maybe I should have bought some different shoes. As my thoughts drifted around, noises began to infiltrate them. I wasn't sure at first, then I realised – *Oh, shit. My brother and Daisy are fucking. Oh, shit!...*

Two minutes later I was going mad, not knowing what to do. Sit there and listen to two squealing pigs fuck, or go and sit in the bar, in constant fear of someone coming in and recognising me. I chose the bar.

Little John was still there. It was early evening. I spied a menu, and suddenly felt hungry. I ordered myself the good old fashioned favourite: Fish, chips, and peas. Then I sat with my orange juice at a small table. I felt content just to sit and be soaking up the pleasure of being back in Devon.

Little John brought my dinner over for me. It smelt, and looked absolutely delicious.

"Any condiments, Miss?" he asked, lingering.

"Oh. Yes please, and call me Janet." I smiled.

"You got a real good English accent there. Well done. You could almost say you were English."

"Well, gee thanks, Little John. That's just *swell* of you to say so," I said, having fun putting on my Texan accent.

Virtually the rest of my meal was uninterrupted, until someone came in I recognised.

I knew who it was, before I even looked up.

"Evening, Lawrence. Usual?"

Standing at the bar, right in front of me was Sergeant Lawrence Cole. I began to blink rapidly.

I must be having hallucinations…

"Yes please, John."

No, it definitely is him. This is real… I searched the pub around me, trying not to be too frantic.

What the fuck is going on? Maybe he's a stalker, or he's following me for some police reason. Shitting shit…

87

I lost my appetite instantly. I placed the knife on the edge of the table, within easy reach. This situation was freaking me out, and I became more animated, looking left to right, left to right, as if an invisible person was slapping me hard on each side of my face. Little John had cause to look over, and called out:

"Oh dear. Are you alright, Janet?"

Lawrence looked over, as well. I instantly stopped doing my unintentional horrendous imitation of Stevie Wonder.

"Yes, Sir," I said, finding my Southern accent once again.

I fumbled as I became edgy, playing with everything on the table.

"Got some Yanks staying here," Little John told Lawrence." So where's that lovely Jenny, then?"

"I'm meeting her here, John." Lawrence's words pushed my *Full Panic Mode* button. My arm came down fast, hitting the knife on the way, which flipped high in the air and somersaulted towards Lawrence, smacking him fully on the head with the handle end. If I had tried a thousand times I bet I wouldn't have been able to make that same shot again.

I stood quickly and came round to the side of my table.

"Oh, my god! I'm so sorry, sir."

I was wobbling in my heels, and I lost my balance. As I went down hard towards the floor, I reached out, trying to grab at whatever I could, which in the event was only my plate. I flung it randomly; peas, fish and chips flying everywhere.

Lawrence helped me to sit back down.

"Oh, my word!" exclaimed Little John, as he came round and began to pick bits up.

I kept my head down.

"Are you alright, Miss? Can I get you anything?" Lawrence asked, softly.

Kind, caring, Sergeant Cole. At least now I know why he was here; He was waiting for Jenny. How funny, what a strange turn of events. Last time I was worried Jenny would see me and Nick, and this time I'm worried Lawrence will recognise me...

I had to get back to my room.

"I do so apologise. I *ahm* prone to mild fainting spells," I explained, thinking that my Texan accent was convincing to a seasoned police officer. I went to stand up.

"No, no. I'll get you some water, stay there."

"No need, really, sir. I have juice." I reached for the glass and knocked the whole thing over. Orange trickled steadily down onto the floor, along with any dignity I had left.

Lawrence went to the bar and poured some water. He brought it over to me, sat down and remained silent while I sipped carefully. Little John cleaned up the mess, and the moment he had finished and gone back to the bar, Lawrence turned and leant closely towards me.

"So, Lauren, what the hell is going on?" he whispered.

My mind froze. *Shit! What's the right answer?...* I sighed. "How did you know?" I asked, whispering back.

He couldn't help but smile. "I don't know anyone as clumsy as you."

Shit. He's a cop, you idiot...

"Although my powers of detection must be failing me, because I don't know why you're here, or why you're undercover. Good accent by the way."

I had actually missed him. He looked well.

"I'm here to find Nick, Lawrence. You look good, are you meeting Jenny here?" I asked, glancing furtively about.

"Okay, so after weeks and weeks, you turn up dressed as a mousy librarian. You didn't return any of my calls. I was worried about you, Lauren." His handsome face was full of concern.

"I'm Janet now," I corrected him. This conversation was throwing me. I was thinking; *Isn't this what Nick should be saying?*...

"Shitting hell, Lawrence. I am spinning out. What the freaky shit?..." I trailed off.

"You're asking me that? I'm the copper, and I'm bollocked if I know." He took my hand and held it. "It's good to see you, even if you are in disguise. I didn't know if we could have had a friendship, you know, what with me seeing Jenny, and you were seeing Nick, even though David was your ex -"

I pulled my hand from his. Hearing the past tense of me and Nick sent a jolt through my body. It all sounded like an episode of Jerry Springer.

"Sorry, Laur... Janet."

For a few moments neither of us said anything. I could sense we were being watched, so I tried to take care.

"Sorry, Lawrence. So, you and Jenny, eh?" I said, diverting the conversation away from Nick.

"Yep. That's why I'm up here. I'm meeting her parents, and I'm staying at David and Angela's bed and breakfast." His words began strong, but ended sheepish.

"Wow. It sounds serious. I bet she loves the fact that your father is a big judge," I said, and heard myself sounding bitchy, trying to cover my pain.

"No, I haven't told her yet."

"Oh... Oh." I was genuinely surprised. "I'm being a total bitch again, I'm so sorry. Then why did you tell someone like me?"

"In my heart I knew we'd never be together. I'm drawn to your disarray because it's such a contrast to my normal structured world. My ex wife was a bit like you. I know it's not good for me. I really need a solid and dependable partner. However, despite all your dizziness I still believe I can trust you."

I replaced the hand that I'd violently withdrawn.

"I'm happy for you. Honestly, I really am."

"Normally I'd invite you to stay for longer and meet her, but that's probably not such a good idea." He looked at his watch. "I've still got about half an hour. Where are you staying?"

"Upstairs, so it's not too far to scuttle off if I need to," I said, pointing at the ceiling.

I didn't want to leave him. I knew I wanted his friendship, despite my own paranoia that he was still *Police*. I was almost sure I could hear Dr Beber saying; *'Go on Lauren, let him give you his friendship.'*

"Has Jenny met your parents yet?" I asked.

He smiled wryly. "No. I doubt she will, unless it's at the wedding, and that's if we get married, which is early days at the moment." The normally composed Mr Cole was becoming tongue tied.

"Well. If you do, and they do, I'm sure they'll love her."

"I'm sure they will. Thanks. Jenny studied Social sciences and Politics. She thinks she wants to be an M.P., and my father would love that, especially as she would run for the Conservatives. I fully support her. Anyway, why are we talking about me? Where have *you* been? Why are you here?"

"Okay, I was staying at my Aunt's house, in Norwich, just so

I could get my head together. Now I'm here to see Nick. Have you seen him?"

Finally, I'd asked the dreaded question.

"Yes. I've seen him, of course. I'm staying at his parent's bed and breakfast, so it's hard not to really," he explained, shifting uncomfortably. He called over to Little John and asked for more of the same, making sure to offer me a drink, politely.

"Oh, no thanks. I'm fine, and - how is he?" I asked. My whole body felt like it was going to burst into a trillion molecules. I gripped Lawrence's hand tightly.

"He looks terrible. It's bad. Sorry, Lauren. I don't want to say too much, not if you're going to talk to him. Nobody knows anything, because he's not mentioned a thing. All he's said to me and Jenny is that he's happy for us, and that seemed genuine."

My heart lurched. I wanted to run to Nick. Comfort him. Love him. Tell him everything.

I removed my hand when Little John came over with the drink. He towered above us and gave me the feeling that I was somehow cheating. We resumed our whispering once he'd left.

"Maybe you can help me, Lawrence. You could let me know where he goes, so I can talk to him, alone."

"What? Spy on him? Lauren, firstly I'm here visiting my girlfriend's parents. Secondly, I'm a police officer; a sergeant. Thirdly, here I am again to help you, but only when it suits you. I can only allow myself to be a fool for you so many times."

The bell above the door tinkled. *Jenny, that's Jenny...* I vaulted up quickly just as she looked over.

"Well, it sure was mighty fine talking with you, sir." I tipped my head down as I passed her, and went back to my room as fast as my high heels would let me.

Nick, I must find Nick... I decided I would start spying the next morning, bright and early.

***

I was awoken a little too bright and early by familiar noises coming from the next room.

I groaned. *Oh, please. Not this early...*

It was nearly the end of October, it was dark and it was cold. I didn't have the modern convenience of an en-suite bathroom, so I plodded down the hall in my slippers and overcoat. On the way back from that heinous experience I realised I didn't have my wig or glasses on.

I really must be more careful...

I got ready, and thankfully I didn't hear any more noises. It was so cold my hands were shaking. I wanted to borrow the car so at about eight AM, I knocked quietly on my brother's room. I waited a minute, and was about to knock again when the door flew open.

Standing there was Daisy, with a huge cock and full set of big heavy balls strapped to her. A glittery red Alice-band was in her hair, that had springs on with small red glitter balls on the end. Her hair was in schoolgirl bunches. Her face had a cream coloured liquid all over it, which also ran in globs from her mouth, and down over her beautifully formed bare breasts. I stumbled back on my heels.

"Dear god, and all that breathes!" I gasped.

She wiped some of the liquid into her mouth and giggled. "Oh, my. What must you think, Lauren?"

I was trying not to. This tiny woman was wearing *that*, with my brother in there. My senses were being assaulted on every level.

"It's Devon ice-cream," she explained, wiping more into her mouth. "I know. You must be thinking, what is this crazy shit? How the hell did they get ice-cream at this hour? And in October?" She shook her pom-poms, and released the mandatory giggle.

I watched the panting playful Red Setter performing in front of me. I didn't have the heart to inform her that ice-cream was sold all year round here, and besides, that was the furthest thing from my mind.

"Come in, sis!" my brother called.

I shook my head meekly at Daisy. I didn't want to see any more.

"Could I just get the car keys?"

She turned and went to fetch them. Mumbling, I informed them that I might be gone most of the day. She just giggled as she handed them over. I had a feeling they would be able to amuse themselves.

The air was icy cold. Grey depressing clouds were my only companion. As soon as I started to drive, I knew where I was going. I pulled into the lane and parked a good way before the bed and breakfast, keeping the engine running. I was back in my Janet outfit, on my stake-out for Love. I waited for the family truck that I'd recognise, or for Nick to go past on his bicycle. Even then, I wasn't sure what I'd do if David was driving the truck, or if I'd try to follow it, and then I realised that if it came to that, I'd also seem a bit conspicuous trailing a bicycle. I just knew I needed to talk to Nick on my own.

It began to rain lightly. Roughly an hour later, a maroon *Fiat* went past, and for the next three hours, nothing happened. I wished I'd bought some supplies, and was starting to feel very, very bored. I had turned the engine off for some time and I was getting cold. I didn't think I would be able to stand too many days of this. A car passed, but it was the same Fiat from earlier.

As it went past, I turned my engine on again. Shortly after that, a dark blue *BMW* pulled up in front of me and stopped. At first I panicked, but then I recognised Lawrence Cole. He came round to my passenger door, opened it and jumped in. It began to rain even harder.

"So, you're on stake out?" he asked, shaking the water off himself like a dog." I thought it was you."

How did he?... "Lawrence, I, I never -" I trailed off, flummoxed.

"So, luckily for you, I was in the reception when one of the guests came in saying they'd noticed a virtually brand new *Mercedes* parked in the lane all morning, and they asked if the local police should be informed."

"You're joking?" I spluttered, feeling slightly indignant.

"Lauren. You're in a very small community, where people notice everything. I've only been in *The Thirsty Nun* twice before, and the last time was two weeks ago. Look at how it was last night. Little John remembered my whole name, what I drink, and why I'm here. Shit, half the people here could happily work for the police."

He was right; I hadn't thought it through properly. I scratched my head as the wig began to itch and sighed deeply.

"So, are the police coming?" I asked, naively.

Lawrence smiled and showed off his set of great teeth. "Yes. I'm here aren't I? I told them I would make a stop, and I flashed the receptionist my badge." He seemed to be parodying himself.

"So it begins. Thank you for helping me again, Mr Cole." I must have sounded almost depressed at the realisation that once more Lawrence was to be my substitute knight in shining armour.

"Well, and here we go again with the; *'I couldn't give a shit,'* attitude, until you need my help, of course!" he said, his voice raised an octave.

I have no idea why, but as we exchanged flaring nostrils, we both began to chuckle.

"God, we sound like an old married couple," Lawrence said.

"Yes, we do. I am sorry, Lawrence for always being such a bitch and I know I must seem ungrateful. In truth I sometimes am, but I'm working on my issues."

"You're not unique. Most people are naturally self-centred, but I appreciate you saying that."

I'd turned the engine off and once again all the windows had streamed up. I started it back up, unsure of what to do next.

He broke the silence. "So, it appears that whether we like it or not we are in each other's lives."

"It certainly looks that way, Mr Cole, but not everyone will be thrilled about that."

"I'm a grown man. I have who I want in my life." He said it as if it was a new year's resolution.

"So, Miss Bowman. What are we to do?"

I wasn't sure what he meant. "Mm. Tell Jenny we're friends?" I suggested.

He smiled. "I meant about you stalking Nick."

"I'm not sure, and I'm not exactly stalking him." I pushed his shoulder, playfully. I wanted things to be easy between us.

"Look. I'll try and help. Let me see if I can find anything out. It's obvious you want to see Nick, and I can't see *this* working." He opened his arms out to illustrate.

The heavy rain fell steadily, and I knew he was right. I couldn't do it this way. I decided to give up the fight and let him help.

"Thank you, Lawrence. Shall I buy a t-shirt with those words on?"

"Yes. It'll save time, anyway," he teased, and pushed his shoulder against mine, allowing himself a tiny indulgence of playfulness. "I know where you're staying, and I still have your mobile number. I'll be in touch."

He opened the door and was gone.

I drove back to the pub and went up to my room. I was feeling tired so I lay down to sleep.

The next thing I knew there was a knocking on the door. I opened it to find Lawrence standing there.

"So, I know where he goes."

I let him in immediately.

TOO LATE, TOO LATE

My heart was racing so badly that I had to take deep breaths to control myself. A day on, and the weather was even worse. Rain pelted down from a pitch black sky. All the cars had their lights on as we drove to where Nick would be. Lawrence had tried to talk me out of seeing him that day, and tried to convince me there was a possibility that the weather would improve later. He didn't like my plan: That he would leave me out in the sticks, twenty miles away from Elderton, in this hellish weather, in the faint hope that Nick would talk to me.

Lawrence had found out the day before that Nick would be felling trees near a certain address: somewhere near a barn. From nine AM he'd be on his own. Lawrence had copied out a little map, which I held in trembling hands.

Lawrence glanced over at me. "We're nearly there. I still wish you would wait, Lauren."

"I've waited long enough. Have you told Jenny what you're up to?"

His silence told me he hadn't.

Through the rain up ahead I saw a large barn, and behind that a huge house.

"There it is - *Quigley Manor*." Lawrence motioned towards the house as we pulled up in front of the barn.

There was a gravel courtyard, with open metal gates. All different kinds of vehicles were parked up and straw lay everywhere. Amongst it all I saw the truck, and I knew he was there.

Lawrence pleaded with me to stick to our loose plan, insisted I call him on his mobile to let him know I'd got back safely, and drove off.

I pulled the thick Parka jacket around me and the hood engulfed my head. That day I wore no disguise, I was simply myself. Once in the yard I tried to quickly decide which direction to start looking for Nick. The rain became torrential.

I could make out a figure running, with what looked like a chainsaw in their hand. They got closer, and I could make out a very pale thin boy. He ran towards me, shouting.

"Better find shelter, Miss. It's gonna get nasty!"

I pulled my hood down and revealed myself to Nick.

Immediately he stopped, jolted and froze with the terror of seeing my face. He tipped his head slowly to the side and scanned me. Perhaps two minutes passed, and he said nothing. Cold rain hammered down onto my face and head, but I too stood in shock. Nick looked haunted. Dark rings under his eyes told of his lack of sleep. He was pale and thin, wearing his feelings outwardly. Luckily my tears mingled with the rain, as I screamed at myself inwardly not to run to him.

"Get in your car, and fuck off!" he shouted, and then he turned and ran to his truck.

"I don't have any transport!" I shouted through the wall of water.

He opened the gates, ran back to the truck, started the engine and drove off. He didn't even stop to close them. Then a hailstorm began. The gods threw their little rocks at me, having their fun. I ran into the barn and sat on a bale of hay, sobbing.

About fifteen minutes passed. Fifteen minutes in which to berate myself.

What was I thinking? I obviously wasn't thinking I'd need a lift back or a car at this point...

Now I wished I'd brought the comfortable Mercedes that my brother didn't seem so keen on using. I must've truly believed that Nick would take me back.

Lauren, you're still being a naive fool...

Poor Lawrence. I'd sent him away only to have to call him for help once more. When I thought of Nick, my heart lurched. It was only too apparent that I had wounded him deeply. I was faced by my true flighty form, my obligations. It seemed as if I'd created a kind of living *Dorian Grey* in reverse. On that fatal day I had clearly made the wrong decision by not telling Nick about his father coming to warn me off. At the time I'd justified it, saying it was all for love, but seeing the state of Nick now, I knew love should not look like that.

As I shivered, I pondered if the babies could feel the cold. I didn't know there was someone standing in front of me, and their words made me start, as I produced a little scream.

"I'm only back because the weather's so bad," Nick said, sat on a bale on the other side of the barn. I naturally kept my head down. The thunderous noise of the rain hitting the roof filled the air.

Don't be a coward, Lauren...

I stood and started to walk towards him. "Nick?" I whispered, and he looked up.

"Oh. Hi, Love."

His words cut into me. He knew that was how David always used to greet me. He was using the pain from my past to hurt me in the present.

"Your turn. Now you speak some more bullshit," Nick spat. His words dripped with hatred, but I deserved the punishment.

"Nick, I need to talk to you," I said, trying to keep my voice steady.

"Well, I didn't think you were here to give me a fucking lap-dance," he mocked.

I began to falter. I wasn't sure what to say.

"Oh, sorry. I thought that's how the game is played. You hurt me, now I hurt you. You seem to prefer that good old fashioned way. I wish you'd never come here." He looked down, dejectedly.

He was succeeding. His words were hurting me.

"I only want to talk to you. Please, I don't understand why you're being nasty."

"What? You didn't think I could be *Nasty Nick*? You want the other one? I'm afraid he's left." He hadn't looked up yet. The bitterness in his voice sent a chill through me.

"You had your chances to talk to me and you missed them."

"This isn't you, Nick," I protested.

101

He lifted his head sharply, and stared me straight in the eyes. I saw no twinkle or light in his dull and lifeless eyes. I felt ashamed when I thought about how I had acted.

He stood abruptly and lurched towards me. I thought he was going to hit me.

"No. You're right. It's not. This is shocked, crushed, bewildered, mystified, DESTROYED NICK!" he shouted, full in my face. He was scaring me, and I stumbled back as he continued. "Trust me, this is definitely not the Nick you want. I told you already, you want the one you are never going to see again. As you said to my dad all those years ago – 'What? You don't like what you've created?'"

Bang, it worked and I staggered back, almost falling onto a bale of hay. For a moment I wanted to hurt him back. I was tempted to shout at him and tell him he was going to be a father of twins. I swallowed my anger, knowing that would only hurt him more. The decent human being in me rose, and I kept quiet. We both sat in our own little worlds, him wishing the rain would stop, and me scared that it would.

I panicked as I clutched for the right words and found none.

This is definitely not how I thought this was going to be...

I wanted to tell Nick that I was seeing a psychiatrist, and that I was sorting through my mental wardrobe. I heard Hyam in my head again; "You should never try to anticipate or predict human behaviour." It was one of my biggest failings.

I really wanted to tell him, and I wished with all my heart that I'd told him about David coming to see me. I needed to unburden myself, but I realised that that would really only be for my benefit. I wanted to be forgiven, but I knew it would be a selfish act.

The rain was subsiding along with my hope.

He came over to me. "So, you're a big girl. You found your way out here, and I'm sure you can find your way back."

My spirit crushed, I gazed at the man who changed my life.

"I just wanted to say how sorry I am, that I Love you, and that running away from you will forever remain the worst decision of my life." To hear myself, I sounded pitiful and weak.

"I don't want your Love. Both times you left, all I got was a fucking note. You've saved me the bother of sending one through the post. You won't ever see me again. I took your advice and I'm going to Australia on a year's working holiday visa. I leave in one week." He retrieved his keys from his pocket.

"Goodbye, Lauren. I don't want to see you again."

He walked out of the barn and out of my life, and then he drove away while I cried and cried.

I don't remember calling Lawrence or the subsequent journey back to my room. I was babbling and blubbering. I was devastated and I was unable to fight it.

***

I awoke to the sound of gentle repeated knocking. I slowly got out of bed, disoriented, only just aware that I was still fully dressed. Carelessly, I opened the door. Lawrence stood there with a cup of tea in each hand. Without giving any sign of acknowledgement I simply got back into bed and pulled the threadbare blankets up under my chin. Lawrence closed the door with his foot, placed the teas down on the small white wooden bedside table, and sat respectfully near the foot of the bed.

"Jesus, Lauren. I was so worried about you. I've only ever seen people behave like that when they're freshly bereaved. You were pretty deranged." He leant forward and passed me the tea. I didn't want it but I took it anyway.

I am in bereavement...

Fight? How can I fight if Nick is in Australia? It's not exactly round the bloody corner...

"You, you said some things..." Lawrence's voice faltered.

I stayed silent.

"You asked how you could cope being a single mother," he said, and let that hang in the air.

Shit! Why is this happening?...

Lawrence took his cup and both of us sipped our tea. I replaced my cup and dropped the bomb.

"I'm pregnant with twins." *It's my turn now...*

The cup stopped just before his mouth, and he seemed genuinely stunned.

"I haven't told Nick, and now you and Nora are the only ones who know. I want it to stay that way please, Lawrence?" I pleaded firmly.

He nodded, still in shock.

"I want to leave today. Nick is going to Australia, so that's it."

Lawrence put his tea down and hugged me. I felt like a cold dead fish.

"I'm sorry, Lauren. I knew he'd got his visa," he said as he let go of me. He obviously viewed me pitifully.

I shrugged. I intended to call Nora and tell him I would be back that day. I needed to tell my brother, but I was reluctant, not to mention apprehensive about what was going to greet me in his room.

"I have to go back to London today, so I can take you," Lawrence offered.

"So I can ruin more lives? No thanks. I can't have any more on my conscience," I replied sardonically.

"Jenny knows everything. I told her last night. I don't want her to be hurt by the gossip. She was fine about it. If I take you to London, I'll tell her," he offered, with a reassuring smile.

I liked the thought of travelling with him. Then at least my brother and Daisy could continue their holiday marathon of sexual depravity in peace.

"If that's alright, then maybe I would come with you. I need to talk to my brother though, and I've no idea what he's up to."

His face turned red, and he shifted uncomfortably. "Well, I knocked on your brother's door late yesterday afternoon. I wanted to tell him how upset you were, and ask him if he would maybe keep an eye on you. At some points you were ranting, and," He paused, and his forehead wrinkled. "Him and his girlfriend were dressed in Japanese kimonos, and there was a strong smell of goat's cheese, so... Well, he knows the situation now."

His face was still beaming red as he stood. "I'm going to get ready to leave and talk to Jenny. I'll be back in two hours, and I'll meet you here."

I started to panic.

"I won't tell anyone about your pregnancy. I promise," he said, and then he was gone.

I called Nora, who immediately said:

"Tweet me, darlink!"

"Nora, no, just listen. I'm coming back today."

I didn't tell him anything else, not even who was bringing me back. What did it matter?

The obvious sorrow in my voice alerted him.

"Sorry, darlink. Hurry home. I'll take care of you." he said, and hung up quickly.

In a state of resurrected limbo I threw my things into my bag. I wasn't even wearing my disguise. Finally I knocked on the door to my brother's room, who luckily for me answered the door clothed and looking normal.

I told him what I was doing, and he told me that himself and Daisy would like to stay for the rest of the week.

"You alright, sis? You seen pretty bummed out."

"I've had better days, but as Nora would say, *Que cera, cera.* What will be, will be."

"See you soon then. Let me know when you next want a ride to Norwich." He beamed at me and closed the door.

As Lawrence drove us back, we listened to the radio, and the weather remained suitably crap all the way to London. I tried to push Nick's tormented face from my mind. He had truly Loved me, and I hadn't known how to take care of it. I hadn't then been equipped with the tools I was only now learning to use.

I wished I hadn't waited so long to check myself. *As if it would have made a difference...* I had a feeling it wouldn't have mattered. Australia. *Australia!...* A twenty-four hour flight away. The one year working holiday visa Nick had was the same one I also once travelled with. It was granted only once, and not if you were over thirty, or had a criminal record. I felt hopeless, it all seemed interminably futile. Australia was a massive country of never ending desert. He was right; I would never see him again.

NORA'S GRAND PLAN

For the whole of that Wednesday and Thursday I stayed in bed. I told Nora what had happened, and he remained totally animated throughout the story. He took one photo - a close-up of half my face, and said, "Hashtag *#BrokenLove.*"

I begged to be left in peace, and he kindly did. I was only thankful that he had kept on Eros and Danny, who didn't ask any questions, and just looked after me. I took the coward's way out and rang Hyam's clinic. I told his receptionist that I didn't know when I could have my next session. Then just I lay in bed and rotted, somehow fighting the raging battle between good and evil.

Get up and do something or lay here, what does it matter?...

Think of your babies - Worry about yourself...

I can't just wallow. Must fight...

It felt like all of it was happening again. Perhaps this was really the end this time, but this time with added fun - Twins.

When Nora popped in to see me that Friday morning I felt just as depressed, but as luck would have it, the early signs of morning sickness had begun. I felt wretched.

He looked at my phone and started writing things down.

"What are you up to?" I swallowed rapidly in an effort to hold down the nausea. "I don't want any surprises for my birthday Nora, just let the day pass, and no fucking photos for Twitter either."

"Oh, so *dramatico*. No, you don' worry. You lay there and slowly fade away," he advised, sweeping his arm across me and placing his hand on his chest.

"Yes, okay you're the queen of tact," I grumbled, allowing a smidgen of humour into my '*feeling sorry for myself* ' world.

Nora hummed, and kissed my forehead gaily.

"Okay, darlink. I leave you to your little pigsty," he snorted, and left.

He didn't intrude on me again that day. I only saw Danny when he served me some food and asked me when it would be a good time to freshen the room.

I must have looked like shit. I told myself I should have a bath the next morning, making that the only birthday resolution I could manage. Then I slept for most of the day.

***

I awoke bright and early, and kept my resolution. I chose Lavender and Clary Sage to go in the bath. Apparently they would make me feel alive, and invigorated, if it really was possible that a few drops of oil could do all that. I doubted the wild claims.

I could hear movements from the bedroom, but I didn't concern myself. The water did feel particularly good. I stared at my stomach and could still see no change.

"Sorry that there's no father around for you two," I said out loud for some reason.

108

From the other side of the door Danny called out. "Lauren, is everything okay in there?"

"Yes," I replied, lying. Although the bath was starting to help me to feel slightly more human.

I got dressed in a sloppy, comfy tracksuit, opened the bathroom door, and there in front of me, beautifully laid out on the bed, was breakfast. Two huge bouquets of exquisite flowers stood on the table, their cloying fragrance already filling the air.

Danny walked over to me, handed me a small package and kissed me shyly on the cheek.

"Happy birthday, beautiful," he said. He was so fresh, young and new looking. He radiated everything I was not.

I smiled, so I didn't appear like the ungrateful bitch that I really was. I unwrapped the gift and discovered it was a delicate silver necklace. Hanging from it was a fairy with small pink diamante-looking stones on the tips of her wings. It was beautiful. Tears stung my eyes and I flung my arms round him, hugging him hard as I sobbed quietly.

"So, I hope that means you like it," he said as he hugged me back.

That unselfish gesture snapped me out of my pity party spell.

I handed the necklace to Danny. "Please, could you put it on for me?" I asked, pulling down the neckline of my most unsexy tracksuit.

The tiny fairy felt cold on my skin. She fitted perfectly in the dip of my neck. I went to the mirror on the wall and saw how the light reflected off her wings, making her look alive.

"I love it. It's like my very own *Tinkerbelle*!" I said excitedly as I felt more precious life-force surging into me. I ran to the bed and slapped the luxurious red silk sheets that Danny had put on.

"Please sit down. I'd really like it if you joined me," I asked, picking up one of the bouquets.

All the blooms were pink and purple, so I knew they were from Nora. The card read:

If you don't enjoy your birthday I'll dry slap you. Love you,

Nora xxx

I smiled involuntarily and sniffed their perfume while Danny poured the coffee. The other bouquet was a bunch of traditional red roses from Lawrence.

How did he know it's my birthday?...

The sentiments in the card were more traditional than Nora's.

Have a lovely birthday. Your good friend, Lawrence Cole. X

"I'll put them in fresh water soon," Danny said, as he buttered croissants.

I glanced at him longer and noticed his highly defined cheekbones, dusted with light brown freckles.

"I'm sorry I've been such a nightmare. It's all been about Nick, the boy I told you about. I tried to save something that had already gone... I can't believe you've got me such a stunning gift," I suddenly gushed, feeling embarrassed and taking a croissant to hide behind.

"I'm so sorry. It must be hard," He blushed. "I got it for you just because I spotted it when I was out and it reminded me of you."

Then it was my turn to blush. "This heartbreak will be one of the hardest things I will ever have to get over, but I'm sure I will. I'd like you to know that your gift has lifted me up out of a worse place," I told him, smiling and truly feeling that it had.

110

He blushed again. "Lauren, you know I'm totally Gay, but I am also a little in Love with you in the sense that you're more than just a fabulous faghag. You're very attractive for a woman, you're fun, and you're sexy and intelligent..." He trailed off.

I swelled with pride. "I - I'm flattered, Danny."

He made himself busy pouring more tea, and chopping up greener-than-green apples. "No, I'm sorry. I shouldn't have sprung that on you. That's not fair. It's obvious you have enough men in your life who love you, it's just that some of them aren't the ones you want."

I stopped him by placing my hand on his. "Thank you, really. I feel it's even more of a compliment coming from a Gay guy."

I squeezed his hand in an attempt to quell his awkwardness.

"Because gay men *can* sometimes fall in Love with women, contrary to the belief of everyday Neanderthals. Look at *Cher*, and *Kylie*, who I totally Love."

Like me, Danny babbled when he was nervous, but at least his easy chatter filled the pollen clouded air over breakfast.

And so, at least I'm letting another new friend into my life...

Nora came in about an hour later, and Danny got up from the bed as Nora approached me and kissed me on both cheeks.

"*Buenas días, guapa. Feliz cumpleaños!*" His beautiful emerald green shirt lit up his handsome face.

"I'll put these in water," Danny said as he took the bouquets. "Morning, Nora," he whispered lightly.

First name terms now, I see...

Nora smiled sweetly at Danny as he quickly took the flowers and left the room.

"So, you two are getting on better?" I enquired.

"Let's just say we reached an understanding while you were away. I'm keeping him here, as long as you are staying here." He poured himself some coffee.

"I like him very much. I'm pleased you have him here. Look what he bought me." I said, pointing to my fairy necklace, just as Danny came back with a vase full of flowers. He placed them on the dressing table, and began rearranging them.

Nora's eyes became slits. "Real diamonds, darlink?"

I opened my mouth, but nothing came out.

"I must be paying you too much, Danny," he called over.

It made me wonder what kind of arrangement they had reached. *Real diamonds?...*

"They are tiny stones, Nora," Danny replied.

"Unlike mine, darlink. *Aaiiee!*"

"You shouldn't have. It's too much!" I protested, finding my voice.

"Phooey. Will there be anything else?"

"*No, gracias.*" Nora replied, and waved his hand royally.

Nora smiled wryly as soon as Danny had left the room. "So, someone has a *Gaymirer*..." He broke open the last croissant and spread strawberry jam onto it.

"What?" I asked, pouring myself tea. I was allowing myself to be happy.

"A Gaymirer is when a female has a gay male admirer. *Joder,* Lauren. Get with the programme." He ate the croissant with a napkin held under his chin in order to catch any falling crumbs that might have spoiled his immaculate attire.

As he told me that Nora's Pearls now had six hundred thousand followers on Twitter, and then made me laugh with some of his pearls of wisdom, I could see that he was excited, happy and truly in his element. I did Love him.

"Oh, go on then, take a photo of us, and hashtag it #Gaymirer," I suggested.

We pulled funny faces, in a rare momentary lapse of poise for Nora.

"So, one of your presents is coming here this afternoon."

"Nick?" I enquired, smiling sarcastically.

"It's a surprise, and I am not Jesus, darlink."

I pouted playfully.

"Tonight we are going to dinner at *La Boheme*, no argument. And don't worry, you'll have something nice to wear as well." He sipped his coffee.

La Boheme was Nora's favourite restaurant, in *Old Compton Street*, the queerest street in *Soho*. We'd be rubbing shoulders with the rich and famous, and the food was French and delicious.

I held my arms up in defeat. "Okay, okay." As I leant forward and kissed him full on the lips I felt him squeal inwardly.

I released him and he used both hands to pat his hair down as his cheeks flushed red.

"So, I must go and check my Tweets. I'll ask Danny to clear everything away," he said as he headed for the door. "And don't worry, darlink. I have a *fabuloso* plan."

After Danny had cleared away the breakfast, my parents called on the phone to wish me a Happy Birthday, shortly followed by my brother. He told me that Daisy and himself were now in Milton Keynes, having decided to spend a couple of days there, and that my present was on its way by courier.

Privately, I still wished that package was Nick.

After a light nap, Nora woke me with a gentle knock on the door and poked his head into the room.

"Here's your first present," he announced, and Hyam Beber walked in.

I sat up quickly, and just as people in India greet each other, he put his hands together and bowed his head slightly.

"*Shalom,* Lauren. Happy birthday." He walked towards the bed and indicated with his hand that he wished to sit.

"Please, sit down," I said, happily. I was genuinely pleased he was there.

He sat professionally near the end of the bed.

"I believe I am one of your gifts?" he proffered with a smile.

"To me you're always a gift. How corny is that? Today is a perfect day for being *Hyamized.*"

He nodded coyly, "Is that how you think of it? May I have your permission to be unconventional?"

I nodded. He kicked off his shoes and sat cross-legged in a Lotus position.

"I will have to be honest. Your friend Nora has paid me handsomely to do a private session here in London on a Saturday, and I've broken sacrament because it is your birthday after all, and because I've heard a loose account of what has happened. As always, I only want you to chat freely about whatever you like." A brief smile danced at the edge of his mouth.

I told him everything. I unburdened myself to my own private travelling confessional.

114

"...and in two days Nick will be going to Australia."

"And I suppose you feel a bit cheated. You weren't really able to state your case. Now you're left with a loose ending that you'd hoped to tie up and conclude."

My god, how does he do it?... "That's exactly it. I thought at least we'd get to a point of - I don't know."

I searched Hyam's face for the answer I knew he would make me find for myself.

"You have no control over final conclusions, or other people's actions. You can simply try to guide people, based on honesty. Nick is coming from a place of hurt and rage. You know that now. I'm sure even if you'd gone there three weeks ago the outcome would still have been the same, maybe worse. As we've talked about before, it's the countless - *What if?'s*, that drive us to insanity."

"I know. You're right. I do know that."

"It's easier to go over to the dark side, as Yoda would say," he teased, with a twinkle in his eye.

"So, you are really very human. Do you like Star Wars?"

He smiled. "With two boys, it's hard not to." He was entrusting me with a tiny piece of information about his private life. "Well, sorry but our time is nearly up." He uncrossed his legs.

"I think the biggest reason I was so upset is because I didn't get to tell Nick about the twins," I blurted out as I suddenly pieced my mind together.

His face told me I had reached another enlightening moment.

"Events may never follow anyone's plans, but maybe Nick does need to know about the pregnancy. Only you can decide. It depends on how he's told, and it's important that you don't assume anything about his response," he said as he put his shoes on.

115

I was going to protest, but I managed to control myself. *No buts, Lauren. Only action...*

We both stood, and he hugged me as if I was a long lost friend. His company warmed my soul.

"I'll see you soon, Hyam," I told him. Little did I know that I would not see him for a long time.

A courier delivered my brother's present, which was a huge hamper of luxurious chocolates. Danny bought me up an additional gift wrapped box, which contained my second present from Nora - A beautiful *Yves Saint Lauren* all-in-one silk catsuit with a plunging neckline. It was black with sparkling lines of emerald green thread. There were brand new black shoes with low heels to go with it. Danny and I wowed appropriately at both presents.

Around seven PM another present arrived from Nora in the form of *Jeffery Claude*, who was a hairdresser. Gayer than a Gay penguin, he played with my hair, teased me and bitched about my ends. He told me I should have been spanked hard on my bare bottom with a hairbrush, for letting the condition of my hair go. God knows what he would have done to me if I'd told him how long my armpit hair was.

However, when my hair was finished it looked wicked. He fixed it up with large chopsticks at the back, leaving strands of my fringe, then took thin sections and twisted them into my crown, securing them with miniature chopsticks. It galled me to tell him and feed his inflated ego, but I loved it. Jeffrey Claude screamed and pinched me, told me I was a lazy hair-whore, and left.

With my new outfit, and my fairy necklace I felt ready to face going out.

Nora looked sensational as well, of course. He wore a black bolero jacket, black high-waisted trousers with a very pale green silk sash, and a matching green shirt. Diamonds sparkled on his cufflinks and buttons, and his shoes were black Cuban heels. He looked like a Tango-dancing matador.

Together we looked sensational. He made Danny take a few photos of us before we went out. "Hashtag #*GlamourCouple* #*GayIsGlamour* #*Headturners*."

We caught a taxi, and Nora's phone constantly beeped throughout the journey. We pulled up outside *La Boheme* to find the street pulsing with life, and he promised to turn his phone to vibrate only. I loved it there. With *Ronnie Scott's* jazz club almost opposite, and theatres surrounding I could always count on being submerged in a world of diverse people.

We went in to the crowded bar, and the smell of the scrumptious food made my stomach grumble. Waiters in traditional white shirts and black trousers ran about delivering all the goodies to the tables. The *Maître D'* spied Nora coming in and his smile stretched to full capacity.

"Darling, Nora," he greeted him. He was on first name terms, because Nora was there so often and he always spent copious amounts of money.

"Marcus, darlink. I have a table for two booked. It's my best friend's birthday," he explained, flourishing a hand towards me. I too looked stinking rich, especially with the full length black fur coat, belonging to Nora's mother that was on loan to me just for the night.

Marcus took my hand and kissed it gracefully. He showed us over to a circular table with thick wooden semi-circular benches around it. Plush thick blood-red cushions were dotted all over them.

Nora ordered a red wine and I went for a freshly squeezed orange juice.

Shit, it's hard not drinking...

However, we did both have mussels in white wine sauce for starters. I was sure I only had them for the alcohol in the sauce.

For the main course, I had barbecued ribs with a fresh salad, and Nora had salmon pasta. It was all simply delicious and we started chatting easily.

"Okay, so now I understand about your counsellor. If mine had looked like that? Oh, *carino*."

"Mmm. There's a bit more to it than that I think, Nora. Like the invaluable help he gives my mental health?"

Nora smirked wryly. "I think I will definitely have to have some sessions with him," he teased, and giggled.

"My birthday wish is that you stay well away from Hyam. I mean it, Nora!" I flashed him my serious look.

When we'd finished our main course, Nora's tone became more serious. He dabbed the corners of his mouth daintily with his napkin.

"So. Now to my plan. Please listen without interruption. Afterwards you can speak, but you must *escuchar* first, okay?"

I nodded, too full to speak anyway.

"I have been looking into going to Australia. We can get a three month visa to visit. I am going to pay for everything, so you are not to worry. So far as I know, Nick is flying into Sydney. Over the last couple of days I have also been looking for a private detective in Sydney, and I've already sent him a picture of Nick."

"Whaaat?" I interrupted, unable to stop myself at that point.

Nora held his hand up. "*Silencio.* Even if he meant what he said to you, you should tell him about the *bambino's*, and he deserves to hear it face to face. Of course, I want to go to Australia anyway. *¡Aaiiee!* It's *so* exciting. The detective will follow Nick so that we know where he is when we get there. I will know what flight Nick is on tomorrow. No arguments, Lauren. *Está es muy necesario.*"

118

He sat back and sipped his wine.

Wow, he has been busy... I was temporarily stunned into silence.

I suspected this was mostly for the benefit of Nora who I was sure would just love to have an excuse to go to *Oz*, but his willingness to go through all this organization humbled me. I was still trying to process it all.

"So, where are you getting your information from?" I asked.

He raised an eyebrow and smugness shrouded him.

"Our very own; Sergeant Lawrence Cole."

"What?" I sat upright. "Nora, what have you done? He'd never willingly spy for you."

"Darlink. I *simplemente* said that I might drop into where he works more often."

Poor Lawrence... I felt sorry he was being blackmailed in that way, but secretly I began to have a little more hope. If I was being honest, it would be fun with Nora, and not worrying about money would definitely be a plus. When I had travelled Australia previously it had been back breaking hard work. I'd worked picking fruit on farms from morning till night.

I picked up my orange juice. "Here's to you having stinking rich parents, I suppose."

Nora squealed and raised his glass to mine.

A very handsome and well kept man came over to our table. Nora stood excitedly.

"*Spencer*, darlink." They embraced affectionately.

"Nora, how are you?" Spencer said boldly. He seemed like a strong and attractive type.

"Busy, darlink. *Stupido* busy. I'm going to Australia, and I'm a huge tweeter. Check me out on Twitter, darlink. I'm *Nora's Pearls*."

Spencer seemed amused. "Will do. See you soon, honey," he replied, and strode off with a purpose.

Nora sighed, hand on chest.

Both of us noticed a man at a table to the right of us who'd turned in his chair and was clicking his fingers in Nora's direction.

"Waiter! Waiter!" he shouted, tutting and rolling his eyes.

"Waiter!"

The increasing volume of his voice made others turn to stare, alongside Nora, whose face seemed to suggest that he had encountered a disgusting smell. His eyes became slits and he looked at the man as if he were a human douche.

"Where's our order?" The man demanded, and eight pairs of eyes swivelled over at Nora.

Nora straightened up and clasped his hands together. I had no idea what he was about to do. Nora's style was never to embarrass himself.

"I find out," he said finally, and turning sharply on his heels he marched towards the kitchen.

I played nervously with my serviette as five minutes slipped past. Nora reappeared, walked back to our table and sat down.

"Sorry, Lauren. I had to do something." He picked up his wine glass.

The pompous man turned round again. He was sweaty and bright red as his flabby bottom jaw flapped. "How dare you!"

Nora's response was quiet but ripe with poison. "I, *tú cono*, am a customer here. You racist son of a bitch."

The man glared back for a split second longer before turning away. His dinner guests glowed with embarrassment.

"Can you believe that *puta*? Just because I'm wearing this outfit, oh, and of course because my skin is brown." He composed himself and began to smile broadly as the offending table were served their food.

"What have you done?" I asked.

"Well, most of the kitchen staff are Hispanic, and I already know them all. Let's say they are getting more than what they ordered," Nora crooned.

They all began to tuck in, and Nora shrilled quietly.

"Stop with the suspense and tell me," I whispered.

"Will you allow me to get my phone out?"

I nodded.

"The secret ingredient - is spunk," he revealed, as he showed me a photo of seven kitchen staff with their cocks in hand, standing around the plates with grins on all their faces.

"Please tell me you are not going to tweet that?"

"Of course not, darlink. This is *For Your Eyes Only.*"

I pulled a face, and together we witnessed their foul feast.

In the taxi on the way back to Nora's, I hugged him sloppily, told him I loved him, which made him embarrassed, and I told him what a good time I thought we were going to have in Oz. I kissed him on both cheeks repeatedly with thanks for my wonderful birthday. We agreed to get the visa forms filled in immediately.

As I fell asleep that night I genuinely felt the warmth of happiness.

The next day I relaxed, reading, and eating all the scrummy chocolate my brother had sent. Around tea time there was a light knock on the door, and Lawrence Cole popped his head round. He seemed uncomfortable.

"Lawrence. Please, come in," I invited, happiness shining through my words. I gave him a big smile and a hug. "Thank you so much for the flowers."

He reciprocated the hug and his cheeks flushed. "Don't be silly, they're only flowers."

I patted the bed next to me.

He held his hand up. "I can't stop. Jenny's in the car. I literally popped in to give your blackmailing friend the information he needed."

"Sorry, Lawrence. I had no idea, but it seems Nora and I are going to Australia."

"The only reason I'm doing this is because you are pregnant, and in all honesty I really don't want Nora to come and see me at work. I'm going now, but I'll see you soon."

"I know you will. I think Nora's jealous that you know about me being pregnant as well, although he'd never admit to that." I stood and kissed him on the cheek.

He turned and left hurriedly, probably to hide his embarrassment.

I thought he would be followed very shortly by Nora, but he left me my own for the next two hours, before rushing in excitedly to tell me that everything was set up, the detective had Nick's flight details, and he would start surveillance immediately.

"*Aaiiee!* It's so exciting." He held my hands and his eyes twinkled.

"We are going to have *adventures grandes.*"

The next day, as Nick was on the plane flying to Oz, I was receiving my test results, and I found out that everything was good with the twins. I took that to be a good omen. Nora *Rumba'd* with me around the house, as I relaxed and felt more bonded with the babies inside me.

The Australian embassy had told us to allow up to one month for our application to be processed. Two weeks later we'd still heard nothing. Nora was waiting for the first report on Nick's movements, and I was having morning sickness, which luckily wasn't too violent. Our excitement turned into anxious bickering, for which Danny told us both off.

Both Nora and I tried to be patient. Nora concentrated on his pearls; taking pics of his life and giving out his sage advice. Sometimes I was curious and involved myself. One of his pearls was about arse cream.

"You can brighten your tired sagging face, with some haemorrhoid cream. A thin layer across the cheekbones lifts for about 8 hours. Hashtag #SaggyArse #haemorrhoids #BumCream."

At the beginning of the third week of waiting, Nora came to my room holding some A4 paper. I had just had a two hour long puking session, and I was recovering on the bed. I curled up, trying to comfort myself.

"Oh, Lauren. *Que pasa*? Can I help?"

"No thanks. I'll be fine soon. What's that?"

"This is the detective's report." he announced, and slapped his hand on it.

I sat up. "Go on then, let's find out."

He made himself comfortable and started to relay the information.

"So, when he arrived at Sydney airport he was not alone. He was with a certain *Patrick Flannery*, thirty-one years old. Father, Australian born *Bruce Wilson*, Mother, *Mary Flannery*, Irish born. They've got a ranch outside *Kalgoorlie*, which is a mining town. Patrick chooses to use his mother's maiden name, which is why he's Flannery, for reasons unknown at this time." His eyes scanned the text.

"Oi! No reading without talking."

"It is boring stuff, like how far that *Goolie* place is, and stuff, and -" He faltered as he turned the page. "*Si, si. Es Nada*, blah, blah. So Nick is staying with this Patrick guy. Mmm, he seems to have money. Nice. He's got a small ranch at a place called *Medlow Bath*. It's at the highest point in the *Blue Mountains*, near *Sydney*." He paused when he heard me gasp slightly, and gave me an irritated glance.

"Sorry, but I've been there. It's beautiful. I went to *Katoomba*. The mist is blue from the eucalyptus trees. I would imagine that this Patrick guy does have some money, if the ranch is his?" I pondered.

Nora scanned the papers. "Yes, he owns it outright." He raised an eyebrow as he suddenly became more interested in Mr Patrick Flannery.

I let out a low whistle.

He read some more, and then screamed as he threw his head back. "*Aaiiee!*"

"*Que pasa?* He lives in a suburb called *Willygong*. I love it."

I remembered that about Australia. All the funny place names they had.

"He stays away a lot, in a place called *Surrey Hills*, that's also in the suburbs outside Sydney. He's got friends, someone called *Mr. S. Chu* who's got Chinese and Korean parents. Mr Chu is thirty-four years old, and a professional gambler. When Patrick is away a girl called *Matilda Jones* looks after his ranch. They're not related. She's got Australian parents and she's twenty-three. Not sure at this point what the relationship is between them." He paused as he turned to a new page.

Oh great, a nimble twenty-three year old staying where Nick is...

Nora continued to scan until he gasped, opened his mouth, and put his hand in front of his face in blatant shock mode.

He had my full attention. "What? What is it? Tell me, no matter what," I insisted, as panic overtook me.

What if Nick's met someone?...

Nora said nothing at first. I shouted at him, and followed that up by throwing a cushion in his direction.

"*Vale, vale.* Okay. It would seem that our Mr Flannery earns his living by, well, by being a very well paid Drag Queen, and Nick..." He looked me straight in the eye. "...is working as a Stripper."

Neither of us said anything for a minute.

"What? Sorry, I thought you said he was stripping."

Nora looked back at the report.

"Yes. He's working with Patrick. They can do up to five strips a night at..." he said, then just stopped.

I screamed at him, and he looked up slowly.

"Four hundred dollars a strip? *Puta madre!*"

Shit. That's a lot of money... I thought about Nick stripping in front of those horny women and lost all hope.

"Shit, Nora. He's only been there two weeks. Oh shit. That's it. You and your bloody report. I don't want to know." I could feel inappropriate anger rising in me.

He looked hurt. "Lauren, I do this for you."

I got up and went to the bathroom without looking up. "No you're not, you're doing this for *you*. I'm having a bath. I don't want to know anymore." I slammed the door behind me.

I ran a bath, angrily wishing that I hadn't found out what Nick was doing. He wouldn't be thinking of me now. *Shit, two weeks...* As I lay in the water and rubbed my tummy I talked to those beings who were inside me. I didn't want to know what gender they were going to be born, they were non-binary as far as I was concerned at that stage. The fact they were healthy so far was enough for me.

"So it seems that your charming, beautiful, devastatingly handsome father is stripping, I informed them." *What woman wouldn't want that young English stallion? And who the fuck is this Patrick?*

I decided that I didn't like him. If Nick hadn't met him, then he would not be doing this. I placed all the blame neatly at Patrick's feet.

I started to feel bad that I had shouted at Nora. *It isn't his fault that all this is happening, no it was obviously that bloody man, Flannery...*

There was a knock on the door. "It's open, Danny," I called. An almost green Nora entered. "Nora, I'm so sorry. I was mean to you and you don't deserve it."

Like a ghost, he glided over and sat on the edge of the bath, saying nothing.

That was very strange behaviour for him. It suddenly occurred to me that he might have read something else in the report.

"Nora, what is it? Nora, is it Nick?"

He was somewhere else far away. I splashed some water on him.

"Nora!" I shouted.

"My - my parents are coming here, in two days. They want to talk to me."

Oh dear God...

Nora's parents' coming to see him was some big shit. Big, big, shit.

HECTOR & ANGELICA

Two days later, on the same dreaded day of the arrival of Nora's parents, we received our visas for Australia. Normally Nora would have been ecstatic, but he was so consumed he barely mentioned it. For the previous two days he had been charging around as if he'd smoked some crystal meth. He screamed at Danny frequently, telling him that he should make sure the house was spotless. He smoked as much weed as he could so he could be as stoned as possible, and screamed at me as well when I crossed his path.

He was afflicted with a kind of man-period. *Man-struation*. Bouts of anger were quickly replaced by those of sobbing and wailing; "You wouldn't understand. Nobody knows what it's like."

Both Danny and I did very well to keep our cool, while all around us *Rome* burned. Nora screeched at Danny, told him he wouldn't be needed while his parents were there and that he would ring the agency when he needed him again.

Nora's parents were due to arrive at the house around seven that evening. They'd be arriving in a private car with a chauffeur. Around five PM, Danny and I hugged and said our goodbyes. I had his number, and I knew we'd see each other again.

Nora, by then wide eyed and chanting voodoo nonsense, had begged me on pain of death to stay with him while his parents were there.

He had concocted a story for his parents about why we were going to Australia, and it was shaky to say the least. To placate his father, he was going to say that he had fallen in Love with a beautiful Nigerian princess, and that she lived in Australia. I pointed out some flaws, and got screamed at, so I decided to let him sink in his own shit.

In between all this Nora was chain smoking joints outside. His father hated smoking, and especially if it involved drugs. Nora's father had very strong ideas about drugs and their users. He only accepted one drug - alcohol, and even that was to be kept to a minimum.

One hour before they arrived, a very stoned Nora changed into parent-appropriate clothing. He still wore *Armani*, but toned it down with plain dark blue trousers and a black *Prada* shirt. He wasn't even wearing silk. We sat in the tropical room, with images of exotic birds and butterflies adorning the walls. A huge gold birdcage, devoid of birds, sat next to a priceless Chippendale table and chairs. Nora told me that birds always unsettled his mother. Just as the prospect of their visit was unsettling me.

Nora paced back and forth, too scared to leave the room in case they came and his father smelt the smoke. In an attempt to be supportive, I tried to chat.

"I'm very excited about the visas. It's going to be so much fun."

"If I don't satisfy my father on every level, we are not going anywhere."

I decided to shut up.

Time crawled excruciatingly slowly in the last minutes until the doorbell finally rang and we both jumped. Nora composed himself, and as he left the room I could see he was trying not to walk so Gay.

At least I felt like I could breathe normally again. I wasn't able to make out the words, but I could hear a lot of commotion going on. It wasn't exactly shouting, but one voice rose above the others. I assumed that it was Nora's father. Maybe fifteen minutes passed and I still hadn't seen a sign of anyone. I wasn't sure what to do.

Should I stay here or go to my room? Is that okay for me to do? Has Nora told them I'm here?...

I knew I would have to move shortly, as I needed the toilet desperately. Then the door opened and in came a tiny old woman, whose appearance reminded me of a dry roasted peanut. She quickly scanned the room and left. That was followed by Nora's head popping round the door.

"Darlink, *molesta*. I will be in here soon," he assured me, clearly flustered.

"Is your mother a very small woman?"

"*Que?* What?"

"A very small woman came in here a moment ago."

130

His mouth opened in shock. Then he threw back his head with laughter.

"*Aaiiee!* That's so funny. O-M-G, so funny." He placed a hand over his mouth to catch the screams. "She is, *aaiiee*," He paused to giggle. "She is my mother's seventy-one year old *Mema*. She is a personal attendant. My mother doesn't even get out of bed without her. You thought she was my mother? Oh, Lauren. You've cheered me up." Nora swished around and was gone before I could ask him anything else.

I decided I needed to pee. I didn't want my bladder to overspill and drown the babies. I peeked out and saw the coast was clear. On my return from the toilet, I passed a room with the door slightly ajar. A powerful, commanding and penetrating voice boomed through the crack in the door and into the hallway.

"I mean it, Noel. If not, you know what will happen."

I scuttled back to the birds and butterflies.

Half an hour passed and I was already bored stiff. Finally I had enough and decided to go to my room. I'd already begun to rise from the chair when a godly beast of a man strode in. He was about six foot four, with beautiful almost ebony black skin and shoulders seemingly hewed from tree trunks. His big nostrils flared quickly like a purebred race horse, just back from a long run. I half expected him to rear up on me. The sheer intensity of energy that radiated from him made me stumble, and I saved myself by falling onto a very small ornamental table. It wobbled precariously, and five small Chinese figurines wobbled, along with my heart.

Please, god. Don't let anything fall...

Obviously it was god's day off.

As with all hideous accidents, time seemed to slow down. As I watched, Hector Sanchez watched, and it became obvious that no amount of us looking at them would have prevented one of them from falling to the floor. With perfect timing, Nora came in, and his initial smile was replaced by a look of fear.

The impact on the carpet was feather light, but the head of the figurine came clean off. Nora gasped as I bent down quickly and picked up the two parts.

"I'm so sorry. I - I think I can glue it back together," I said, holding the head on to see if it would still fit.

Hector strode towards me.

"That is one of the earliest pieces from the *Ming* period. It *was* valued at a quarter of a million pounds. You will observe I used the past tense," he said flatly as he took the broken candy from the baby and put it in his pocket with a shovel-like hand.

"It's one of my wife's favourite pieces. There's no need for her to hate you on sight." He glared at me.

I felt like a proper shit, and my anxiety grew.

Nora came over to me and held my hand. He pulled me towards a very uncomfortable, yet priceless looking sofa. We sat down, and Hector sat almost exactly opposite us, perhaps in case he needed to pounce. He crossed his legs exactly as Nora did.

Shit. I must remember not to call him Nora...

He glared at us both and the white of his eyes, stood out against his skin. I realised then that Hector Sanchez terrified me.

No wonder Nora gets so anxious...

I imagined heads of business and industry instantly giving in to any demand Hector asked for.

"So, Miss Bowman. My son tells me that you are also involved in this Australian escapade, on my money?"

He caught me off guard, and my mind went totally blank. I nodded dumbly.

"My son has informed me it is because of a woman, can you tell me something about her?" he asked. His nostrils flared for dramatic effect, and he sucked his cheeks violently.

I bet he could suck a clitoris clean off... The thought of it made mine shrink inside me.

Nora squeezed my hand, just as the door opened and the small peanut woman came back in, thankfully postponing my answer to Hector, which was good as I had no idea what Nora had told his father.

Hector and Nora stood, and so did I. Although I didn't have a clue why, but I just sensed I should comply. He let go of my hand, and his mother entered the room. My breath caught in my throat, and all became apparent as to why Nora had laughed earlier. There was a universe of difference between that old crone, and this stunning pedigree of a woman. Hector greeted his wife with a kiss, whilst *Mema* plumped and fussed as she readied a chair. He talked to her in Cuban Spanish and I understood none of it. Nora, like his father, went to his mother and greeted her. She smiled weakly, air-kissed both his cheeks and talked to him in their mother tongue.

Nora gestured towards me.

"Mamma, this is my best friend; Lauren Bowman."

She looked down at me; the specimen who was staying in *her* house.

I didn't know how to react, but I felt I was under the gaze of this individual's power, harnessed by this powerful couple.

I decided to do a small curtsy. Out of the corner of my eye I saw Nora suppress a smile.

"Lauren, this is my *Madre. Angelica Sanchez.*"

I curtsied again out of sheer fear.

Hector sat back down, and told *Mema* what to do. She got

busy fixing drinks at the bar. Nora held his arm out so his mother could take hold of it. She didn't walk; it was more of an undulation. She sat down as if she were being filmed.

"*Gracias, bonita,*" she said, weakly feigning a smile. Nora returned to my side.

His mother was perfectly exquisite, dressed from head to toe in designer labels. A silky caramel *Yves Saint Laurent* dress clung to her perfect six foot body, shaping her perfect breasts. Her Mocha skin shone from health and wealth. Her light brown hair had caramel highlights and swayed across her back. Her hair was straightened poker-straight, just as her son's was.

I could tell her beauty was natural, which only enhanced her appeal. The jaws of time had only yet bitten gently upon her. Still, she seemed just as delicate as the priceless ornament I had just broken. I imagined that even a strong orgasm would cause a near death experience for her. Every movement seemed acted to perfection, as if she was constantly auditioning for a part. I realised that this was a woman who could be emotionally draining.

Nora's father began to speak in what I once again assumed was Cuban. Angelica adopted a look very familiar to me. I had seen it on her son's face many times. Clearly Nora had seen how successfully it had worked for his mother, and taken it on as his own. *The look* said that life itself was inanely, tediously and acutely boring. Drawing breath itself was a chore and if they could, they would employ someone to do that for them.

Nora allowed his father to bark at him, whilst he clasped and unclasped his hands on his uncrossed legs. The old woman bought over a box and opened it, presenting various cigars. Hector took out a huge one, which for some reason I found very intimidating. The little old *Mema* replaced the box and left the room that I wished I wasn't in.

No one said or did anything while Hector sniffed his way along the cigar. His horse's nostrils flared open as he inhaled, and his eyes opened wide. As I watched this simple ritual I almost fainted.

Poor, poor, Nora...

I had thought Hector didn't smoke, but I knew that was definitely not up for debate.

After his cigar was lit, he resumed where he had left off. He directed his power towards his only son and heir. Nora eventually retaliated and began to argue. He pleaded his case to his mother, which in turn made Angelica argue with her husband in defence of her only son. I was astounded that she'd managed to conceive even once.

She looks like she might buy a child for charity..., I mused to myself. I could hear Nora calling my name.

"Darl - Lauren. My father is being very unreasonable. Money, money, it's always about money," he complained. He looked over at his father and gave him a look of utter disgust.

"Seeing as you have involved your friend, Noel, it's a perfect time for me to finish asking her my previously interrupted question." He turned to me with a purpose, and made me squirm as he puffed on his cigar. Nora tried to remain casual. I shifted awkwardly as I felt the babies inside me do the same. It was making me feel sick.

"So I am to believe that my son has met a Nigerian princess, who happens to live in Australia, and that he has fallen desperately in love with her?" he demanded, his voice booming. My rattling nerves were helping to stir the cauldron in my stomach.

I nodded like a performing dog, and started to babble. "Oh yes, desperately, desperately."

"What does she look like?" he commanded.

Nora interrupted, "Papa, please. You cannot interrogate my friend."

Hector Sanchez didn't even flinch.

"I have every right, *Noel*. She is living in my house. You tell me she is going with you, and you have already spent forty-five thousand dollars of my money in the last couple of months, Noel. *My* money. Even when I die, it still won't be your money, unless I have a grandchild."

I went into shock upon hearing the amount of money Nora had spent. My mind was so much in turmoil that I didn't even think about the question he'd asked me.

"Well, Miss Bowman?"

I had completely forgotten the question, so I just stabbed in the dark. "Yes it's a lot of money. Terrible, just terrible…"

Hector closed his eyes, and his nostrils began to flare again, so I knew I had answered the question wrong. No points for me.

"The Princess!" he reminded me, impatiently.

"Oh yes, yes." I began to giggle with terror. "She's beautiful, very beautiful, and definitely black, er…"

Both parents sank their incredulous glare into me.

"I'm sorry, I don't know why I said that. Of course she's black, being from Nigeria. All I was doing was confirming that. It doesn't mean she's less beautiful," I babbled, and my mind was screaming at my mouth to stop. I was making things so much worse.

"Where's my favourite Ming piece?" Nora's mother asked in a slightly raised voice.

There was silence.

I shot a look at Hector. Nora stood up and walked casually over to the bar. He was trying to deflect his mother's attention. His left hand fanned out.

Hector reacted. "Don't walk like a faggot, Noel."

136

Nora retracted his hand. Angelica moved to the edge of her chair, and spoke to Hector in whispered Cuban.

Hector tried to placate his highly agitated wife. He went over to her, as Nora made as much noise as he could making drinks.

"Noel, darling. Where is my Ming piece? You know that is one of my favourites of the collection." She clutched her throat, dramatically, just as Nora always did.

I wanted to leave the room, and tried frantically to think of an excuse. I really felt sick.

"Héctor, call *Mema*. She will know where it is." She stood, and Hector put his hand in his pocket. My never ending puke factory cranked up its engines.

Oh dear, I really must go...

He pulled the broken figure from his pocket and held it out. Angelica stood and screamed as she took the already dead piece of ceramic and cradled it in both hands. Wild eyed and highly dramatic, she sobbed and held it out as if she had *The Holy Grail* in her hands.

I felt I had to confess. "I'm so sorry, Mrs Sanchez, It was me. I'm so sorry. It was a terrible accident," I explained, and was promptly sick on the rug in front of me.

She fell back, screaming, and swooned as if she were really fainting. Her screams brought her *Mema,* who berated me, though it seemed more like she was cursing me.

Whilst all the attention was on Nora's mother, I crept out of the room and trotted back to my sanctuary. Every now and then raised Hispanic voices penetrated the wall.

I contemplated calling my brother and going home for a few days but I knew my Mother was going round there to interrogate Jonathan's girlfriend, Daisy, and I knew I would be in the firing line there too. I sat on the bed and thought about Nick, until I had to run to the bathroom to be sick again.

Very attractive, I'm sure, compared to who Nick will be meeting...

I vomited a couple of times, before deciding to have a bath and I chose Juniper oil, because the label told me it would heal my mood. The door opened and made me jump. It was Nora. He immediately lit a joint and sat on the edge of the bath.

"Oh, my darlink. I'm so sorry. *Es un bastardo*," he said, bitterly, and spat into the bath.

"Erm, excuse me? I probably do deserve to be spat at, but I don't want to sit in it."

"*Molestas, guapa*," he said, and sucked hard on his joint.

"Was the rug expensive as well?" I asked, in a tone that suggested I didn't really want to know.

"It was a personal gift to my mother from *Jackie Kennedy*," Nora answered.

My mouth dropped open, and Nora gestured in the air as if it was nothing.

"I shouldn't be here, Nora. They hate me. I'm in the way while they're living in *their* house. I feel as if I can't do anything or go anywhere now. The whole house is spun from leprechaun's pubes, and the furniture's made from *Queen Victoria's* eyelashes."

Nora choked on his joint as he laughed and smoke billowed out.

"Oh, my god! You're so funny. Darlink, you are not going to abandon me in my hour of need. My Mother cares a lot about objects and charities, always talking about save the something or other, except her family, and let's not forget *money*, her biggest love of all. When she was nineteen, she swam up a *Rio De Mierda*, and beat off all the competition to be with my papa. It was her looks that secured her place at his side. She clings in fear to these things."

138

"She *is* breathtakingly beautiful," I sighed.

"My Mamma has the depth of a tissue," he said, snorting. "And all that my papa cares about is that I spunk into the appropriate receptacle that will bear him a grandchild and prove to the world that his son is not gay. I know that secretly, my Mamma doesn't really want to be an *Abuela*. She would rather drink cocktails with shards of glass in than be called *that*. She loves the fact I am gay, and she secretly embraces it. My father outwardly condemns it, loudly. When I was five she had a leopard print outfit made for me by her personal friends, *Dolce* and *Gabbana*. Whenever my father went out, she would dress me up in it and parade me around the house. The only other person who witnessed that was my *Mema*. By the time I was ten I possessed my own secret wardrobe, full of clothes made by the most famous designers. I had pink silks and coats made from ermine. I had shoes that had been clubbed to death and transported all the way from the Arctic, just to be placed on my feet."

He finished the joint and removed a small pipe from his inside pocket, which had high-grade weed already packed into it. He lit it, inhaled deeply and paused for a few seconds before finally exhaling with utter pleasure and relief. I delighted in the fragrant smell, and was jealous of the obvious gratification he was feeling.

"Mmm, that smells so nice."

He offered me the pipe. I shook my head.

He held it out. "Lauren, it's not heroin. *Todos es buena.* The test results were good, *vamos*."

I took the pipe, guiltily, and Nora stood up and lit it for me. I inhaled the smoke greedily and then sank down into the water, submerging myself and drowning all my doubts.

"So, if the babies have arses for heads, then I can blame you."

"You are *loco*. We all know that doing drugs turns your children gay."

That started us off giggling, and we had trouble stopping. I laughed along with him, and we soothed each other's tired souls.

"Do you think that you would have naturally been gay, or did your Mother's influence help you to choose men?" I asked.

"Oh, she always knew. I thought she was so clever and wise, and that's why she did it all for me." He made a scoffing noise.

I suddenly remembered the money that Hector had mentioned.

"Nora, about the money, it's way too much to spend. I don't want to cause you to lose all that."

"Darlink. I've taken that money out. I have twenty thousand in my pants drawer, *aaiiee!* We gonna have fun, *chica*. If power and money is all they care about, then I shall try my best to undermine that." He kissed my forehead, stood and smoothed his hair. "Trust me, they will only be here at the very most for *dos dias*."

They lasted until just after breakfast the next day. Raised voices and slamming of doors informed me of their departure, right before Nora came in with a huge joint, jumped up on the bed and started dancing. That made me laugh.

"They're gone. *Whoopee, aaiiee, salsa!*"

Eventually I had to hold up my hand and stop his fun, as the bouncing was making me feel sick. He sat down, looking jubilant.

"Lauren, Australia 'eh? So many men, so big *aaiiee!*"

"You managed to satisfy your father then?" I enquired quizzically.

"He told me that if I do not come back from Australia with a wife, then I will be cut off."

140

For a moment we were both serious, and then we began to laugh.

"I don't know how you do it. I'm sure you'll wriggle out of it somehow," I said.

He clapped his hands, gleefully.

"Christmas in Australia means *mucho sexo*."

And Nick... I couldn't stop the thought from popping in.

He squealed with pleasure and jumped up.

"I'm going to look at flights now. *Aaiiee!*" he screeched and headed swiftly for the door.

I shouted at him. "Nora, no one is to know about the babies yet. Including the Airlines."

"*Vale, vale,*" he agreed, and trotted off. I didn't see him for the rest of the day. I was happy his parents had gone, and I daydreamed freely about Australia. I had fond memories of the place, I was excited to be going back there this time with Nora, and I was thankful we'd have money this time.

At least if Nick's really shitty to me again, Nora will cheer me up...

***

The following morning he came running into my room and shook me awake.

"Wake up, Lauren. I've done it. It's done. We are going to Australia in one week!" He screeched in my ear. "We are going. *Aaiiee!*" He took a selfie of us both, with me looking startled. "Hashtag #Australia #BumFun #HunkyMen."

141

GET READY

The week that followed was mayhem. Our nerves mixed with excitement and we clashed frequently. Small bouts of bickering broke out between us. There seemed to be so much to do. I blamed Nora for booking it so quickly, and he screamed at me that he was under the impression that time was precious and life was short. Of course the fact that he was right just pissed me off even more.

We were flying Air New Zealand, from *Gatwick* - first class, and I certainly wasn't complaining about that. We had the luxury of an open return ticket, and could return home anytime within our three month visa. I told my brother, and then took the cowards way out when I phoned my parents, lying easily as I told them my made-up reasons for going. My mother told me it was probably just what I needed, and I knew that secretly she was happy I was going to be so far away, as my absence would save her the embarrassment of fending off any awkward questions. This tactic of mutual denial suited us both very well. My father sounded genuinely upset, and though I wanted to tell him he was going to be a grandfather, I knew he would crack under questioning. He would love to hear that news, especially since I was going to have twins, but his opinion was usually the complete opposite of my Mother's.

Danny and Sergeant Cole both visited me on separate occasions during that week, and both said they'd miss me, although Lawrence seemed more concerned, probably because he knew about my pregnancy.

"Are you sure it's safe for you to fly? And so far away?" he asked, taking my hand as we sat on my bed.

"They do have medical care there, Lawrence. It's not a load of kangaroos doing the operating."

He smiled. That day his aura looked especially relaxed and casual. His eyes twinkled with happiness, and he seemed more attractive. My hormones raged as I stamped and snorted around my bullring of sexual desire. I rubbed his hand and gave him my best flirty hair flick.

"You look good, Lawrence. Being with Jenny obviously agrees with you."

He blushed. I knew I was flirting but I didn't care. After all, Nick was already showing half of Australia his cock for money.

"I'm sure too, that Nora has paid to have a *Gucci* helicopter standing by for any emergency," I reassured him.

Lawrence looked around at my environment.

"Stupid me. Of course. How can I forget when everything here is made of money. It must be hard not to be spoilt."

I withdrew my hand from his.

"Nora is *not* spoilt, Lawrence. I can assure you of that, despite his surroundings. You of all people should know that. He has restricted personal freedom, just as you do. I remember that story you told me about the lake at your house and never being allowed in it," I reprimanded him, angrily. "People in glass houses, and all that, Lawrence."

He held his hands up. "Whoa, there. Okay, I get the message. I wasn't actually saying your friend is spoilt. I do understand,

143

Lauren. When you're born into money it's all you know." He swallowed nervously. "But you sure do look pretty when you're angry."

"Passion can also turn around and snap off your manhood, Lawrence."

Without thinking he lowered his hands and protected his most prized possession. We both smiled.

"But I don't think I've quite reached that point yet," I said, back at ease.

"I really will miss you," he said, and his voice seemed different somehow. I took his hand again. "Please stay in contact. Someone should really know what's going on, and I definitely have the qualifications," he implored me.

"I will. I promise," I assured him, and at that moment Nora burst into the room, causing Lawrence to jump, and make his excuses to leave.

I kissed him discretely goodbye, and then Nora did; on both cheeks, while pushing up against and grinding on him.

When Lawrence had gone, Nora flounced down onto the bed. "I think I make him nervous," he said, smoothing his trousers.

I sat next to him and pushed him, playfully. "You are such a bitch," I accused him, giggling.

"*Darlink*. A rich bitch if you don't mind."

"Have you been having fun?" I asked. We only had three more days to go, and I knew the next day was the big packing day. I was actually already packed. I'd prepared extra early in case of any unforeseen dramas, which made a change for me. I hoped and prayed to the Goddess that there would be no dramas, although I knew from experience that praying was futile.

"Not really, darling. I've been shopping. *Muchas compras*. So boring," Nora complained as he examined his nails and sighed. "Also I spoke to my detective. He is going to meet us at the airport and take us to a hotel that he has booked. He'll fill us in on what the current situation is," Nora told me, and sighed again.

I slapped him. "Nora! This is exciting. Do you think you could show a little more enthusiasm? You look like you're watching an insect die."

"*Aaiiee!* You're so funny. Yes, *carino, es* exciting. Like a movie. I bought so many things though. *Tan mal.* How are you today, darlink? *Como está?*"

My morning sickness, which had cunningly disguised itself as lunchtime sickness, teatime sickness and even bedtime sickness had finally abated.

"Better thanks, honey. I'm probably going to have a nap." I realised I was feeling tired a lot.

***

That was the last thing I remembered until I was woken by the sound of high pitched screaming on repeat. I listened again, and again, until eventually I got up and rushed to the source of the distressing sound; Nora's room.

I flung the double doors open to reveal a vision of chaos. Clothes were spread thickly around the room, and six large suitcases stood open. I could see the label on the one closest to me; it was a *Louis Vuitton*, a set of six. In the middle of all this was Nora, still screaming. His hair had bounced out, and I could tell he'd been exerting himself for quite some time. He stopped screaming, abruptly, and began rambling in Cuban as he threw things around. I watched this pitiful display until I couldn't stand it anymore.

145

"Okay, I'll ask you. It's worked. What is wrong?"

"Sons of *puta* whores, Lauren," he wailed at me. I said nothing, willing to let the drama of the missing comb, or whatever it was, unfurl.

"I don't have enough room," he said, clutching an item of clothing to his chest as if he was at a Black Friday sale.

"In which one?" I asked, tipping my head towards one of the suitcases closest to me.

Nora arched his eyebrows and gasped incredulously.

"In all of them, darlink. *Todos.*"

Of course... I smiled at the foolishness of my question. "Nora. We are going for at the very most, three months, not three years. I know you can afford the extra baggage charges, but I am not travelling with you and six cases." I was already playing out the theatre of it in my head.

"You are *loco*. I said I don't have *enough* cases. I don't want to cut down on them."

I foolishly chose to help, and bent towards a case that had underpants on the top. As I lifted them up they just became more underpants. I lifted up more and more, only to reveal countless *Calvin Kline* in various colours.

"Nora is this only filled with underpants?"

"Of course," he answered, wallowing.

I was beginning to see where the problem lay.

"Right. For one thing, they do have underpants in Australia - yes even your beloved *Calvins*. Also they have washing machines that clean clothes. Honestly, Nora. I don't know what you think it's like over there, but it is actually inhabited by talking humans who have managed to harness the rudimentary power of speech, and not by some feral, cock-dangling,

146

bushmen." Although in truth I had seen some people like that there, I was not about to tell Nora that.

He threw some clothes at me and pouted his lips. My natural bemusement calmed him, and he closed the curtain on that particular stage production.

"Will you let me help?" I asked, and approached him tentatively. I helped him up from his hot mess of brattyness and took him over to his bed. His room made mine look like a cupboard. His huge oak four poster bed, as he had told me before, had been owned by *England's Henry VIII*, and given as a gift to the first colonial governor of *Cuba, Diego Velázquez de Cuéllar,* in the fifteen-twenties. Subsequently Nora's family had inherited it. He often told people that *Ann Boleyn* and the king of England had *sexo* in that bed.

"I like to think I have a little bit of your king in me," he would say to bemused listeners of his recanted tale. There was exquisite detail in the carvings, and you could practically smell the history seeping from it. I thought it was a great bed, but I definitely didn't ever want to sleep in it.

I sat him down on the red silk sheets, which didn't seem authentic, and I suspected they didn't come originally with the bed.

I began to clear the underpants suitcase and removed fourteen pairs as I listened to Nora whimpering in the background. There were three cases full of clothes and accessories. One whole case was dedicated to shoes. Another held a red duvet with a picture of *Shirley Bassey* on it, together with two pillows and three blankets, which Nora informed me was because he needed different thicknesses, depending on what the need was.

The final one I looked in contained random items, so I took them out carefully.

I held up a fairly large box, which said on the top, in bold letters:

Anal Waxing Kit.

The makers of the product: *Waxy Hoop,* guaranteed their kit would remove every stray hair.

"Mmm. That's probably not needed," I said, and shook it in the air.

Nora let out a small whimper. "You never know, *darlink*. Best to be prepared."

I retrieved fifteen packets of wet wipes made by *Soft Queen* from the case. We argued it down to three packets, which took about fifteen minutes. I sensed this was going to take a while. Next, I pulled out a wheel of cheese, which pushed me over the edge.

"For god's sake, Nora. They do have cheese in Australia."

"This is not just any old knob cheese, darlink."

"In what situation do you think you will need to whip out the cheese?" I demanded, and placed it to one side. I insisted that the cheese stay at home, and promised him that I would eat my words if that dreaded moment of cheese crisis should arise while we were away.

"Now you'll see. Aboriginal men will kidnap you, and perhaps they will sodomize you and chop you up, and all they wanted was a very good round cheese," Nora protested.

He did make me laugh. "I'll kill you with it myself if you don't shut up about it."

There were pots of jam, different selections of condoms and thirty-one bottles of sun creams and blocks, all factors, and for different areas where they should be applied.

There were unguents for the lips, the face and for around the eyes. Products for the neck, the breasts, and incredibly, one bottle was actually for the testicles. I removed them all gingerly.

Nora squealed and protested. "No way, darlink. I heard they have a really thin sky, caused by some oozy layer, and just walking to your car you can get cancer."

"I think you'll find it's called the Ozone layer, and if that is the case, do you suppose they might have stocked up on bottles of sun cream, as a nation?" I asked, and I couldn't help but smile. He offered no argument.

I took out a curious pouch with about ten different small round headed brushes.

"What are these?"

"Tongue brushes," he replied, walking over to me.

"What the hell are they?"

Nora arched one eyebrow and took the packet from me. "Mm, I would have thought that was obviously in the name. They're not ball brushes," he tittered. "And I am taking them."

"Jesus. Why not just one?"

He rolled his eyes. "Because they're for different parts of the tongue."

I couldn't help but laugh. "Fucking hell, how big is this tongue? Giant sized I imagine."

Nora threw the packet on the floor. "I think a nice big tongue like that *es estupendo. Aaiiee!* Where is this tongue? Oh, *por favor.*" His mood improved once we'd finally got the packing down to two cases, without too many tears, and with lots of promises that we'd do some shopping when we got there.

The packing was done, and all our goodbyes had been said. Nora was tweeting his little pearls like crazy. He was worried that he might not be able to tweet while he was away, but I assured him repeatedly that Australia had modern technology. By this time we were both very excited, and even if things could not be resolved with Nick I was determined to make the best of it.

On the final day we were happy to leave the appalling British weather. It was bitterly cold, and constantly raining. I called out to Nora to tell him the taxi was loaded with our cases. He came out of the front door, locked it and took me by the hand, squeezing it hard.

"Cariña, vamos. Una adventura grande. Arriba!"

AUSTRALIANA

I was in mad depths of comfort as I sipped my orange juice. I'd never owned a chair as plush as the one I was sitting in, even my own bed wasn't as luxurious, let alone on a plane. I knew this experience would spoil me forever, and I'd probably harbour a snobby disdain for battery farm economy class in future. Nora was in the toilet again, for what was probably his fifteenth time, as he joined the mile high club with a passenger who had boarded on the stopover at Los Angeles. Older and Australian, the man had simply ordered a glass of champagne. Nora had been on the bubbly too, and was halfway through his second one, when the attractive stranger had merely tilted his glass towards Nora, and that was it. Now the two of them were at it like flying bunnies.

Finally Nora slipped back into his seat, glowing. He looked sensational, and when I had seen him that morning, I'd been speechless. In a way I had been secretly worried about his potential choice of flight attire, but in the event I was completely surprised. He wore a dark blue *Don Lorenzo* suit, with a black *Armani* shirt and no hats or gadgets. I'd kissed him on the cheek and told him how handsome he looked. He oozed panache, and I understood why men were so sexually attracted to him, despite his bitchy manner. So far there hadn't even been a minor infraction, and what was now the three of us silently thanked him.

"Oh, so nice to have you back," I teased.

Nora said nothing, and simply picked up where he left off, sipping his champagne. A moment later the man returned to his seat.

"Have you no shame? It must be obvious what you're doing. The air stewardess must know."

"I have paid enough money for them not to care. We are first class, darlink, not bog-standard cattle class."

He was right there. The air stewardesses were stunning, and their smiles and makeup were un-crackable. They glided up and down the aisle like catwalk models, catering to the passengers every whim.

"I hate to point out that if the plane crashes we will all plummet towards our death together. First class won't magically disengage itself from the rest of the plane, and miraculously grow new wings and fly off, jetting us to a limousine that will take us to a resort to recover from the ordeal. In fact it's the opposite, as we are at the front of the plane and have paid more money for us to hit the ground first." I smiled smugly at Nora.

His loathsome look told me he couldn't find the words to argue, and he resorted instead to mumbling obscenities in Cuban, as he took two angry photos of me.

"Hashtag *#FirstClass #SecondClassScum*."

152

I slapped him playfully. "Anyway, you amaze me."

"What just me personally, or do all us gays amaze you?"

"Mmm, I'll go with the latter, but it really does amaze me because it's all so swift. No mucking about. I didn't even seen you speak to him, buy him a drink, nothing, and yet you still get the goods. No howdy-do, no nothing. Just a small gesture, and it's all worked out. It just seems so quick and easy."

"Is it better to be like straight people? Wait for three months for them to fart in your direction, or buy them a few drinks, and then take some girl home whose self worth is about the cost of the drinks you bought her. Darlink! At least whores price themselves extremely well, and if you want the ten dollar 'round the back of the station' one, well then, at least you don't have to talk to them." He snorted at me.

"I suppose it's just my jealousy, at the ease of it all." I sipped my orange juice.

"Darlink, you should be. AIDS is so *estupendo*. One big laugh and very easy. One giant sneeze, and its *adiós*. As my papa said: 'It's god's antidote.'"

I felt foolish and ashamed and turned my head away.

"Lauren, darlink, I love you. I'm taking the piss, and anyway, maybe it's not so casual. I have his phone number. His name is *Brian*, but everyone calls him *Aunt Fanny*."

I leaned forward to peek at the large, black haired man. He was rugged, with glowing red cheeks, and I found it hard to imagine he was called Fanny.

"He lives in a place called, er, *Darwin*, and he's one of the best chefs in Australia. He's got a channel four TV show called *Brian's Barbie's*. His father used to call him *Fanny Craddock*, you know, she was a famous TV cook in the sixties, and well, to his father's horror the name stuck."

"So, you managed to do some talking as well? Darwin's in the Northern Territory," I giggled.

"Yes, even with a full mouth. *Aaiiee!* So naughty. What? O.M.G. *Que?* They have a North-South divide all the way over here?" Nora asked, truly puzzled.

"No, silly. It's just what they call the area where it is."

"We'll have to pop up there one day from Sydney."

I said nothing and just let the smile play on my lips. He had no idea how big and vast a county Australia is. You cannot *pop* to the next town. You have to plan your route and make sure you have all the supplies. I knew he was in for a big surprise.

Nora managed to squeeze in one more visit to the washroom with Aunt Fanny before we were told to take our seats as the plane began its descent. After strapping ourselves in, we instinctively held hands. I remembered how much I had liked Sydney. I had only stayed one week back then, and I was looking forward to exploring it more. I hadn't felt queasy throughout this whole trip, and I took that to be a good sign. Even now, having had hardly any sleep, I was wide awake and filled with adrenaline and excitement as we dived towards Sydney airport, and Nick.

***

It was five-thirty in the morning Sydney-time when we finally stepped from the plane. A whole day had passed since we'd boarded, and the first blast of heat felt very pleasant on our faces. Before landing, the captain had informed us that it was nineteen degrees Celsius, a whole seventeen more than London was at that moment.

We waited for our luggage, having successfully completed the airport's assault course.

154

"So this detective, he's meeting us in arrivals then?" I asked, as I spied the first of the cases coming through the flaps. Nora seemed preoccupied, and began his penguin dance, as he tried to spot his luggage.

He waved his hand dismissively. "*Sí, sí.*"

"Does he know what we look like? Or are we looking for yours or his name, being held up on a card?"

Nora turned to me and smiled. "That would be so funny if he has his name up on a big card."

"Why?" I asked, dreading what he might be called. *Wayne Kerr? Bobby Sandyballs? Mike Colon?...*

"His name is *Gene Kelly*," he answered, without even glancing at me.

"What? He's called what? Do you mean we're going to meet a dead singing and dancing movie star?"

Nora laughed. "I picked him because of his name. So funny!" He screamed and pointed towards his emerging bags.

"So you didn't pick him based on his spectacular performance as a detective?"

I imagined him tap dancing his way over to us and delivering the news through the medium of song.

Nora was struggling with his bags, so I helped him catch the third one before it ran away. I knew I should probably just get a trolley, so I set about fetching one, and lifted one of the cases onto it while Nora hand-fanned himself.

I was incredulous. "Oh please, don't struggle. I wouldn't want you to pull an eyelash," I said sardonically, and released the case with a bang.

He pulled a face and continued to fan himself.

"Nora I *am* pregnant. A little help is needed here!"

He pursed his lips and blew air out, whilst raising one eyebrow. He then feebly attempted to lift a case, before he gave up, dropped it back down and dragged it across the floor, noisily.

"Nora, pull the handle out and use the wheels that you paid nine hundred pounds for." I was feeling tense and I wanted to get some real fresh air, the kind that even first class couldn't have pumped into the cabin.

Nora made a slight show of it as he did my bidding. "Lauren, darlink. It's only a case. What next? You can't lift a toothbrush, or a cup? Maybe you need help holding your mascara tube."

"I don't have to wait with you. I've been here before. I know where to go. I'll go and meet this singing detective myself." I said indignantly, puffing up my chest and acting pompous.

Nora paused, laughed and then continued without further complaint.

We finally made it through arrivals, but only after Nora had taken a flurry of photos capturing our arrival in Australia.

We both fervently searched about and it was Nora who spotted the sign being held up saying **N. Sánchez**. The man holding the sign looked nothing like his deceased dancer and actor namesake. The closer we got to him the further the resemblance became. Finally, as we stood in front of him, he seemed more to resemble the corpse of the star. Considering this Gene Kelly was a man who lived in one of the hottest countries in the world, it looked like he'd never seen the sun. Five foot nothing; he resembled some kind of insect. An unhealthy sheen of moisture veiled his grey skin. I was half expecting him to pull back his neck and lash out his long marsupial insect tongue.

He took Nora's hand and shook it vigorously. "*G'day*, Mr. Sanchez. I'm Mr. Kelly. Welcome to Australia."

Nora smiled thinly.

Mr. Kelly tipped his invisible hat towards me. "*G'day*, Miss."

I felt sorry for this wretched man, saddled with the same name as such a handsome, dashing and charismatic legend. I imagined working alone and following other people around suited Gene very much, as none of those flattering adjectives sprang into my head when I looked at him.

"*G'day*, Mr. Kelly. I'm Lauren Bowman." I was still fluent in Aussie and I wanted to impress with my native language skills.

He helped us with the trolley and we headed to his car. He asked us if we wanted to go straight to our hotel, and I said I thought that would be best.

As he packed our luggage into the trunk of his shabby brown station wagon he chatted. "Because you wanted to stay in top accommodation near a gay area, I've made a reservation for you in a hotel in *Darlinghurst* on the edge of *Kings Cross*."

Nora looked surprised. "What? Like London? So what's the name of the hotel?"

"It's The *Bong Willamaloomoo*," he said as he opened the car door for us to get in.

We both stared at Gene, and pursed our lips tight to suppress our laughter. His skin tone visibly changed to a puce-grey.

"It's a five star hotel. It's a *beaut*," he said meekly, and smiled.

We sat in the back childishly giggling whilst he told us that he had up to date information of which he would inform us once we had settled into our rooms.

The rest of the journey we were all quiet. Nora and I looked out of the windows as the Sydney sky birthed a new day, we sat in a vehicle being driven by *Gene Kelly*, and made our way to Kings Cross, destination: *Bong Willtoiletcow* or something like that. Along the way, the warmth of the day built up, along with my hopes. It was so nice to be back.

Mr Kelly had been right; the hotel really was a *beaut*. As we entered the live art installation known as *Bong Willamaloomoo* I knew we were in for a treat. Sparkly glass baubles in all different sizes and colours cascaded from the ceiling. Trees made from the same baubles branched throughout the lobby with laser beams fracturing and bouncing between them, splitting the lights into rainbow colours.

Seriously cool...

I glanced at Nora, who glided past me, unimpressed. As we neared the counter, which was completely plastic and transparent, I blinked. There were two staff behind it, a stunning looking girl, and an equally stunning looking man. On the top half both of them seemed immaculately dressed, but when you looked down below the counter level, the woman wore suspenders, black stockings and high heels. The man wore a rubber codpiece. They must always have been approached by customers with beaming smiles. I even noticed Nora do a double-take, so I knew he was finally impressed. It was so exceptionally clean, I felt like I was checking into heaven.

I heard poor Gene Kelly's *Aussie* tones which brought me slightly back down to earth.

Even as he approached, I couldn't resist staring at the beautiful female receptionist. Ever since my previous trip here, I had developed a particular liking for Aussie women, or *Sheilas*, as they call them. I'd even thought about staying permanently when I'd nearly fallen head over heels in Love with *Christina*, who was a textile millionaire from *Perth*. The lifestyle had been fantastic and if I had been that shallow, I would have stayed and pretended to be more infatuated than I really was. For a second I thought about my present situation; *I'm single, old, pregnant with twins and totally broke. I'm being supported by a real queen; my best friend, who in turn is being supported by his unsuspecting wealthy parents. At least I'm keeping it real...* I thought, and made myself smile.

I heard my name, and looked round to see Nora being escorted to the lift.

It was Gene talking to me. "So, two hours then, Miss. *G'day*." he said, cocking his hat again before scurrying off.

The male receptionist handed Nora the key. "The elevator will tell you where to go, sir. You're in room two-oh-four," he said loudly as we headed off keenly. The lift door opened and I joined Nora inside. The doors closed and the walls began to change colour from pale blue, to lilac, to light green. We were so entranced that when the elevator stopped and talked it made us jump. "Room two-oh-four. Turn left and follow to left," it said, in a soft female voice. "Your luggage will be brought to your room in two minutes."

"Thank you," I replied.

Nora giggled. "So now you talk to lifts? *Vamos*," he said, and strode off purposely.

He had only just opened the door to our room and I could hear him squealing, which was always a good sign. As I entered I could see the pure white walled hallway inside. I felt uneasy, and looked down to see a thick glass floor, with fish, yes *real* fish swimming happily beneath my feet. The colours were beautiful and I was in awe. The corridor carried on for several metres and I stared down as the room opened out. I was so entranced I was unable to take my eyes off the fish, until a huge scream pierced my tranquillity. Of course, I knew it was Nora but I didn't know where, or why. A cry of "*Aaiiee!*" came from above my head. I scanned the room and saw a door on one side of a huge balcony. I moved hastily towards it and flung it open. Individual *Perspex* stairs stuck out of the wall, leading up to another door. I made my way up carefully as I realised what a dangerous nightmare they would be if you were pissed up.

I got to the top and stepped through the door. "Nor-" His name caught in my throat, and my jaw began to drop.

We found ourselves on the roof of the hotel. A glass railing encircled the large space. There were two swimming pools, one with light blue tiles, and the other with black. There were two *Jacuzzis* with fountains and lights which jetted up into the air to make the colours of the rainbow flag. Marble pillars held up glass roofs above the pools. In between the pillars hung long swish pale lilac curtains. Nora was stood at the railing. I joined him and we linked arms, both entranced as we surveyed Sydney.

I couldn't help but remember my previous arrival in Sydney. I had been on a backpacker's budget, and things could not have been more different. I'd stayed in the *Kings Cross* red light district, in a hostel called *Kanga House*. It was owned by a huge Aboriginal man with long white hair. He never actually spoke to me in words, but performed various grunts instead, which only intimidated me more. He only added to the authentic atmosphere that you only find in hostels. I think someone went to hell, came back as a zombie and created hostels to serve the walking dead. I loathed them but they're always cheap. My very first night I'd witnessed a large woman from *Wales* called *Mary* shitting into a plastic carrier bag. It seemed it was also compulsory to get so paralytic as to lose control of your faculties.

I'd got caught in the middle of three large arguments; one row had been about who had had the most chips, and many were based around poor *Judy* who was apparently a right slag according to her 'Cock and balls on display' boyfriend. I witnessed regular vomiting and once I saw two couples copulating simultaneously in the same dormitory, complete with running commentary throughout, just in case the other people in the room two inches away from them somehow missed what was happening. At least their shouts of; "I'm coming!" let me know their horrible deeds were nearly done.

Here is some of the advice offered to me that first night in a hostel;

"It's best to sleep with money and passports between your legs, for security."

"Don't go to the toilet, or you will be robbed."

"Hang a sheet or bath towel over your bunk if dirty stuff is happening on it." (Apparently it's okay to hear but not to see.)

I told the person who enlightened me about this gem that I was travelling alone, but that if I felt like a good old masturbation session on this, my first ever terrifying night in a hostel, of course I would hang my towel.

I was told to embrace god at length by four of the other tenants, and by that time my state of mind was that strung out I was looking round the twenty-eight bed dorm and beginning to think that maybe that wasn't such a bad idea.

Finally I had the pleasure of meeting *Jennie*, a true *Aussie* whose most profound words of wisdom imparted to me were; "See when you get pissed, and fuck a fella? Well, afterwards you gotta crouch down on the floor, cough a whole lot and get those little bastards out've your cunny. Wash it all off in the *dunny* (toilet), and you're good to go."

Yes, my previous visit had been very, very different.

"Darlink, okay. It's fucking amazing. Stupendous. Fabulous. I love it. *Aaiiee!*"

"Come on, I want to look at the rest of our rooms," I asked, impatiently

Nora shooed me away with his hands. "You go. *Un momento, por favor.*"

I left him, knowing that much tweeting would be occurring, and explored the rest of this little paradise. I discovered the fur lined bathroom, and the heated water bed in my room.

Just as Nora came down the stairs there was a knock at the door. Feeling giddy and blissful, I opened it to the sight of a very sweaty Mr Kelly holding the latest information on Nick, in his hand.

"Come in Mr Kelly, Gene." I opened the heavy door just wide enough for him to slither past me.

Nora was already waiting, sitting on a cream leather couch, his arms spread wide along the tops. It seemed he was spreading them ready to fly, just in case things became messy. Gene sat opposite him and I sat next to Nora.

"This is the latest information about Mr Nick Palmer," Gene said, fumbling with the envelope. Our stressed out silence was clearly unnerving him.

"This Saturday, Mr Palmer will be with his business partner at a venue called *The Lucky Sheila*. They are booked to do a striptease at eight PM, for the Sydney Ladies Cricket team," He looked up. "For about five hundred women, I reckon, judging by the size of the place."

Nora raised an eyebrow, and I felt a look of shock settle on my face.

"I've had a word with the proprietor, and she said as long as the brown *fella* here blends in, then there shouldn't be a problem with you both going in, if yer wanna?"

Nora sat up stiffly and a wry smile played across his face. He leant forward slowly.

"I'll try very hard not to be so *brown*." He stood up and sashayed across the room to the bar.

"I definitely want to go and see him, but that's nearly six days away," I complained. The thought of waiting that long deflated me.

"Ah, good. Gives me time to lose a bit of my colour," Nora said, a perfect blend of acid tongue and smiling lips.

Gene stood up, clearly feeling nervous.

"Here are the directions to the club. I'll meet you at the front door and take you inside. I'm assuming my work will be concluded after that event?"

"You will be paid in full on that evening, Mr Kelly," Nora said clearly, his back turned.

"I'll see myself out," Gene said, with a tiny bow, and then he was gone.

I threw myself on the couch and pulled my lip down. "Six days, Nora? It's going to kill me with the suspense of it all. The waiting."

He came over to me. "Darlink, you need to rest. Think of the *bambinos*. It's a long long way here, *puta madre*. We'll have fun and explore later. Shopping and cock." He kissed my forehead.

I smiled. "Can we do them in that order? And I think I'll miss the cock."

"Darlink, I know how you feel. I miss it too. *Aaiiee!*"

Nora's humour always helped to put me at ease. We unpacked and I tried to get some sleep, but I just couldn't manage. Eventually, after I'd moaned enough at Nora, we went out. Jetlag seemingly had nothing on us, and we went out and explored the city with gusto. We went shopping, we ate amazing food, and that evening we went to a drag bar where a female drag artist did a show in which she spoke fourteen different languages. We were still up at five the next morning, eating banana pancakes from an all-night vegetarian cafe.

Nora had bought new clothes for me to wear the coming Saturday night. I was happy for him to take the lead, and I allowed him to shine at what he was best at.

"Tomorrow we will get the jewellery to go with it," he told me. "And we must go to a good hairdresser."

Finally, at seven AM, we arrived back at the hotel.

I sat on the sofa and put the bags down on the floor. "I still can't believe I'm not tired."

"Me too, darlink. I feel incredible." Nora said, as he sat next to me.

That was the last thing I remember.

**

I could feel a very dry sensation in my mouth,   and light flashed on my eyelids as they flickered open and I sucked in the arid air.

Nora was asleep next to me, and we were both dressed. I could tell by the light coming through the windows that it was evening. I desperately needed a drink of water before anything else. I took a swig from a nearby bottle and looked at the time. It said eleven PM.

Bloody hell, we slept for sixteen hours...

After so many hours of sleep, I felt like crap. I sludged along with misty eyes, feeling sure that the babies felt better than I did. *They bloody should be, they are feeding off me...*

I wanted to wake Nora, so I shook him gently by the shoulder.

He sat bolt upright, screamed *"Puta!"* in my face, and quickly followed that up with apologies and lots of kisses.

"It must be your split personality that your short term lovers find so endearing."

"They love it, darlink, and my big black *polla,*" he retorted as he patted down his slightly unkempt hair, which had lost none of its smoothness.

"Nora, can you believe we've slept sixteen hours? It's Tuesday night."

"Que?"

"I know, it's crazy. I didn't do that before. Maybe it's the two extra passengers on board." I patted my stomach and smiled.

Nora focused on his *Cartier* watch and gasped slightly. "Darlink, *por favor,* turn on the light."

I looked around, located the switch and turned it on, Illuminating us.

"Puta. Mierde. Lauren?"

"Yes?"

"It's not Tuesday night, its *Wednesday* night, eleven-fifteen PM."

I sat down. "No way. Your watch must be wrong then. We haven't slept that long."

Nora's voice tightened. "Wrong, darlink, so wrong. This is a hundred thousand dollar watch. It's a *Cartier.* It's encrusted with blood diamonds and emeralds. Wrong." He sniffed and stuck his nose in the air.

"Oh sorry, Lord Snob. I forgot that you're wearing the blood of young children around your wrist. Maybe their haunted spirits within those diamonds gave you false information."

We both stood, our tempers rising, and I immediately felt so dizzy that I almost fell over.

Nora rushed towards me, *"Carino!"*

Without thinking my hand went to my stomach and I rubbed it.

"Los bambinos. Darlink, I'm sorry. What can I do?"

"I'm fine. Really, I just feel a bit dizzy. I'm sorry, I don't want to fight over something as small as what day it is, but that was a hell of a sleep. Nearly two days!"

165

"Of course, you feel dizzy. You must eat. You need to feed your angels. I will get room service, and we will eat like royalty."

I hugged him, inwardly thanking the Goddess that he was here with me.

We spent a magical night up on our private roof terrace ordering different dishes from room service, including kangaroo, which Nora wanted to try. I'd had it before, and like nearly everything, it tasted like chicken. Nora was taking one of his rare nights off from impressing the world, and he kicked back and relaxed. We laughed, ate food and chatted right through to the next morning. Our body clocks were being thrown everywhere. We slept all that day, and by the next evening I was still disorientated. My body didn't know what day, or what time zone we were in. I did notice however, that I hadn't felt nauseous. This side of the world obviously suited my mental health, and I felt relieved.

Nora wanted to go out to find "Drugs and cock." He ordered a taxi and told me he planned to be out for a while. I preferred to stay in and watch local Australian TV, which is hysterically funny, although it's not always meant to be. After a full evening of eating and giggling, I finally made it to my waterbed at the respectable hour of three AM, and fell straight to sleep.

When I awoke, my first thought was that it was Friday, and so I only had one day to go before I saw Nick.

At least I think it's Friday?...

I decided I would go out for breakfast. I needed some fresh air, and I had a craving for lush blueberry muffins. I got up to shower and check if Nora was awake. From my room I could hear voices, and as I came through to the lounge I could see that Nora was on the couch with someone. A third man was standing and removing his clothes.

I coughed. No one took a blind bit of notice. I coughed harder. Nothing.

"Nora!" I shouted.

He jumped up, kissed the naked man who stood before him and danced over to me.

"*Cariño*. You understand." He hugged me.

"Of course. I'm going out. My needs are different, and right now I need a little air. "He smiled a soppy *'I'm happy and high on drugs'* smile, and returned to his play.

I grabbed my bag and left. I spent that day walking and sightseeing. I ate at restaurants and daydreamed. I remembered what happened when I was there before. It felt like I was travelling on my own again as I explored this amazing antipodean city.

I didn't really mind being on my own, in fact it was nice to have my own thoughts. I didn't care about jewellery or accessories, but I didn't know what to do about the state of my hair. Just at the moment when I was thinking that, I saw a hairdresser's shop in front of me. Its name was *Hair by Lucy*.

I stared, curiously. It had to be an omen. I walked into the shop to see a pretty girl sitting behind a plain reception.

She smiled and stood.

"*G'day*. What can I do you for?"

"Mmm, I'm not sure. It's a last minute thing. Are you *Lucy*?"

"Yep, that's me," she replied, smiling her best reassuring hairdresser's smile.

I didn't know why, but it seemed important to me that she was the same Lucy whose name was on the sign outside, otherwise there would be no positive karma.

"Well, take a seat, and let's see what I can do for a very pretty lady." She flung a cape around me and began to play with my hair.

167

"I would say cut it off. It's quite dry and you have good bone structure," Lucy suggested.

I shook my head violently. "No, definitely not short. It doesn't suit me."

I remembered the few times I'd had my hair cut short. Like when I was nine years old and my mother cut my hair very short, including the fringe. I looked like I had stepped from a performance of *Hamlet*. I'd looked like a cone head, and my face bore a look of permanent shock. At fourteen my mother took me to the hairdresser. She wanted my hair to be short and tightly permed, for the sake of neatness. When it was finished it looked exactly like a bird's nest, and I cried in secret for a week. I kept finding things in my hair that, during school, the other kids had placed in there; chewing gum, feathers, condoms, and chocolate. One day I even found a little stapler in there.

No, short hair and me did not have a good history.

"I can see you're not too keen, but honestly you have got a face that suits short hair."

Her smile was winning my trust, and I was starting to think that maybe a complete change was what I needed.

"Well okay, if we're doing this then maybe we can change the colour to a dark brown?" I suggested.

Lucy's smile grew. "That's the kind of spirit I like."

"There's only one rule though: No cutting higher than the top of my ears."

"Agreed."

As she went to get her tools, I thought: *Oh well. Either way, I will look different by the end of this session...* I just hoped it would look good.

***

It was better than good; it looked amazing, outstanding and unbelievable. I absolutely loved it. I turned my head from side to side and marvelled at the miracle Lucy had created. She had razor cut it short at the back, and just to the tops of my ears. My fringe was thick, poker straight and hung a millimetre above my eyebrows. Dark hair framed my eyes in a way that made them look very big, and made the blue even bluer.

"Wow, if you don't mind me saying, you look like a model for *Mary Quant*. You are truly stunning," she told me, blushing fiercely.

I stood, and for a moment I felt so full of confidence that I kissed her fully on the lips.

"Lucy, I am in Love," I said, and gave her my best sexy playful smile.

I turned again and looked at myself in the mirror. It sure didn't look like me, but I loved it.

I tipped her generously, as I felt she had given me more than just a haircut. She'd also *shamanised* me. With my new hair came new hope. I was glad Nora had decided to have a cock-fest.

I walked all the way back to the hotel smiling as if I had found life's secret. I felt ready and prepared to see Nick. The next day I would find out how that worked out, and how a simple haircut can delude you.

STRIPPER'S DELIGHT

I managed to wake up at a good hour, which reinforced my positive attitude. I hummed cheerfully as I ordered breakfast, and then lunch. I spent the day by myself out on the terrace as Nora was still not up. The curtains gently billowed like my mood, and time passed pleasantly. I dangled my toes carefully in the pool, but nothing more as I wanted to keep my hair intact. As I was doing exactly that, I spied Nora hauling himself to the top of the stairs, where he paused and stood, studying me. He began to wave.

"*Hola, hola! Señora, hola!*" He walked towards me. "Hello? This is private here. *Privado!*"

As he stood in front of me, I grinned at him and waited for the penny to drop.

His hand clutched his chest, and then Bang! He jumped back and screamed as he realised.

"Lauren. Lauren. *Puta madre!*" he exclaimed. He was breathing so heavily it was as if my hair had hit him. His chest rose and fell rapidly.

"I, I, - I fucking love it. O.M.G. *Guapa*, I didn't even know it was you."

"It was a last minute decision. Thank flip it paid off."

"It is an amazing creation. I'm sorry I didn't come with you but maybe it was meant to be," he said, showing me the insides of his pockets.

"*Exactamente.*"

"How do you feel about tonight?"

"I feel good, Nora. No matter what happens."

He walked over to the phone and ordered food.

"*Cariño*, do we stay here today?"

I nodded happily.

By seven PM we were both getting ready, and by eight, I was sitting waiting for Nora.

I had a simple sapphire-blue dress on, with long sleeves, a hem just above the knee and an ample neckline. The colour went perfectly with my new hairstyle, and my eyes shone as brightly as the dress did.

Nora emerged from his room dressed like an Edwardian. His face was plastered white and he was wearing heavy red lipstick. He was dressed in a frilly shirt with a flowery waistcoat over the top. His pantaloons had frills on, and he held a gold-topped cane in his hand. His hair was all his, and combed back slickly. He walked over to me confidently.

I was caught between shock and laughter, tittering and giggling.

"Too much?" he asked, his arms open and eyes wide.

My mirth came out on top. "Ha ha! Have you gone jetlag mad? What the hell?"

"I was asked to blend. You remember? So I'm making myself white. I'm blending."

He smiled, and he looked like *The Joker*.

Nora insisted I take photos, which were all slightly blurred because of my sniggering.

"Hashtag #whiteface #knickerbockers #blend," Nora said, and pressed *tweet*.

"That's what I love about you: Your subtlety. Let's go, Mary Ann Tudor Rose. I think we need a taxi."

"*Aaiiee!*"

Linking arms *Wizard of Oz* style, we went out together as comrades.

We ended up sitting at the back of a very crowded venue, which looked like it was an old cinema with rows of seats. Off to one side were dining tables that seemed to be booked solid, although when you're staring at men's willies all night it's hard to say which food would be the best accompaniment. Chicken in a basket? Sausage and chips? Scampi?

We had already fought our way through the foyer and found Mr Kelly, who'd clearly been bowled over with Nora's look. Most of the women just thought he was part of the night's entertainment.

By this time I was getting a bit nervous. There were three strippers on before Nick and his new best bloody friend, Patrick.

First, *The Destroyer* took the stage. He was a huge muscle-bound guy, who stumbled around and tried in vain to perform a basic dance routine, filling in the gaps by flexing his formidable muscles. At least he could do that well, and he even kissed them. He picked up a woman, flung her around on stage for a while and then rubbed cream all over his body, before he gave her the treat of her life by stuffing his crotch in her face as he pulled off his G-string. Her face met with his sweaty creamy balls, and then he helped her up as the crowd went mad.

It was a real mixture of people as well, not what I'd thought it would be. I'd imagined them all wearing some sort of cricket clothing, seeing as it was a cricket club, but I was wrong. It was like lots of different small groups clustered together. There were feminists and lesbians, stood next to sex starved, feral looking creatures. There were classy ladies ready for a posh night out. Despite their differences, there was one thing that obviously united these women. As soon as the men came out, the screaming began. Nora was loving it.

Next was *Laser Man* who went round dipping his penis in women's drinks and slapping it on their foreheads, which is always quite amusing as long as it's not *your* drink, or *your* forehead. I thought that one would be hard to top, but I was wrong again.

Captain Hard taught me some stuff that night that I never quite forgot, and that will always linger in the depths of my subconscious, ready to disturb me at a moment's notice.

Dressed in black and red, he looked like nothing fancy at first. Doing a poor impression of *Freddie Mercury*, he made disgusting gestures with his tongue.

Nora held a white lace hanky up in front of his face, so I wasn't sure what expression he was pulling.

Captain Hard stripped down and finally pulled off his pants. Unlike the other acts, he didn't bother to conceal anything. A very healthy penis hung down and all the women clamoured to look at it.

"Ooh, it's a fuckin' *beaut*, Doris. Like a baby's arm!" one of the women on the next table shouted.

He opened his legs and it hung comfortably as he raised his arms up like a muscle man. The lights dimmed and strobe lights slashed across his manhood.

Then it moved up, independently. His shaft slapped his stomach loudly and a surprised lull settled over the women. I was also, naturally, bewitched. Nora let his hanky down. Captain Hard's shlong moved again, this time to the beat of a rock song, to the side, down and double tap.

How the hell?... I was mystified. As the music reached its climax he bent right over, his hands on the floor and his arse sticking up in the air. There was a big loud drum roll, and something that glowed bright red shot out of his bum and sailed through the air. All who could followed its trajectory, until it came down and landed precisely in someone's drink. The room fell very quiet at this point, as a fairly respectable looking woman fished it out, inspected it and then holding it up, yelled: "It's a love heart!" The women went crazy.

I looked at Nora, and then at the lucky woman - who lifted her drink and took a sip of it.

"Good to go!" she shouted, which only made the woman more frenzied.

I took a sip of my drink, gingerly. Nora looked as disgusted as I did.

"Why are you disgusted? You eat arse all the time," I said.

"*Si*, but not the shit that flies out of it. *Puta madre*. He could have had that up his *culo* all day."

I choked on my drink.

By now the audience were highly excited. The smell of hormones hung heavily in the air, and they seemed like a huge group of caged animals, ready to pounce. I began to feel a little uneasy as fists slammed tables wanting more meat.

174

The compere came out, looking a little on edge himself.

"Ladies, ladies. You are about to get a real shaker. Please put your hands together for *Miss Topsy-Turvy*!"

Women who had been poised, with their hands ready to clap together, faltered. "A woman?" "A bloody woman?" On came Patrick.

A murmur went round, and someone shouted, "We haven't paid to see a fuckin' *Sheila*."

I kind of hoped they would throw things and make it hard for him. The music began, and though I did not know the song, his routine was admittedly good. He entertained the women and engaged them by shaking his hips just like *Shakira*.

He had fantastic legs, from what I could see. *Shit, now I'm staring as intently as Nora...*

Topsy was charming us, weaving her magic.

Right in front of our eyes, we watched a pretty woman strip down to reveal a sexy man. Each layer he peeled off revealed a more tantalising man. The crescendo of encouragement from the women echoed my thoughts. As the excitement mounted, there were screams and cries for him to go quicker. Nora clutched my leg, which was unusually tactile for him.

Topsy was now *Turvey*. In his tight leather shorts and chained top, his arse would have won prizes. It looked solid, as it stuck out slightly, proud and tight.

He slid his top off and stood before the audience, studying us as he tugged at his shorts and goaded the crowd until they were screaming for cock. He pulled them off quickly, covered his jewels with his hand, and the stage went black.

The women wolf-whistled and called out, baying as a pack. The lights came back on, but he had gone.

The compere came out again. "Bloody marvellous. Put your hands together, ladies," he commanded, and they did. "Okay now we're going to let you all have a well earned five minute break, before our final two *fellas*."

I sighed. Now I'd have to wait even longer. Nora had removed his Elizabethan fan, and was waving it lazily.

"Darlink, I'm sorry but he was good. Did you see that *culo*? I could eat all my food from that, *aaiiee!*" He threw his head back and laughed wickedly.

"I feel sick, Nora, at the thought of seeing Nick."

Nora leant forward, took my hand and squeezed it tightly.

A very drunk woman passed, stopped and stared at the dressed up Nora. "Oy, when are you up there?" she asked, trying to point to the stage.

He smiled "You madam, are an aesthetic crime, please move away."

I smiled as she swayed in incomprehension, and then staggered away.

The compere asked the ladies to take their seats, loudly.

The babies felt my anxiousness rise up, and made motions that only increased my nausea. My stomach churned around and I took Nora's hand again.

Out came the fat and balding compere and quietened down the women.

"Now then, ladies. We've got a real treat for you now. Our next act is all the way from England, the country of our sovereign queen. I think you'll love him, so let's hear it for *Mr Exposure!*"

176

The woman reacted exactly the same as they had with all the others. Now I really did feel sick. The music began; *Bang, bang, bang*, and I knew it was him.

He started his show wearing an old Macintosh raincoat, buttoned up. A black trilby with a white ribbon round it was tipped forwards on his head, hiding his face. After the fourth bar of the music he jerked his head up, and thrust his raincoat open. The breath caught in my throat, and all the other women's screams faded away around me. I could only hear, "*I'm Horny, Horny Horny, Horny*," whilst I watched the only man I had ever really loved strip his clothes off in front of five hundred screaming women. He had a gangster's suit on under the raincoat, and his devastating looks matched his body, with its newfound healthy tan. He was sensational. He jumped on tables, lifted women up in his arms, and poured baby oil on his tight muscular chest and abs, rubbing it in.

I ached for him and yearned for his touch, as did nearly all the women in that room.

I realized he was finished when I heard loud banging on tables as reality came back to me, and then Nora's voice broke my trance. "Lauren, we must go now. *Vamos*."

I couldn't move. I felt so unsure about everything. Any confidence I'd gathered had been peeled away like the clothes from the stripper's bodies.

Nora pulled at me, insistently. He took me over to a door that was set to one side of the stage, and we slipped inside. We found ourselves in a small dark corridor, which led to what sounded like the changing room.

"I'm not going in there, Nora. We'll have to wait outside."

He pouted, obviously disappointed, but he followed me outside, and we waited by the stage door, watching faces as they left. We clearly looked like a neurotic looking woman with a man from the nineteenth century.

I thought I saw Patrick, and then I heard Nick's voice.

As Nora made a bold move towards them, I scuttled behind him, using him as a human shield. Patrick stopped, and stared at Nora, as Nick did the same. Nora pushed me in front of him and Nick stared at me. He looked at Nora, the white painted freak, and back to me, without a glimmer of recognition on his face.

"Can I help you?" Patrick asked, in his heavy Australian accent.

No one said a word. I watched as Nick's mouth began to open very slowly, but no words seemed able to come out.

"Look, I don't know what's going on here, but you both need to move away," Patrick warned, as he took a step towards Nora.

"Lauren!" Nick finally managed to blurt out.

"Yes?" I answered, smiling.

"Lauren," he said again, and then he just broke away and ran as fast as he could.

"Nick!" I called after him, but he was gone.

I burst into tears. The whole thing was overwhelming me.

"What the hell is going on?" demanded Patrick. Nora brought his hand up and slapped him across his face. "This is your fault, you *bastido*."

Patrick began to protest, but Nora grabbed my hand and both of us fled just as swiftly as Nick had.

After a while of running away, I stopped, wracked with grief. Nora hailed a cab and we went back to the hotel. I curled up in the back seat, unable to talk, and Nora left me to my thoughts.

When we got back, I went to my room. "Sorry, Nora. I need to be alone. I can't process this."

He kissed my forehead, and quietly told me he was going out again.

*****

I lay in bed, stuck with the image of Nick running away from me. Rather than see me again, he'd always run away. Thousands of miles away from home and he still ran. I knew it was the end. It was over. I had to come to terms with the fact that he really didn't want me ever again. Even though I had promised myself I wouldn't cry all the time, I did. I cried all through the night and most of the next morning until I worried that the babies would get dehydrated with all the tears I'd shed.

Nora was still not back at breakfast and I allowed myself to wallow in self pity. I sobbed as I rubbed my stomach and talked to its occupants.

"That's it, I'm afraid. You're both stuck with me. Which is crap," I told them, and triggered another sobbing episode.

Luckily, Nora returned alone. He hugged me tightly. "I have a plan, darlink."

He looked scary. Patches of his white make-up had worn off, giving the illusion his skin was peeling off, as if he had zombie disease, or leprosy. His wig had disappeared, and his swish pantaloons were very dirty. His dishevelled appearance stopped my blues in their tracks and made me smile.

I tried to hush him, but he swayed in front of me and placed his finger on my lips.

"Shush, shush. I called Gene straight away last night. Luckily, he managed to follow them, and he told me they are at the ranch. He will stay there and monitor the situation. We are going there and you can tell him about babies, then we go. *Simplemente*," he said, and smiled as if he had solved all our problems.

'Nora. I don't want to. I've had enough. We've come halfway round the world to see him, and he's made it clear what he wants. I can't keep chasing him."

He hugged me again. "*Cariño*. Just tell him, *por favor?* It is correct. Then *vamos*, we can go.

It seemed there was no way to argue with him.

"How will we get there?"

He clapped his hands, sensing triumph. "We will hire a beautiful car, darlink. So, come on, chop, chop. We leave soon."

"I'm not going today, Nora," I said incredulously.

"*Sí, sí*. Gene is there, darlink. My father is paying him by the hour," he said, and laughed.

I sighed and raised an eyebrow at him. *Maybe it's a good thing...* I found myself thinking as I was getting ready. Nora was right, after all. Nick did have the right to know he was going to be a father. What he did with that information was up to Nick.

I dressed casually in tight jeans and a pale yellow shirt, which really suited my short dark hair. I had no show at all yet, despite the fact I was now fourteen weeks pregnant. I'd had no more sickness, and it seemed that being down under suited my passengers.

An hour later we were sitting in the hired car that had been brought to the entrance of the hotel. We simply got in, set the Satnav, and I drove towards my destiny again.

WHO LOVES WHO?

When I'd come to Sydney all those years ago, I hadn't had time to visit *The Blue Mountains*, although I'd always wanted to. Now I was finally at the foothills and just about to enter them, I felt calm, and pleased we had come. Nora had snored most of the way as he slept off the events of the previous night, and I'd enjoyed some peaceful me-time. I snaked the car up the mountain road, and headed towards *Willygong*.

The sign made me giggle. Nora had said *Willygong* made him visualise a man with his willy hitting a gong, and that maybe that was the picture on their flag? I smiled as I remembered his words, and silently thanked him for making me come here. The road was damp with dew, fallen from what seemed like layers of clouds with smudges of blue and purple dancing within them. I opened the window and the scent of eucalyptus trees lifted my body and soul. My blood pumped in my ears, and I felt cleansed from the inhalation. It looked breathtaking and felt truly magical. As I looked off the side of the road I watched it fall away into big valleys and steep bluffs. There were eucalyptus trees everywhere.

"Stunning. I hope you two in there can smell this," I said out loud. I figured it would help, like a giant lozenge.

181

Nora stirred as the fresh lunchtime air came through the window. At altitude, I felt like I was in fairyland at the tips of the trees, or perhaps outer space. For some reason the mountain air gave me hope and lifted me up until I was floating and alive within the clouds. All my senses were resurrected, and I was glad to just be. I smiled, I sighed and I laughed as we got higher and higher.

"*Que pasa? Cariño, es muy frío.*" Nora said as he woke up. He hugged himself theatrically.

I smiled beatifically, and closed the window. The woman on the Satnav told us we'd reach our destination in thirty-five minutes.

"I have such a thirst. *Joder!* Thirty-five minutes. Can we stop?"

"No, you'll have to suffer. I want to get there now and get it over and done with. Then we can explore, and maybe even stay the night somewhere.

"Darlink. I only want a drink."

"You are terrible. It was your idea to come up here today, and just look around you. It's stunning. It's not my fault you've got cock throat."

He gasped as he tried to cough but could only rasp painfully. He raised both eyebrows, but he stopped bitching.

The mountains renewed me and gave me the clarity of mind to think rationally about what I was going to say to Nick. I resolved to approach him, no matter what, and then we would leave.

The roads seemed to be winding up to heaven, where soul-filled clouds uplifted me.

The woman inside the Satnav spoke up in her honeyed Australian accent. "Less than two kilometers to your final destination. *Willygong*."

We both sniggered in unison.

As we drove through the tiny town of *Willygong*, which was bathed in blue beams of sunlight, I felt no anxiety at all.

We turned onto a dusty track, and I saw the battered vehicle of Mr Gene Kelly just as he was getting out.

I pulled over, and Nora looked apprehensive as we both got out to meet him.

"*G'day*," Gene greeted us, and bowed his head slightly.

"Mr Kelly, here is your cash. *Por favor,* be ready just in case we need you again." Nora said, and handed him a fat wallet. I knew his parents would have a fit about all that money.

I saw Hector again in my imagination, and this time he was blowing fire from that powerful nose and cooking his son, the heir to his money machine.

Back in reality, I noticed Nora's hair was having a slight afro-frizz problem. The moisture of the atmosphere was already playing havoc with it. I knew he'd hate that.

I shook Mr Kelly's hand and watched him leave hurriedly.

We got back into our car. "So we go to the gates where it says *Freedom Ranch*. We can open them, and then we just keep going. *Vamos*, "Nora commanded, motioning ahead with his hands.

We drove through lush green fields which seemed to contradict the normal arid landscape of Australia. Eucalyptus trees were everywhere, with the mist siphoning through them.

Presently, I saw the huge gates ahead. They appeared to be freestanding, and big letters of wrought iron across them spelt out:

FREEDOM RANCH

"Well?" I asked, as I stopped the car in front of the gates and looked at Nora.

"I thirsty."

"I pregnant."

Nora got out and cussed loudly all the way over to the gates, as he opened them, as he closed them, and all the way back to the car.

"I would have thought all that cursing takes precious spit," I said, once he was seated.

"I found some sperm at the back of my throat."

My mouth fell open, and laughter gripped me.

"That's disgusting. You are so wrong, my Cuban friend."

"*Aaiiee!*"

We got the giggles and I drove on in happiness.

"*Porque*, you are so calm? *Normalmente* you vomit and *caca, siempre.*"

"I don't know. It's some kind of spiritual thing."

He scoffed. "*Puta.*"

"Yes, it's possible that the goddess of whores is watching over me," I teased.

Just as I spied the roof of a house in the distance, *Mad Max* descended upon us. Two quads came flying over a hill towards us, preceded by a huge pack of variously sized dogs, running and barking. They were crazy, mangy looking things. Nora screamed, and foolishly I accelerated, which only made the whole pack of chasers, well, chase us more.

In front of us I could see people waving us down, as something else approached us at speed. Nora and I screamed as a rider and their horse appeared directly in front of us.

"What the fuck?" I shouted, and slammed the brakes on. The car skidded fantastically and stopped sideways. The horse rider sped over to us, and pulled the magnificent beast to a halt, alighting as the horse still moved and dragging the heels of his cowboy boots along the floor.

We both gasped in perfect unison. For a moment, admiration replaced fear. However, that moment was fleeting, as the dogs joined us and circled the car. Some were as high as the window, and the noise from their barking was phenomenal. A quad came from behind us, then another came from the side. The riders both cut their engines immediately and jumped off.

Nora gripped my arm, and all my saliva drained from my body as a cowboy walked towards us in his tight jeans.

"*G'day*! Friends or foes? Gotta check," he shouted, and standing in front of our car, he took his cowboy hat off and craned closer to its occupants. It seemed neither of us could talk.

"Please, get out of the car," he said.

"I think its Patrick," I managed to croak.

"I don't care if it's the fucking Pope. *Muchos perros.*"

One of the quad drivers took their crash helmet off. She was a pretty girl, with chestnut ringlets in her tied back hair.

Matilda... I guessed. I turned to see Nick remove his helmet on the other quad.

I gasped and Nora screamed.

Nick cocked his head. "Nora?" he said. He leant down to look at us, saw me, and his face was a picture of utter shock.

"Do you know these people, Nick?" Patrick asked.

Nick couldn't speak either.

"Down!" shouted Patrick, and every single dog stopped barking and laid down.

Nora gasped again, and I gripped his arm. "I think we should get out, Nora."

We both got out of the car gingerly. None of the dogs moved a whisker.

"Sorry about all this, but you never know who might come here. You could be some crazy gay killing scum," Patrick said, as he smiled and offered his hand.

I shook hands and tried to collect myself. "I'm sorry. We should have announced ourselves. We are friends of Nick. I'm Lauren, and this is my friend Nora."

Patrick offered his hand and Nora shook it gently, without saying anything, which was very unlike him.

"Nick, I think we should all go back to the ranch."

Nick nodded, and there was a glimmer of hope in my heart.

"Well, okay, and over here is Matilda," Patrick said, and indicated towards the quiet girl, who simply waved.

"We will all meet each other there," he said, smiling.

He was very handsome. His eyes were full of sparks that swam in emerald green pools. He replaced his hat onto his unruly strawberry blonde hair, swung a tight muscular leg over the horse and gave the reins a sharp pull. The horse turned adeptly and he cantered off, obviously a superb horseman because his animal let him take total control. The dogs followed in a blaze of jubilant barking, with Nick and Matilda herding them all on the quads.

I headed for the car and opened the door. I called for Nora, who hadn't moved.

"Nora! Nora!" I had to shout.

"Okay, okay. *Vale, vale*. I hear you," Nora groaned, and got in. At first, we didn't speak, each lost in our own thoughts. Then, as we approached, Nora said; "Did you see the way he handled that horse?" He sighed, and I had the answer to my question before I'd even formulated it. *Patrick*.

The house at Freedom Ranch was typical of rough wooden outback houses. A giant skirt went round the entire house, creating a wide porch with a roof that was a great place to stay cool in the normally murderous desert heat. Up here, the climate was much more forgiving, and a stubborn chill refused to leave. Spring spewed forth colour all round the ranch.

"Wow!" was all I could manage as we got out of the car.

Nora screamed in panic, and I knew he'd seen his hair in the mirror. Filthy swearing confirmed it.

I waited, and watched Patrick open a big double set of wooden doors. He smiled at us though I was trying not to like him, despite myself. I saw Nora desperately apply what tiny amount of spit he had left to survive onto his hand, and use it to try to smooth his hair down.

"Nora, for God's sake. Get out. Leave your hair."

He pouted.

"Now."

He got out, looking sheepish.

Patrick walked over to a round wicker table, with matching chairs.

"Please, let's take a seat. Nick said he'll be here very soon."

We did as we were told. The doors opened and my heart steadied itself. It was Matilda, holding a tray. She had the most beautiful smile, and goodness emulated from her. Her hair was down and the ringlets cascaded round her pretty face. She flashed her amber eyes at me as she laid the tray on the table.

She's so young. Shit...

"*G'day,* again. Here's a few *stubbies* for ya."

She went over to Patrick, flung her arms around him and kissed him on the cheek.

"That was awesome," she said, breaking away and sitting down. I reached for the water and poured a glass out. As I downed it I was definitely starting to feel more nervous.

Nora coughed lightly. " *Por favor, que* is *stubbies?*" he asked, almost whispering.

"It's beer," I told him, and smiled. He pulled a face that said; *'Water, please.'*

I poured and heard the doors open behind me. *That can only be Nick. Yes, now I'm nervous...*

"So I am right in thinking I know you two from last night, and you're the ghosty lookin' *fella* that hit me?" Patrick asked, just as Nick sat down, turned and looked at Nora, clearly horrified.

Matilda immediately got up to pour a drink for Nick. When she'd finished, she hugged and kissed him as well.

My back straightened. *What the fuck?...*

"*Si. Es la verdad.* It was me. *Señor*, I apologise. I am totally in the wrong." Nora said, owning up most humbly.

I thought I was going mad. What was happening? No catty comeback or self righteous indignation? He actually sounded genuine.

Nick still hadn't looked at me.

"Well. It was almost worth it," Patrick said, and smiled at Nora.

Nora blushed "We have travelled so far, and then when Nick ran, I lashed out. *Lo siento, otra vez.*" He looked at Nick, "*Es no tu culpa, mi amor.*"

Nick managed half a smile. "No it's not. Bit of a shock seeing you both here, all the way from London. I have no idea how you found me in such a hidden location. It's almost like you had me followed!" He ran his hand through his hair.

I desperately loved him.

"We did, darlink." Nora dropped the truth flippantly.

Nick turned a shade of angry red and looked at me.

"Well it must be for a good reason, to go to all that trouble?" Patrick cut in.

Nick stood up. "Lauren, I think we need to talk."

I stood up and followed Nick as I heard Patrick say to Nora: "I'll show you round."

I followed Nick through two large dark and dusty rooms. He pushed open a door, and we were on the veranda at the back of the house. There was another set of wicker furniture, and a long swing chair. I sat in a high backed seat at the table. Nick sat a chair away from me, staring out at the beautiful landscape. I had no idea what was going through his head, and the silence hung as heavy as the clouds. All I was sure of was that we had to start talking. I knew what I was going to say. He hung his head and sighed, then looked me straight in the eye.

"I really have no idea what to say. I'm literally speechless. You had someone follow me? For how long?"

"Since you came here."

More silence.

"I really don't know if I should be flattered that you went to all this effort, or fucking furious, for not letting me go." His eyes stared into mine, and the words I'd rehearsed began to slip away.

"We came here because I have something important to tell you. Something that can't be said in a mail or by phone. I'm sorry Nick. It is a lot to take on that we're here."

"Mm, yep just a bit. You both turn up to where I'm stripping, across the other side of the world. You got to admit, that's fucking freaky. That's why I ran last night." He looked at me. "I didn't have a clue what to do," he admitted, and his expression changed as he stared at me. I saw softness, and concern. "Why do you have to come all this way to talk to me? Are you sick? Oh my god, you're dying!" he exclaimed. He went to reach out, but stopped himself.

My breath slowed. He cared. He totally still cared. The look was real, he still wore no mask, and hid nothing. My voice squeaked in my throat as no words came out.

He threw himself on me and hugged me tightly.

"Oh please, Lucy. Lucy, my darling, please, please, don't die."

With the sound of those words, everything fell away. *Lucy*...

I still couldn't speak. Heavy emotion gelded my words.

He took my silence as an affirmative admission.

"It was so hard for me last time I saw you. I even had to make my dad drive me to the airport in case I changed my mind, and now, now you are here," he babbled as he held my hands. I had to tell him.

"Nick. I'm not dying. In fact it's the opposite. I am more than alive." He looked puzzled, and he relaxed his grip.

"I am producing life, well lives technically. I'm pregnant with twins, Nick. Your twins," I said, and stopped to check he'd heard.

His head cocked strangely to one side.

"I'm almost three and a half months gone. Funnily enough, they are due near your birthday at the end of May."

All the colour had drained from his face. He let go of my hands as if he'd been stung and jumped up from the chair.

My hope teetered on a cliff edge, resuming the position it knew so well.

Nick put his hands on his head. "Twins, twins, *feckin'* twins, *feckin'* holy Mary!" he said out loud in his deepest Irish accent.

My body and soul lurched back from the edge, and moved towards possible ecstasy.

He covered his groin with his hands. "Jesus. I'm terrified. I think me *feckin'* dick has shrunk."

We both grinned. He started laughing, and I joined in. I loved his Irish accent, which he obviously reserved for moments of true Love and affection.

He came to me and lifted me up. He spun me round and kissed my face.

"*Valentines spin in my brain,*

Without you there is only pain.

From now on I'll never be the same,

Something now, I can explain, it's Love, it's Love..."

He stopped spinning. That was our song that Nick had written for me. He'd changed the lyrics at the end to be more appropriate for us.

Tears welled in our eyes as we kissed. Time slowed down and my heart shattered into happiness, each shard pulsing with ecstasy. It was a kiss worthy of time travel, let alone across the world. He put me down, howled like a wolf and screamed.

"So you're happy?"

I heard the sound of boots running on wooden boards. Matilda charged round the corner like a bull. Seeing us both laughing, she halted. Her cheeks were flushed, which highlighted her amber eyes.

She's so pretty...

"*Strewth*, I thought something was wrong," Matilda panted, which only added to her appeal.

Nick picked her up and spun her round.

"*Valentines spins in my brain!*" he sang, laughing. "Everything is so right." He hugged her. Nothing could spoil my relief and elation at Nick's response. Even if he'd taken her then and there and shagged her, I still would have been elated.

Patrick drove up on the quad, with Nora as his passenger. He cut the engine and jumped the veranda fence in one stride.

Everyone's turned sexy...

Patrick saw Nick spinning Matilda round, and then he saw me standing and staring with the look of a street-dwelling peasant girl who'd just found a pair of clean knickers.

Nora got off the quad and joined us.

"So, we heard screams, and now I see you're hugging Matilda ecstatically. I am definitely curious," Patrick enquired in his delicious accent. A very gentle Irish accent softened the Australian twang, and the two blended perfectly.

I do actually like him...

Nick put down Matilda and turned to me. "Can I say?" Nick asked, and his face shone with the kind of happiness and stunning beauty that my soul loved, and even ached for. He came over and placed an arm around me as I nodded blissfully.

Nora leant against the fence and I noticed an unusual look on his face. He looked like a homeless gay *campasino* boy who'd found the perfect cock.

Patrick and Matilda sat down.

"I'm going to be a father - of twins," Nick said, and he sounded young and joyful. I looked into his watery eyes as he turned back to me. "We are going to be parents."

I didn't think I would ever see such joy contained within one person ever again. I wished it could be bottled and distributed to all the sad and disillusioned people. Everyone should experience that joy at least once before they die. He placed his hand on my stomach, and transferred the feeling to us.

I could never have imagined his reaction. That meant everything to me. Even multi-millionaire's couldn't have bought this for me. I hugged him tightly.

"Nick. Nick. I'm..."

"Pregnant, laughing and hysterical, darlink. Thank god he knows," Nora said, and sashayed over for hugs and air-kisses. Then Patrick and Matilda hugged everyone, blanketing the whole place with Love. I cried even harder.

"Of course, you will stay here with us," Patrick insisted.

I had no idea where we would stay, or what was happening. Or who loved who, except the one thing I did know for certain was that I had Nick nearby, and he still loved me.

Its okay, kids. Panic over. Your father is here now to add some rationality to our lives... I quietly confided to my completely loved and wanted babies.

DECISIONS, DECISIONS

I woke up from the best night's sleep I'd had for a long time, wrapped in Nick's arms again and feeling protected. That day was mostly spent with Nick fussing over me and making sure I was all right.

Nora protested his lack of clothes, and tried in vain to flatten his hair, until Patrick told him he looked very attractive with his natural afro, whereupon he suddenly stopped trying to hide it. I was stultified. In all the time I had known Nora, he had never, ever let his own natural hair out. Once I'd caught a glimpse, I agreed with Patrick. It really suited Nora.

I asked Nick if perhaps he wanted to talk about what had happened, but he assured me there would be time for us to talk soon.

Matilda wanted to show me round the farm, especially the stables, which she was clearly particularly proud of. I relished her carefree and easy manner, and readily tagged along. Nick came with us. At first, he was enthusiastic about taking his own horse with me on the back and Matilda on another, but I had to explain to them that horses and I had never really gelled.

I had tried horse-riding at least five times and actually loved the romantic idea of hacking through forests, with your sexy partner galloping alongside, both astride these huge and powerfully strong beasts. I understood the dream of emerging onto the beach and thundering along on wet sand, always ending with making mad passionate love at the edge of the waves. None of my real-life experiences had bore even a hint of any of that.

My first ride, at the age of eleven, was at a reputable horse riding stables where you could pay to take the horse out on your own, within the boundaries of the grounds. My horse was called *Norris*. The girl assured me that Norris was very, very docile. I was with a friend called Elaine, who'd had some experience, and she was given *Prince* to ride, whom she was told had a little more spirit.

We had exited the paddock perfectly, and as we entered the wide open lush green fields, Elaine opened up Prince and started trotting around. Prince performed impeccably, whilst Norris just stood, and stood, and stood. No amount of cajoling him, pulling lightly on the reins or giving him little kicks seemed to help. Elaine even gave him a little pat on the bottom but that horse would not move. Eventually I resorted to threats, whispering in his ear;

"Listen here, my friend. You are glue when we get back, get that? Glue, you bastard."

He didn't even flinch. In fact he just lowered his head to eat grass. To make it even worse, I had to endure watching Elaine having a breathtaking ride on her obedient beast. She was laughing gaily and enjoying herself. When the hour was up she led Prince back to the stables, and it was only then that life emerged from the bowels of Norris, and he slowly followed them back.

Of course I complained, but I didn't get my money back. So Elaine and I decided to try a different, less prestigious establishment. I had told the stable boy there that I wanted one that wasn't too docile, so when he brought out a horse called *Titan*, I should have had some suspicion that this was not going to end well, which of course it didn't.

With hardly any horsey experience, and only ten minutes into the hour, I was having trouble communicating with my mount again. I'd merely given Titan a first gentle nudge with my heels, when his black ears went flat against his head, and he thought he had entered the Grand National derby. He quickly went from the speed of a *Mini* in second gear, to the blur of a *Ferrari* racing car in top gear. I screamed, and unable to hold on, I star-jumped off rigidly, my arms and legs stuck straight out. I broke an arm badly and shattered my right ankle.

Once I was better, I attempted to ride one more time, without even leaving the paddock. I'd put my own saddle on, as there was no one about to help. This time I wanted my shame to be mine alone, and so I made sure I was on my own.

I lifted my leg into the stirrup and it felt good, but as the horse trotted into the cobbled courtyard, the saddle began to slip to the side, taking me with it. I banged my head on the stones, cut it open and had to have six stitches.

So, I considered my riding days done. The fourth time, I wasn't even on a horse. I was running through a field very close to a horse's behind and got a nice kick, which luckily only grazed my leg and caused a huge bruise that lasted for two months.

The fifth and final time I had been anywhere near a horse, I was merely stroking their face. I don't know if I was being too rough with the horse or if he was just being playful, but he'd just bent his head down and bitten my tit. The pain was unbearable and my left breast was swollen for about six weeks, which earned me a nickname at work; *Big One-tit Lauren*.

I didn't want to change now for anyone. Horses just clearly did not like me.

"I think it would be safer not to risk it in my present condition," I pretended, and showed Nick and Matilda my biggest, '*I could easily do it otherwise,*' smile.

"You go ahead, Matilda. We'll meet you at the stables. I'll take us on a quad, Lucy. Of course, you're right, you have a precious cargo."

"What, and I wasn't precious before?" I teased, and our easy familiarity made me feel so happy.

When we got near the stables, we saw Matilda was petting a beautiful gray horse. Nick put the brakes on and stared over at her.

"She's pretty isn't she? Well, I'm only human," I commented.

"Yes, she really is stunning. Nice and young. She'll handle well. I can't wait to get a go on her."

My eyes opened wide in the face of such sheer blase-ness, until I realized. "You're talking about the horse, aren't you?"

He nodded, and began to laugh. I knew that stupid questions deserved a similar response.

"No, I'm not attracted to Matilda. After only knowing her for such a short time however, I do admire her. She's *not* a victim of the world, I'm sure she wouldn't mind me telling you. Both her parents were killed in a car crash when she was fifteen. Since then she's been through a lot, living rough, and trying to survive," Nick concluded. I knew she had confided in him, and he was no doubt keeping a few more secrets for her, and I loved him for that. I'd tried to live without him, but it had felt like life in a cardboard cut out world.

I got off the quad and placed my hand on his arm. "I already liked her. She's got a fierce will to live, you can see that in her."

"There's still so much to say, Lucy."

"Yes, but for the moment, let's just take today, and then maybe tomorrow, as naturally as we can. If that's okay with you?"

He smiled boldly, with beautiful full lips. I leant forward and kissed them.

"The stables," he mumbled.

The stables were beautiful; in fact they looked nicer than the main house. I could see the wooden panelling and all the poles that made up the fencing were practically new. Three horses mused quietly around the paddock. I knew I wasn't going to enjoy this, and I wondered if my fear of horses would be transmitted to the occupants of my womb. Matilda bounded out as we approached the huge main stable doors. On one door was written FREE and on the other DOM. As we walked in, Matilda hugged us both, warmly.

"My favourite place to be!" she exclaimed, and opened her arms, clearly proud of her sweaty, smelly, unpredictable horse heaven.

"How many are there?" I asked, trying to sound interested.

"Twenty-five," she answered, beaming.

Oh dear...

"Come and meet some."

I took Nick's arm and we came up to the first stable door where a hood-eyed, dozy looking chestnut head looked out at us.

"This is *Meaty*, he's a real *hoon*. Love this *fella*."

We went along the line and I met *Tucker*, *Fried Beans* and *Pearly Bulb*. My favourite was *Willie's Revenge*. She told me about each one and their character and I began to daydream. *Cock Ferret* was racing *Fanny's Bang*, *Dangly Balls* was trailing far behind, and even further back limped *Infertile Sperm*.

I could hear Nick's voice; "Don't you think so, Lucy?"

"Oh, yes. Sorry, I wasn't paying attention for a moment, there."

"This one is Matilda's favourite, *Shlong*. He's a show horse, and a real stud."

"Oh," I responded, still not having a clue.

"He's got his name for good reason. I can show you if you want. I have to clean him now anyway."

I smiled with stupidity, though I wish I'd known what was happening. She fetched a bucket and a cloth, and then started to perform what I can only describe as a sexual stimulation for the horse.

Bloody hell, what kind of a wash is this special horse getting?...

The answer was a *Jacuzzi* and a shiatsu massage. Then *IT* slowly began to come out. Time for me seemed to stand still, as I watched his huge python slip very, very slowly out of it's sheath.

It almost reached the floor. She bent over, lifted it into the bucket and washed it down, thoroughly.

Revolting...

The look on the horse's face said: "I've been here a million times a day, mate."

"You really should charge money if this is how you end every tour," I managed to joke. I allowed myself some nervous laughter.

Once she'd finished her penis maintenance, we went to look at the paddock.

"This is what I do here," she told me. "Patrick lets me live here, feeds me, and I look after the horses. He's horse daft. Could be one of the best if he wanted to," she boasted proudly, and then stopped herself, not wanting to gossip any further.

200

"So, let's see some more, if you want?"

I nodded vigorously. So far no accidents had happened, and I wanted to keep it that way. In fact since I'd gone to see Hyam, and he'd told me to try and be more mindful of myself, I'd had a lot less mishaps. I thought that his aura must have been powerful to be reaching me still from so far away.

It was all quite naturally impressive and stunning, and we returned to find the house enriched with homely smells and sounds with Patrick and Nora the source, in the kitchen.

Patrick was cooking and talking, whilst Nora stared at him, enthralled. Matilda came in and greeted Patrick with a kiss.

They obviously had a strong bond with each other in this house, and yes, there was Love, but I could see now that there was a different kind of Love blooming. For one thing, it was plain to see that Nora was infatuated with Patrick, and I thought Patrick was definitely attracted to him. I'd never seen Nora like this, but I hadn't yet been alone with him for one minute to talk.

Love's young dream: *Us*, sat down at a big plainly made wooden table. A big old wood-fired stove heated the cooker, and dust lay about the floor. Matilda busied herself making a *brew*, as she also called it.

"Australians are as mad about tea as the English," Patrick said, as he battered down his dough.

"So I showed Lucy round, and showed her my job. She nearly spat when I got *Shlong*'s todger out, and cleaned it."

Nora raised an eyebrow. "*Por favor*. I never got that tour. I want the horse-pleasuring experience," he demanded, pouting at Patrick.

Patrick giggled. "For you, anything," he replied, flirting blatantly. Nick and I exchanged glances.

Patrick returned to his dough-pounding. "I was just asking Nora his opinion about a plan I have."

We indicated that he should continue.

"A friend of mine has a house east of *Manly*, near Sydney, in a place called *Palm Beach*. It's stunning there. I'm sure you both need some private time, and dear Nora is concerned about his clothes," he said, smiling playfully at him. "You can take my *Ute*, I'll take your hired car back to Sydney with Nora to get clothes, and we'll just hire it for longer." He took a breath.

It sounded perfect to me. "That sounds like a very generous offer, Patrick. I think I would say yes to that."

Nick's gaze settled on me, and I smiled to let him know everything was okay.

"It's probably best to leave in the morning. The mountains can be treacherous at this time of year with these clouds."

"Yes we will, and thank you, Patrick." I got up to hug him. It felt like a house full of Love there, and I hadn't experienced that since I was a child, staying with my adopted Irish family. The memory of that warm feeling had long been pushed away. It had never had cause to resurface until now. The babies hadn't been unwell, and they seemed to suckle on my positive emotions, giving them even more strength.

We stayed the night. We all ate at the big rough table in the kitchen, which had an open grate that always had hot water ready above a witches' fire. This was clearly the heart of the house. We bonded, laughed and became acquainted. Freedom of speech flowed without prejudice, as did Patrick's delicious, simple home-cooked food. In a way, I didn't want to leave this simple tribe, this small but safe family.

Matilda asked Nick how he felt about being a prospective father of two.

Nick explained that he was terrified, but also ecstatic simultaneously.

202

Patrick asked Nora why he embraced his gayness, but had issues with his black heritage. His hair, for example. That one made us all go quiet.

"I would have to say that is a very good question, but far too complicated to go into right now," Nora answered, and I was proud of how he reacted.

"You are right, I probably shouldn't have asked you something that personal," Patrick said, putting his hand on top of Nora's.

Yes, there's definitely something smouldering there...

Later that evening, Patrick gave us the keys to the house and those for his pick-up truck, along with instructions for the best route.

Nick and I went up to bed. The night before we'd just slept in each other's arms. I was still nervous tonight, after all, so much had passed between us. I wanted him, but I was scared, and I didn't want to be rejected. I ached for him and now I wanted more than just contact. It was only our second night back together.

"I'm scared, but I want you," he whispered, and that was it. I pounced on him, almost tearing at his flesh, as if he was a zombie. He reacted likewise, and as he entered me, a million droplets of blood exploded inside my head. His body felt sublime to the touch, chiselled by *Zeus*. He gently enraptured me at first, before basic lust took control and his muscular thighs crushed down on me, encapsulating us into a perfect capsule of ecstasy.

Afterwards we lay there panting and unable to speak for a few minutes, until Nick found his voice. "I'm sorry I lost control, I hope I didn't hurt you, with the babies."

I smiled. "Of course not, they're only tadpoles."

He laughed and pulled me closer.

We fell asleep in each other's arms once again. Sexual contentment enveloped us and ensured our deep slumber.

***

The next morning, I reluctantly said goodbye to Matilda.

"Don't spew, mate," were her parting words. "We'll see each other soon."

Patrick gave us the keys to his *Ute*, and Nick drove, increasing his sex appeal by the moment. The beautiful, shiny black pick-up truck had leather seats and seemed brand new.

"How old is this car?" I inquired.

"Two weeks," Nick grinned.

"Flipping heck. Wow, and he lent it to us."

"Patrick is a really good guy. It was definitely fate that he sat next to me on the plane. Plus he dropped his ticket as he sat down. The stewardess said; 'Mr Flannery. I believe you dropped this,' and handed it to him. I offered him my hand, introduced myself as *Corcoran*, we shook hands, and that was it," Nick said, and raised his hands briefly from the steering wheel as if that explained it all.

The dumb expression on my face was asking him; *What are you talking about?*...

"Oh yes sorry. My mother's maiden name is Cocoran. *Tis'* an unwritten rule, no matter what your politics, or where you're from, you are united Irish brothers. We help each other. *Tis'* always so," he explained, smiling. "He took me in and showed me the ropes."

"Cock ropes? Covered in gold no doubt, judging by this car, and the ranch?"

"Yes, cock ropes."

I whistled. "I don't blame you for doing it, and from what I

204

saw the other night, especially the behaviour of those women, your wages must be justified as danger-money."

"That crowd was quite well behaved, but I do love it, and it's a lot of fun as work goes. Do you want me to stop?" he asked nervously, stealing glances at me as he tried to gage my reaction.

I had already thought about it. "To me, you looked sexy and alive, plus you were entertaining. Your looks shone high above the others. I thought at the time; *I don't want to take this away from you. If I really Loved you I'd let your star shine, and I must let it happen...*"

He stared ahead as he drove, and I saw tears roll down his cheeks.

"I truly Love you, Lucy. Thank you for fighting for me."

"You can thank my best friend and his rich father, whom I've now had the privilege of meeting."

We chatted about my meeting with Nora's parents until we got to Sydney. We stopped at the hotel and collected some things, then set off to *Palm Beach*. Navigation was easy with the Satnav.

Nick was relaxed, and asked me a question unaware of the gravity of recent events. "So, how did you find out you were pregnant?"

A heavy silence hung in the air.

"Lucy?" he asked.

"I don't think I should tell you while you're driving." I knew that even that evasive answer would probably make him worry, and it did.

"That doesn't sound good. Shall I pull over so you can tell me?"

I wasn't sure I wanted to talk about this either.

"No, no. Seeing as I don't know when the right moment will be," I took a deep breath. "I tried to kill myself."

The *Ute* swerved across the road, and his arms let go of the steering wheel, as he stared at me, clearly in shock.

I let out a gasp, and he immediately pulled it back into lane.

"Fucking hell. Shit, Lucy. Yes, I definitely should have pulled over. What the hell? I mean, no, wait a minute." He put his foot down and applied some speed. He wanted to pull over somewhere and I wished I hadn't said anything.

Luckily Australia has big wide straight roads, with lots of stops. Some you can just pull over onto a bit of dirt, while others have showers, and wash places with electricity, or with barbecue areas. If you are really lucky they have a small trucker's stand nearby, where you can get beer, drinks, and snacks.

Lady Luck was smiling on us, and when we both spotted the truck stand amid a small copse of trees, Nick pulled in and cut the engine.

"I... I really don't know what to say. I'm horrified that it was meeting me that caused that to happen. Oh my god, and you were - pregnant." He gulped. His beautiful face seemed contorted with pain.

I took his hands. "Nick. It was my fault. I should have been honest, and then none of that would have happened, but it did, and maybe it was for a reason. If all that hadn't have happened, then I would never have found Hyam, and his counselling has been invaluable. He is so wise, he taught me to see clearly, and challenge myself, fairly. He set me free. I was at a very low ebb, and I just couldn't see a way through. As Hyam said, 'That's the most dangerous way to cry for help. I came through it with his help. I'll tell you more about him later, and the counselling."

Nick said nothing at first. He lowered his head into his hands for what seemed like ages before speaking. "I want to be honest with you. I also thought about it." He raised his head and looked me directly in the eyes. "I had my dad's sawn-off

206

shotgun. I took it with me to the barn. I wanted relief from the pain that consumed me. I'd never felt like that. Darkness and doom seemed destined to be my constant companions. I just felt like shooting my brains out. I sat with the gun on my lap for a whole afternoon, trying to embrace the concept." He laughed nervously at the memory.

I was uncharacteristically dumbfounded, and for a few seconds I found myself temporarily unable to form coherent speech.

"Well, uh, it probably sounds crazy of me to say, that in some ways, it seems hopelessly romantic. Almost *Romeo and Juliet*. We can thank the Goddess that she intervened, and maybe that divine intervention was an omen that we are meant to be together." I was trying to add some positivity to an otherwise insane moment.

He leant towards me and kissed me tenderly. "You definitely put a good spin on it," he said, and grinned. "I think we are fated to be together, Miss Bowman, and I thank the Goddess you survived with our twins intact. You do seem different now, I can see you've changed for the better, I have noticed that, and if this Hyam helped you to transform, I Love the man as well.

We hugged, and a feeling of security flowed between us.

"So shall we stop here? Are you hungry or thirsty? Do you need water to take your vitamins?" Nick asked, clearly concerned about the lives inside me. "I know all these questions seem weird after what we have just confessed to each other."

"I'm not sure which one to answer first, but; No, no, and yes. Let's get back in and keep going. Thank you for caring, and I know I have to be careful being an older mum, especially with twins. Especially with twins," I reiterated as my voice drifted away.

"Are you OK?"

"Yep, I just have to keep reaffirming it, to make it feel real."

"I'm sure that when you're screaming in agony and blaming me, it will feel very real," he teased.

"Oh thanks. You are filling me with hope for the prospect of an easy birth, which as I have just said doesn't seem real."

He squeezed my cheeks together. "Oh, it's real, baby. It's real."

Just like that, it felt like the heartache was over. Our past actions lost that lingering bitterness. I giggled and felt like a girl, a feeling that only Nick could invoke.

The rest of the journey we looked at the landscape which Nick had never seen before. I too had never been to this part of Australia. Wide open roads were edged by crisp white sandy beaches and ocean which sparkled by our side all the way. Huge unfamiliar trees bowed before us, as if welcoming us to this special place. Late that afternoon we drove onto a small side road and the Satnav told us where to park. It was chilly, and there was a light sea mist in the air. Thickly lush plants towered decadently around us. It reminded me of the film *Day of the Triffids*. On the other side of the road stood big white gates, and inside them something that looked like a tower.

"That's it," Nick said, as he got the bags and retrieved the key from his pocket.

What a strange building... I thought. *What is it?...* Through the gate I could see that the cylindrical tower went up through the trees and rocks, up and up until it went into the bottom of a round white saucer-like building, with lots of windows, embedded high in the rock face. It appeared to be a very, very plush spaceship.

Nick read out the name on the gates; "*Mr. S. Chu.* Yep, this is it. He's a good friend of Patrick." He unlocked them with a clunk.

I did know of Mr Chu, thanks to Gene Kelly's notes, but I

felt at that moment it was superfluous information.

After Nick had locked the gates behind us, we walked over to the foot of the cylinder and discovered an elevator door. A simple one button panel indicated up or down with glowing arrows. He pressed it.

"This is exciting," I had to concede.

The lift opened, and appeared to be space-age, bedecked with buttons and flashing lights.

"Hold on mothers, you in the Chu Tube," a voice with an Asian accent informed us, the doors closed, and then within a second we were being catapulted skywards. I clung to a grab rail, which was clearly there for more than just aesthetics.

It stopped as rapidly as it began. As the doors opened we heard the same voice cackle with laughter;

"You here. Get out."

"That was wicked fun," I enthused, and it was, but that was only the beginning. We stepped out into a kind of honeyed moneyed wonderland. I had thought the hotel me and Nora were staying in had been outstanding, but this was astonishing. We stepped out slowly, in order to take it all in.

The whole house was one big circular space, each room divided by walls that appeared to be full of water. Each wall was a different colour, and constantly moved and flowed, making them look alive. The breathtaking luxury of it all hooked us both, and we explored wonderland as children. When we came to the last waterfall wall, I finally spoke. "You can definitely keep getting your cock out if it brings these kinds of perks," I said approvingly. Nick giggled.

Each section had a window, making up a totally panoramic view. As I gazed out, Nick hugged me from behind. His carved arms snaked around my waist and sent my hormones into overdrive. *Now showing: Knickers On Fire 4...* I pounced on him, acting as if I was one of the women from the audience of his

ate kangaroo steaks, *gambas*, which turned out to be delicious giant prawns, blueberry muffins and strawberry smoothies. It was, in retrospect, a repulsive mixture of dishes.

"We have to stop, I think I'm going to be sick," I protested. Even the babies were full up.

"I think maybe we've overdone it, and I'm sure we've eaten a lot of Mr Chu's food," Nick said, trying to look concerned.

"Good acting. We can replace it, I'm sure we could arrange it with Patrick."

"I suppose so," Nick said, and hugged me tightly.

The storm out at sea took our attention once more, it seemed so very angry.

We fell asleep in each other's arms on the revolving couch.

***

The following morning brought perfectly blue skies over a crystal calm sea. It seemed the perfect time to go for a walk.

As soon as the lift door opened, I heard the noise of the lift announcing its arrival, as well as a voice coming from within that sounded almost identical.

"More! Harder, you're slacking -"

Nick had seen the door of the lift open and shook his head to warn me not to approach.

"Come on! Lift knees to chin. LIFT!"

I heard cackling followed by murmuring, then;

lonely travelling on my own. Now we can do it together. I can be your stripper's groupie."

I knew he was thinking intently by the look on his face.

"What about the babies? The checkups? Will we be able to tell people?" he asked, and they were legitimate questions.

"We can afford the checkups, and I can have them here. I really don't want to tell my mother or father, though. Not yet."

Nick turned to the storm, pensively. I stayed quiet and left him to his thoughts for a few minutes.

"Let's find out how you can stay here legally for the rest of the year. I don't want the children to be illegitimate here because you are breaking the law somehow. I can't go through that, Lucy. Let's talk to Patrick and Nora when we get back."

I agreed, hoping fervently there would be a way.

"I won't tell my family yet, either," Nick said, hugging me and kissing me on the side of the head. "I do know it's going to be a one hell of an adventure."

I had one confession left.

"There is one person that does know about the pregnancy, and I know it's going to sting. Sergeant Cole."

Nick puffed his cheeks up and blew the air out slowly.

"He was with Jenny when I came up to see you in Devon. I was very upset, I needed to tell someone, and it just sort of came out. He drove me back to London. He was very kind, Nick."

Nick's embrace stayed firm. "I think if he stays with Jenny, he is going to be in our lives. We have to accept that. I'm glad he was there to help you."

Contentment held us captive and we held hands all evening, as we replicated and sampled food from the magic fridge. We

"STOP! Take off top. Now run."

"Chu-Chu!" said the female voice, and she ran anti-clockwise around the house. I desperately hoped she would stop before she got to me, but the sound of her panting grew nearer and she stopped right in front of us. She eyed us sideways. Her big heavy breasts swung like a pendulum and shiny black sweatpants clung to an oversized body on a petite frame.

A very small Asian man took the opportunity and caught her from behind, begging to lick the sweat off her. He was dressed in very old fashioned underpants, which had several holes deliberately cut out. He stuck his finger into a hole near his penis. Neither Nick nor I dared to breathe. Our combined energies prayed hard for our invisibility cloak to start working, but *no*. No one was listening.

As this latecomer slurped his tongue down his companion's midriff, he spied the two other people stood in front of him, and stopped. His tongue however, stayed stuck out, and the moment stood frozen in time, as he was. He didn't move until finally, the girl screamed. Then he came back to life and lurched forward, his right leg stuck out rigidly. He screamed "Possession!" and that made me scream too. Nick tried to tell him who we were, but *Mr Chu* was not ready to hear it.

He kicked Nick in the stomach as he ranted in a language we were not familiar with.

"Chop, chop, and chop."

Nick was stronger however. He caught Mr Chu's foot, twisted his leg, and propelled him backwards onto the floor. His companion screamed again and ran off.

We headed for the elevator. "Let's get out of here! Push the button, Nick. Push it!" I urged him as Mr Chu rose, newly enraged.

"I kill you! I use peeler on your cock," Mr Chu screeched.

We got in the lift and Nick hit the button rapidly. The door started to close and Mr Chu sprang forwards into action, holding the doors open with skinny arms that seemed thinner than my eyelashes.

"Mr Chu?" Nick pleaded one last time, but it didn't work. Nick pushed him back, and as the doors closed he screamed;

"You dirty fuckers, you ate my food, ate my -"

My heart was not only in my mouth, it was banging against the roof of it.

"Shit! Oh, wow. Shit. He was like *Jackie Chan* on crack. What a scary little dude," Nick said, keeping his finger pressed on the button. When we stopped at the bottom, we flew through the small gap in the door as it opened, and ran to the gates.

Above us, more swearing came out of a window. "I peel your soft eyeball with fucking peeler!"

Objects began to fall on us, thrown from the window above, and we stampeded towards the car. Nick had already got the keys out, and both of us jumped in *Dukes of Hazzard* style. Nick put the *Ute* into reverse with a crunch, and we fled like amateur bank robbers.

Scared shitless, neither of us could talk, for at least two kilometres. Nick constantly checked the rear view mirror.

"Anything?" I asked, the alarm bells still ringing loudly in my brain.

He shook his head.

Had the whole world gone that sexually bizarre? I'd often thought that my bisexuality sat uncomfortably for most people. I'd never hidden it, and I wasn't afraid to talk about the subject, but I had witnessed first my brother and nurse Urmsham *en flagrante*, and now Mr Chu.

"No, no. Seeing as I don't know when the right moment will be," I took a deep breath. "I tried to kill myself."

The *Ute* swerved across the road, and his arms let go of the steering wheel, as he stared at me, clearly in shock.

I let out a gasp, and he immediately pulled it back into lane.

"Fucking hell. Shit, Lucy. Yes, I definitely should have pulled over. What the hell? I mean, no, wait a minute." He put his foot down and applied some speed. He wanted to pull over somewhere and I wished I hadn't said anything.

Luckily Australia has big wide straight roads, with lots of stops. Some you can just pull over onto a bit of dirt, while others have showers, and wash places with electricity, or with barbecue areas. If you are really lucky they have a small trucker's stand nearby, where you can get beer, drinks, and snacks.

Lady Luck was smiling on us, and when we both spotted the truck stand amid a small copse of trees, Nick pulled in and cut the engine.

"I... I really don't know what to say. I'm horrified that it was meeting me that caused that to happen. Oh my god, and you were - pregnant." He gulped. His beautiful face seemed contorted with pain.

I took his hands. "Nick. It was my fault. I should have been honest, and then none of that would have happened, but it did, and maybe it was for a reason. If all that hadn't have happened, then I would never have found Hyam, and his counselling has been invaluable. He is so wise, he taught me to see clearly, and challenge myself, fairly. He set me free. I was at a very low ebb, and I just couldn't see a way through. As Hyam said, 'That's the most dangerous way to cry for help. I came through it with his help. I'll tell you more about him later, and the counselling."

Nick said nothing at first. He lowered his head into his hands for what seemed like ages before speaking. "I want to be honest with you. I also thought about it." He raised his head and looked me directly in the eyes. "I had my dad's sawn-off shotgun. I took it with me to the barn. I wanted relief from the pain that consumed me. I'd never felt like that. Darkness and doom seemed destined to be my constant companions. I just felt like shooting my brains out. I sat with the gun on my lap for a whole afternoon, trying to embrace the concept." He laughed nervously at the memory.

I was uncharacteristically dumbfounded, and for a few seconds I found myself temporarily unable to form coherent speech.

"Well, uh, it probably sounds crazy of me to say, that in some ways, it seems hopelessly romantic. Almost *Romeo and Juliet.* We can thank the Goddess that she intervened, and maybe that divine intervention was an omen that we are meant to be together." I was trying to add some positivity to an otherwise insane moment.

He leant towards me and kissed me tenderly. "You definitely put a good spin on it," he said, and grinned. "I think we are fated to be together, Miss Bowman, and I thank the Goddess you survived with our twins intact. You do seem different now, I can see you've changed for the better, I have noticed that, and if this Hyam helped you to transform, I Love the man as well.

We hugged, and a feeling of security flowed between us.

"So shall we stop here? Are you hungry or thirsty? Do you need water to take your vitamins?" Nick asked, clearly concerned about the lives inside me. "I know all these questions seem weird after what we have just confessed to each other."

"I'm not sure which one to answer first, but; No, no, and yes. Let's get back in and keep going. Thank you for caring, and I know I have to be careful being an older mum, especially with twins. Especially with twins," I reiterated as my voice drifted away.

"Are you OK?"

"Yep, I just have to keep reaffirming it, to make it feel real."

strip show, broken free. Guttural noises freely gushed, as did my *pum-pum*. We went into the kitchen, where I pushed him onto every available surface. Perfectly clean large stainless steel worktops aided my sexual fury. We slid around on what looked like *Star Trek* replicators, abandoning any respect for Mr Chu's stuff. As I leant over a unit with Nick behind me, we must have triggered something. A dishwasher shot out, and I fell head first into it, my face pressing against wire metal plate dividers. I was on the brink however, and shouted at him to keep going. He carried on and I screamed my orgasm down the drain hole during the rinse cycle. Nick adeptly lifted me to a standing position, and climaxed himself. Almost immediately I began to chuckle.

"You're a dirty girl. I should put you back in there," he growled, motioning towards the dishwasher.

I couldn't suppress my amusement. We stayed naked and explored the flat, totally bemused while we tried to find everything. It took us an hour to find the bath, which we eventually discovered under the floor by pressing buttons on a hidden panel. Then Nick danced around, holding his cock, like a small boy does, whilst we tried to find the toilet. Eventually, in desperation, he peed in the bath, and it was only then when I discovered the toilet came out from a panel in the wall.

"All I can say is; It's a good job it was only a wee," I said, and sniggered.

A huge American fridge took our order of not only drinks, but ice cream. We had to punch in the numbers indicated on a wall chart beside it.

We both chose Devonshire ice cream, and ate it whilst sat naked on a huge round sofa that slowly revolved and allowed us to look at the changing view.

I was sure I'd dreamt this. Every single cell and molecule in my body gladly surrendered my soul to complete liberation, including our incubating twins.

Over the next four days we explored our surroundings and talked about how we felt. We discussed at length the virtues of honesty, which I admitted Hyam had helped me with. I told Nick that facing issues from my past had opened my eyes to what had happened. I explained why I didn't have many friends, and why I was scared to let people close to me. I had tried to heal myself like a patchwork quilt, sewing all my different emotions together, and in my mind, *Voila!*... I'd thought everything was fixed. Now, I told him, it's different. I'd become totally committed to the path of honesty, primarily with myself, and from that had followed these truthful answers.

He was impressed, and told me I was now some kind of little *Buddha*. He said he felt that this time, in contrast with before, I was really being true to my thoughts and feelings.

"Let's face it, relationships, as we know, are hard enough, so I know that our bond can only be strengthened by our reciprocal confessions of attempted suicide."

I thought he should speak out at world summits. His words of profound wisdom would reduce mere mortals to tears.

We abused Chu's house for hours, at least sexually. We walked along the nearby stretch of most beautiful golden beach, whose constantly glittering choppy waves dared us to enter. A lighthouse on the other end added extra romance. Nick admitted he too was enraptured with it all.

On the fourth day, we were eating fruit dipped in chocolate, and watching a battle in the sky. An electric storm, of the kind that only Australia can produce, captivated us with its show.

"This is bloody unreal. I've never seen anything like it," Nick enthused. He was bewitched. "I bet there's some really diverse weather in this country."

Which all lead me perfectly on to what I had been thinking about. "Well then, let's stay," I suggested, pulling his attention from the storm. "I want to stay. You planned to be away for a year. Let's find out how to extend my visa. I don't have to work, and I could risk it anyway. When I was here before I was a bit

211

I was beginning to realise quite how naive I was. My sexuality paled into insignificance, compared to these sweat-drinking, ball-gag-wearing, ice-cream-smearing goings on.

My heart slowed to a nearly normal pace. "He doesn't know you then?" I asked sweetly, trying to lighten the mood.

"I think you know the answer to that one. Maybe Patrick has told him about me, but he obviously doesn't remember. I've seen his other house in *Surrey Hills*, in the suburbs of *Sydney*, but I've never been inside. I waited in the car."

"Our stuff is back there," I moaned as I realised.

"I don't care. We'll get more stuff." His *La Bamba* ringtone sang muffled from a back pocket. Nick lifted an arse cheek. "Can you get that?"

I squeezed his butt hard.

"The phone," he said, bemused.

I retrieved and answered it. It was Patrick. He proceeded to explain how sorry he was that we had both been caught out like that. Chu had called him after he'd recognised the *Ute*.

I recanted the tale to Nick. "- and then Chu told off Patrick for not telling him, and Patrick said he was really sorry. He thought he was going to be away. So it's not our fault."

"In fact," I added with a dramatic pause. "Mr Chu wants all of us to go over there for dinner."

"Well I sure as hell don't think I want to refuse. He'll probably get a gang of triads onto us," he joked, and although we both laughed, I could tell he wasn't sure how true or funny that really was.

For the rest of the drive I knew both our thoughts were on our upcoming dinner engagement.

MR CHU

The last two days had gone so quickly they had seemed almost like a dream. Nora had checked us out of the hotel and we were staying with Patrick at the ranch. Nick and I told him and Nora about our plans to stay. Nora was not acting like himself at all, to the point of being quiet and listening to everyone. He was even ignoring those constant damn tweets.

They both seemed very happy that we wanted to stay. Nick mentioned that he intended to continue stripping. Nora had told Patrick he wanted to stay longer than three months, and Patrick had insisted that we all stay with him and Matilda. He assured us there was more than enough room. Matilda seemed overjoyed, and I decided I liked her very much. She was genuinely a sweet girl, with a relaxing aura. Her constant smile was infectious, and she was easy to be around.

Patrick suggested that we should definitely talk to a lawyer about an extended visa. As he reminded me, I was pregnant, and my babies would probably be born here now.

Nora told me not to worry, because he would pay any amount of money to extend our visas. He was clearly on a constant high, and didn't care about the consequences of his extravagance.

Myself, Nick, Patrick, and Nora, got out of the *Ute*, about to meet Mr Chu for the second time. Nick and I were visibly nervous.

"Please, don't worry. He's great," Patrick reassured us smoothly as he rang the doorbell.

We'd walked up a few plain concrete steps, to what seemed like quite a modest house in the suburbs of Sydney. He rang the bell again.

As the door opened, three of us took a step backwards while Patrick remained in front and spoke in what seemed like Chinese to the very petite Asian woman dressed as *Wonder Woman* who'd answered.

"*Cha cha.*"

"*Hi*," she responded quickly, and ran off.

A familiar figure came down the hallway towards us. He was dressed in a dark salmon silk suit. His jet-black poker-straight hair was clearly stuck down with tons of products. His round face seemed unnecessarily large for his tiny features. Thin feminine lips matched his cat-like eyes.

"Ah, Patrick, I see you bring robbers to my house!" he said, and cackled at his own joke. He hugged Patrick around his thighs, then he thrust one arm out to shake Nora's hand, the other fanned across his chest.

"I -" he began, pausing for effect. "I Suk Chu."

Nora turned and looked at us, confusedly. "I've never even met the man, let alone have him suck me."

I bit on my lips to stop my laughter.

218

"*Hola*, You never sucked me, *hombre*." Nora was back on form it seemed.

"Oh! I see, you're the funny man. Ha-ha!" Mr Chu leant very close to Nora and stood on his tiptoes. "I never heard that before, I must write it down," he said sarcastically, scribbling with an imaginary pen and paper. "You may call me Suk."

Nora simply smiled and offered his hand limply.

Patrick introduced us properly, and Nick and I both shook Mr. Chu's hand vigorously to indicate our wish for peace.

He leaned towards us. "If you ever speak of it, I kill you." He cackled with laughter and threw his head back violently, before escorting us into a huge open lounge where very loud *Drum and Bass* music was playing. Wonder Woman was already fixing drinks from a bar that had flashing disco lights all round it. Another two beautiful Asian girls were in the room. One was dressed as *Storm*, from *X-men*, the other as the eighties *Catwoman* from the series of *Batman*. She was hula-hooping. Mr. Chu screamed in the direction of the girl at the bar.

I felt as if I had entered a cult Chinese movie. Mr. Chu sat down and lit a cigarette which he held in a long holder. He motioned to us to do the same.

"You want drugs?" he yelled at us all. Without waiting for an answer he shouted something at Wonder Woman, who left the vast white-walled room instantly. None of us had responded. I thought perhaps it was a trick question. It was hard to take it all in.

Mr. Chu seemed an unusual friend for Patrick. I knew that they were very good friends because Mr Kelly had already informed us.

Wonder Woman returned carrying a huge tray, which she laid on the table. The raver in me lurched forward, and Nora physically jumped on sight of this smorgasbord of drugs.

White powders were piled high, and there were even lines of pink stuff. Pipes were stuffed full with Meth, Crack or Heroin. As for pills and weed, there seemed to be a bewildering variety.

Nora sniffed hungrily at the big mountain. "*Aaiiee! Buena.* Darlink, this is better than Brazil," he remarked to Suk.

Mr. Chu tried to stretch a smile across the expanse of his face in response. It made him look as if someone was pulling his cheeks out really hard. "I know, I *am* Brazil," he laughed. "You want to know what's what, ask this girl."

Mr. Chu sashayed over to Patrick and sat beside him, rubbing his leg and making "Ah, ay, ha, hee," noises all the while. Wonder Woman brought our drinks over. There was a wide selection, including freshly squeezed orange juice. Nick poured some out from the decanter for *us*.

Nora helped himself to a rum, poured Patrick one out and ignored our host, pointedly.

"Patrick. Your room's ready. You like?" Mr. Chu asked, rubbing his hand right up into Patrick's groin. Nora stirred the ice in his glass loudly.

"You want drugs?" Mr. Chu asked Patrick, gesturing towards the tray.

Patrick shook his head and smiled. "No thanks, Suk. Not tonight."

Surely that wasn't the connection. Patrick seemed way too clear-headed to be involved in any of that.

Nora pointed out a large shiny looking crystal.

"Amphetamine," said a very quiet but helpful Catwoman.

Nora chipped some off and chopped some lines out. "Oh well, when in Rome, or China," he sighed, and sniffed hard as he snorted a big fat one up.

I've got no doubt that this is going to get more interesting...

"I am Chinese Korean mix," Mr. Chu declared, as he wet a finger, dipped it into an unknown substance and wiped it liberally onto his gums.

I felt it was time to talk, and this seemed like a perfect opening.

"That's an exotic mix. Is that unusual?"

His eyes narrowed, and I thought I'd gone too far.

"I not here, lady, to give you Chinese and Korean history lesson," he said, deadly serious. At which Nora began to laugh, encouraging Mr. Chu's taunting. I knew it was going to be a long night.

Standing abruptly, Mr. Chu clapped his hands.

"Come. My mother's cooking a meal. She's the best cook in Australia."

We all followed, feeling compelled to do as we were told. Through a small door, we entered a huge kitchen, full of people cooking. Steam from the food flew through the air. Delicious smells accompanied the orchestral movement of the kitchen.

A vaguely familiar screaming came from somewhere within. I held Nick's hand firmly as we investigated. Between two counters, the tiniest of women sat in a huge wheelchair. A *Chihuahua* was curled up in her lap, contentedly sleeping amidst the chaos.

In one of her hands, she held a long thin length of bamboo. She slapped it down onto the counter tops frequently to emphasize her point. She seemed totally terrifying. She noticed our small crowd, and whipped her stick in the air, pointing it towards Mr. Chu. He ran over and placed his hands either side of her face, kissing her fully on the lips, over and over, until it made me want to turn away in disgust.

221

He spoke to her in Mandarin and beckoned to us. We shuffled forward, nothing more than lambs to the slaughter.

"Forward!" Mr. Chu urged.

The woman's face had seemingly collapsed into itself. Wrinkles opened into channels, which opened into gullies. It was a challenge to tell exactly where her eyes or mouth were. She looked more than a hundred years old.

"Mrs Chu!" he announced, introducing us.

"Oh, how lovely, this is your Grandmother," I exclaimed, thinking that that's who we were meeting.

Mr. Chu leant towards me and prodded me hard, speaking slowly. "No-o, she is my mother: *Mrs Chu.*"

I definitely wasn't making many friends that week.

"These are Patrick's friends; Lucy, and Nick," Mr. Chu informed his mother.

She craned her neck, presumably in order to study us, and prodded me hard with her stick. "He too young for you," she told me, by way of greeting.

I stepped back, left with a feeling I'd been verbally slapped.

"Mrs Chu," Nick said, as he took her hand, kissed the back of it, and successfully seduced the creature to croon.

"This one I like," she informed her son. Then she opened her arms wide. "Patrick, Patrick." He went to her and she hugged him, stroking his hair until he pulled himself free.

"Mrs. Chu. You know it's always a pleasure."

It seemed like the chewed toffee in front of me was smiling, but it was actually really hard to tell. Most of her wrinkles were pointing upwards from her nose area, so I had to assume she was happy. One of the chefs came to her and held a huge wok out for her inspection.

Delicious smells pirouetted round us. Mrs. Chu tasted it, spat it out onto the floor, and then proceeded to attack the chef, hitting him with the cane, and issuing a string of profanities in Mandarin. The cook scuttled off, ashamed.

Mr. Chu spoke to his mother quietly, kissed her again, and took the small dog from her lap.

"Come!"

We all followed him back into the lounge. Mr Chu began kissing the dog, just as he had been doing to his mother a few moments before.

"This *Merkin*," he said, getting the little dog's paw and waving with it. "*Hawo, hawo.*" He kissed the animal again.

I decided right then that I never wanted to kiss Mr Chu. Nora did some more drugs, and rolled a joint. Mr. Chu barked at Storm, who put the telly on in response. That telly was bigger than my local cinema screen. A spinning roulette wheel juggled the dice, propelling it from one number to the next. It entranced me. Secretly I bet on the number *10* in my head. All of us were transfixed as it slowed down and finally stopped with a little bounce on *Black 25*.

"Ahh, yes. *Ah hi.*" Mr. Chu picked up poor Merkin and took the petting a step further by licking the dog sensually on the mouth.

Good God! What next?...

"Patrick, I just made nearly a million dollars, uh huh," Mr. Chu remarked, nodding and pulling at an imaginary beard.

"That's a real *beaut*," Patrick replied, his Aussie twang coming through.

Personally I was stunned. Nick squeezed my hand as both of us tried to stay quiet. I felt like we were *Hansel and Gretel,*

223

ironically trying to abstain from all the goodies that actually would have helped us to get through this *Alice Through the Looking Glass* story.

Could this be the connection between Chu and Patrick? Patrick doesn't seem like a gambler...

"Suk, darlink. Suk," Nora said as he giggled, high on his drug concoctions. "I must congratulate you. *Es stupendo. Fabuloso. Fantástico.*"

"Mandarin or Korean! No talky other crazy language. It's bad enough I have to speak English, for stupid English who don't understand my languages," Mr. Chu growled, cutting Nora down with his mental karate chops.

Nora's eyebrows rose, and his eyes flickered over at the Aladdin's cave of drugs, but he said nothing in response.

Mr. Chu spoke to Patrick in one of his aforementioned languages, and Patrick smiled and nodded. "Suk says I am learning very well," he said, translating for us Neanderthals.

Nora sighed deeply as he clutched his chest and stared at Patrick.

He really, really likes him. I've never seen that kind of look on him, even on chemical enhancements...

A huge gong was being struck by Catwoman.

That was the signal for the kitchen door to fly open. Behind us we heard the whirring sound of machinery being operated. We turned to see a table and chairs rising out of the floor. Plush and pure white, it seated twelve people. A parade of dishes began to be placed on the table. Mr. Chu shouted, and we all stood, knowing whatever he'd said, it meant food. He told us where to sit and we all complied. Mrs Chu was the last dish through the door, and was being wheeled by one of the cooks. He was clearly nonplussed by her constant yapping. As she neared the table she brought her stick down and indicated her place. Lastly, the fancy dressed girls sat down.

A small gong was placed to the left side of Mrs Chu. She hit it three times and said something that sounded like *"Poo, poo, goo."* She lit an incense stick, opened her arms, and Mr. Chu and Patrick began to help themselves. Then we all did, apart from Mrs. Chu, who produced a long thin pipe from her pocket, and proceeded to smoke it throughout the whole meal. Later, in the car, Patrick would tell us it was opium she was smoking.

The food was amazing, even though Nora pushed his round the plate. Drugs had taken his appetite away, but I could not seem to stop myself gorging. Eating for three was taking its toll on my stretching stomach. Occasionally Mrs. Chu would smile, exposing stubby black teeth.

"My mother likes to watch people eat. She have a tiny, tiny appetite. Like a tiny precious bird. She is as soft as the breeze," Mr. Chu said, and genuine Love soaked his words.

From where I sat, she looked like she could ingest razor blades.

"Hey you, pretty boy. Your girlfriend eats like pig. She soon be whale fat," Mrs. Chu shouted.

Nick stopped and looked at me, then at Mrs Chu. It took him a few seconds to respond.

"Er, Mrs. Chu, Lucy is pregnant with twins," Nick explained, smiling, in order to excuse the pig next to him.

She began to cackle, and started speaking to her son, who also joined in the laughter.

How rude!... I thought, wanting to extricate myself from the situation.

"Please can I use the bathroom?" I said loudly. I actually did want a pee.

"Yes, you need. Babies peeing inside you. Food squash those little things," Mrs. Chu advised, puffing hard on her pipe and blowing the smoke helpfully towards me, only two seats away.

Nick asked me if I was alright. I nodded.

"*Chi Cha* show you," Mr. Chu said, and Catwoman rose from her seat. She escorted me through to a pure white house, with stunning vases scattered throughout, the flowers within them the only hint of colour. The flowers were not mixed, and so in the bathroom there was only red roses.

I think there was music playing. A tortured, wailing woman was trying to scream whilst being intermittently drowned out by a tinny plucking sound. Washing my hands showed me how much dirt had been living on them. I splashed the sides of the sink and felt compelled to wipe it up.

Who would want to live in such a sterile environment?...

I didn't want to use the pure white towels, so I fanned my hands in the air to dry, and hoped we could leave soon. I thought Mrs. Chu was hideous. I managed to make myself smile thinking about her face and how it was like the backside of an elephant. Wonder Woman was still waiting there, and she was probably wondering why I was smiling inanely.

The chatter at the table relaxed me as I approached. The previous tensions seemed to have eased slightly. I gave my best smile, pulled my chair out and sat down.

A strange squeak came from my vagina area. The silence grew as everyone's gaze settled on me. I heard another noise, only this time it sounded fainter. I shrugged my shoulders and looked at Nick, and then we heard another small squeak. It certainly didn't feel as if anything was up there. I stood up slowly, and Nick groaned. Mr. Chu stood abruptly, and I saw that I'd sat on his little dog, Merkin. I lifted it up and Mrs. Chu and son screamed in unison. Mr. Chu ran over to me and snatched the dog that hung limply from my hands.

226

I hoped to god it was still alive. Mr Chu rubbed the little dog's chest and put him on the table, which Patrick was frantically making a space on. He performed full CPR, blowing into the little dog's mouth, and pumped his tiny little Chihuahua chest with his fists. Mrs. Chu wheeled herself over and started slapping the stick on my backside.

"Please, Mrs. Chu, there's no need for that," Nick pleaded, trying to placate her.

"Your big pig, she has killed my poor little Merkin with her fat pregnant arse. We're not in Korea now, killing dog for dinner!"

Nora had crept back over to the drugs, and I heard him giggling, until Mr. Chu spotted him.

"Hey you, little fag spick boy. I hit you on face with stick. You get Spanish inquisition."

"Please, Mrs. Chu, it was an accident. Look, Merkin's moving." Patrick's calm voice cut through the storm, and Mrs. Chu retreated.

"Yes, you are very forgiving, Patrick," she crooned.

The little shit of a dog moved some more, and Mr. Chu lifted it up and squeezed it tightly as he hugged it.

"My mother is wise as *Buddha*. Precious as a raindrop." He handed her the tiny sack of skin that was meant to be a dog, and kissed her just as he did before.

When will this night end?...

Nick hugged me and kissed me on my face to let me know everything was fine. Nora came back over and sat at the table ignoring all of us. I knew then that he would be in a murderous mood. The gong sounded again, and trays of fresh coffee were brought out. I decided I was going to have one. I watched Patrick massage Nora's shoulders.

'Coffee,' Nora said, nodding.

Patrick poured it out. "I'll be *Mother*. So let me tell you how I met my good friend Suk Chu, and his lovely mother here." He was trying to smooth things out, and it was already working. Mother and son beamed with pride.

"Patrick saved my, delicate as snowdrop, Chu Chu," Mr. Chu explained, gesturing towards his mother.

In an effort to redeem myself, I said; "Did it involve a runaway horse?"

Mr. Chu's eyes narrowed and he pushed his crescent moon chin up. "Firstly, this is not a competition to guess what happened. Second, we live in middle of *Sydney*, who gonna come here on a horse? Maybe *Colombo's* in town, he swoops my mother up on horse and they ride to *Sydney Opera House*. Happens all the time. NO. My mother was crossing the street, and this crazy car driver nearly killed her. Patrick pushed her out of the way. He rolled over the bonnet like a big star movie man. He's family now."

There was applause and clapping for Patrick.

So that was the connection, and what a belter it was. Saving this living alligator skin purse had elevated him to Triad status with twenty-four hour batman protection. He always had a place to stay here.

Patrick simply bowed his head humbly, and raised his coffee. It seemed like we were all rushing, so much so I even burnt my throat a little.

Patrick made some excuses and assured Mr. Chu that he would look at his room next time. "*Che che hi,*" he said, and Mr. Chu came over and hugged him.

"So anyway, my mother needs beauty sleep. She is light as feather."

Nora said something in Spanish that made Nick smile.

"Oh, the cotton pickin' boy understands his own language; Spanish." Mrs. Chu's voice sliced like a knife.

I stopped breathing for a moment. Had this all been too much for Nora? His face was unreadable and I had no idea what he was going to do. His skin colour was entirely a different matter.

"I'm sure, Madam, that when your vagina tragically fell out, it took your humanity with it," Nora said coolly. He walked to the front door, opened it, and then slammed it behind him.

It took a while for the rest of us to leave the hysterical Suk and his mother, while Patrick tried to smooth things over. Fifteen minutes later myself, Nick and Patrick finally got in the car. Nora was sitting in the front, waiting. Nick and I stayed quiet while Patrick started the car and drove.

"I understand why you're pissed," Patrick said finally, breaking the silence.

"Patrick, darlink, if that woman had not been a friend of yours, I would have tipped her from that chair onto her back, and watched her frantically squirming like a stuck beetle, until she stopped struggling."

Patrick put his hand on top of Nora's. "Thanks for being so awesome about it."

Nora pouted sulkily, but then he smiled his sweetest of sweet, sweet smiles directly at him.

I definitely have to talk to Nora...

I hoped then and there that we wouldn't have to see that wretched creature Mrs Chu too often. Little did I know it would be too soon.

NORA'S IN LOVE

For the next few days we all hung around the ranch generally chilling, and I decided I loved it there. It was sublimely relaxing. At night on the veranda we gazed at stars that shone like diamonds, and the days were cool but pleasant.

The early morning mist smelled minty because of the countless eucalyptus trees. Tendrils of fog crawled over the grass and around the horses. I sat in a wicker chair one morning, drinking hot coffee and absorbing the view. I could see that when life was this simple it brought harmony and contentment. A pretty brown horse stood in what looked like smoke and took on a magical quality.

I didn't hear Nick approach, and only realised when he sat next to me.

"Hey! Are you in there?"

The spell broke and I greeted him with a kiss.

"Are you okay?" he asked, and he sounded calming. He took my free hand and held it.

I smiled. "I feel that everything is just right in my life now. I know that sounds funny, but for me that means no more hiding or concealing the truth, no running away from myself, but just simply playing my part in it all, no matter how crazy things seem to get."

Nick admired the view with me. "It does feel that since we met loads of crazy stuff has happened, but at least I feel alive, I feel real. It's a cliché, but it's better to ride the rollercoaster than stick with the same old merry-go-round."

I broke my gaze off to look at him. "I feel exactly the same. I have a witch-like premonition that there'll be more craziness, and I'm ready for it, even if I can't identify why it's happening." At that moment I couldn't have imagined what an understatement that would prove to be.

The horses began to gallop, flushing big black crows out that flew squawking from their rooks.

"Patrick and Matilda have asked me to go riding today, and I said I'd love to. Nora said he would rather lick a dog," Nick informed me. We both laughed at the thought.

"Of course you should enjoy the horses," I agreed, thinking that would give me a perfect opportunity to talk to Nora.

Later that morning it was especially quiet. All the dogs had gone running after the horses, howling and barking with the joy of it all. As they gambolled dangerously around the horses, I heard Patrick shout:

"Get out of here, you mongrels."

I found Nora in his room playing with his hair. By the way he was patting it down, I could tell he still wasn't sure about his big new afro. I knocked as I entered, and I startled him. He had clearly forgotten he was not alone.

He lowered his hands from his face. "Lauren, darlink," he whispered, and smiled a rare genuine smile.

I did love him dearly. He actually looked stunning with his new hair, and I felt such pride that he was my best friend.

"You look amazing, you know?" I told him softly.

He held his arms out for a hug.

"*Cariño,*" he murmured as he stroked my hair.

This was a new Nora. One who wasn't stuck in *Constant hysterical queen* mode, always ready with a mouth full of acid to spew over everyone. This was kind, considerate, Nora instead. He finally released me and looked back into the mirror.

"My mother would be ashamed if she saw it, but... Patrick likes it, so I try." He smiled as he said Patrick's name.

"Why would your impeccable, sculptured mother hate it? Surely your hair is a part of your heritage?"

"My father's heritage, darlink, and she thinks we have gone into tribal bush mode when our hair is like this, but Patrick..." He drifted off for a few moments. "So, Patrick, he's really something. I like him a lot." Nora sighed and held his heart.

I saw my cue and sat on the bed. Reaching over, I slapped his arm gently. "Right, come on. Tell me. What's going on in that Cuban head of yours?"

He clutched my hands together so tightly I thought he was going to break out in song.

"*Mi amor, mi amor*. I'm in Love," he announced to the ceiling above. Then he faced me as if he was possessed. His eyes lit up as he grabbed my hands and squeezed them together. He stood, and actually did sing;

"Tonight, tonight, the stars they seem so bright," he began, and proceeded to sing nearly the whole song, followed by *Maria,* all from *West Side Story,*

"I feel pretty, oh so pretty,"

I let him sing, amused by his performance as he truthfully got it out of his system.

Once finished however, he was panting hard, and slammed back down into his chair.

I started to laugh. "That was like watching you audition for *The Voice.*" I could tell from the look on his face that that was not the response he thought he would get. His expressions only increased my mirth. Gradually he couldn't help but join in, easing the electric tension we were feeling.

"I'm sorry, darling. That's not fair of me, especially after you have just proclaimed your Love for someone. I'm used to you Loving some*thing*, objects, like I find it funny the way you Love your *Louis Vuitton* handbags, but I'm not used to it when it's a real life breathing person."

"*Aaiiee!* You are so bad, *muy malo*. I love you, I love me and I love my mother and father's money. *Aaiiee!*" he screamed again. I had actually missed that scream. Suddenly he became more serious. "And I Love Patrick, Lauren. Nothing about him bothers me. I want, in fact I need to be around him. I feel comfortable and confident with him, as if I can really be myself. No acting required," he said, and stared directly into my eyes. "Keeping up an act can be very, very tiring."

I felt for my friend. I knew all about the weight and tragedy in his life, all the things that money could never change.

"Nora, let yourself Love. I know you're afraid. I know some things happened to make you afraid, but you've got to let it in." I'd always assumed that what held him back was the Love he never received from his parents, but I was wrong. In the future when the truth would reveal itself, I would end up wishing my prognosis had been correct.

"Look at how scared I am to Love," I appealed to him.

Nora went quiet, and his mind obviously drifted away somewhere. He shook his head as if to rid himself of unwelcome thoughts.

"Does Patrick know how you feel?" I asked.

"He knows I like him a lot, but I'm not sure if he knows I *Love* him. I'm too scared to tell him. His ex-partner died of AIDS, and they'd been together ten years."

"Well I've seen the way he is with you, and I think he likes you a lot too, so I think you two should definitely date, and then see what happens. Why not take the risk?"

"Lauren, it is a very big risk. I'll tell you why. His boyfriend, well in the end it was his husband, never told his family he was gay, ever. He pretended to have girlfriends, and always carried fake photos of girls, that he pretended he'd broken up with for one reason or another, whenever he had to produce evidence of a girlfriend. Patrick put up with it because he Loved him. They got married alone, and when *Cory* got HIV, he told his family he had cancer. He moved purposely to the other end of Australia, making it very difficult for his low income family to visit. When he died his mother and father got the bus from *Kalgoorlie* to Sydney, where Patrick had to greet them as a friend of Cory's, because he didn't want to go against what Cory had wanted. Patrick said it was one of the hardest things he ever had to do. He cannot go through that deceit again," Nora insisted, pensively.

"So you would have to tell your parents?" I asked carefully, as the penny dropped.

"For Patrick, I can tell the truth, or should I continue to lie so I don't lose the money? *Mierda!* I fall in Love, but my father will cut my money off, or maybe my balls if I have to come out to his face." He screeched at the ceiling, desperately. "Lauren, I have nice balls. They are one of my best features. *Buenos cojones.* If someone is wondering whether or not to sleep with me, I get out my balls, *y buena,* it's all good."

"It's fine, really Nora, I don't need to know. If there is a police line-up I don't think that will be the thing that gives you away," I assured him, and he cracked a smile. "I think you should still take a chance. Patrick is too good a catch to throw him back in this very overcrowded pond. It's not like you have to call your parents right now this minute and tell them you're a bum bandit, eh?" Nora looked horrified.

"What? Too much?" I teased, and began to giggle.

"*Tu eres un puta blanca!*" He laughed and pushed me weakly.

"I'm a pregnant whore, so lay off, *Mohammed Ali,*" I said as I pushed back limply. Giggling together helped Nora with his big decision, temporarily at least. He told me that Patrick wasn't pressing him for a quick decision, but he had strong feelings for Nora that he had told him about only that morning.

"Let the two of you spend a little more time together, and then make a decision," I suggested.

He nodded. "I haven't even shagged him yet. What fuck is worth thirty-four million?"

I coughed loudly as my breath caught in my throat. I had nothing for that one.

After a while, Nora spoke. "I suppose I could look at the goods first, and then decide if they're worth buying." That set us off giggling.

"I bet it's a beauty," I said, and I imagined it would be a good one.

"I bet when he gets it out you want to kneel and worship it. *Si, es la verdad.*" Nora suppressed a snigger.

"Not like a little button mushroom one, or a big helmet plunger," I suggested, joining in.

Nora picked up the theme. "Or one that goes off to one side and you never know which angle to tackle it from, or the little child-like willy that doesn't get any bigger when it's hard, or even the cock-ferret with a huge eye."

Both of us were in such fits of laughter we did not notice Nick and Patrick standing in the bedroom doorway. When we did catch sight of them it only made it worse, and our laughter turned to howling.

"So I see you girls have been having a hoot this morning?" Patrick said, and winked at Nora. "I'll make a brew. See you lovely ladies in the kitchen," he said, and was gone.

"I'm jumping in the shower. I'll see you in a bit," Nick said, grinning at me.

Nora and I calmed ourselves, and went to find Matilda.

"Could we ask Patrick if we could have a little look?" I whispered.

"Okay, but then I want to see Nick's."

"No way!" I protested, but the idea of it set us off giggling again. We found Matilda in the kitchen starting to prepare dinner.

"That was a bloody good ride, *strewth* they've got some energy today," she said, and she shone with the health and enthusiasm which always infected her after she'd been with the horses. She was a natural horsewoman who enjoyed company of the hoofed variety more than she did humans. She told us she had ridden her favourite today; *Shlong*, and began to describe the whole ride in detail. I lost my interest when I heard Patrick on the phone in the adjoining room, swearing. He mentioned Nick a couple of times.

Nick came into the kitchen, his hair wet and rough. He looked sexy as hell as he leaned across the counter to get a cup, and all three of us checked out his fantastic arse. I smiled with the knowledge that it was all mine.

Patrick came in and told us what the phone call had been about. It was a booking for a strip show starring himself and Nick, for the coming weekend, and it was for a birthday party. Patrick hesitated before revealing the last piece of information. "It's for Mrs. Chu's birthday, and it's being held at the Korean nightclub."

What? Not the Mother from hell?...

He could tell that none of us were enthusiastic.

"You can all come. Lauren and Matilda will be allowed in the audience. Nora can be backstage so he can hold my handbag," Patrick explained, and we all smiled to think of such a handsome and rugged horseman with a handbag. "Personally, I am obligated. There was going to be traditional Chinese dancing, but Suk Chu wants to surprise all the ladies."

They'll certainly be surprised...

Nora spoke presumptuously for all of us. "Darlink, of course we will all go with you. *Everyone is Kung Fu fighting,*" he sang, happily.

Wow, he really, really does love him...

To forgive at all had never been Nora's style, but his willingness to forgive Suk Chu and his mother so quickly after that disastrous evening was a first time experience for me.

The day after the dinner party however, I had pointed out to Nora what an awful thing he had said to Mrs Chu, and he'd had to admit it had been a little harsh.

I was determined to look up and learn some history and culture of the Korean and Chinese people, so I could seem less ignorant, and after all, I was genuinely interested.

237

I looked at Nick quizzically.

Well, I did say to him that if he wanted to continue stripping, it was fine by me...

He shrugged at me, as if to say; 'I don't think we have much of a choice.'

I smiled grimly as I thought: *It's going to be one hell of a night...* And it was.

MRS. CHU

The dreaded night came round way too quickly. Choosing costumes had been difficult, and Patrick and Nick spent two days frantically rehearsing, all the while checking with Suk Chu that everything was still on track. In the end it was decided that Patrick would start off dressed as a Chinese dancer - a woman, and then he would strip down to a g-string as a man. Nick would be dressed identically to the waiters, and when his music came on it would be his cue to go to Mrs. Chu's table, begin the strip and then wind his way through the tables to the stage. I was a little concerned about that part, but Patrick assured me that Chinese and Korean women would not act like the wild Australian animals that we had witnessed previously. Nick tried to make the best of it and told us all how much fun it could be. Patrick and Matilda agreed.

"And the plus part is that Suk is going to pay us five thousand each," Patrick mentioned casually.

I was washing up and Nick was drying, just the two of us. We froze in our tasks, and Nick's mouth began to hang slightly open. "I, I…" Nick stammered.

"I have never heard of such an amount for a strip. *Nunca!*" Nora's voice floated down the stairs.

"How on earth did you hear that from all the way up there?" Patrick asked with a smile.

"Darlink, it's about money. Of course I hear." Nora came in to the kitchen and kissed Patrick on the cheek, which threw us all a little off guard. Patrick blushed and then so did Nora.

This is serious. Thirty-four million serious. That kind of money makes five thousand seem like you could wipe your bottom with it…

Nick was reanimated. "Wow, that's a lot. I never thought I could make so much money just for stripping down to my scants. It's great news, although I am bloody nervous about tonight."

"Nick, don't worry. Suk makes that kind of money every minute," Patrick reassured him.

"Maybe he is okay, I will give him another try. *Puta coño.* Calling me a *Spic*," Nora cussed, smiling and fluttering his eyelashes at Patrick.

Patrick was staring back at Nora, and the look in his eyes told us he was very fond of him. They sparkled with life, and the desire to Love again.

I felt like I had a real family round me. I was experiencing true warmth and affection and I had nothing much to go back to in London. My brother had the means to visit me anywhere, anytime, and the two most important people in my life were already there with me.

Patrick was touching my heart as well as Nora's. Tears welled up in my eyes, and Nick put down his cup and came to me, concerned.

"I'm fine, it's just the hormones. It must be the kiddies," I explained, using them conveniently. *Mm, they could be a great excuse for me, in case I go all cry-baby again...*

Nick hugged me. "We'd better start getting ready. It takes a while to get to Sydney. We'll get ready at the nightclub. Normally I'd get ready at Suk's place, but well, tonight's a bit different."

We all nodded in agreement, and prepared to leave.

***

We pulled up into Chinatown, and I assumed we were heading to meet Suk Chu. All of us had been animated the whole way, in full chitter-chatter mode because we were so excited and nervous. The journey seemed quick and we reached our destination rapidly, pulling up in front of what looked like a temple. Red and gold columns adorned the entrance and huge flags hung down with beautiful different coloured dragons embroidered on them. We all stopped talking. Suk Chu was there, standing at the bottom of the gold steps talking to a huge doorman. Both men wore black tuxedos, but there the likeness ended. The doorman looked as if his mere breath could cut off one of Suk's limbs.

Patrick wound the window down. "Hey Suk, you bludger," he said with a real Aussie twang.

The little man spun round ready for trouble, but upon seeing who it was, he smiled, at least I thought that's what he was trying to do.

"Patrick. Ahh! Beloved brother, come come," he beckoned, waving his hands. "All, come."

Suk whispered something to the huge man, who walked round us and got into the car to park it. Suk firstly hugged Patrick, and then he offered a limp wrist to Nick, completely ignoring the rest of us. I heard Nora mumble something vicious under his breath.

He led us round the side of the building, until we came to a set of black metal double doors. He pushed them open and we walked into a big round nightclub with three big bars and two stages with Karaoke machines. I hated Karaoke. Pissed up people *'singing'* (Well, some might call it that.) into a microphone to anyone that will listen. They always think they are the next big X Factor winner, about to be discovered. They always choose a song that you've heard a thousand times too many before.

If I hear *Love lifts me up where you belong*, sung badly one more time, if I had anything to do with it then I'd make sure that person would never be able to Love again. Or in the case of *Gloria Gaynor - I Will Survive*, I would do my best to ensure that the person who was recanting it would not, in fact, survive.

It looked and felt very plush as Suk took us across a marble dance floor. Adorning the walls were glass coffee tables and gold arm chairs with purple felt cushions. One elaborate brass coffee machine served each table. He took us around the bar and through another door, into a large room with mirrors and dressing tables, which I guessed was the changing room.

Suk stopped, confirming my suspicions. "So, you get ready here. Before you go on, we're gonna have the world renowned Chinese harp player, *Chi lua Lui*. She will play for half an hour. When she's finished, you, Nick, will get changed into the waiter's outfit while Patrick is on stage."

Who the hell is Chi Lua Lui?...

242

My mouth opened but then my brain engaged just in time, warning me; *Don't ask, don't...* I closed my mouth for a second, thinking it best that I ask a sensible question that wouldn't get me into trouble. "When do we all sit outside?"

Chu leaned towards my face until he was about three inches away.

"Oh, I see. We have a super intelligent one here. Sharp as a knife. So my mother sees you all, and of course she is an intelligent woman, and she wonders why that silly one is here. Oh no, now she knows something is happening, there is no surprise, no nothing."

Taking a step back he did a karate chop in front of me. I felt dumb. Yes of course she'd know something was going on if she saw us all. I really was not fighting my corner very well.

Chu spun on his heels, and then thankfully he was gone. I turned to Nick and Patrick, sheepishly.

"You really will get to like him, honest," Patrick murmured abashedly. He tossed his bag onto the side and Nora flounced over to a chair, flopping down into it.

"It won't be much fun if we can't see. *Strewth!*" grumbled Matilda.

"You can peek through the doors, I'm sure you can see everything from there and you won't be seen" Patrick suggested, pointing.

The doors flew open as we were looking at them, which made us all jump, and a dejected small oriental woman came in and shuffled over to us bearing a tray of alcoholic drinks. She put them down shakily, and then proceeded to cough all over them.

"Not you, you don't touch," she said to me, before shuffling back to wherever she'd come from.

"Darlink, the hospitality is pitiful." Nora said, and kissed his teeth, something he rarely did.

243

While Patrick got ready, he carried on apologising for his friend again.

We all heard a commotion outside the doors and turned our heads. Patrick had done most of his makeup and looked very much like a Japanese geisha girl. The doors flew open and lots and lots of people started to come in, all talking at once in various Asian languages. There was some random slapping of heads and some small cries of delight. All our visitors carried stunning bouquets of flowers, and the room was quickly beginning to fill up. Silver trays were brought in, bearing drinks and snacks in abundance. Chairs were wiped down respectfully, then a short silence was followed by much bowing and small ripples of pleasure. A very proud, short but upright man held what appeared to me to be a cardboard box that had a stick coming out of it with some wire attached. He placed it down like a new born baby, and again there was a short silence. A woman entered who made the small man look tall. She must have been barely four feet tall. One of my shoes would have been heavier than her. She had a yellow dress on, and resembled a tiny canary, albeit with a huge black bobbed hairstyle.

This must be the famous Chi La Luna, and the instrument of shit...

As she walked, people bowed and pulled her chair out, while us peasants could only watch on from the other end of the room. Suk Chu came in, bowed as he approached her and talked quickly, servile in his actions. Then he clicked his fingers and men rushed towards the delicate little thing, taking her coat and pouring her a drink. Suk Chu left shortly afterwards, leaving an admiring entourage around her. To my knowledge she had not yet said a word. I smiled as I thought that words were probably too heavy for her little mouth.

A waiter came in and gave Nick his waiter's outfit costume, a jug of water and some cups, before leaving hurriedly.

"*Hombre, cono*, I'm sorry, *molestas*. There is a five star treatment for us after all, look," Nick said, opening his arms out to show us what wonders he'd just been brought.

244

Then we all heard the level of noise rise from the disco area, so Matilda went and peeked out. She smiled weakly.

"What?" asked Nora.

"Mm, well it's a bit packed." She shrugged and went over to help Patrick.

I went to see for myself. As I pushed the door ajar I gasped slightly. In front of me there must have been about a thousand women. It was like a version of *The Matrix*, where everyone was Mrs Chu. Excited chatter catapulted around the room. I shut the door and thought of poor Nick. *How did they manage to get all those tables and chairs packed in there so quickly, spilling all over the dance floor?...* Nick could see I was anxious. "You've got a good crowd in." I said, smiling faintly.

His colour drained a little. He was nervous anyway, and all this was not helping. His outfit underneath the waiter's uniform was a silky black pyjama suit, with a black square hat. His mission was to keep his head down and avoid being spotted. Patrick was fully dressed, and was already sat relaxed and waiting. Nora got up and put his arms around his shoulders.

A loud gong sounded and echoed out. The murmur of chatting grew louder still. On a microphone I recognised Suk's voice, followed by a large round of applause. Then I heard some more announcements that were met with lots of *ooh's* and *aah's* and vigorous clapping as they awaited the tiny bird-like lady and her box of who knew what?

As she went out and glided onto the stage the audience began clapping, screaming and shouting in earnest. She was such a real live Elvis to them that they stood and gave her a standing ovation. This went on for ten minutes. *Who is this woman?...*

Eventually she began her show. We were all peeking through the door, curiously. I thought she was going to do tricks, and pull stuff out of her magic box, but I soon realised it was a musical instrument that she was playing. Accompanying this awful sound, another equally painful noise joined in; her voice. She seemed to be intermittently portraying different levels of agony with random plucks and bangs on her instrument. She held a bow which she ran slowly along a wire, making my teeth go on edge. All of us were absolutely bemused. I suddenly remembered the *music*, though I use the word in the loosest of terms, in the toilet at Suk Chu's house. One could never have forgotten such a heart wrenching sound.

For some strange reason we all felt compelled to stay by the door and listen to the whole hour and a half performance, even though Patrick was complaining how hot he was in his outfit.

Once she'd finished, everyone in the audience stood up to applaud apart from one small woman in the front who was sitting in a wheelchair. *Mrs. Chu.* Personally I would rather listen to cats fighting in the alleyway at the back of my house, but I must stress, that's just my personal musical taste. The applause went on and on, and after fifteen minutes even Patrick became impatient.

"It's bloody hot in this clobber," he complained, unleashing his Aussie charm. His wig was a huge black glamorous classical Asian hairstyle, ornately decked out with hanging trinkets and small chimes. Eventually the world famous singer and string-plucker took her leave, shooing the motley gang that was hanging around the dressing room door away from her as she returned.

Chu went back on stage and talked some more, telling them, I assumed, that now they were meant to see dancing. The door was still open and I took a better look. It was like spying on a belly button convention. Their ages seemed to range from ninety to two hundred.

Has this been thought through properly?... I speculated.

Were they ready for a big thrusting white male who's gyrating his groin only inches from their faces? Were they truly ready for the *Tom Jones* cover of *Kiss* by the fantastic *Prince*? I was morbidly compelled to watch and find out.

The music started with some traditional Chinese melodies. Patrick, ever resourceful, moved slowly, just as he'd practiced in the house watching lessons online. His fan gracefully glided through the air, and little sounds of approval came from all the ladies mouths.

"Ahh, oooh. Ahh, oooh!"

The suspense was killing me. All four of us pressed hard against each other so we could look through the slit in the door. Nora was breathing heavily. Once again, he was back on his phone, clicking away as he took photos.

"Darlink, these pearls are too good not to shoot over everyone. I can tweet them *luego*."

Patrick bowed very deeply, almost to the floor, which all of us knew was the sign for everything to change.

The familiar beat started, and the lyrics came in *"You don't have be beautiful, to turn me on -"*

Patrick stood bolt upright and threw his fan into the ancient audience, as simultaneously every mouth puckered and every neck pulled back in surprise. As he peeled off gold and white gloves and threw them out as well, women began to look at each other.

"Think I gotta dance now," instructed Tom, so Patrick did, as he pulled the wig off and put it at the back of the stage. He tousled his hair and then ripped off his dress, revealing a purple g-string, and stockings with suspenders. Mrs Chu held her hands frozen in the air, and time seemed to slow down. Mouths opened, necks coiled out even further, and hands went to mouths which had no sound coming from them. This was the utter opposite of the strips I had seen before. Patrick, a true professional, carried on. He turned and bent slightly, slapping his buttocks.

Mrs. Chu began to smile as wide as she could, showing her black stumps. Nodding, grinning and pointing, she pulled out a long pipe from under her chair, and lit the opium. Patrick leapt from the stage in front of a very old woman, moving his pelvis in circles. She began to smile, and then nodded her head vigorously, her eyes glinting and full of life. As Patrick went round the room the atmosphere took on a youthfully charged sensation. He ripped off his bodice to reveal nipples painted with chocolate, and there was lots of clapping accompanied by noises of wonder. He stopped right in front of Mrs. Chu and bent over, his hands touching the floor. Mrs. Chu's eyebrows went to the top of her head as she beamed with delight and slapped Patrick on the bottom. He shook his glutes and laughed as he waved his body about. The other ladies clapped, and there were titters and laughter all around. They were loving it. Above all the noise, which never got too raucous, you could hear a man laughing loudly, and we knew it was her son, Suk Chu.

Patrick jumped around provocatively as she puffed hard on her pipe, and then, because he jumped back onto the stage I knew it was nearing the end of his performance. He turned his back to the audience, and pulled the G-string off in perfect time with the lights going out.

He pulled the towel around his waist as the lights went back on, clearly startled, as he quickly began to be surrounded by tiny old Chinese and Korean women, holding pens and bits of paper.

Shit! Those old women can move quickly when they want to...

Patrick signed his autograph for them, which made all the women go "Ooh!"

Now clearly a true star in the Asian community, he went up to Mrs. Chu, and kissed her cheek whilst a thousand hands patted his bottom.

Then Patrick stood while Mrs Chu spoke to everyone and explained the story of her and how she met the mystery stripper, ending with "Yes, he's an angel. Save my life."

There was so much coo-ing it sounded like a pigeon convention. Patrick made his way back to the dressing room, and I gasped slightly as I saw Nick, who'd got changed.

"Not very sexy, is it?" he mumbled. He was nervous, I could tell.

"You would be sexy even if you were disguised as a bucket of shit."

He laughed. We had gone over the plan several times: Serve some drinks, keeping his head down, then when he was next to Mrs. Chu he was to rip open his top and throw it. Nick wore nothing underneath. His now perfectly chiselled body and six pack were enough to make anyone swoon. I felt confident. After all, it had gone much better than I had anticipated with Patrick.

Chu came flying in and ushered out the box-playing lady and her entourage, bowing profusely as they left.

He shouted excitedly. "Patrick, sensational, amazing! I give you two thousand extra. I have not laughed so much since I saw my next door neighbour get run over!" He cackled and snapped his fingers at Nick. "Your turn, pretty boy. Follow me NOW."

I kissed Nick quickly, before he scuttled after Suk, head down.

The four of us held our faces pressed to the crack in the door once again. Nick went over to the bar where Suk explained the subterfuge to the barman, who then proceeded to give Nick a tray of drinks. He carried them skilfully and placed them on a table next to Mrs. Chu with about ten women round it. Gently in the background the music from earlier was playing, which was to be replaced as soon as he got near the target by Guns and Roses - He's a maniac for Love. No sooner had he put the tray down and the music came on, Nick turned to Mrs. Chu, ripping open his top and swinging it above his head.

Mrs Chu didn't just scream, she screamed for China. Nick lifted his head to show his face and moved towards her, but judging by her elevation in pitch, this just made matters worse. Still screaming shrilly and adeptly, Mrs Chu was looking for something under her wheelchair, desperately. The whole time her little dog had sat quietly on the lap, but now Merkin began to growl and yap.

"Mrs. Chu, it's me," Nick said, and as he went to take his hat off, he was prevented by a lash to his arm.

The old lady had produced a weapon of some kind, and began to beat Nick with it, mercilessly. Her shouting made the other ladies react, and after one picked up the tray and began softly beating Nick with it, then like a huge elderly female gang of Triads they came to defend their leader.

Nora was frantically taking pictures and laughing. I pushed past him angrily and pulled open the door, followed by everyone else. Bouncers as big as bulls began to appear.

Patrick was shouting at Mrs. Chu - "Mrs. Chu, its Nick - my friend."

"He try to rob me, he steal my dog, my dog!" she screamed. I was manhandling some old women who seemed to be stuck fast like glue. They all joined together in a chorus of unnerving laughter. Nora called them all "Putas!" as he jumped in and tried with me to prise them apart.

Matilda stood in front of the bouncers.

"I might be little, but I'm quick. I'll have them balls off in a second," she shouted, and grinned.

Suk Chu shouted "Chu chu, ha hi se chu kow, Mumma, Mumma!"

Then he turned and screamed instructions to the doormen.

It was bedlam. No one really knew what was going on. Finally Nick's hands came reaching out of the heap of Asian geriatrics. Frantically I rushed over and started pulling on one arm, and then Patrick started pulling on the other. Nick's hat had come off, and he was gasping for air.

Nora by this time was spitting out Cuban curses, and Suk was explaining who Nick was to his mother, who was clutching her dog, Merkin, and still tapping away with her stick. She shouted out to the other ladies, and they moved slowly and reluctantly back to their seats.

Who needs doormen when you've got this lot?...

I pulled Nick from the human rubble and sat him down. I could see he appeared dazed and confused. Matilda poured him some water. The Chu's were both laughing, our concern for Nick seeming to amuse them highly.

I wanted to jump over and throttle the life out of her little dog, in front of all of them, and then stamp up and down on its dead tiny carcass, while Nora took photos, tweeting Hashtag #DeadFuckingChiuhuahua.

Nora came over "Putas! Darlink, Nick, are you okay?"

Nick rubbed his head and sipped the water Matilda had offered. "I think so. I was beginning to think what a ludicrous way to die that would be."

I kissed him on the cheek, just as Chu came over, still laughing. I tried to contain my anger.

"Oh, Nick. So sorry, my mother didn't know, it was so funny though, and she agrees now that it was funny. I'm a funny son for pulling such a big surprise."

"Chu, that was a bit of a shocker. Strewth, poor Nick," Patrick said in a soothing tone.

Suk waved his hand flippantly. "Don' worry. I'll pay, I'll pay. So hilarious, Mama Chu loved it."

I was just about to say that money cannot buy everything, when he offered Nick an extra three thousand, and I realised that sometimes it could.

"Eight thousand bastard dollars, just for being jumped on by some old Sheilas," Matilda ruminated from the back of the changing room. "I reckon if he survives, it'll be worth it, but."

Patrick added fresh make-up and changed into an outfit that made him look like a giant pink cake.

I was confused. "Is there more?"

"Not here. I'm getting a cab to Kings Cross. I've got more work now; for the Buttered Buns Tea Party tonight."

"We go together, junto," Nora crooned.

"Nora, could you take a piccy please, and hashtag it #ButteredBunsTeaParty ?"

"Aaiieee! Of course, darlink, my Twitter feed is todo mundo"

I felt left out, but I knew my emotions were childish and unnecessary. Let them have time together, for christ's sake...

"I'm afraid you're both stuck with me," grinned Matilda. I did not actually mind at all.

Chu came in waving cash at both our stars. "Take, take." They took.

Patrick asked me and Nick to look after the money for him, as he felt it was way too much to be carrying with him.

"I can come too? I want to get sooo drunk. Mummy will be singing the whole night with her friends now. I'll come back later," Chu asked.

"Of course," Patrick replied, smiling, then shrugged as Nora shot him a W.T.F.? glance.

We all walked together to the taxi rank. Chu was clearly in a very good mood, and hummed to himself as he spun round to face Nora.

"What are you thinking about?" Nora asked him, bemused and curious.

"Yay, yay, I've been thinkin' bout Chu," he sang, and carried on humming *Fine Young Cannibals* eighties hit. He cackled with laughter at his own joke. The rest of us failed to join in.

From behind us we heard voices with thick Australian accents.

"You're a fuckin' queer bunch. Who's the fuckin' *hoon* inside the cake?"

Chu stopped laughing. A sense of danger, and imminent animosity cloaked the air.

Instinctively, none of us said a word in reply, and we quickened our pace slightly.

"Oy, you mangy dogs, we're fuckin' talkin' to you." A strong smell of alcohol exuded from whoever was speaking and wafted up from behind us.

"Hey, *wog*. What you doin' with a fuckin' *Abo*? Oy, little *chinky* fella - You got a *stubby*?"

Nora only knew one definition of that word; *wog*, and he immediately spun round, cat-like. I knew that had pushed him too far.

"*Senor*, a stubby what, eh? A stubby cock, like you? And that's probably only because you were spat from an interbred convict whore's diseased cunt."

253

He narrowly dodged a can that was meant to hit his head.

Oh, no...

Suk Chu joined in: "Ah, big words from the swamp dwelling Australians. I'll send my mother round to lick your balls," He and Nora bellowed with laughter. "Oh no, I forget - you don't have any." Suk pointed out where their balls should have been.

They pounced. There were four of them. They were white suburban males in their mid-twenties, quite drunk, and very stupid. Luckily they weren't huge *fellas*. Patrick began to hit the two that were attacking Nora and I joined him, grabbing and pulling at them. Nick and Matilda became involved and stepped forward to help.

I screamed as the other two flung Nick to the ground, and then one straddled his chest and pushed on his face. Letting go of Nora's attackers, I ran over and repeatedly kicked the boy until he lost his balance, and Nick was able to get up.

A high pitched scream made me spin round, just in time to see Chu actually biting down on one of our assailants' penises. Sinking down to his knees, the man screamed in agony, and at this the others stopped fighting. Clearly they had realised that what they thought was an easy group to pick on, was actually not, and they began to flee.

"Come back," Chu screeched. "I bite all of your balls, I bite your kneecaps off, I bite your tongue, yes!"

Shakily adjusting ourselves, we all hugged, and our hearts seemed to pound in unison. We kissed and laughed nervously as a flame of real kinship spread through us. In a heartbeat we were all united.

Nick grabbed me by the shoulders. "Lucy, are you mad? The babies and you - that could have gone wrong, really wrong."

I opened my eyes wide and saw that one of Nick's eyes was totally red. "Your eye, there's something's wrong with it," I told him.

"It does feel painful. He pushed his thumb into it."

The others looked. "*Strewth*. Can you see? Might have to go to the hospital, mate," Patrick said, clearly worried.

"No, I can see - sort of. My vision is blurred, and I'm getting a bit of a headache. Let's see how it is tomorrow."

"I'll pay for a cab. You go back to the ranch and rest, Nick," cooed Suk.

A cab back to the ranch? Is he mad? That's loads of money!... But Suk had insisted.

It took more than two hours to get back, with Matilda and myself fussing over Nick all the way.

We all slept well, especially poor Nick, considering he had been attacked twice in one night. I insisted on making him breakfast while he stayed in bed. One eye was particularly bloodshot, and I was worried. He tried to reassure me by telling me it was fine, but I could tell he was in pain.

Down in the kitchen I was surprised to see Nora. He was sitting down, his upper half sprawled across the big wooden table.

"Morning!" I said very loudly.

A moaning came from the apparently living corpse. I busied myself with breakfast.

"So you had a good time?" I asked.

More groaning.

"Is Patrick here?"

Nothing.

Wow... I had seen Nora in a lot of states, but he seemed truly wretched this time.

I couldn't help myself. "What about a nice runny greasy snotty egg, served in a dirty ashtray?" I suggested, smiling.

Nora bolted to his feet, and ran outside. This was followed by the sound of vomiting. When he staggered back in, he looked green.

"*Gracias,* you bitch. Oh please, *por favor, ayuda mi!*" he said as he resumed the position.

"I am making coffee if you want one?" I offered.

He retched, and I took that as a *No.*

Matilda came in and viewed the decaying body. "Bit of a rough night, there."

Nora stayed quiet.

"Hell of a night, but how's Nick?" Matilda asked, seeming genuinely concerned.

"Oh, he says he's okay, but I'm worried about his eye. He said he can see, and his vision is still a little blurry, and painful, but he insists on not seeing a doctor. I think he's trying not to worry me."

"If he's *crook,* he should see one," Matilda said, frowning.

I nodded in agreement. "Is Patrick here?" I enquired again.

"Yep, he's at the stables. Getting ready to do some jumping this morning," Matilda answered.

Nora groaned. "Please, God. Give me drugs anytime, not alcohol. I hate it. My head *es muy mal.* Someone did a shit in my mouth."

"What, literally? Crikey, you must have been even more drunk than you thought," I said, and giggled, purely because I was in the luxurious position of not having a hangover.

"*Puta!*" was his only response. Not about to miss a good opportunity, I grabbed Nora's phone and took a quick snap of him, just as he lifted his head and a whispered zombie groan escaped from his mouth, too weak to protest.

"Aaggghhhhh..."

I swiftly uploaded and tagged it out loud: "Hashtag *#CrackWhore #NoStyle #AlcoholBitch #tragic #Gaydire.*"

A growling issued forth from what sounded like an extra in the *Thriller* video.

I left the kitchen, letting Matilda know that Nick and I might come to where Patrick was jumping, depending on how Nick felt. I had no choice but to leave Nora to wade through his own shit alone.

Nick and I enjoyed our breakfast, even though I was responsible for cooking it; the boiled eggs resembled two eggcups of ectoplasm accompanied by burnt toast and the two pieces of meat remained unidentified even after we'd eaten them.

"So, still enjoying the rollercoaster?" asked Nick. He smiled and winced with pain at the same time.

"Got to take the rough with the smooth, so to speak," I answered, smiling back.

"I'm more worried about you and your *Kung Fu*. How are you and the babies? You did put yourself at risk last night."

"I couldn't just stand there and let that happen. Although, yes, I suppose it could have all turned very nasty. Still, a bit of *Karate* is worth it for eight thousand dollars, and saving my man." I said, and grinned.

He couldn't help but laugh. "I see you put the money first," he teased, poking me gently.

257

"I could also say the same for you. I want the father of my children alive, please." I leant over and kissed him on the forehead.

After breakfast we both went down to the kitchen. Matilda was ladling coffee down Nora's throat, which was upright now at least.

"Whoah! You look worse than my eye feels," Nick exclaimed.

"*Gracias*, that makes me feel better" croaked Nora, whose normal voice had given up after so much retching. He squinted over at Nick, and winced at the sight of his bloodshot eye.

"I'm going to the jumping field soon to see Patrick if you want to come?" Matilda asked us.

I nodded. "I know you want to go," I said, motioning to Nick. "What about you, Nora?"

Nora groaned and lay back down on the table. I took that as a *No*.

Matilda rode her own quad. I was happy to sit on the back of Nick's. It was such fun roaring along around the sprawling land of the farm. Beautiful lush greenness grew everywhere, and most days there was a heady scent from the eucalyptus trees, that day being no exception. Thoughts ran through my head, and it occurred to me that maybe in the past this kind of activity would have been a disaster. Since I had become pregnant, and had counselling with Hyam I was no longer such a disaster zone. Maybe the odd mishap, but nothing compared to the trail of catastrophes that had always followed me through my life previously. I wondered how Hyam was, and thought about Sergeant Cole. *I'll check my email tonight...*

We pulled up to a large open field full of lots of horse jumps of all different kinds. Patrick was already there, going full pelt at them. He soared expertly over each jump, turning beautifully while hardly seeming to steer his animal.

He knocked nothing over, and we all watched, transfixed by the show of expert horsemanship. It seemed as if the hand of the Goddess lifted the horse and took them both over each jump effortlessly. I felt as if I were watching music being composed in front of me. Horse and rider were clearly one.

"He's very good!" exclaimed Nick, to no one in particular.

"He could have been an Australian champion," Matilda said, and sighed. "He only jumps when he's stressed or upset now. When Cory died he'd spend hours and hours out here. I couldn't get him to come in the house, and he slept in the stables for over a month." Her voice quavered.

I wondered what was bothering him this time and realised I was going to get my answer quicker than I thought, as Patrick finally noticed us and rode over.

"*G'day,* didn't see you lot there," he said, and by the way he stared at Nick as he spoke, I could see he was upset about what had happened the previous night. "How's that eye?"

"Oh, I won't make pirate status," Nick answered jokingly. Patrick did not smile.

Nick tried to placate him, as sensitive as always. "It was no one's fault, Patrick, only the arseholes that started on us."

"If I hadn't been in drag it wouldn't have happened," Patrick moaned.

I had been right. "Patrick, you should be able to wear what you like, it's not you. It's uneducated people, they are the threat, not you. If I want to parade around in a pink tutu with glitter falling out my arse, shouting, 'I only eat fish dinners!' that is my prerogative. We don't beat up the straights for wearing the utterly hideous shit they wear. Fuck them."

Patrick smiled slightly and the love and pride in my heart swelled. I felt honoured that I had him in my life.

Matilda managed to convince him to come back for some *tucker*, as the *Aussies* say.

"We'll meet you at the stables," she shouted over her shoulder as the quads sped off. Patrick galloped alongside, looking far more dignified than we did, rattling around like jumping beans on our quads. I wished Nora could see him looking this spectacular. Nick could not have sat next to a better person on the plane.

PATRICK

We arrived at the stables. The weather hung heavy in the air,
illustrating Patrick's mood. He put away the horse while we
went into the tack room. Even though I'd definitely never been
a natural horsewoman, the smell of leather and saddle soap
in the stables intoxicated me. Matilda obviously blossomed in
this environment, humming as she picked up saddles to hang
on the wall. Nick and I sat on a bench, waiting happily. One of
the saddles that hung there particularly interested me. Different
from the rest, it shone a beautiful chestnut colour, bordered
with a cream piping.

"That's a nice saddle," I remarked to Matilda.

"It was Cory's," Patrick said, and his voice made me
jump. "Or at least it would have been." He strode over to
the beautifully cared for saddle and ran his hands over it
sentimentally. No one said a word. As he turned away I could
see the sadness tinged with melancholy in his eyes.

261

"This was the one he was going to buy when I won Australia a gold for jumping. Or so we naively thought." He sat down on an old beaten up chair and sighed.

My mind raced. *What? Olympics? Gold? Shit, he must have been good...*

He shook his head and began to talk, almost as if to himself.

"You see, I was tipped to win in the Olympics. Australia's finest. I've always been around horses. My parents have a small ranch just outside *Kalgoorlie*, which is a mining town, and full of men. That's great when you're gay and merely window shopping but God help you if you want anything more. My father, the great arsehole *Bruce Wilson* is *Aussie* through and through. He used to scream at the *'fuckin' poofty fellas'* on TV. My mother is a lot softer, but unfortunately she's totally afraid of him, and usually does his bidding even when she doesn't want to. He's a violent man, especially when he drinks, and he drinks all the time.

I could ride before I could walk, my mother told me. I was never happier than when I was trotting bareback round the harsh scrub land of Kalgoorlie. Jumping just seemed a natural enhancement to the riding, but even I knew I was good. My father boasted and made bets on me, knowing I would win every competition. By the time I was sixteen no one could touch me.

I knew I was gay. I'd known for a long time, but nothing would have made me tell my father, and I didn't want to dump it on my mother, who had enough to deal with, being married to a racist homophobic pig. I often wondered why he'd chosen my mother, and not an Australian woman, but I never questioned either of them about it.

In that summer, in my sixteenth year, I was jumping at the Kalgoorlie state fair when a divine intervention occurred, some kind of huge fluke. One of the men watching was from *Canberra*, the capital of Australia. His car had broken down and he was having it repaired. Whilst he waited he was enjoying all we had to offer as a large mostly male-populated mining town.

After he saw me win, he approached me. His name was *Kenny Brown*, and he was a trainer at the stables in Canberra where all the top riders trained. He told me he wanted me to go there, and try out for the Australian team. He said he'd never seen anyone as good. Of course at first I thought it was a joke. My father came over bristling and demanding to know what was going on. As soon as Kenny produced a card and confirmed what he was saying, my father's attitude changed. He could smell the possibility of money and mild fame.

"I'll bring the boy myself. Still, you gotta cough up the coins, it's a long way from here." I can remember his exact words. A week later, my mother in tears, I left.

Canberra was a huge bustling new metropolis compared with the old fashioned shacks I'd left behind. So, true to his word Kenny met up with me and introduced me to some of the other people in charge. I tried out for them, and was immediately asked to do a four year apprenticeship. They paid for my bed and board and I trained every day. The best thing was saying goodbye to my father, and embracing the gay life I now felt free to discover, and wow, did I! I missed my mother but I sent her photos along with my regular letters. I styled my hair, changed my clothes, and well I suppose I started to look Gay! I've only been home to visit twice, and not since I was selected to jump in the Olympics.

Just before I was twenty I met Cory. It sounds corny but it was Love at first sight. We were so at ease together. Everything was brighter and better when I was around him. He added so much joy to my life. He was so proud when I got selected and told everyone, except for his family. His excitement kept me on a constant high. He called me *The Horse Flyer* because that's what he thought I looked like when he watched me.

I decided to go to Kalgoorlie and tell my parents firstly that I was in the Olympics, and secondly about Cory. It turned out to be the worst decision I ever made.

On my arrival my father already started complaining that I looked too feminine with my hair, clothes and mannerisms, but once I told them the news that I was in the Olympics both my parents were ecstatic, for different reasons.

263

That night he took me all over town telling all his mates and slapping my back as if he had been responsible for the whole thing. He told anyone that would care to listen. I honestly think that was the only time my father seemed to genuinely like me."

Patrick stopped for a few moments and sighed, taking a pause from his painful memories. "I told them. It was extremely difficult but I told them. My father beat me so badly that I spent three months in hospital, and five more recovering. I missed the Olympics, and never went back to Canberra again. As he beat me he was roaring that no *poof* son of his was going to show him up in front of the world, he would rather kill me, and in fact he almost did.

While I was in hospital Cory gave up his job, moved near me and was my only companion for all that time. My father forbade my mother to visit. The moment I was out Cory and I went to Sydney together. We wanted our own ranch, even though he was a terrible rider, and on our eighth anniversary I bought him that saddle. He always said it was the saddle I would win the Olympics on, forever the optimist. Shortly after that he was diagnosed with *Aids*. He liked his drugs, and he'd been stupid enough to share a needle with *go-ey* in: speed. He paid the ultimate price. Not long after we found out he was infected I saved Mrs Chu, and Suk came into our lives. Suk put down the deposit on Freedom ranch, and Cory and I lived here. He died here. Suk did everything. He arranged the funeral and paid for it even though I told him not to. I'll admit I was inconsolable. After the funeral he paid for me to go to his private island off of Korea where I stayed for two months, sheltering my pain." He paused, lost in his painful memories.

None of us said a word. We were new friends, voluntarily tangled in his web of sadness.

He stood eventually, and sighed, placing the riding tack he'd been holding tightly in his hand to one side. "I definitely have difficulty handling intimacy, or any kind of strong feelings that I haven't had since Cory."

Even though his back was to us, the underlying message, I thought, was that he must like Nora. <u>A lot.</u> He had revealed such a personal, upsetting chapter in his life. He was letting us know that he couldn't stand any more pain, that he was scared of these rare feelings. I knew immediately that I was going to relay most of his story to Nora. I resolved to tell him that this man was not a pair of *Gaultier* shoes that you can discard, or a *Louis Vuitton* bag to be slung in the river. Although I had never seen Nora this smitten, a chat was still definitely needed.

Slowly movement began. Matilda wiped away silent tears. Nick just stood, dumbfounded as to what to do next. Patrick looked around, and upon seeing Matilda looking upset he instantly strode towards her and embraced her protectively, every inch a close and loving friend.

He drew back and stared into her eyes, seeking forgiveness. "Matilda, I'm so sorry, I didn't mean to upset you. I wasn't thinking, I'm sorry," he effused while hugging her.

Nick and I looked at each other and shared our lack of comprehension about what exactly was happening. Later, we would find out.

She pushed him away. "Silly bugger. I'm not upset," she insisted, jutting her pretty little chin out just as she had done to the doorman the night before.

Patrick spun on his heel to face Nick. "Again, sorry about your eye, *mate*. I'm cooking the best *tucker* today for all of us." He placed his arm around Nick's neck. "How's Nora?" he asked me, managing a weak smile.

"When I just saw him, he looked like some kind of holy resurrection, laying across the kitchen table," I replied, smiling.

Patrick threw his head back and laughed. "I bet. Him and Suk Chu got roaring drunk. That whole terrible event brought them together in comradeship. They celebrated with Cocaine™ and *Jack Daniels*, and somehow ended up with a puppy each! God only knows how they got hold of them. They were pedigree puppies. Suk has them with him. Mrs Chu is going to have a fit if she or Merkin sees them."

We jumped on the quads and headed back to the ranch, all of us consumed with our individual thoughts.

A now almost fully resurrected Nora, showered and freshly dressed, was in the kitchen patting down his newly grown afro as he tried to get used to it. A beautiful pale cream cheesecloth two piece suit accentuated his perfect deep chocolate skin, although his normally perfect sashaying walk that morning looked shaky. He shooed his hand at me as he sat down gently. "Coffee, darlink," he whispered, shielding dark alcohol soaked eyes.

Queen Nora had clearly dropped his good manners and put on his bitchy queen's robe. He clicked his fingers.

I was about to tell him that Patrick had already started to make the coffee, he clearly found Nora equally as loveable as Nora did him.

It must be Love or why would he have told us all that?... My theory was reinforced by a little chat we had later. For now, Nora was the hero of the hour, and still as delicate as a tissue. Our gracious host was preparing delicious food.

"This is an honourable lunch for the hero of the night - Nick," Patrick announced as we all sat down, and spread his arms out towards Nick, who was blushing fiercely. A small incredulous gasp escaped from Nora, who'd clearly thought it was going to be in honour of himself. Matilda was yet to join us, late from shouldering the bulk of the responsibility with so many horses. Patrick put the radio on and danced while he cooked, shaking a very tight tush at us. Nora peeked through his fingers, apparently reading some kind of arse conveyed Morse code. As he got up and went to fetch his coffee he almost swooned.

He leant towards Patrick as he picked the mug up. "*Gracias,* Patrick. Thank you, darlink, for cooking for Nora," he said slyly, implying it was all for him in the third person. Patrick accepted it nobly.

Matilda bounded in, acting like a new *filly* freshly released into the grazing field. She handed Patrick an Australian white wine and kissed him on the cheek before joining us at the table.

"So, I heard that y'all had a good night?" Nick asked cheekily as he casually stirred the pot.

Nora, trying to be understated, agreed that they'd had a good night, although the alcohol had been a little bit overly consumed. Suk and he had sorted out their differences and naturally, a little celebration had been called for. When Patrick asked about the puppies, Nora told him he was mad. Patrick seemed pretty sure, although he didn't push the point.

Almost on cue, the radio went to Local and Sydney news.

We listened idly, and nearly everything sounded uninteresting, until the very last item.

"...Lastly, An incident took place in *Darlinghurst Park* late last night. Two men are wanted for indecent exposure and theft. Namely, the abduction of two pedigree *Pit-bull* puppies..."

We all froze in time.

"...The robbers were totally naked, apart from a beauty pageant crown," said the newsreader, and all eyes swivelled towards the elephant in the room, who grinned naively from his chair.

"A *Mrs Judith Preacher*, the owner of the nine week old pups, had been taking them for a late night walk when the incident took place. Mrs Preacher described the event to our reporter on the scene."

A gnarly voice crackled out of the radio.

"We-ll, it was late, cos I like to take the little buggers out and get a bit of fresh air, when I saw two *fellas*, they was running at me screaming, wearing crowns, and bugger all else. Then they snatched two of my prize Pit-bull pups!"

"Would you be able to identify the attackers, Mrs Preacher?" the reporter croaked.

"I sure would, one was a little *yella fella*, and the other was brown." That appeared to conclude her detailed description.

"That was Ted Smith reporting. If you have any information, please call the *Darlinghurst* police on five-five-five-eight-one. The puppies' names are - *Little Piddle the third*, and *James Doodoo Crumple*. Thank you and *g'day*."

The radio station returned to playing music, whilst Nora shrivelled as all eyes fell upon him.

"So as I was saying, about those puppies?" Patrick asked sweetly, with a big fat helping of *I told you so*.

"I think I'll have to call Suk," Patrick said, putting his phone on loudspeaker so Nora and the rest of us could also listen. A small voice answered; "Yes?" and Patrick explained the situation.

"Patrick, I don't know where the bloody puppies are. My mother found me naked in her biggest saucepan in the kitchen. Then she goes crazy and smacked me right on my balls. She told me she was gonna cook them. How could I bring those dogs here? Merkin could be eaten by those killing machines. She threw me out, now I can't find her. Oh no, my mother's boiling up some food!" he shouted and the line went dead, leaving us all suspended.

Oh no, really she couldn't, wouldn't. Could she?...

I searched Patrick's face for any sign that she would do what I imagined.

"I don't understand, I hate dogs, and I'm deep chocolate, not brown," Nora coo-ed.

"Those are the two things you gleaned from all that?" I said, shaking my head.

"Well, you could hardly call that a detailed description," Nick said, and smirked. "I think you're both safe on that count."

"I just hope Mrs Chu is not boiling them," I whispered, my throat drying out at the thought of it. "I hardly think they're killing machines at nine weeks old."

"Mrs Chu is very passionate about Merkin. She sent her for a two week holiday in Hawaii once."

We all stared at Patrick, incredulously.

"A dog, a fucking dog!" I exclaimed.

He shook his head. "All we can do is wait and see what happens." He shrugged. "For now, let's eat this celebratory lunch."

It was delicious, and all our moods grew lighter as we ate. A fit of giggling caught hold of me as I imagined two naked men wearing tiaras and running through the park, cocks bouncing around as they thrust themselves at Mrs Preacher and her puppies, before gaily carrying them off. No one needed to ask me why I was laughing, my giggles had an infectious effect, and pretty soon we were all close to hysterical.

Luckily, Suk called back with some good news. His mother had made one of his chefs put the puppies in a box on the steps of the local police station, with a note saying it was "-from the yellow people". That caused more jollification.

Thank goodness for that...

After lunch Nick wanted to go out for a ride, so Matilda and Patrick joined him. That gave me the perfect chance to talk to Nora, who was unusually receptive. I relayed the story that Patrick had told us and asked him to think seriously about his feelings towards him. He acknowledged the seriousness of what I was saying and said he needed a rest to think more

269

clearly, so I left him in his room.

Once on my own I decided to check my emails. I'd been thinking about Sergeant Cole, and how things were back in *England*. My list of unread mails was a very small one; just my brother, and Lawrence Cole. A part of me felt sad that it consisted of so few names. My brother would ask my mother's questions for her, which my father would have filtered through to him and deemed what was necessary. First I looked at Lawrence's email. My brother; Jonathan's would be harder. I intended to tell him about the twins, and about staying in Australia for longer.

At least Sergeant Cole had written me an email. There was mostly good news. He and Jenny were going to get married, early the next spring. He explained how much he enjoyed being with her, and how he'd decided to give himself a second chance. The lyrics Nick had written, which had been turned into a song by the legendary *Frankie Bubbles*, had been at number two for six weeks, and had only just gone down to number five in the pop charts. Once, when Lawrence had visited Jenny, Nick's family had been in the pub, and had seemed apparently relaxed as they'd told him that Nick had gone to Australia for a year, and was having a fantastic time. Meanwhile Lawrence Cole knew the truth. He reminded me that acting was not his strong point, but he hoped all had turned out well in reality. The email was signed - *With Love from Lawrence*.

I beamed at the memory of that song. It had been so painful for me to hear before. I hadn't listened to it for a long while.

"Without you there is only pain, from now on I'll never be the same, something that I can't explain, Desire..." I sang quietly and hummed to myself as I sent a reply.

All was fabulous, I reported, between Nick and me. The babies are healthy, wanted, and I felt them nourishing my spirit. They were keeping me strong and happy. We were going to find out how we could stay longer, and Nora was definitely staying, which wasn't a problem as he could probably afford to buy Australia if he was inclined to do so. Of course, I left lots of stuff out that he didn't need to know. There is such a thing as too much information. I signed off, - *Love, Lauren. xxx*

My reply to my brother's email took longer. I insisted that he keep the pregnancy a secret from my parents. I told him that I hoped my flat was still in one piece and had not been transformed into a whore's circus.

When I'd finished I gazed out of the window and watched the brooding sun set, unaware of the time and unaware that I was being watched. Minutes slipped away before I finally sensed someone behind me. I spun round to see Nick leant against the doorway. His hair was wet and his face gleamed from the exhilaration of the ride as he breathed deeply.

No talking was needed as our passions met and we made love for most of that night. Words seemed unnecessary and woefully inadequate. Eventually we fell asleep, content and enriched. I dreamed of a birthing lake where both of us swam like dolphins, and the twins glided gently out of my vagina, and rode on their father's back to get to the shore. Funny how sometimes your dreams turn out to be the complete opposite to reality.

XMAS DOWN UNDER

Nick and Nora were giddily excited about the Christmas day that approached in two days time. I had never spent an enjoyable *Navidad*, not that I could remember, anyway. Even when I was young, going out with David, he'd always managed to spoil it somehow. I felt guilty remembering that, but I decided not to be so hard on myself. I couldn't eradicate my memories, but at least now I had better tools to equip me with a more appropriate response to life. I cast my mind to Hyam and remembered that in the Jewish faith they did not celebrate Christmas.

I looked out of the window, and felt a million miles away from it all. Glorious weather surrounded us every day, while a proud throbbing sun gave life to stunning flowers that looked like swans: *Birds of Paradise*. Their succulent heady scent mixed with the incredible fragrance of the *Frangipanis* and their beautiful white flowers. I wanted to take a bite from the invisible summery cake that floated on the air. Nothing was there to suggest that 'HO, HO, HO! Santa's coming,' and it felt great.

Nick and Nora were getting animated while Patrick made tea. The day before, we'd gone to Sydney to see the lawyer to apply for our three month visa, followed by an appointment at immigration. I was four months pregnant by then but I didn't show at all, so we said nothing to anyone about that. Patrick had contacted Mr Kelly who had recommended a lawyer, *Duncan Brown*. Mr Brown was middle aged with brown thinning hair and a brown suit, although his skin was definitely more of a clammy yellow. I was pleased we hadn't brought Nora, as I felt sure he would have left in disgust with so many shades of beige on display. Instead we just passed on his information.

"Mr Sanchez will have to come with you when you come down to see if you have been accepted for the three month extension of your tourist visa." We nodded shyly.

I liked Mr Duncan Brown, he reminded me of a little shrew, who burrowed through people's lives unobserved, winning cases for them like a small Australian *Colombo*. He seemed like a hero of the people.

Afterwards, I told Nick that I felt confident Duncan could get it done, and without us going to prison, which naturally we feared. We imagined leaving the twins with the Australian authorities while we were sent back to England. Patrick had laughed at that and told us; "It's not like the days of convicts anymore. We are actually quite civilized nowadays in Australia."

Back home in the kitchen we knew we'd have to wait nearly a week to hear if we could have the visa, so I suspended my anxiety to better absorb the holiday festivities.

Nick and Patrick were doing a strip show in Sydney on Christmas Eve, and then we were going to Suk's house afterwards to stay the night and wake up all together on the twenty-fifth. We all knew that the soup dragon; his mother, was going to be there, but Suk had almost begged us all to come. Patrick told us every one of Chu's friends was busy over the holiday time, and he thought it might be nice to bond more. Nick had practically jumped in agreement.

I was really looking forward to the strip. Nick and Patrick were performing with two other strippers, at a club called *The Pink Teacup*, in Darlinghurst Road. It was a big venue which seated a thousand people, and it had been booked out for weeks. There was to be a giant fireplace with four big stockings hanging up, each one containing a man. *Mariah Cary* singing *All I Want For Christmas Is You*, was to be followed by the classic *It's Raining Men* by *The Weather Girls*. Cannons were primed to shower the audience with snow. Afterwards there was going to be a guest appearance by Australia's fantastic *Marsha Hines*, who was as talented as *Tina Turner*, and then a long list of guest DJ's would play. Nick and I talked the evening before. I said I wanted to try to stay the whole night and he said as long as I was okay, he was happy to stay up with me.

The plan was to meet the manager of The Pink Teacup at seven. The show started at eight PM, when Suk would also arrive.

Nora was very animated with the excitement that his BOYFRIEND, his *NOVIO*, as he told us at least twenty times that day, was in the line-up. "*Darlink*, they could have had anyone, just anyone, but no, they ask you!" he enthused, sizing up his impressive new catch.

Luckily for all of us, Mrs Chu was over at a friend's house, and wouldn't be at home while we were there. When we learned that, relief flooded from all of us, heightening our state of excitement.

Patrick educated us, and told us that normally, Chinese and Korean cultures don't celebrate Christmas. In China they have a kind of Santa known as "*Sheng dan lao ren*" meaning Old Christmas Man. They don't have pine trees in the house, and they eat more traditional foods associated with the Chinese New Year, like barbecued pork, dumplings and *jiaozi* soup. As Suk's mother was not there, Suk wanted a real Aussie '*Shrimps on the barbie*' day with a huge tree, or so he'd told Patrick, which is why he was very excited about us all coming. Mrs Chu would be away for two days, and it sounded like Suk wanted to make the most of it.

At eight PM, on Christmas Eve, all of us were there promptly, dressed in our best clothes and ready for a night of fun. Patrick was shaking hands with the Manager of The Pink Teacup, *Cliff Robinson*, who was not what I had expected. He was a true hippy, with long flowing hair and a caftan. Numerous beads garnished his attire.

"How's it goin'? It's bloody heavin' in there. I'm stoked about the whole thing, what a trip!"

He took Nick and Patrick to the dressing room and then showed us to our table. Nora graciously pulled out a chair for Matilda, who blushed, uncomfortable without her horsey clothes, which she clearly preferred.

"*Strewth*. Thanks, Nora."

As I watched, I thought she resembled *Kylie Minogue*. She was all clean in her best *clobber*. Her chestnut ringlets shone as bright as the manes on the horses that she cared for so lovingly. A simple knee-length baby-blue dress made her look very pretty and understated, in contrast to Nora who was wearing a *Jason Wu* designer suit over a plain silk black shirt. The simulated print of newspapers adorned the material of the jacket and trousers. A big wide brimmed black hat snuggled happily onto his afro.

Suk joined us only moments afterwards, also dressed for the occasion. He complimented Nora on his choice of designer, while he himself wore a *Vivienne Tam*; a two piece dark suit with a yellow shirt. A Santa hat sat jauntily on his head. He did a little dance before sitting down, wiggling his head to jingle the bell that was on the hat, before launching into song -

"I've been thinking 'bout Chu… doo-dee-doo, I've been thinking 'bout Chuu…"

Nora took photos, and hashtagged them *#FagsXmas #PinkHolidays #PinkTeacup #DiverseFriends #faghags*, although that latter one caused myself and Matilda to protest.

I had chosen a pinstripe halter neck suit, with a zip all the way up the front. It suited my short hair, which Nick loved and so did I.

Funny that people treat you so differently, purely based on your hair colour, and even length. Short hair? Then you're a lesbian, a *Friend of Dorothy's*, a carpet-muncher, someone that bats for the other team, a scissor sister.

A chic bob cut? Then maybe you're straight, but it's too business-like, too *'woman with balls'*. Straight men generally like to be the only one running things and could do without that kind of competition.

Long hair? Really long, and blonde? Oh no, then you're a bimbo, and your hair colour obviously defines your I.Q.

How about bleached short hair? No, that just takes us back to the '*Lezby friends – homo you don't.*'

Grey hair? Then you're old. Long grey hair? No, no. You're a granny, a hippy or a herbalist.

Blue, red or perhaps even green hair? No, because that's a: 'Punk, you're going to burn my house down,' hair colour.

Long black hair? Are you mad? It makes you look dead, so very, very pale, ages you terribly, and makes you look like a witch.

Got an Afro, or dreadlocks? Oh no! Now you look as if you are going to rob them senselessly.

I felt my hair added a fake window display of confidence and knowledge. *Would I ever change it now?...*

The audience filled up quickly; a montage of interweaved sexualities and looks. Fabulous drag queens sat alongside various transgender and gay men and women and even some straight couples. Here was a bubbling blanket of different cultures and races, connected together by their differences, and uniqueness.

As the lights went down, a hush descended upon the crowd. The compère's voice boomed from the PA speakers:

276

"Welcome, your royal queens. Here at The Pink Teacup, have we got a night for you!"

Huge blasts made us all jump as indoor snow rained down on us and in our drinks as well.

"To start us all off, let's see what Santa has stuffed in our stockings!"

The boom of the snow cannons sounded again, and hands sped to cover expensive drinks and cocktails.

The big deep red music-hall curtains swept back to reveal a big fireplace in which a fire seemed to be fiercely burning. Four giant bulging stockings hung, two either side of the hearth. The music started, and one by one each stocking started to move as a man stepped out of them. If I found any of these men in my stocking, I would know that all my prayers had been answered in one hit. Nick climbed out first.

He must be so scared..., I'd thought when they'd told him he was coming out first, but as it turned out he had no need to worry. Fists thumped tables, hands clapped in applause, and lips wolf-whistled. The mercury in my pride-o-meter went shooting up.
Secondly, a big, big man with huge muscles emerged from another stocking. Unusually stunning and handsome, he looked as if he was possibly *Maori*, from New Zealand.
Then Patrick got out of his stocking, and Nora and Suk stood up and screamed out like star-struck schoolgirls.
The fourth man appeared to have been chiselled by the gods; his dark black skin shone and his muscles jumped for the joy of being trapped in that glorious body. We all went mad as they strutted their stuff on stage, with a tight dance routine that Mariah would have been proud off.

The clothes started coming off in the second song, *It's Raining Men*. As *The Weather Girls* belted it out - "Tall, dark..." all the performers on stage stopped, and several more men who were painted gold, covered in glitter and wearing Santa hats, sprang from all the exits in the club in a parade of deliciousness. They wove through the crowd sprinkling glitter from little pouches.

Bang! The strip began, and all the men stopped throwing glitter and stood like statues.

The crowd went mad, including all of us at our table who knew we were witnessing a true show. The climax came as each man faced each other and ripped the other's g-string off as the lights flashed and went down, in time with the snow cannons going off for one final boom. As the lights came back on, we could see all four performers had put on a Santa jacket. We all stood and cheered in unison, clapping enthusiastically, while they accepted the glory gracefully.

The compère encouraged us: "That's right you *bludgers*, make some noise for *Hard Exposure!*" They waved their way off the stage, and then it took a minute or so for the noise to diminish. Suk and Nora were already ordering more shots of tequila, while Matilda stuck with her *stubbie*; beer in Aussie slang. A very unfortunate turn of phrase I'd always thought, especially for Australian men.

Patrick and Nick joined us at the table just as the compère announced that Marsha Hines was in the house. Whoops and whispers reverberated around the room, and we waited with excited anticipation.

"Now put those hands together for the salivacious, salubrious, Miss *Marsha Hines!*" The curtains went back and the whole room stood, manically clapping. She was stunning. Although she was probably in her fifties by then, she could have easily passed for thirty. I had seen her perform when I'd been in Australia before, and I'd purchased her album immediately.

She sang four songs, and nearly everyone knew all the words. I didn't need to drink because the atmosphere was intoxicating enough, and besides, Suk and Nora were doing my share for me. After a five minute standing ovation for Marsha, *DJ Sticky*, a very well known DJ in Oz, appeared behind the decks.

"So everyone, get ready to shake your booties. Hold on to your drinks, the tables are going down," the invisible compère told us. All the tables began to slowly move down into the floor until they'd disappeared, and round mirrored discs slid out to cover the holes, leaving the floor shining brightly. "Boom!", went the cannons again.

***

I remembered falling asleep on a chair after dancing for what seemed like hours. Nick had checked I was feeling good, and I was. A night of dancing and fun was just what the doctor ordered.

We got a cab to *Surrey Hills* in the early hours of the morning to stay at Chu's. We were having the guest bedroom, Nora was with Patrick in his room, and Matilda was on the sofa-bed in Suk Chu's mother's room, where Suk normally slept. Nora and Suk were already very drunk, while Patrick, Matilda and Nick had managed to stay fairly sober. Nick and I fell asleep immediately, after such a fantastic Christmas Eve.

The next morning; the twenty-fifth, we were the first up, and we crept downstairs like naughty children, stopping and wowing in the lounge. A huge decorated pine tree stood in the middle of the room, with tons of presents piled underneath. A small alpine looking house had a sign outside that read *'Santa's Grotto'*, with a real live man dressed as Santa who greeted us with a "HO, HO, HO!" The big table was brimming over with food. We heard the double doors to the kitchen open and for a moment, our hearts stopped as we thought Mrs Chu was there, but it was just a very happy looking cook. She put hot scrambled eggs and sausages down next to some smoothies. As Nick and I began to tuck in, I realised I felt ravenous. We chatted casually between mouthfuls, before Matilda arrived, shortly followed by Patrick, who poured himself a hot coffee.

"So, anyone had Santa visit them yet?" Patrick asked, grinning at his own wit.

"I'm a bit nervous of what might be in that grotto," Nick admitted, lowering his voice.

Patrick laughed, "Yeah, you never know what Suk could have planned."

279

For the next two hours our little gang sat chatting and eating, until Nora, closely followed by Chu, finally came to join us. Dead corpses would have looked better than they did, but their moods were light nevertheless. Suk drank down some coffee before announcing that we were all going to gather round the tree to open the presents.

Santa 'Ho, Ho, Ho!'ed his way over and called our names as he dished out the presents. I was dreading that moment, not because I am an ungrateful wench, but because we were not in a position financially to compete with the lavish gifts that were so often bestowed upon Chu's friends. However I was taken by surprise, and all of the presents turned out to be fun and inexpensive. There was a Mrs Santa's baby-doll outfit for me, with some delicious mint chocolate nipples and bust boosting cream. I laughed to show I was in the spirit of things. I got lots of different body lotions, one cookies and cream flavour, even one called *Essence of Vagina*.

Nora got a glass bottle-like dick pump, which you place your penis into and squeeze the hand pump to inflate your member. Nora was hung-over, but in good spirits. He guffawed at the sight of the pump, and also at his oversized gold Afro comb, which he stuck directly into his hair for safekeeping.

He must be in Love...

Nick got a cock-ring, a stainless steel ring which when placed around the shaft and plums, plumps the little man into a very keen size, looking ready for action at any moment, and a blow-up sex doll, which Suk really tittered at.

Patrick got a blow-up sheep called *Flossie the Love Sheep*, some *stubbie* can holders shaped like testicles and drinks straws shaped as penises. All of us were laughing at the funny presents, and the real live Santa just added to the specialness of the day.

Matilda had sat and joined in the laughter, even though she herself had not yet received one gift. Lastly, the man in the big red suit handed her a single envelope. She opened it, her eyes absorbed the contents, and then in a dream-like state, she slowly brought the letter down onto her lap. Her deep brown eyes filled with tears which spilled down onto her cheeks. I had no idea what was going on, and nor did Nick, judging by his expression.

"Can this be fuckin' true? I, I..." she stuttered. Her words faltered with emotion, and she was unable to continue.

Patrick explained briefly. "I've given her the deeds to a little outhouse I own on Freedom Ranch, it's nothing really."

A noise came from Matilda that was unintelligible.

He continued. "And Suk has bought *Shlong* off me, to give to her."

Matilda jumped up and propelled herself towards Patrick, and then Suk, hugging them fiercely. She was still unable to speak.

"I wanted you to have your own home that no one can take away. It's been written up legally by Mr Brown, the lawyer, so that even if something happens to me... and well, I know how much you love that bloody horse." Patrick's words were thick with emotion as well.

"HO, HO, HORSE!" bellowed Santa, ringing his bell. We all smiled.

"I'm afraid our gifts are very simple," I said, almost stuttering. I winked at Nick, and in unison we said:

"*Ha ha te che che, meh ta cha cha.*" Nick and I beamed proudly.

Suk at first didn't react as we'd thought he might, but then he began to laugh. "At first it took me a moment to understand you, and then I wondered why you'd say that, you're so funny!"

"What did we say?" Nick asked.

"You wished me good holidays and may my year be filled with monkey sacks, that's so funny."

Nick went red, "Er, no we meant to say; May your year be filled with good wishes. We've been learning some Mandarin."

Suk pushed his smiling round face upwards. "I'm very proud. I love my pressie."

"Monkey sacks!" Matilda had found her voice. "Can we put them on the *barbie*?" she asked, and we all laughed. Nick explained that our gifts to them were only small gestures but they were very private and personal. We had been briefly but seriously discussing who the *Goddess Parents* of the babies would be. Both of us had agreed to Nora, and hopefully Patrick, if he agreed, because even though we had only known him for a short time, we both loved and trusted him already. Of course primarily, we just wanted the twins to be born healthy, and then worry about all that other stuff. I was after all, only four months pregnant.

Suk took us all outside, telling Santa to stay indoors in case we needed his cottage, and cackling to himself the whole time.

We entered a garden that I'd never seen, where about six Asian girls were dressed as elves and cooking a barbecue.

"Right, you *bludgers*. We got shrimps on the *barbie*!" Suk screeched out loud.

"See, Patrick? I can talk *Aussie*, now I'm a real Australian."

You could clearly see he was in Aussie Christmas heaven.

The rest of the afternoon was idyllic. The weather was stunningly warm, and there is definitely something warm and comforting about the smell of a barbecue. Thick juicy kangaroo steaks complimented potatoes in their jackets with sour cream. Giant *Gambas*, prawns, sat next to huge slabs of fresh tuna steak. We all started chatting freely and soaking up the delightful atmosphere.

At around seven PM one of the elves came over to see Suk, who was quite drunk now, along with Nora. Patrick preferred, like Matilda, to stick to *stubbies*.

"Oh fuck, what have you all done?" Suk cried, and wagged his finger at us.

"Come on then, I'll play. We have a surprise now," he cackled. He held his full glass of whisky above his head and sang *Waltzing Matilda*, to a bemused Matilda.

All of us sat expectantly, and I whispered to Nick: "What's going on?"

"I don't know," Nick answered, and beckoned Patrick over. "What's happening?"

"No idea," answered Patrick.

A giant cake was wheeled in, a bit like the one you see in movies that a stripper jumps out of. Before I could think about that, Suk jumped up. "Oh, you bad people. I know my present!" He jumped up onto his feet, and in one adept move began swinging his drink, while pumping his groin into an imaginary vagina. "Suk, Suk, I'm gonna Suk Chu, yes Suk Chu baby."

An elf brought an old fashioned cassette tape player with a medium sized speaker attached to it, and pressed play. None of us moved, as *Right Said Fred*'s classic intro blared out.

"I'm too sexy for my car, too sexy by far. I'm a dancer, you know what I mean,"

We all witnessed the top of the cake beginning to crack.

"On the catwalk, yeah, I shake my little tush..." More tiny cracks appeared, and then I noticed a very small fist emerging. It looked like a baby bird breaking out of its egg for the first time. In fact it took so long the song played out, and an elf came running quickly to rewind and replay the tape. Our whole group was baffled, surely if it was a stripper, he/she would have just burst out, instead of taking six or seven minutes?

Fred was onto the second chorus again *"...and I'm too sexy for my shirt..."*

There was a final push, and as the top of the cake broke, nothing could have prepared me for what happened next.

An extremely old Asian woman stepped out, gasping for air and wearing nothing but a pink furry g-string.

"Aaahhhh!" screamed Suk with delight.

"Aaaiiiieeeee!" Nora screamed, looked back at the contents of the cake again, reached, and promptly vomited.

"Jesus," Patrick reacted, as Matilda froze like Suk. The gasping ancient mummy that stood before us picked up the two hanging sacks of skin that went down to her stomach, and squeezed them tightly, increasing the hideous effect. I realized these were one hundred year old breasts as the woman began to swing the ends around and twist them simultaneously. This grotesque animal balloon display using breasts began to make me feel sick as well.

"*Puta madre,* make it stop," whimpered Nora, as the woman bent over and parted her butt cheeks a little, before slapping them loudly. It sounded like a baby bird hitting the windshield of a car.

Suk craned his head forward. "Mrs Cha?"

She opened her puckered mouth and laughed at his realisation.

"Dear god it's Mrs Chu's friend," I said, and before I could go on, Mrs Cha opened up the front of the cake and then even Nick gasped, so it had to be bad.

There, inside, in her wheelchair was Mrs Chu, who, as she prised herself out, we could see wore no clothes at all. She stopped as another elf played the song for the fourth time. Luckily for us she didn't twist and turn her boobs, but her approach was to caress them softly instead.

There are certain things in life that will never leave you, photos in your memory that you can never erase, or gloss over. Mrs Cha seemed to be loving playing her part and was now rubbing her fluffy pink thong with her skeletal hands.

None of us could stop watching this horror film, or even react. All of us were frozen as we watched two one-hundred-year-old Asian women sexually stimulate themselves in front of us.

Suddenly Suk's spell broke and he lurched up, grabbing the tape player and smashing it on the floor. He spoke rapidly in a very high pitched Mandarin to both women and gestured with his arm towards us as he screamed at them. Both old ladies laughed at him, and Suk seemed like he was going to blow until his mother produced the famous stick, and proceeded to beat her son with it, while talking over him. His protests stopped but the beating didn't. She went on and on, before finally getting Mrs Cha to wheel her away.

Nora spoke first, "What the fuck was that? Darlink, a million lives will never eradicate what I've seen here today".

"My, my mother said she thought it was very funny. She got me back for surprising her on her birthday with the strippers, and she was very angry hearing me sing *Waltzing Matilda*, without proper Asian food here, and she wants to know why there is a Christmas tree, so I know she will beat me again later for disrespect to our culture." He hung his head and I truly felt for him, having to end the day seeing his mother try to milk her dead ninety year old mammaries.

Patrick asked if we should go, and Suk simply nodded sadly.

In the *ute* on the way back to Freedom Farm, light laughter escaped from the occupants, which gradually escalated to mildly hysterical laughter. Nora had tears running down his face,

"*Coño*, I mean it. I want to bleach my eyes, this is going to haunt me when I'm old," he complained, but still he couldn't stop laughing.

"Speaking personally, that was the best friggin' Christmas I've ever had," Nick said as he smiled from ear to ear, "It'll take something to beat that."

I totally and wholeheartedly agreed with him.

GETTING READY

Time seemed to pass rapidly. Life was amazing and Australia
suited me perfectly. You could count on the heat for most of
the year, depending on where you were in the country. When
I'd previously been in *Darwin*, English summertime was their
so-called equivalent to winter, known as the rainy season. I had
loved Darwin, and I'd stayed there over five months. I suggested
to Nick that maybe we could visit after I'd given birth, and told
him about the expansive country and how long it would take
to get there. Nick had embraced Australia like an old friend,
and wanted to explore more of it. Strangely enough Nora had
kept in contact with Brian, whom he'd shagged on the plane.
This was because when we were first in Sydney he'd seen a TV
commercial for a cooking program called *Brian's Barbecue*. He'd
phoned *Aunt Fanny*, alias Brian, and kept an ongoing rapport.
Patrick asked him how he knew the Australian acclaimed top
cook, and admirably, Nora told him the truth. Patrick was just
"*Stoked* that Nora *rooted* the right person."

I was heavily pregnant, with just over five weeks to go, and my healthy lifestyle was keeping me glowing. We were still living on the farm, and I had obtained my visa just before Christmas. I was able to get one for three months, and it could continue as long as there was enough money in the bank. We did however omit to reveal the fact I was pregnant, not thinking it could be a problem, and besides, until then I hadn't been showing. Nick was fine because his year's working holiday visa was still valid. He had made very good money from the royalties from *Desire* thanks to *Frankie Bubbles*, and his stripping, which he was still doing regularly, brought in plenty more. Nora had secured a three month visa, but it had definitely been more difficult for him to obtain.

Christmas had clearly been one of the best ever. Nora and Patrick were totally in Love. Whether Nora wanted that or not, he couldn't control his feelings, and said he was determined to tell his parents eventually, knowing how important it was to Patrick not to live a lie. None of us could have known just how quickly he would have to reveal himself.

As my stomach got bigger the love grew equally in Freedom ranch. Matilda helped me so much. We'd become good friends, and as she finally began to tell me her back-story I realised we'd only been scratching the surface. Her parents had died tragically in a car crash, and she had met Patrick shortly after that. He, and the horses, had saved her. She was also totally in Love with Patrick, albeit platonic, and even though she understood there could never be anything between them, she would rather be near him than anyone else.

Myself and Nick got to see Suk Chu often, but we preferred not to run into Mrs Chu, who seemed hideous to us. When she saw me she always said: "You fat, big old woman. You will not lose that huge belly. I can cut off the fat and cook with it!" Then she would laugh, opening her mouth so we could view her peasant-like stumps.

"Look, you waddle like big ugly duckling. He will leave you after, for a nice slim swan."

She was always puffing on her opium pipe and blowing it in my face. Suk was always saying "My mother is as delicate as the morning dew. As fragile as a glass slipper." She nevertheless always appeared to me as if she could ingest razor blades. She always carried round her bloody dog, who constantly yapped at me.

Nick's eye had healed slowly. In the end he finally surrendered and went to the doctor. It took its time healing and Nick spent four months wearing a pirate's eye patch and playing a pirate on stage, which only made him even sexier.

We met lots of amazingly fun loving people, who were all either a friend of Chu's or Patrick's. *Francesca*, otherwise known as *Frans the Trans*, was from Perth. Sporting a full beard and moustache, he only ever wore blue or pink checked gingham dresses, together with pearl earrings and open-toed sandals with a low heel. On Sundays he played a type of rugby football called *Aussie Rules*, which is probably one of the most dangerous sports I ever saw. To me it seemed like a misnomer - the complete opposite to its name because there were in fact no rules. Some people say rugby is dangerous, but I'd challenge any rugby player to try a game of Aussie Rules. If you can smash, kick and punch your way to the end of the pitch whilst still holding the ball, wearing a loose fitting pair of short shorts, and a t-shirt with the sleeves cut off so you can't use them to strangle the opposition, then I applaud you. Francesca also could, and did, make some of the best cakes I ever tasted.

Golden Mike, from Darwin, had, you guessed it, gold coloured hair, and he was just the sweetest thing. Always positive and smiling, I loved having him around. Mike's orange freckles sparkled with mischief. His parents, *Dougie* and *Suzie*, were sensational, often getting the bus down to visit him. They utterly supported him when it came to being gay, in fact they took a keen interest, to the point of match-making: "Ooh, he's a nice boy, what about him?"

Scott, who was Chinese, was a very good friend of Suk's. Sexy as hell, he nearly always wore cream or red clothes with small round sunglasses. His body was tuned to perfection, and he really was one of Sydney's best *Kung Fu* masters. He could snap a brick in half with one eyelash. Ironically, he was never without a cigarette. Scott's parents lived in China, whilst he resided in Sydney, with another place in *Cairns*, which is near Darwin and just as tropical. He wasn't a gambler, but he'd made his millions when he was only sixteen, inventing a new app for phones that had gone viral in a good way.

Sammy was a constant moaner. Extremely overweight and always bright red in the face, he also nurtured what always looked like a nine months pregnant stomach. I never saw him when he wasn't stoned or eating. He was an utter bitch, but unbelievably generous. He was from *Townsville*, and he was always bemoaning that: "There's a town that'd make anyone gay."

Troy was my absolute favourite. He also worked as a stripper and ran his own dance company. He was very attractive, although with the perfect amount of confidence to match. He dressed sharply and was always clean shaven, not to mention interesting, clever and funny. This was the kind of guy that you would beg your boyfriend to please try it with just once, just to get that second hand sexual energy from him. I had mentioned it to Nick, maybe once, or a thousand times. His responses made me laugh:

"Lucy, please. One new thing at a time," he said as he stroked my bump.

Of course, we saw Troy the least. Although he lived in Sydney, his work and dancing took him all over Australia.

Lydia was a stunning transgender woman with a perfect figure, who made me feel jealous when I first met her. She had breasts that you wanted to spend a holiday in, and her long champagne hair tickled her bottom below her waist. One day she surprised us when she said she wanted us to see her most striking feature, and we were presented with one of the finest cocks we had ever seen. Nick and I talked about that for a while, both being so naive at that time. Her husband was a hairdresser from L.A. called *Nicky*, who had huge biceps. Nicky was gay, as was

Lydia and it twisted our ridiculously uninformed brains. They were an amazing couple, and created a famous atmosphere around them. Lydia had done some small acting parts, and was considered quite a local celebrity in her own right.

Lastly there was *Charles*, who was Aboriginal. This man did his hair while he slept. You could smell his aftershave 3 streets away. He had fantastic long dark hair, with perfectly tight ringlets that shone in the sun. He was more immaculate than Nora. Nora said to me one day, "Can you imagine his twinkle cave, darlink? Like an empty toothpaste tube." That made me laugh, and of course then I thought about those sparkles escaping from the cleanest hoop in Oz whenever I was with him. He was a stripper as well, although mostly for gay parties. He told us that his own tribe would take him out to the bush and spear him if they knew about his sexuality. Constantly smiling and chewing gum, he loved to drink *Strawberry Daiquiris*.

Despite being a very diverse bunch of people, they were all very good friends who somehow fitted together in their non judgmental world.

I was sitting thinking all this as I surveyed the women sitting round the room. Nick and I were sitting in a stuffy waiting room, waiting for my final check-up. We had arranged a private clinic for the births, but we were having our check-ups on Medicare, which was cheap.

To me it seemed as if the whole world was pregnant. There were four Asian women, two Indonesian and eleven white women who I assumed were Australian. Some had men with them who looked like they were planning their exit from it all. One Australian guy constantly told his wife what she was doing wrong:

"Sheila, you're not sitting properly. Drink more liquid, don't cross your legs, look, you're slouching again." I imagined what a comfort he would be during the birth. 'Sheila, you're not pushing enough. Sheila, the baby's bent funny. Right, that's it. I'm taking over.' *Arsehole...* I thought.

Nick stayed quiet and held my hand. He didn't seem bothered at all, not like in the beginning when he'd been a bundle of gangly raw nerves at every check-up, putting me and the other expectant mothers on edge. He'd sweated, paced, wrought his hands and his breathing had been so shallow and rapid that I'd thought he was having a stroke. Now he was relaxed and ready to be a father, even though he was only twenty-three. In three weeks he was going to turn twenty-four. Internally I was beginning to get slightly nervous. Of course all new parents secretly question if they will be any good at their new role, one that they never receive any training for. I was still painfully aware that two watermelons were going to have to pass through a straw. The larger I got, the worse the stories of childbirth became, and I nearly always heard them here at the check-ups. I sat still and tried not to make eye contact. Luckily everyone was usually engaged with themselves.

A bedraggled white Australian woman sat next to me. She was encased by five children who were all yapping at her and each other.

"Right, you fuckin' *bludgers*. Go to the *chinky* shop, bring me some beers, and make sure you bring me the fuckin' change!" she screamed after them as they ran off. Then she turned her attention to me.

Oh, no...

"Like a pack of bloody hyenas."

I tried to smile in a way that said, 'Please stop talking,' but it didn't work.

"So, this your first?" she asked, flicking thin yellow hair, which luckily matched her teeth, in our direction.

"Yes," Nick answered, and as he smiled at her, I could have smacked his face off.

"And you the father, what a *beaut*, bound to be a right *beaut* in there. I got a pack of mongrels, nine of the little buggers."

I shuddered for her. A true breeder sat before me.

"They're twins," Nick informed her, his voice thick with pride.

I stared at Nick. He seemed unaware that she would have licked out his toilet bowl and drank his bath water if he'd let her.

"Twins, that's a hoot, whooh! Gotta get them buggers out. You'll be able to shout up her *cunny* after, you'll be able to reach inside and pull the next lot out!" she shouted, and cranked up her amusement park laugh a notch. "You would've been fine, normally, with just the one, but now I'd say goodbye to that shiny fresh *cunny* of yours. Still, my first one was, well Sheila, you wouldn't have fuckin' believed..."

My mind tried to zone out. As I have said, I'd already heard a lot of gruesome stories, but now I had a feeling this woman was about to exceed them all.

Her mouth stopped moving and creased into a vague smile, giving me false hope she had stopped. Wrong.

I raised my eyebrows and tried to look sympathetic. "Oh dear."

"Well," she began, as she grabbed my arm and held it tight.

My eyes scanned the room for a toilet. Since I had begun to grow larger, my bladder had done the opposite, shrinking to about the size of a peanut. Even shedding a single tear made it fill up, sending me dashing and waddling to the nearest loo. My one weird craving hadn't helped there, although people said I was lucky to only have one: Kiwi juice. Without it I felt I could easily rip heads off.

There in the corner, I spied the washroom door and caught the last part of her story:

"...Well, by this time my *cunny* was like a train wreck in a tunnel. Then his huge bloody head split me from me arsehole right down to me *cunny*. Seventeen bastard stitches. I had to sit on a special cushion 'cause my cunt was falling out for two whole months. I used to shit myself when I farted 'cause part of my arse had collapsed in on itself."

I glanced sideways at Nick, apparently cheerfully ignoring this old Australian witch. I wondered what it was about my face that indicated I wanted to listen to all this. I retracted my neck back and opened my eyes and mouth in genuine horror.

"We always have a right fuckin' laugh about it, especially the kids. Me old man calls it a *fanarse*. Fuckin' funny as... well, as a fuckin..."

All I could think was; *Please stop...*

"...a tiny bit of skin between me holes, like a Chihuahua's neck," she screeched, and cackled, throwing her head back. "By the time my sixth one had come out, I could sling my tit across a table for them to suck on," she said proudly. Her brood burst through the door at that moment, making a cacophony of noise and stealing her attention.

There is a certain moment when you realise you are truly pregnant. It could be a glance in the mirror, someone offering you a seat on the bus or failing to fit into the biggest sweatpants you ever bought. This was my moment.

Panic readily magnified my fears, and my brain began to regurgitate all those horrible stories, instead of remembering the good. I'd had a couple of nightmares where one twin had come out easily, but the other had been stuck high up and came down in their own time, making me go through two lots of hell. During one nightmare, they came out so quick they shot across the room, smacking the wall and dying. I feared my inability to tolerate any serious pain.

Nick wanted to help, and he'd found an exclusive workshop in the centre of Sydney filled with the most amazing women. The total opposites, in fact, of the woman next to me now.

They'd helped Nick and I quell our fears, empowering us to enjoy, embrace and even love the birth experience. It had become a sacred personal experience. We wanted to be able to have a home birth in a comfortable and nurturing environment, surrounded by Love and support.

Eventually we both decided to book the clinic and go to them for a water birth. It was a culturally aware maternity clinic, sensitive to women's ethnic and cultural needs. Having first been unburdened from the misconceptions about home births, we'd come to embrace the other different styles.

Mercifully, my name was called and we managed to escape from the rabbiting rabbit sat next to me.

As with every previous scan, Nick marvelled and coo-ed at the lives within me. We told the very nice lady who performed it that we didn't want to know the sexes. We only wanted to know they were healthy, and they were. One of my biggest fears early on had been the prospect of *Twin Mialga,* where one of the babies takes more than the other from the mother, leaving one of them very small and weak, and even causing death, as I'd been reminded by a mother with no experience of twins.

The twins looked healthy however, and that made us feel soft, fluffy, excited and thankful all at once. Later on that evening, back at Freedom ranch, we placed the photo of the successful scan on the table and breathed a sigh of relief.

Life for the next four weeks took on an electric air. A surprise party was being organised for Nick's twenty-fourth birthday, and there was the added anticipated arrival of the twins. The level of excitement had risen further with the addition of Brian from *Brian's Barbies*, who was cooking the meal which had to feed sixteen people. Luckily he happened to be there in Sydney that week. Suk Chu's mother had been outraged that she was being replaced as master chef. She predicted food poisoning, and death to most of us. Apparently, we were to expect food that tasted like Merkin's little dog shits. Nevertheless, she was coming to the meal, and we dreaded what she might say.

"My mother loves to have fun, she must be there. She is as fragile as a lotus flower," Suk insisted, defending her.

Organising it all quietly was a challenge because Nick was always very good at sensing if something was going on. His birthday was the sixteenth of May, which that year fell on a Friday. Preparations were in full swing, but luckily the others didn't need my help much, as tiredness often overwhelmed me and I found myself sleeping a lot. Before I realized it was only two days away, and Patrick, Nick, Nora and I were having drinks with Brian, who liked to be called *Aunt Fanny*.

He was very funny and we could all see why he had his own show. In an attempt to fit in with the kitchen at Chu's house he had promised he would be doing Sushi and Tempura as well as other Chinese and Australian dishes like kangaroo steaks with a thick plum sauce. Aunt Fanny was so very Australian.

"Jeez I was *crook*, I'd been on the *grog* and I was in the *dunny* half the night. I felt like a right *hoon*. All sweaty, sitting there like a prize *Galah*."

Nora laughed. "Darlink, I have no idea what you are saying. I overheard a man saying he had 'fucked her in the *dunny*,' and I thought he meant her *culo*; her arse." That sent me, Patrick and Brian into paroxysms of laughter.

"It's a toilet," Patrick said, and smiled, squeezing Nora round the shoulders.

"I prefer my version, *si, es mejor*."

We all got on so well that evening. It was very pleasant, though it was interspersed with fans approaching Brian for autographs.

He coped very well: "Mate, oy mate, you're that bloke ain't yer? Aint yer? With the barbecue, oy, bloody funny mate. That cheese and pineapple pizza bit, bloody hilarious."

"I should probably tell the *bludgers* I'm gay, that would soon stop them, but I'm contractually bound so I can't," Brian confided.

"Brian, Brian, how did you barbecue that *Roo* steak ?"

"Well I stuck it on the fiery flames, and it cooked," Brian revealed as the enthusiastic fan shook his hand vigorously.

"Bloody genius!"

 It seemed Brian was very well known throughout Australia for his *Kangaroo Jerky Turkey Tucker*.

"That bloody *Tucker* has made me a lot of money, not to mention a celebrity. I'm gonna make it..." he paused suddenly. Immediately I knew he had been about to mention Nick's birthday

"...er, round a mate's house," he concluded.

Nicely saved... I thought as he changed colour slightly.

Chu liked Brian purely because he had his own programme and because Chu enjoyed the food of a good chef, a good chef being the complete opposite to his mother, whom Brian had yet to meet. Speaking sadistically, I wanted to be there for that show.

As I returned from my seventh dash to the toilet I could feel the enjoyment radiating from the group, and I felt confident the surprise meal would be one to remember. How right I would turn out to be.

***

Nick and I were staying in a hotel in Sydney. Matilda was at the same hotel but in a different room which was probably a good thing, as my hormones were raging and Lust swam through my veins. At first Nick was superstitious and worried that he would hurt the babies. I responded by saying he would be hurt a lot more if he didn't give in to my demands.

296

Eventually Nick totally succumbed to my desires. I told him the truth about me lusting after Matilda, the Japanese maid who cleaned the room, and the Swedish girl who waited the tables in the hotel. Taking on the mannerisms of a drugged bull, I snorted and sniffed the air, then decided to stay longer in the room. Nick pretended to order the Japanese maid, on room service.

"Well, it is nearly my birthday," he shrugged boyishly. I sensed that I'd possibly get my special room service after all. He thought we were having a quiet, no fuss meal and then back to the hotel.

Patrick and Nora were plotted up in Chu's house, staying in the room reserved for Patrick. That gave them the perfect excuse to decorate the house in preparation.

Brian, a.k.a. Aunt Fanny was residing in a very discreet and exclusive gay hotel.

"While I'm away, Fanny will play," he said, winking a big round eye at us all.

On the morning of the big day, I awoke early, wired with excitement and nerves. I'd bought one gift for him, a white gold necklace made of two snakes intertwined with rubies for eyes. *Perfect...* They seemed to represent our soon to be new souls, our children. I decided to give it to him later, because right then I wanted to give him something else.

I woke him gently and my lust engorged us. Afterwards the twins gave approving kicks as the blood pumped round my healthy body. I'd been doing moderate exercise every day for the last four months and every part of me felt alive. I was enjoying pregnancy so much more than I thought I would, even though my breasts swung heavily, and every material teased and milked them. I was even contemplating old sack cloth in an attempt to eradicate my sexually silky clothes.

I chose a very thick bra, and a loose fitting understated green emerald top with matching baggy trousers. Comfort was steering my choice at this point.

Nick, of course, looked sensational. A short-sleeved powder-blue cotton shirt clung to his perfect body, happily sinking into the contours of his muscles. Cream shorts ended just above his knees, complimenting his tan. The blue shirt brought out his eyes.

I will feast on him forever...

The plot had been planned for mid-afternoon at two-thirty, so we'd be able to go outside in that beautiful garden in Surrey Hills. The weather was predicted to be slightly cloudy as the summer was coming to an end. A mild breeze elbowed its way in and the air felt damp. Nora began to moan about it. His new afro style didn't agree with the climate and he was complaining.

"Darlink, my afro is getting so big that other gay men are hiding in it." I tried to reassure him that it wasn't that big.

The three of us jumped in a cab outside the hotel. Matilda looked naturally pretty in a flowery dress and an old fashioned crocheted pink shawl. Her aura of happiness felt genuine, the best gift she could have brought. Nick told us he was pleased he was having a low key birthday as Matilda and I tried not to reveal anything about the surprise.

We both knocked on Suk Chu's door and Patrick opened it. From that moment, nothing seemed the same again.

QUEER BIRTHDAY

The three of us stepped into a different world. A forest had appeared, consisting of untold different trees, bushes and plants. There appeared to be a real living vine trailing up the walls.

Between the three of us we were unable to speak a word. Chinese lanterns hung everywhere and real birds flew around. Patrick put his finger to his lips to signify hush, but we were all already speechless. We navigated our way through the forest and stepped into a central clearing, where we found a beautiful, massive hand-carved oak table. Above it hung a pale green silk shade, protecting the table, I imagined from the bird shit.

A chorus of voices shouted "Happy Birthday!" and Nick stood stock still. Aunt Fanny stood at an indoor barbecue, creating delicious smells. Suk walked towards Nick with open arms, while behind at the table I spied Mrs Chu and a friend. Nora stood, and as he came towards us he managed to take a barrage of photos.

Suk hugged Nick and slapped his back. Pushing him back roughly, he beamed proudly. "I bring the outside, inside. I don't like it too cold, and just imagine my mother going out into that weather. She's as frail as a new born baby, so that could not happen."

Nora was wearing green as well: A dark emerald suit with a pale pink shirt underneath. "Darlinks, let me finish my tweet, hashtag *#SurpriseBirthday* *#IWantSexWithHim* - Joke, joke!" A real happiness encompassed him and made him appear utterly sensational. His amber eyes shone wickedly. He hugged first me, then Nick, who slyly edged a glance at me.

As we approached the table people stood and introductions were made. At each end of the table were three chairs. At the far end were Scott, Suk, and Mrs Chu, with her friend Mrs Cha next to her on one side of the table. Next to Mrs Cha sat the stunning Lydia, with Nicky, her husband. Next to him was Charles, and next to him was Sammy. The three chairs on the nearest end were for Aunt Fanny in the middle, with Golden Mike and Frans the Trans either side. The other side sat Nora first, next to Patrick, then Troy who was next to Nick, with me last. I was next to Scott, and opposite Mrs Chu and her friend, Mrs Cha, who whispered and giggled like wise old hags on crack. Scott stood and hugged us both warmly. He was wearing a cream suit and black shirt, still with the obligatory round shades. He made my hair stand on end, even the way he flicked his cigarette seemed sexual. Troy sat next to Nick wearing a pair of orange fur chaps and a *thong* (g-string). A dog collar was round his neck and he held the lead in his hand. A very tight and almost transparent top in a burnt red was so tight it looked like a second skin. His smile was tantalising and almost immediately I began fantasizing about him and Nick, without listening to the rest of the introductions.

Mrs Chu wheeled herself off to the kitchen complaining loudly and bumping into everything along the way. A sensation of being pinched abruptly took me away from my sexual fantasies. Nick was trying to get my attention.

"No, I really had no idea, honest," I lied transparently to his beautiful face that was tinged red with mild embarrassment.

Nicky was pouring wine out for everyone. "It has been hard keeping it a secret, and managing to get us all together. I was meant to be in L.A. doing a cover, but it's cancelled. Meant to be." I covered my glass with my hand and he seemed uncomfortable.

"Don't worry, everyone forgets," I reassured him, pointing at my bump, which began to move as I shifted in my seat.

Glasses were raised, and Patrick proposed a toast. "I haven't known him long, he's also a *Pom*, he's straight, disgustingly attractive, and who couldn't love him? To a lifelong friendship: Happy Birthday, Nick!"

Everyone raised their glasses and cheered. African dance music played softly in the background whilst petite Chinese and Korean women dressed as Peter Pan and Tinkerbelle brought dishes to the table. Aunt Fanny's gastronomic creations sizzled away at the barbecue, and I could hear Mrs Chu barking orders. A stick thrashed its way out of a tree and she shouted at her friend as she wheeled towards her. Scott tried not to laugh too loudly.

"Please, could you translate?" I asked in my politest voice.

"Of course," Scott answered and leaned towards me, thankfully whispering, as I didn't want a lecture about my abysmal language skills. "Mrs Chu cannot find her bathroom, so she has had to shit at the bottom of the tree. Suk has gone mad, but she said that since the birds were shitting everywhere, she did too." He grinned and lit a cigarette.

I smiled, that *was* funny. Lydia came up to Nick and kissed him fully on the lips. She looked sensational in a tight red dress tailored to the floor with a plunging neckline. Her long champagne hair snaked down and nestled between the best breasts ever. She handed Nick a bottle. It was a cut glass decanter, containing a very rare cognac. Mrs Chu was still rattling on to Mrs Cha.

301

The dishes all looked spectacular, and very different.

"Mumma," Suk moaned, hugging her as well as you could hug a sack of bones, but she carried on complaining, even when released.

He laughed, and kissed her fully on the lips, making sucking sounds as he did so. "So delicate," he cried. "My mother complains about Brian's cooking, but I say it's traditional."

"Traditional like dog shit!" Mrs Chu shouted. "Like a kangaroo did a shit, and he cooked it. What does it taste like then? Like shit!" she concluded, lighting her opium pipe in disgust.

Sammy shouted down from the other end of the table. "I hope you're wrong, Mrs Chu. Who wants to eat dog shit?" He drank down a huge mouthful of wine.

"I think that's enough about shit, thanks," Patrick called out, calming us all. Nora and Matilda both gazed at him with pure Love. Golden Mike and Frans were with Aunt Fanny at the barbecue.

The babies started to kick inside me again. Hoping to settle them down, I stood up to mingle. The spread was amazing. The table was packed with fresh rice, salads, spring rolls, cooked meats, steak and *sushi*, which I knew was best to avoid in my condition. I sipped my orange juice and felt the good vibes in the room.

Nora hugged me, "So darlink, what do you think?" He splayed his arms wide.

"It's amazing. Utterly surreal. How on earth did you manage it all?"

"Well darlink, all it took was lots and lots of money," he answered and we both started laughing.

At that very moment Mrs Chu struck her gong. "Sit down!" she barked at everyone, who unwittingly and automatically followed her command. Frans, who had chosen his blue check dress to wear that day, was the last one to sit down. The lanterns lit up, and stars shone out from a fake night sky complete with a full moon, which only made everything more surreal. The gong struck again. "Eat!" Mrs Chu commanded. While everyone ate enthusiastically I gave Nick his present.

He clearly loved it, and as he put it on I could see that it suited him. He hugged me and whispered in my ear. "I wasn't sure about all this at first, but it's actually pretty great. To think of the trouble you've all gone to." He kissed me passionately on the lips, which caused Mrs Chu and her friend to cackle amongst themselves. Scott gave Nick tickets for a weekend cruise with a guest around Easter Island, and Nick was clearly embarrassed by the scale of his generosity. Chu had made a bet on his behalf, and he'd had some luck and won two thousand dollars, which he presented, tucked inside an alligator wallet with the winning receipt. Nick ran his hand through his hair and stuttered.

Suk flapped his hands in front of him. "It's nothing, no really, nothing. Just for luck."

Wayne and Frans presented their gift jointly - a half day at a spa in Sydney, with a massage. I was beginning to wish I'd had my birthday there.

Gently, Chinese music began to play, in a hypnotic style I'd never heard before. Spookily, the rhythm matched the trees' eerie sway.

Nora and Patrick presented Nick with a beautiful horse's saddle. I could see that all this attention and love was overwhelming him somewhat.

My womb distracted me slightly with a sudden movement again. I ignored it. The afternoon was rapidly turning into night and everyone was having a great time, enjoying the sensational food. As the charmed atmosphere grew, so did my discomfort.

No matter how I stood or sat, it didn't help. For once, unbelievably, I was in agreement with Mrs Chu about not being able to find the bloody toilet. I tried asking one of the Peter Pans for help but I got lost every time. Nick was becoming a little drunk, but he was still very endearing. I didn't want to mention anything.

Mrs Chu even seemed almost content as she puffed on her long slender drug pipe and chatted with her friend. In front of her lay an almost empty plate.

Aunt Fanny was casually clearing away, and as he lifted up her plate he said: "So, Mrs Chu. You must really love dog shit, you've eaten the whole plate." He scoffed, pulled a face, and nearly all of us froze. Lydia and Nicky, who were slow dancing, came almost to a complete stop.

Suk's hands automatically went flat as he switched into Kung Fu mode. Mrs Cha did the whole E.T. thing, retracting her neck, and flattening her face into itself, as if the face had left the room, but the body was still there. Then an opening appeared in her tiny, lined face, and emitted a screeching sound. This did not help to determine Mrs Chu's reaction as she banged her wheelchair and garbled at Mrs Cha. Her friend pushed her neck back out and began to nod.

"It's okay, she said it's very funny. Apparently, the big fat man is funny," Scott told us, grinning. Both ladies by this time were alternately nodding and laughing.

Chu slapped Brian's back. "Thank god my mother is happy, for one second I thought I'd have to get my *Triad* friends here." He laughed, slapping him again.

Even though Aunt Fanny was a hulk of a man, you could see he was visibly nervous.

Suk laughed. "I joke. I joke, funny, I joke," he protested, waving his hands. Clearly it was one of those half-jokes where you don't know if it's a joke or if they are absolutely serious. He returned to his seat next to Scott, just as at that very same second, a pain shot through me and caused me to blanche.

Nick was dancing with Troy.

Suk noticed my discomfort. "What's wrong?" he asked, sounding genuinely concerned.

It eased off as quickly as it came. I pointed to the origin of my pain. "Near my ovaries. Don't worry, it's gone."

"You are getting *ovary* excited," he cried, and screamed at his wit as he clutched Scott's arm.

I smiled weakly.

"You get it, yes, ovary excited," he repeated, throwing back his round head and cackling to himself.

Oh dear, Nora has retired from being a hysterical queen and he's been replaced by a maniacal gambling triad. The phrase - 'better the devil you know' springs to mind...

He got up from the table to recant the joke to everyone. "Ovary excited. I know, so funny."

The hilarity filtered through to Nick, and he rushed over to me, concerned. I wanted his face to remain perfect, and unmarred by worry.

"Lucy, are you alright?" he asked, and his breath was heavy with anxiety.

I placed my hand on his cheek to reassure him. "Yes. Just a couple of twinges, nothing to worry about, really," I wanted him to continue with his special day. "Go on, run and play. I'm fine here." I smiled my best *'I'm fine'* smile for appearances sake.

Scott stayed sitting next to me, but was busy chatting and flirting with Charles. Everyone else was up and dancing to *I'm a Barbie Girl*. Only Mrs Chu stayed in her seat at the end of the table, watching Mrs Cha move her stuff, and wow, could she ever! As she performed a high kick and caused people to rush forward she laughed like a devil. Mrs Chu clapped supportively for her elastic little friend, while Merkin yapped pathetically from her lap. Frans was trying to climb a tree, and Aunt Fanny was trying to chase him.

This is definitely not an everyday birthday, hopefully it's one he won't forget... How could I have known my thoughts were to prove so poignant?

At first I didn't even realise there was a puddle of water, except my bottom and legs begin to feel cold.

It was Charles who jumped up and flicked his lush hair back with surprise. "What the fuck is that?" he asked, his face contorted with disgust. "I've never seen so much piss."

Scott jack-knifed out of his chair and propelled himself away from me. I wanted to defend myself, but a deep, deep pain, racked my body and rendered me speechless. Mrs Chu stopped puffing and started screeching.

"Oh, she's dirty. She gonna piss everywhere, like a big fat horse. Ah, look she pissing so much!"

It was happening. *O.M.G., it's actually happening. One week early, right now, in this bed of madness...*

"I'm, I'm..." I tried unsuccessfully to speak as the pain wrenched through me. I could still hear the music playing; it was *Enough is Enough* by *Barbara Streisand* and *Donna Summer*, ironically enough. I gripped the arms of the chair and tried to lift myself up, holding onto the edge of the table.

Nick had obviously seen me. "What's wrong, Lucy?"

More pain. I screamed loudly. "Bastard!"

"Me? Oh no…"

"Water's broke... Babies coming," I managed to say, though my breathing was becoming deep and hard. My whole being wanted to push, needed to.

Marilyn and Rochelle had told me at the antenatal classes that if the contractions are close, so are the babies. I leant against the table and threw my head back, screaming profanities. "Donkey bastard, whore face, shit breath, wanker!"

Nick reacted by going to pieces. All the groovy training in the world had not prepared him for this eventuality.

Mrs Chu finally realised what was happening. "She having babies on table. Suk!" she shouted loudly.

He came running over to me, and a ripple of realisation went round the room as everyone became aware of what was happening.

I started to push regularly. I could feel a baby's head trying anxiously to get out. Nick wasn't the only one, I wasn't prepared either. It was happening way too fast. *Is this normal?...* I felt a terrible sadness that they were coming into existence. I had loved being pregnant, more than I could have ever imagined, and now it was all to end so quickly, so abruptly. I began to cry, which only made things far worse for Nick.

He squeezed my hand, tightly. "Oh my god, oh my god, what do I do? I can't remember. What do I do?"

I pushed again, and as a tiny head started to emerge, the circus began. Sammy began to scream, before fleeing up a tree and bending the branch over with his weight until it almost touched the ground. He carried on screaming.

"Now? They can't fucking come now! Not now..."

Charles began to vomit into a passing tumbleweed, while Golden Mike crossed his arms in front of his face in an effort to prevent this reality. Frans clung fiercely to Golden Mike, wringing the shirt he was wearing. His fear of the antichrist was coming true.

Nora was fussing futilely around myself and Nick, constantly yapping in Cuban. *"Por favor, Dios, escúchame. Está niños que bien, no molestas, por favor!* Darlink, you're not even shaved, isn't that a health hazard?"* he reprimanded me disgustedly.

I heard a clicking. "Nora! If I find out you are tweeting the length of my pubic hair whilst..." Indescribable pain roared through me. People were speaking but I couldn't comprehend any words. "I really don't think that my big bush is a complication," I heard myself say.

PAIN... "Drugs! Give me some fucking drugs!" I spurted out between gasps.

Lydia and Nicky shouted out: "Hot towels, water," and "*Dom Perignon*, wash her down"

One of the Peter Pans was attempting to make me more comfortable with some cushions.

I carried on pushing and heard a voice of calm, a steady hand on my stomach.

"The head's out and your contractions are very close. Remember your classes, and your breathing."

That was Patrick, guiding me.

"Ring Marilyn, Nick," I shouted, as I tried to remember her advice. The twins were coming whether I wanted them to or not.

Patrick's calm words helped me to control my breathing. "On the next contraction, Lauren, really push."

I was there almost immediately. As I began to push hard, I knew the first baby was already out.

Sammy climbed even further up the tree in order to indulge in some hugely deep, bowel-moving retching. Sat right next to my face was Aunt Fanny, who Troy, in turn, was fanning with a napkin.

"I can't bloody take this. Fuckin' great vagina opening up and spitting children at me. Worse than any steak I've ever seen," Aunt Fanny moaned.

I heard a smacking sound.

"Oh no, baby not breathing. It's dead," remarked Mrs Chu, casually.

There was more smacking.

"Yep, baby dead."

"Mrs Chu, please!" Patrick scolded, and just as I considered strangling her with the umbilical cord from my first child, a piercing cry rang out. Patrick handed me HER! It was a girl, complete with healthy, shouting lungs. Nick was crying and chanting: "A girl, a girl, a girl…"

Another big twinge yanked me back into the moment.

"Number two's on their way," Patrick's calm voice said, and I could hear more vomiting in the distance.

"*Strewth*, I can't take another one," Aunt Fanny implored me, as if it was him that was giving birth.

Nick cut the cord, and Patrick took over. Tinkerbelle handed him hot towels whilst Lydia and Nicky stared at me like it was a new entertainment show. Golden Mike had gone behind a tree to be sick, and Chu was shouting at Scott in Chinese. Everyone seemed to be comforting someone. Nora was still chanting, screaming and irrationally taking photos, tweeting the bizarre events live as *Brown Girl in the Ring by Boney M*, played.

I desperately tried to find my safe space, my happy place, where I would get some peace. I tried to imagine every musical I'd ever seen. Instead I had a feeling as if I was running with the forest all around me, being chased by Jack Nicholson, as he was in *The Shining*. My breathing sure sounded that way.

"Push!" shouted Patrick, above the bedlam.

I pushed. "Shit on your dog!" lurched out of my mouth. This being in labour was making me hurl the strangest insults. I pushed again.

"Yes, it's the head," I heard in quadraphonic sound from at least four people. Nick was holding our first-born daughter who was crying constantly.

"Oh no, look! Baby blue, baby dead. Dead long time."

"Mrs Chu!" Patrick reprimanded her. I heard more slapping, and then a new voice crying, although not as loudly as the other.

I must remind people how fantastic Mrs Chu's midwifery skills are...

Patrick placed the infant on my stomach. "Another girl," he said, and his voice cracked with emotion.

Nick came close to me and I saw tears of joy rocketing down his cheeks. "Daughters, we have daughters."

"We do," I agreed, smiling.

There were some short, loud, screeching sounds next to us. "It's guts, fuckin' *strewth*, her guts are hanging out," Aunt Fanny cried, almost hysterical.

Troy and Wayne, who had only just returned, clamped a hand over their mouths, while Sammy vomited right next to me.

"People, please. Get a grip, it's the afterbirth and the umbilical cord," Patrick implored.

"What? An umbrella cord? What? It's disgusting," Charles commented, waving a bottle of aftershave under his nose. "I've never even seen a woman's vagina, and don't forget, this is in real time. It's way too much for me." He took a deep sniff from his bottle of scent.

Patrick cut the cord to a chorus of *"Urrrgghh,"* that echoed throughout, just as I spied Marilyn, the midwife from the International Birthing Centre weaving her way through the trees towards us. She looked like an apparition. An angel gliding through a river of shit.

She took complete control of the situation.

"Dear God, you just gave birth in all this?" she asked disbelievingly, as she opened her arms. Everyone wanted to fuss round me, but Marilyn wanted to take us somewhere more appropriate to wash the new girls, and make sure I was alright. Nora was telling everyone what a hero Patrick was, and I had to agree. I thanked him while he helped us to a room with an en-suite bathroom.

"At least you seem to know what you're doing," Marilyn commented.

"I grew up on a farm, so I've delivered hundreds of animals."

Thank god he didn't have to put his whole arm up there...

Finally in a calmer atmosphere, I became emotional, binding with my girls unexpectedly, and even the thought of that was so strange it made me cry. They were so beautiful. Both had almost-white downy hair and big blue eyes, but one of them had tiny flecks of green in the blue.

I washed myself along with the girls in a shallow bath. The tranquil space was a sharp contrast to the hysteria we had just left. Marilyn told me that all of us were healthy and well. She weighed the girls on the bathroom scales, though I could already see that both of them were quite small for new-borns. One weighed six pounds eight ounces, and the other seven pounds two ounces. Their tiny hands curled around my finger.

"How can we Love them so strongly, we've only just met them?" Nick wondered as he crooned.

I was amazed at how easy the births had been. I was feeling a little sore and tired, but otherwise I felt elated, alive and connected with Mother earth. Once we were all clean I lay on the bed and both girls instantly attached themselves in order to suckle, one on each breast.

311

"Well, this is definitely one job I can't ask you to do," I said to Nick.

"I would if I could," he replied. "A family, my own family for my birthday. I am truly fucking spun out. I'm so sorry I went to pieces. I thought I'd be good in the situation we planned, but nothing could have really prepared me for *that*."

"In truth, it was kind of nice to see you acting like us lesser mortals, and not *Mr Perfect*, unlike our two beautiful perfect daughters," I assured him, beaming.

Marilyn came back in the room. She had been invaluable, turning up at just the right moment, and taking over just at the point where Patrick would have gone into uncharted territory. She reassured me that even though the twins were a week premature, all was well and as it should be.

"So, the party seems to be continuing, and you've got many well wishers wanting to visit, apart from that ghastly woman in the wheelchair," Marilyn said, with a practised midwife' smile. "Don't worry."

"I don't mind but I can't handle visitors just yet while I'm feeding the girls, and I think we should think about names first. I know I've got some idea, what about you?" I asked, rubbing Nick's arm as he sat on the edge of the bed.

"What about *Tabitha*? I've always loved that name, and I know you like it."

"Tabitha it is then, and yes I do. I was thinking of a Spanish name..." I let it hang in the air.

Nick raised his eyebrows. "*Noelia*?" he guessed, and smiled.

"Noel, Nora, Noelia. Okay, I love it too. So is it meant to be that easy to choose the names of your children? They're stuck with them for life."

"For us, apparently yes. So say hello to Tabitha and Noelia, our beautiful daughters." Nick confirmed, his voice thick with pride.

Tabitha had the green flecks in her eyes, and was four minutes older than her sister. We couldn't stop staring at them. After a while, Nick went downstairs to let people know they could visit. I'd asked him to ask Nora and Patrick to visit us last so we could talk properly. I was excited and looking forward to sharing our choice of name with Nora.

While he was down there, Nick let Marilyn out, and she promised him she'd call again late morning the next day.

The first sensation of breastfeeding was actually not as unpleasant as I feared it would be. Tabitha and Noelia fell asleep, tired after their first meal. I loved my huge new breasts, they were so sensitive, and I was only hoping they'd remain that way for a while without the life being chewed out of them.

How different my life has turned out...

Previously, I would have slapped someone if they had told me how hopelessly in love I would be with my babies. Maybe I would have even spat in their face. Now, those things I had despised and even mocked, now seemed intrinsic to my life. Nick and I had somehow created these stunning beings. My clumsiness had almost completely abated, and I was surrounded by such different and wonderful people that I could never have imagined in my life. Nick was right, I did want that rollercoaster, that explosion of senses that opened my eyes to different worlds, full of people with differences that I wanted to embrace wholeheartedly. The girls had come early, but the colourful world they were brought into was a perfect place to start with.

Our first visitors, who knocked on the door giggling like choir girls, were Aunt Fanny, Golden Mike and Sammy. They each took turns hugging me, kissing me and cooing over the girls.

"Well, thank fuck that's over," Aunt Fanny said. "We," he hiccupped, "have gifts." He held up a very rare steak.

I waited to find out what was happening with it.

"It's a steak for your *cunny*. Thought it might be a bit bruised and raw down there. Just place it over the, er, affected area."

"Well, mm, thank you. It's not quite that bad though, I had babies, not a car crash."

"Ooh, I don't know about that. I reckon it was more like a train crash," Sammy offered, swaying as he spoke.

"Yeah, mate. A very slow-motion bloody train crash." Golden Mike agreed. He still looked more like Green Mike, visibly shaken by the experience.

Nick joined us, and grinned when he heard how the steak was to be used. Mike and Sammy had brought a bottle of red wine, which they had mostly drunk. They left quickly and we waited for the next visitors.

"Nora's not very pleased that he's last, but I didn't want to say why. Just be warned, he's pissed," Nick managed to say before we were joined by Frans, Troy, and Charles. Naturally, they were all drunk. They had constructed two little birds-nest looking items, which turned out to be little crowns for the girls. I was beginning to feel like *Mary*, I mean, where was my frankincense and myrrh? As the three of them left hurriedly, we heard Charlie say: "I'm never going into one of them."

Then Scott, Suk, Lydia and Nicky all came in.

They all genuinely seemed interested in the girls. Both Nick and I refused to divulge their names.

Scott gave them each a casino chip. "I don't know what I'm supposed to give, but these black chips are worth three thousand each. You can decide what to do with them."

Nick tried to refuse, but Scott wouldn't have it.

314

Suk gave me a mobile phone and a number on a card. "You call this number, and get whatever you need; double buggies, car, whatever."

Lydia signed a napkin with a kiss, and Nicky wrote out an I.O.U. for his salon in L.A., to be used when the girls were older.

No sooner than they'd gone, an angry looking Nora burst open the doors of the bedroom and came in, with Patrick just behind him.

"Darlink, I am very upset. We must wait the longest? Patrick is a hero, without him your children could be dead," he paused for dramatic effect. "*Y mi*," he sniffed the air. "Your best friend."

"I'm sorry Nora. We wanted you to come in last because we wanted to talk to you. Yes, I do want to thank you Patrick, for being so frickin amazing, and we wanted to tell you both what the girl's names are before we told anyone else, because we also decided that you two should be the Goddess-parents."

Nick pointed to the baby on the right. "Meet Tabitha," he said, smiling down at her. Then he introduced the baby on the left. "And this is Noelia."

Nora suppressed a scream as he fell onto Patrick. Then of course he rushed over to meet his namesake. "Patrick, darlink. Look at her, she is perfect."

I coughed, "Don't forget Tabitha as well."

Patrick came over. "They really are both very sweet."

I beckoned him close to me and kissed him on the cheek. "Thank you ."

Nick shook his hand. "I'm sorry I went to pieces mate, thanks so much for being calm and helping so much."

Patrick blushed while Nora hummed and fussed round Noelia.

I felt very tired and began to fall asleep. Nick took care of the girls while I slept through the night.

***

I was awoken by the sound of crying. *What is that? Oh yes, they're mine, I mean our girls...*

Nick lay beside me holding one of them, although I was still having trouble telling the difference between them. I only knew our babies needed feeding, and that these little lives depended on us from now on. Beside me lay Noelia, I realised when I saw her eyes up close. I released my built-in feeding tools, and definitely enjoyed the experience of quieting their cries.

Marilyn called round to check up on all of us and apparently we were all doing well. I did feel sore, but it was nothing compared to what I had imagined over the last few months. We told Marilyn we intended to go back to the farm that day, and she reassured us that we should be fine. She let us know when I needed to go for a check up, and reminded us that we had to register the births, for their birth certificates. I explained to her that I had extended my Visa twice without mentioning the pregnancy.

Marilyn explained there would definitely be some consequence for that, but the girls were born there in Australia, and had to be registered.

She helped us fill out the details on the necessary forms, but we just wanted to go home.

Funny, we're already thinking of Freedom Ranch as home. I hope myself and Nick won't be sent to prison for the secret births of Tabitha and Noelia...

Later that day we were finally home. Matilda greeted us warmly; she'd decided at the last minute to stay at the ranch, as one of her favourite horses was sick.

She fussed over the baby girls, and had already set up a beautiful double crib, a gift from Suk Chu.

Over the next few days we allowed ourselves to bond with the girls. We surrounded them with calmness, and wrapped them in total Love. I could have watched them all day, I was that mesmerized by their breathing alone.

Nick was affected even worse. "Who would have thought that they began as sticky white goo?"

"Baby goo," I said, and giggled.

"Baby goo, baby goo, pretty pretty pretty pretty baby goo, my baby, my baby goo-ooh-ooh. We-ll I love my girls because they came from my baby goo, ooh, oo-oo-ooh," he sang, Buddy Holly style.

That really made me laugh.

We had talked about what we would do at this point. We had both agreed not to tell our families yet, and to stay there in Australia if we could, where we felt truly loved. We considered the girls Australian now. We wanted them to experience a different world, hopefully one without fear and prejudice. However that depended on the Australian immigration board.

For now our family was contained in Freedom Ranch. We bought some stuff on Suk's card, and though we tried not to go mad, we actually did. Patrick cashed the chips that were gifted from Scott while he was in Sydney. We asked Scott if we could give Nick's birthday present - the cruise, to Patrick and Nora. We wanted to be in our immediate family unit for a while. Scott told us that we were to have '*No worries,*' there.

Our bank balance looked extremely healthy. Tabitha and Noelia got fussed over by all the occupants of the house. Nora began to float about in silk caftans, quoting Jamaican poetry. In an effort to compete with Suk Chu, he also ordered his own gifts. First, two gold Moses baskets were delivered, personally commissioned by Nora from *Gaultier*, each one beautifully inscribed with the girl's names. Then came two tiny diamond bracelets with matching tiaras. At that point we forbade them both from giving us any more gifts. We definitely didn't wish to bring the twins up to be spoiled and privileged.

Nora had been as transformed as me by Love. He'd taken down his queenliness a notch or two, and was discovering the roots that he'd always pushed to one side. He genuinely seemed more concerned with other people's problems. Nora and Patrick started to go out on romantic rides together, and they both ordered special papooses for babies so they could walk them round the farm. Nora always insisted he carried Noelia, and I wondered what I'd done to him.

Matilda was totally enraptured by the twins as well, but mostly we wanted to have them near Nick and I, so we could inhale their pure essence. Patrick had reassured Nick that the stripping would still be there for him. Nick wanted to return to work soon, but first he wanted to spend time with us.

For a whole month, we stayed on the farm, only driving to town once to register the girl's births, and of course, their names. I'd told Nick they could use his surname, making them Tabitha and Noelia Palmer. Nick clearly suited fatherhood, it caused him to radiate competence and undisguised happiness.

For two glorious days we had Freedom ranch to ourselves. Patrick and Nora had gone on the weekend cruise around *Fraser Island*. They'd both been very excited about it. Patrick was happy to leave us here in charge, and Matilda stayed down at the stables just the way she wanted.

I never felt as contented in my life as I was then. Friends called and complained on the phone, they wanted to know why they couldn't come and visit, or demanded to know where Nick was. I remained cocooned in a state of perfection.

At the end of the month, Nick, who'd been scheming with Lydia and Frans, threw me a surprise baby shower. Surprisingly, it was amazing fun.

They all came to Freedom Ranch, where Nick, Nora and Patrick had decorated one of the rooms with pink from top to bottom.

318

There were pink balloons, pink teddies, pink sweets, pink drinks, pink blankets, pink clothes, and pink stuffed toys.

All Lydia's friends were post op, or pre op, or somewhere in-between. As she swigged champagne, Lydia pulled out syringes of Botox, and swayed as she liberally injected them into her friends faces, one syringe after another. Stunning women began to swell up in front of me. Their lips took on a caricature-like hugeness and their cheeks puffed up into giant bruises. Lydia lunged at my face waving the needle about like a loaded gun. I politely but firmly declined. One of the women told me she'd just had her vagina made in London, and her boobs in San Francisco. She offered me a viewing; however, I politely declined again. It was a very unconventional night, but I felt Loved and cared for as a family. The girls were lavished with gifts while being constantly passed around like a bong full of the most fantastic herb. They all made me feel special and they made it a memorable night, with lots of laughs.

As we went into the second month of maternity, our lawyer was working hard on trying to obtain visas for us to stay in Australia. Worryingly, the fact that the girls had been born there did not grant us any special dispensation to stay. Nora wanted to stay as well, and again, he was paying for everything. Apparently not concerned that his father might fly over and castrate him, he said; "Darlink, don't worry I won't see him for *mucho tiempo, no te preocupes,*" he remarked, flamboyantly casual about it all.

I did grab a quick peek at my emails, and what I read totally stunned first me, then Nick, when I told him. Sergeant Laurence Cole had married Jenny, on the sixteenth of May. I was too stunned to reply to Lawrence's mail immediately.

"It's unbelievable how inexplicably we are linked. I have no idea why," Nick commented, shaking his head.

Of all the dates they could have chosen, they'd chosen that one. They had somehow tuned in to us from across the other side of the world. So now the sixteenth of May was their anniversary, Nick's birthday, and Tabitha's and Noelia's birthday.

I had a quick glimpse at a photo in which Jenny and Lawrence were beaming with happiness. Strange, but I didn't think I would see them for a very long time. How wrong can you be? Things can certainly change so abruptly.

NEXT STOP KANSAS

Money apparently does talk. The Australian immigration service decided we could have a three month visa, which had to be renewed again every three months, to prove we still had money, and so we could also prove we had a place to stay. Tabitha and Noelia were automatically Australian citizens, as they'd been born there. The lawyer had negotiated a fine that we had to pay for concealing the fact that I had been pregnant. It was a pretty big fine, though once again Nora took the brunt and paid it. Nick promised he would pay it back very soon.

We were so happy that we were able to stay. We were gladly entrenched into our colourful, and some might say controversial, lifestyle and social circles. Deliriously happy, both of us wanted to hide here forever with our new secret family, on the other side of the world.

It became clear that Nora had decided to be truthful to his parents. Patrick agreed with him that it would be better to tell them face to face, and naturally he would totally support him. They began to arrange a trip to Cuba, while myself, Nick and the girls stayed with Matilda at the ranch.

I was so proud of him. Love had sculpted Nora into something new because Patrick fulfilled him and nurtured his soul. Nora was in a place that he'd wanted to be in for so long, and that was where he could be himself. Just being Nora. He was riding, reading and writing poetry. He was seeking knowledge, and absorbing aboriginal writings. He started talking to Charles about his culture and history and asked lots of questions about the meaning of the *Dreamsnake* to his people. Charles also asked Nora questions about *his* history, unintentionally highlighting the fact that Nora was woefully uninformed. Nora rectified that immediately. I cried when I saw how real Love bloomed within him.

One morning, as I came into the kitchen with Tabitha in my arms, I almost fell over. In real time, there was Nora cooking.

"I can't believe what I'm witnessing. You even seem to know how to use the utensils, and real food is cooking in the pan," I commented, my tongue in my cheek.

"Mm, and that coming from a real pro in the kitchen," Nora retorted.

"*Touche*, darlink," I said, mimicking his Cuban accent. Tabitha gurgled in agreement.

I continued imitating him for Tabitha's amusement. "Yes darlink, *aaiieee*, Uncle Nora is in *la cock-ina*."

Nora laughed without realising my intentional *faux pas*.

"Darlink, whatever you've have had in you this morning does not concern me. I am in the *cocina*."

I giggled and hugged him, squashing Tabitha slightly as I kissed him on the forehead. "I love you. You are going to do a very big thing, and you are acting so calm and cool. You are our family, and you are in our hearts."

As Nora told me to let him get on and cook, I could see he had tears in his eyes.

I knew that being with Patrick Flannery was giving him the power to do and say these things, and I knew he would be free, no matter what the outcome.

When the twins were three months old, Nick appeared in the kitchen looking dishevelled and upset. Immediately I knew something was wrong and stood.

"What - What is it?"

He leant on the table reluctantly. "We, we have to go home. My brother emailed me. It's my dad, they've found a lump." He sat down heavily with a thump that matched my sinking heart. *Home, home?...* This was our home now. Then my mind raced to deal with the concept of David having a lump.

"Nick, I'm so sorry. Did he say where?"

Nick couldn't seem to look at me straight. "Testicle. It's his..." He didn't finish the sentence.

Ouch, that's nasty... Even as a woman, I felt empathy for that ailment.

Testicles reminded me of our twins. That was where fifty percent of both of them had originated.

I glanced at the girls. "It sounds awful, but that would mean we have to tell your family the truth. Shit! The girls, your Mother, my Mother, oh god!..." My voice trailed off as I

323

imagined multiple hideous scenarios. But David had a lump, and I would have hated anything to happen to him. Neither of us mentioned the dreaded word - *Cancer*. Emotions tumbled around as the long forgotten sensation of panic settled back into my bones. I didn't want our old life back, full of suspicions and judgement, and I think Nick could sense that,

"Lucy, he's my dad. I have to go, and I don't want to leave you all here, no way. Maybe it's the pressure of time, making us do this. No more lies. We can always come back," he finished weakly, knowing full well that life could never be that certain. I hugged him tightly, knowing I'd follow him anywhere.

"We'd better get the twins passports," I said.

Later that day we told Patrick and Nora that we would get flights as soon as we had Tabitha and Noelia's passports.

"Okay, I've got a cracking idea, why don't we fly via Cuba? I'll pay. Nora can see his parents and then we can fly to the U.K. to support you both," Patrick proposed, and beamed with pride at his great plan.

"Patrick, darlink, we were planning this trip much later in the year," Nora protested, and his voice was tinged with anxiousness. "And anyway, they need to get back quickly. With babies? No way."

That's when I suddenly saw through the smokescreen. He had perfectly real intentions of coming out to his parents, but it would always be just in the future. He was dragging out the prospect of his inevitable confession by postponing it. Nora himself even believed his own charade.

I directed my attention to Nick. "I think it's actually a good idea. I'm not an invalid just because I have children. We could do a quick stopover on the way to the U.K. It wouldn't take hardly any time out of our schedule."

Nick shrugged. "Well if it's not more than a couple of days I don't see why not, but I don't want to stay long. You understand why."

I reassured him that I understood.

"*Putas! Escuchar mi*, I can say nothing about this, I am not ready."

Patrick said they would discuss it between themselves. He informed us later that they were coming after all, and we agreed to fly via Cuba, where Nick, the twins and I would be staying two days, with a connecting flight to the U.K.

Within six days it was all booked. The required documents were obtained at great expense again so the lawyer could rush through the girl's passports. Guess who paid? Yes - Hector Sanchez.

Nick asked me how I felt about David, and I replied calmly. "Honestly, I don't know. He will never be my David again, Nick. Now he's just your father, and for that reason alone I care that nothing happens to him. In fact, if I was being totally, hideously honest, a tiny part of me blames him for taking us away from here, and I know that's really selfish of me, but it's true."

"Thank you for being honest. I understand Lucy, but we couldn't keep the girls existence, and our location secret forever."

I knew his wise words were true, and I knew that myself and Nora were both extremely anxious for very similar reasons. We were both about to bare ourselves naked with all our lies, to so many people. I wondered how we would both individually manage.

We said our goodbyes to so many tearful people, especially Matilda and Suk Chu. We promised them all we would come back soon, even though Nick and I didn't know if we could fulfil that promise.

Nora had reluctantly called his parents, and he became even more unenthusiastic when he found out they'd both be in Cuba upon his arrival.

Six of us sat on the plane on its way to Cuba, each for totally different reasons, each with their own troubled thoughts. The twins were the only ones who seemed happy, in fact they seemed excited at the prospect of travelling. Nick was trying not to worry about David, and the spectre of Cancer. I was terrified of the moment when Angela would know it was me who birthed her Granddaughters, in fact that the whole family would find out we were not only together, but with children. I'd always been a caterpillar in a cocoon, living my life without taking risks, mostly conforming. Now I'd become a butterfly, flying from one flower to the other and sucking in their complexities, loving the subtle differences between the intoxicating tastes. I refused to return to that stale state of existence. I had a look of terror on my face, as if this was the flight of death. Still, my face did not look as bad as my best friend's.

Nora was terrified because he was on his way to finally come out to his parents, and face the fact he had spent half a million dollars of his father's hard-earned money.

Patrick was anxious that Nora would chicken out, having been so wounded before.

How can you predict what happens when such intricate webs of lies unravel?...

Silently I clicked my heels together three times.

There's no place like home, there's no place like home...

Coming soon, the final instalment in the
Misadventures of a Femme Fatale trilogy -
Instagold

Also by **Trixie Bloom**

TRIXERCISE ~ Loving Yourself Hurts

A humorous diet and excercise parody with real
exercises that anyone can do at home.